Always You

KIRSTY MOSELEY

Acknowledgments

The beautiful cover was made by Hilda at Dalliance Designs. Hilda, your talent never fails to astound me. Thank you for putting up with my 'Can we tweak this, what about that, can this be moved. Actually, change it back to how you first made it because it was perfect the first time'. Your patience is never ending. <3

Dedication

For Adelaine.
Girl, we've never met in person, but some people can come into your life and carve a special place in your heart that is just for them. That's what you did.

prologue

From: rileythecandyeater@hotmail.com
Date: Friday January 20, 2012. 10:21am
To: ClayPreston12@hotmail.com
Subject: Stupid Wi-Fi(less) country!

Hey you,

So, things have changed. I know I was supposed to get online tonight so we could chat BUT this stupid Wi-Fi neglected country has ruined our plans again! The internet has gone down at my aunt's house so I've made David drive me into the town just so I can use the Wi-Fi at McDonalds to send you this email! Now I have a very unhappy stepdad, but at least he's sneaking in a cheeseburger so that should keep him amused while I write this.

I hardly have any cell phone reception here either. I'm really starting to resent this stupid country now LOL. How do people live with no internet? It's like being in the stone ages or something. :(

Anyway, enough ranting and complaining about the bleak sparseness of Devon and how much it sucks. How are you? Did you go to that engineering convention you were talking about? Did they mention the apprenticeship?

What else am I missing out on (apart from the sun, my friends, people driving on the right side of the road, and Fox channel?) Have you done anything fun lately that you can entertain me with?

England is boring. I can't believe I've been living on a stupid cattle farm for the last month; this is probably the worst experience of my life. The only good thing here is catching up with my cousins and uncle! The people here are lovely, but I get so bored that I end up in bed by nine o'clock each night. I miss my own bed, I miss home, I miss my house and car. There was something else that I missed too but for the life of me I can't think what (or who) it is... ;P

I'll be home on Sunday night and I can't freaking wait. Speak to you soon.

Riley xxxx

_____

From: ClayPreston12@hotmail.com
Date: Friday January 20, 2012. 4:16pm.
To: rileythecandyeater@hotmail.com
Subject: Tell me what you honestly think!

Hi Riley Bear!

So it's safe to say that you're enjoying your time in England? LOL. I agree with the stone ages comment though, what kind of place doesn't have free Wi-Fi? Hicksville! Though I bet as soon as you get home you'll miss those cows and being woken up at stupid o'clock by that cockerel that you love so much... ;)

It's okay that you can't get on to chat tonight; it's only a few more days that I have to wait before we can have a proper conversation anyway. Has it seriously only been a month that you've been away? Feels like forever. :(

The convention was great. I got loads of info about the apprenticeship. Hopefully I impressed them, fingers crossed!

As for what you're missing out on, nothing much has happened really. I went to the beach, did a bit of surfing, went to a few more parties than normal, but that's about it.

I can't wait for you to get back. It's been too long since I hung with my Riley Bear; the place is so quiet without you here talking my ear off...

See you soon.

Clay xxx

chapter
one

Oh God, I feel sick. I can't believe I have to go to this stupid school. I only got back from my month's vacation last night, and the following day I have to start a new school? This really sucks!

Half way through junior year was probably the worst time to start a new school. People would already have their own friends and groups, and I was going to be left out and lonely for the next year and a half. I huffed and scowled out of my windshield, seeing the entrance to my new nightmare. South Shore High School. As I approached the gates, I contemplated driving straight past, heading home and begging my stepdad just to let me go back to my old school. I sighed deeply, already knowing that he wouldn't give in because I'd been working on him for the last three months to no avail, so I reluctantly turned the wheel and pulled into the parking lot.

I stopped in the first available space and glanced around nervously, seeing people casually sitting on the hoods of their cars, laughing and flirting, making the most of the sunshine before they had to go into the school. Gulping, I reached up and tilted my rear-view mirror, looking into it at myself, trying to settle my fluttery stomach. I looked okay; my long chocolate brown hair had been pulled into a loose bun. I had applied a tiny bit of mascara to make my blue eyes stand out, and some clear lip gloss. I hadn't gone to too much effort to make myself up today. Being my first day, I was just hoping to make it through school without embarrassing myself.

I pulled my leather jacket on over my red shirt and black skinny jeans, took a deep breath, and stepped out of the car. Almost immediately everyone stopped talking and looked at me. It felt was like one of those movies where the new girl steps out and everyone stops what they're doing so they can analyse everything about her and see where she fits in the social hierarchy of the school.

So much for getting though the day unnoticed!

I pulled my shoulders back and tried to look confident, not letting the nerves show on my face. As if on cue, the boys started to whistle and shout cat calls at me, and the girls stared at me with a mixture of jealousy and hatred. *Looks like I'm not going to fit in here very well after all...*

"RILEY!" I heard my favourite voice in the world shout.

A big goofy grin slipped onto my face as my heart rate seemed to increase at the sound of his voice alone. I turned expectantly, my eyes raking the parking lot for him. My heart almost stopped as I spotted him running towards me with an enormous smile stretched across his beautiful face. His short, messy blond hair was blowing in the wind as he ran across the lot, skilfully dodging around people.

Clay Preston, my best friend in the world, the one I told all my secrets to and who knew me better than anyone else. I sighed contentedly as all the stress and strain, loneliness and heartache that I'd felt for the last month, just ebbed out of my body at the mere sight of him. It had been too long since I'd seen that smile.

I dropped my bag just as he got over to me and jumped into his arms, wrapping my arms and legs around him, squeezing him as tightly as I could. I pressed my face into his neck and breathed in his smell. *My God I've missed him!* It felt like I hadn't been able to breathe for the last month without him. I had barely eaten anything the whole time I was away; I'd just wallowed and missed him as if someone had taken a piece of me away. Here, in his arms, breathing him in again, I felt whole. I sighed contentedly as he squeezed me tighter and spun us in a small circle, laughing.

Everyone in the whole parking lot was staring with wide eyes and open mouths at us. "Clay, I missed you so much!" I told him, unwillingly unwrapping myself from him and kissing his cheek.

He sighed. His beautiful, dark green eyes were sparkling with excitement. "I missed you too, Riley Bear. I didn't think you'd be here today, you only got back last night, right?" he chirped, slinging his arm casually over my shoulder and picking up my schoolbag, his grin still stretched across his face.

"Yeah, I'm so tired, but David said I had to come today because I'd already missed too much school," I whined, rolling my eyes.

"You should have told me, we could have ridden in together." He tightened his arm on my shoulder, guiding me in the direction that he ran from minutes earlier.

"I didn't get back until after one this morning so I didn't think I could call you," I explained. Personally, I would have much rather rode in with him today too, then I wouldn't have had to try and drive here with shaky hands.

He stopped walking and looked me straight in the eye. "Riley Jane Tanner!

You can call me anytime of the day or night, you know that," he said fiercely, looking a little hurt.

I rolled my eyes at him. He always used my full name if he had a point to make. "Come on, Clay Richard Preston," I mocked, using his full name like he did mine and giving him a little shove forward, laughing. He grinned and grabbed me again, tucking me under his arm as he kissed the side of my head. I tried to ignore the stares that were directed at me.

He seemed to be guiding me towards a group of three boys that were sitting on the hood of an old red BMW. As we approached they looked up at me expectantly, smiles plastered on their faces. Their eyes raked over me, curiously, making me feel a little uncomfortable. I guess, being the new girl, I was going to come under scrutiny today. I couldn't help but hope that someone else new started today too so that the attention would be divided.

"Guys, this is my best friend, Riley. Riley, this is Craig, Ben, and Tom," Clay introduced, pointing at the guys in turn. I looked at them carefully, noticing quickly that they were all good-looking in their own way. They all had a confidence that told me that they were in the popular crowd at school and that they knew they were sought-after. Craig had blond hair and blue eyes, Ben and Tom both had brown hair and brown eyes but Tom had really cute dimples in his cheeks when he smiled. They were all the same sort of build, height about six feet, and muscles that you could plainly see under their clothes.

I smiled a seductive smile. *Hmm, maybe this school won't be as bad as I thought!*

"Hey," they greeted almost in unison.

"Hey," I replied with a flirtatious smile. Instantly Clay stiffened next to me.

Crap, I forgot that he gets all protective of me when guys are around. I'd had a few boyfriends before and Clay had scared most of them away with his 'you hurt her, I'll kill you' speech. I slung my arm around his waist and gave him a reassuring squeeze, making him smile at me.

"I can't believe you've kept this little hottie away from us all this time! This is *the* Riley? The girl who lives next-door to you? The girl that you've been best friends with since diapers?" Tom asked Clay, smirking and doing air quotes around the words 'best friends'.

Clay just nodded, seeming rather uncomfortable about something. "Yes, so keep your hands off! She doesn't need players like you chasing her around," he growled with a threatening tone to his voice.

I burst out laughing. "Clay babe, I think I can handle things myself. You don't need to go all protective big brother on me." I shook my head at him and patted him on the chest.

"I'm not trying to be your brother, Riley," he mumbled, frowning.

Just then a group of five extremely attractive girls walked up to us. They all looked the same, short skirts, low cut tops and way too much make-up.

They all stood around with seductive smiles. One draped herself over Ben and immediately started making out with him. Another one walked over to Clay and gave me a sneer, making me pull my arm from around his waist quickly.

"Hey, Clay. How are you doing, baby?" she purred, running her hand up his chest slowly. He smiled at her, but I could tell he was uncomfortable by the way he was clenching his jaw. I smiled and shook my head at him; he could never tell someone what he really thought if it would hurt their feelings, he was way too soft.

"Er, I'm fine Zoë, how are you?" he replied, stepping backwards. The move didn't actually have the desired effect though, because she just stepped with him and pressed her chest against his, smiling seductively.

"Oh I'm much better now that I've seen you," she purred. "How about you take me out tonight? We had lots of fun last time we went out, didn't we?" She raised one eyebrow suggestively, smugly even. Clay squirmed a little and shot a quick glance at me.

I rolled my eyes knowing that was my cue to leave. "I'll see you later. I've gotta go get my schedule." I smiled and picked up my schoolbag, heading off in the direction of the main doors of the school hoping I could find my way or a teacher to ask.

"Riley, wait!" Clay called. I ignored his plea and just carried on walking. I hated watching him get pawed by girls; it turned my stomach for some reason, though I certainly should have gotten used to it by now. I probably saw him with a different girl draped all over him every week. How he'd not caught Mono from all the kissing I'd witnessed over the last couple of years, I didn't know.

I looked up at the huge school, and a shudder tickled down my back as a blush crept onto my face. This place looked a lot bigger than my old school and I was already envisioning getting lost within it. I only got a few yards away when an arm slung lazily around my shoulder. "I'll walk ya, sweetheart," Tom suggested, giving me a wink. I flinched a little when I realised it wasn't Clay, but I decided to go with it, I didn't want to walk on my own anyway.

I smiled gratefully. "Thanks."

"So, why do you think Clay forgot to mention you were a little hottie?" he questioned, smiling.

I shrugged. In my opinion I wasn't exactly a 'hottie', I was just average. Like every girl, I had my flaws and insecurities. "It's probably because he's never noticed. He doesn't look at me that way. We grew up together." I'd known Clay since the day I was born, our parents were friends, and we even lived next door to each other. Clay was slightly over a year older than me, he was a senior here, but the age difference never seemed to matter to us when we were growing up. Since the day I could walk and attempt to say his name we were inseparable.

"Right, *that's* the reason," Tom replied sarcastically, rolling his eyes and chuckling darkly. I looked at him strangely; having no idea what was so funny about that statement.

Just then we reached the office so I went to collect my schedule. Tom waited outside the office door for me. "Let's have a look then," he chirped as soon as I walked out of the office with it. He snatched it out of my hand and looked it over with a smile. "Hey, we get first and fourth together. Clay has those too."

"First and fourth? What are they?" I asked, taking my schedule back flicking my eyes over the writing.

1st - AP English
2nd - Science
3rd - History
LUNCH
4th - Gym
5th - French
6th - AP English literature

Hmm, that's not too bad actually. "Great. Want to walk me to my locker?" I asked with a flirtatious smile. The more I looked at him, the more I found Tom cute. I was pretty sure that Clay wouldn't like me to date one of his friends though. I averted my eyes and saw that everyone was staring at me again. "Do I have something on my face?" I whispered nervously, frowning.

He turned towards me, looking a little confused. "Er, no, why?"

Suddenly, someone grabbed me from behind and pulled me backwards into a hard chest, trapping my arms down by my sides, making me squeak a little.

"Hey, why did you leave? I would have walked you to get your schedule," Clay growled in my ear.

I breathed a sigh of relief and elbowed him in the stomach lightly. "Clay, you jerk! You scared me," I scolded as I spun and pushed him playfully. He just laughed and grabbed my hand with a happy smile. "I thought you were too busy with your new skank," I continued, trying to give him a stern look but failing miserably. I never could get mad at Clay. We had only ever had one argument before in our sixteen year friendship, and even then we had made up within an hour.

He just laughed and pulled me into a hug. "Ooh, is someone jealous?" he teased, laughing.

"Oh yeah I'm so jealous!" I replied sarcastically. "I wish I could drape myself all over you, get used for sex a couple of times then dropped like yesterday's paper." I rolled my eyes as I pushed him off of me and started to walk down the hallway towards where I assumed the lockers were.

"Well you could have just asked. I would have given you a go," he said cockily, catching up with me and wrapping his arm back around my shoulder.

Given me a go? Wow, the cocky player is so overconfident! Hmm, let's have a little fun; I know everyone's staring at me already, so why not give them a show?

I stopped and pushed him against the lockers roughly, stepping right up to him, pressing my whole body against his, our faces inches apart. I put my hands on his thighs and dragged them up slowly, teasingly, across his hips, up his stomach to his chest.

"Oh please, Clay, won't you give me a go right now? I want you so badly, please?" I begged in a breathy voice in his ear.

He made a little moan deep in his throat as his hands landed on my hips, his fingers digging in as he clutched me closer to him. "Er, Riley..." Every inch of my body was pressed against him, so I could feel the stirring that was beginning to happen in his jeans. The movement actually made me catch my breath before I remembered that I was supposed to be messing with him.

I laughed nervously, a little uncomfortable because of his body's reaction. I stepped away quickly and noticed that everyone was staring and whispering. Clay was still standing there, looking a little dazed.

I felt the smile creep onto my face. *Not so overconfident now, huh?*

"Don't mess with me, Clay Preston, you never win and you know it!" I joked, winking at him as I grabbed his hand, pulling him along again. "My locker's two eleven. You know where that is?" I asked, looking around for it. He didn't answer. "Hello, Clay? Two hundred and eleven, do you know where that is?" I repeated, waving my hand in front of his face.

He blushed slightly and then gave me his usual grin, pulling me around the corner. "Yeah, come on."

· · ·

I SAT WITH CLAY and Tom in English which was great because they kept a lot of the unwanted attention away from me, but I wasn't with them again until after lunch. I took a deep breath as the bell rang signalling the end of the lesson. I didn't want to be on my own at all. Clay gave me a sympathetic smile. He knew I didn't like making new friends and that this was going to be hard for me.

"Come on, Riley Bear, I'll walk you to your science class." He grabbed my hand and helped me up off of my chair. We walked to my class hand in hand, we didn't speak. Our friendship was easy, honest and extremely affectionate. We were so comfortable being together, he'd been my best friend and my rock who kept me sane for so long now, that I didn't know how I would have gotten through everything without him.

When we got to the door of my class he took my face in both of his hands and stepped forward until our foreheads were touching. I could hear gasps and whispers coming from the classroom so I closed my eyes and just enjoyed his closeness. My body was starting to tingle, and my stomach felt all fluttery. I was suddenly aware of how incredible he smelt and how his breath tickled across my lips. I didn't want to let go of him. I had no idea why I suddenly felt weird, but it must have just been nerves for my first solo class or something. I swallowed loudly and smiled, pretending I was fine even though he probably saw through that immediately.

"Be confident, you'll be fine. I'll meet you at lunch," he whispered, kissing my forehead before walking away. I turned back to the class to see everyone staring at me again, even the teacher.

After taking a deep breath I walked to the only seat that was empty in the back row. As I passed a cute boy with reddish brown hair, he slapped my ass. I gritted my teeth and ignored it, sitting in my seat and laying my head down on my arms on the desk. I could feel all eyes on me so I just sat there unmoving.

"Hi," chirped a girl beside me. I lifted my head to look at her. She was pretty in a 'not in your face' kind of way, she had short black hair with some blue streaks which she had spiked out stylishly, and big brown eyes. She was smiling a friendly smile.

"Hi," I replied, trying to sound more confident than I felt.

"Are you dating Clay Preston?" she asked, her eyes wide, showing her admiration. It was pretty obvious by her expression that she liked Clay.

I shook my head in response. *Dating Clay, seriously?* "No. He's my best friend. I've known him forever." I smiled. People always thought that Clay and I were together, our parents even thought we would get married one day and used to tease us about it.

"Oh, that's a shame because he is so freaking hot!" she gushed, fanning her face and sighing dreamily. I couldn't help but laugh. Clay wasn't just hot, he looked like a God he was so beautiful - even I could see that and I was his best friend. He had always been gorgeous, but as he got older he just kept getting better and better looking. Honestly, no girl could resist his charm.

"Miss Kent, do you have anything to share with the class?" the teacher asked sarcastically. The girl flushed and shook her head, ending the conversation.

When the bell rang at the end of class, she waited for me. "I'm Rachel, by the way," she chirped, smiling warmly as I picked up my bag. "So, where are you next?" she asked as we walked out of the classroom.

I pulled out my schedule, looking at it. "Er, I have history next."

"No way, me too!" she cried excitedly, linking her arm though mine. As we walked up the hallway, everyone was looking at me again. A few of the guys whistled or made some suggestive remarks, but I just ignored them. "I can't believe this is your first day and you have the whole of the football team after you already. I heard them all talking about you in my first period calculus class.

They're all placing bets on who will sleep with you first," Rachel stated, shaking her head in a disapproving manner.

I gasped. "You're kidding me!"

She chuckled. "Nope, not kidding. You're fresh meat, and you're hot. The cheerleaders will probably approach you at lunchtime to join the squad. You'll easily make the 'it' crowd," she replied, turning up her nose distastefully.

"I don't want to be a cheerleader." I shook my head at the thought. I groaned. *I don't want guys hitting on me all freaking day!*

"Great, then we can be friends!" She grinned and tightened her arm on mine, leading me through the complicated maze-like hallways.

• • •

RACHEL AND I CHATTED whenever we could, whenever the teacher wasn't looking and as we walked between classes. She was extremely nice, and we actually had a lot in common. She told me all about the school and how it worked, pointing out people of interest - hot guys. Or people to stay away from - clingy stalker types. She said that Clay and his three friends that I had met this morning, were part of the football team, and were the most popular and most sought-after boys in school. Apparently, Clay being the hottest was 'alpha male', but that they were all players who only stayed with a girl long enough to get into their pants. I just smiled as she told me that. I already knew this little titbit of information about Clay; he had been with lots of girls. We didn't actually have any secrets from each other; he openly admitted that he didn't want a girlfriend. He always joked that I was the only girl for him and that the others he just used for some fun because I wasn't interested.

After History class, I walked with Rachel to lunch. As soon as I entered the cafeteria, the room fell silent. I turned to Rachel with a grimace; she just linked her arm through mine and pulled me to the lunch line.

"I'm not hungry anymore," I moaned, looking at the wide range of food they had available. I could hear people whispering behind me.

"Hey, Riley Bear. How was your morning?" Clay asked suddenly from behind me, wrapping his arms around my waist and pulling me backwards into his chest. I breathed a sigh of relief at the safeness that I felt when he was near me, and rested my head back on his shoulder.

"It was okay," I mumbled, looking over at Rachel who was completely eye raping Clay, with her mouth hanging open. "Er, Clay, this is Rachel. Rachel, Clay." I waved my hand around in introduction even though they probably knew who the other was, but then again maybe Clay didn't know who she was, she was a junior the same as me, but he was a senior, so their paths had probably never crossed - unless it was a sexual path of course. That last thought made a little frown slip onto my face.

"Hey, Rachel. Been looking after my girl for me?" he asked, smiling politely. She just carried on staring at him as if he hadn't spoken. "O... Kay," he mused, chuckling.

"You obviously have an effect on the girls at this school. They all seem to hate me," I whispered to him.

"They don't hate you. You're being paranoid," he replied, giving me a reassuring squeeze.

"Really? Paranoid, huh?" I answered, turning slightly and nodding my head around.

Clay looked around and took in all the girls giving me hateful and jealous looks, but all of them smiling at him as soon as his eyes went in their direction. "Oh! Okay, maybe I shouldn't hug you anymore then," he suggested, stepping away and grinning at me.

"Get your butt over here now!" I hissed, pointing at my side. He chuckled wickedly as he threw his arm around my shoulder before loading two plates of chilli fries onto my tray and pushing me up to the cash register. I reached into my schoolbag for my purse, but he had already handed over the money and picked up the tray for me.

"So, Rachel, would you and Riley like to come sit with us?" he asked, nodding to the biggest table at the end of the cafeteria. It was filled with all the hottest people in the school, guys and girls alike.

"Sure," Rachel replied, wide eyed. She looked so excited that she was probably fighting to urge to jump up and down.

Clay led us to the table. "Shift down, guys. Make room for my girl and her friend," he ordered, waving his hand. Immediately, everyone moved up to make room for two extras.

Wow, he really is like an alpha male, he says jump and everyone asks how high! I rolled my eyes at him, but he wasn't one to abuse his power, he was too kind and sweet, but he liked to give off a macho image.

"Hey, Riley. I'm looking forward to next period," one boy said, winking slyly at me.

I chewed on the inside of my lip as I looked at him. He was hot again, brown hair sweeping over his forehead and dazzling blue eyes.

Jeez, do they put something in the water in this school? And why the hell haven't I seen any of these guys around? But I knew the answer to that; it was because my mom insisted I go to a stupid private school three towns over. But that was okay, I was happy at that school, I had a lot of friends and everyone knew me. But no, David had convinced my mom that sending me to private school was a waste of money. Hence, I was now at the local public school and the money they would have spent on my education was invested ready for my twenty-first birthday. It wasn't too bad; at least I would get to see Clay a lot more, which was certainly a good thing.

"What have you got next period?" Rachel asked.

I grimaced. "Gym," I moaned, turning my nose up. Clay chuckled wickedly as he started munching on his fries. I was terrible at sports. The only thing I liked to do was running; I usually went for a run every morning with Clay before school.

"Let's see your schedule again," Rachel requested, holding out an expectant hand. I dug it out of my bag and passed it to her. She scanned it over. "Hey I have French and English Lit with you too!"

"Oh I have gym next period too. Maybe we could be partners," another boy suggested, waggling his eyebrows and smirking at me.

Clay visibly stiffened. "Enough! Leave her alone. I've already told you guys!" he barked, looking at them all in turn with an angry expression.

I turned to look at Clay. *Is he serious? He's warned people to stay away from me?* "Clay, what? I can look after myself you know," I retorted, frowning.

He looked at me, his face softening. "I'm just looking out for you, Riley Bear. You don't want anything to do with these jackoffs," he explained, waving his hand around the table at his friends.

"These jackoffs are your friends, Clay," I countered, shaking my head at him.

"Exactly, I know how they think. So stay away," he said venomously. Before I could stop myself I kicked him under the table, my foot connecting with his shin. "Ouch! What was that for?" he accused, leaning down and rubbing his leg, scowling at me.

"For being an ass. I can talk to whoever I want, okay? Please don't start with this whole thing again," I begged, giving him my puppy dog face that I knew he couldn't resist.

He snorted and shook his head. "Fine! Talk to whoever you want. Date whoever you want. Just don't come crying to me when it all goes wrong," he snapped, shoving his plate of food away from him angrily and getting up from the table, stalking off in the direction of the exit.

Wait, he's angry with me? What the hell did I do? He's the one that's being all super possessive and protective!

I looked at his retreating form, confused as to what had just happened. But I knew I couldn't let him be mad at me, I loved that stupid boy with everything I had. Instinctively I jumped out of my chair and ran after him. When I got close enough I jumped on his back, wrapping my arms and legs tightly around him, catching him by surprise and almost knocking him over. I bent my head and kissed the side of his neck which made him laugh quietly. I smiled against his neck because I already knew that all was forgiven and forgotten. A wicked plan formed in my head as I opened my mouth and sucked hard on the soft skin of his neck, giving him a hickey.

"I'm sorry. I didn't mean to be all ungrateful. I know you're looking out for me," I told him.

His body seemed to relax under mine. "No, I'm sorry, Riley Bear, I shouldn't have done that. You can talk to whoever you want; I was just trying to look out for you, honestly. These guys here aren't good enough for you," he said, shaking his head a little sadly.

I sighed and kissed my hickey on his neck as my stomach growled hungrily. "Can we go back and finish lunch now?" I asked. He nodded and turned around, wrapping his arms around my thighs so I didn't have to hold on as much. When we got back to the table, he plopped me back into my chair. Everyone was staring at us again. I rolled my eyes as Clay kissed the top of my head making the girls gasp and glare at me even more.

Clay sat back down opposite me, and immediately Ben's eyes widened. "Holy shit! You let her brand you?" he cried, pointing at Clay's neck.

"Brand me?" Clay repeated, looking confused as he rubbed at his neck.

"Yeah she gave you a freaking hickey!" Ben stated, laughing.

Clay shot his eyes to me. "You didn't," he accused, with a smile.

I nodded in response, trying not to laugh again. He just rolled his eyes and pulled the collar of his shirt up to cover it. He was always doing that to me so this was payback. Since I was ten years old, when he first learnt how to do them, he'd pinned me down and given me a hickey almost every week. He always says that he's marking his territory like a cat marks with scent.

"Paybacks a bitch, huh?" I teased, with a sly smile.

• • •

IN GYM WE WERE running track which was perfect for me. I loved to run and at least I wasn't stuck in some stupid hall playing dodge ball or something. That would really suck. The only trouble was that I didn't have any gym kit yet because as I had been away for a month. Rachel had leant me her shorts, but because I was a lot taller than her, they were actually quite short shorts. I didn't even have a shirt to wear. I grabbed my cell phone and text Clay, asking if he had a spare one. A couple of seconds later he text back that he would wait for me outside the girls' locker room. Everyone was ready so they all made their way out. As I stepped tentatively out of the door in my red shirt, I saw Clay leaning there waiting for me.

"Here." He threw a large white t-shirt at me.

"Hurry up, or it will be fifty push-ups for both of you!" the teacher shouted, turning to walk out of the door.

I quickly stripped off my shirt and replaced it with his t-shirt, then turned back to the locker rooms and threw my top in the pile of my stuff. When I turned back to face Clay, I saw him standing there with a pained look on his face.

"What's up?" I asked, tying a knot in the back of his shirt to make it fit a bit better. He just shook his head but didn't answer. Realisation hit me what was wrong with him. I'd just taken my shirt off in front of him. *Crap, great job, Riley!* But it wasn't really that big of a deal though, he'd seen me in bikinis a lot so it was just the same really. So why was he looking at me like that? I turned and ran for the field, dismissing his obvious unease. "Race ya!" I shouted over my shoulder because he was still standing stock still outside the locker room.

We were supposed to be running a mile, which was five laps of the circuit. I ran as fast as I could. I needed a head start because Clay was a seriously fast runner. After about a minute, I heard him catching up behind me.

As he ran past, he slapped my ass making me squeal from the shock and slight sting. "Keep up, slow poke, or you'll have to buy dinner tonight." He laughed.

I took a deep breath and pushed my legs faster. I caught him up, but I had the strong feeling that he let me, there was no way I could catch him if he wanted to go. We ran alongside each other, sending teasing insults back and forth, the same as every morning when we ran.

We were on our last lap now, and I silently thanked God because I was completely worn out already. "How about we make a bet?" Clay suggested, grinning.

Oh crap, I always lose his bets! "What sort of bet?" I asked hesitantly. I could feel the sweat running down my back because of the effort. We were totally alone because no one else was taking this seriously; they were all just walking and chatting or having a leisurely jog.

"Okay well, if I beat you then you have to kiss someone of my choice. And if you beat me, then I'll kiss someone of your choice. A proper kiss though, with tongues," he suggested, smiling at me.

I looked at the end of the track wondering if I could actually run any faster than I already was, because I knew he could. We were nearing the hundred meter mark now. I quickly weighed my options. I didn't really want to kiss someone, but if I won the bet and Clay had to kiss Rachel, she would owe me forever. The challenge of it won me over.

"Okay deal," I agreed as I bumped him with my hip, making him lose his stride. I needed any advantage I could get when racing him. I ran as fast as possible. My legs were pumping so fast that I could barely even keep up with them. I didn't risk losing my concentration to look over my shoulder to see where he was, so I just focused on the finish line and the victory that was just within reach...

Suddenly, seemingly out of nowhere, he breezed past me and crossed the line. It wasn't even close; he must have beaten me by a solid thirty feet.

Damn it!

I crossed the line too, but we didn't stop running straight away, we just slowed down to a jog and ran a little longer, then slowed again to a walk. I was completely exhausted; I flopped down to the grass, lying on my back under the shade of a tree, gasping for breath. Suddenly, he flopped down on top of me. His whole body pressed me down into the cool, hard ground making the grass tickle my exposed back. Surprisingly he wasn't heavy so he must have been holding his weight off of me.

He laughed as I tried to push him off, but my body was spent and my muscles refused to cooperate. "I won," he taunted, shaking his head like a dog and making sweat drip off onto me, plopping on my cheek.

"You always win! Maybe one day we'll find a bet that isn't so one sided. I am a girl in case you haven't noticed, I have shorter legs," I whined breathlessly.

"I've noticed," he replied, smiling wickedly. I pushed him playfully again, but he just laughed and smirked at me. "So, about my prize..."

I groaned. "Okay fine. Who? Don't make it a teacher or something though because I'm not doing that. And I really don't want it to be a girl," I grumbled, turning my nose up but giggling at the same time.

"Nope, I'll make it easier for you than that," he replied playfully.

I shut my eyes wondering why on earth I had done this in the first place. His bets never went well for me. "Okay, so who do I have to kiss?" I repeated.

I was cooling down now and was actually starting to feel the cold ground and the wind. I shivered and wrapped my arms around his waist, pulling him a little closer to use his body heat. Every inch of him pressed against me as his warmth seeped into me, his hot breath fanned across my face and I smiled as I recognised the sweet scent of strawberry flavoured candy, his favourite. He smiled and wiped the sweat off of my forehead.

Oh God, I must look so sexy right now all covered in sweat - but then again, this is Clay, he sees me like this every day. And I don't mind his sweat; actually, it makes him look hotter when he's all sweaty and breathing heavy. Wait, did I really just think that about my best friend? I mentally slapped myself and looked at him expectantly. He was gazing at me with a weird expression. *Crap, does he know what I was just thinking?*

"Clay? Who do I have to kiss?" I repeated, wanting to change the subject in case he could actually read my mind and knew I just had a weird thought about him and not in the best friend way.

"A proper kiss, with tongues," he clarified, biting his lip. I nodded and rolled my eyes. *Yes, I remember the stupid bet!* "Me," he whispered, bending his head down slowly.

I froze. *What? Holy crap, he's going to kiss me! My best friend is going to kiss me!* He was about an inch away from me; I could feel his breath across my lips. I was frozen, shocked that this was happening.

Suddenly he moved and grabbed my chin, turned my face to the side and sucked hard on my neck. I giggled at the feel of it; it always made me laugh when he did this. I raised my hands trying to push him off, but he just gripped my wrists and pinned them above my head, and carried on sucking on the same spot. After a couple of seconds he pulled back and looked at it, nodding with a satisfied expression on his face.

"What the hell was that for?" I asked, laughing again.

He looked extremely pleased with himself. "Just marking my territory," he answered, kissing my forehead and climbing off of me, pulling me up. We started walking back, and he threw his arm around my shoulder. "Are you cold?" he asked.

I nodded in response. "So, that was a joke?" I asked quietly. *He doesn't actually want me to kiss him, does he?*

"Here." He pulled off his t-shirt and wrapped it around my back to keep me a little warmer. I kept my face forward and tried, unsuccessfully, to keep my eyes off of his glorious body. He had sweat all over his well-muscled chest. I watched as a bead of sweat made its way down his abs. Before I knew what I was doing, I reached out a finger and wiped it off, leaving my hand there for a second longer than needed.

Oops! What the hell was that? I gritted my teeth and looked up at him; he had the pained expression back again like outside the locker room.

I smiled weakly. "Sorry, you, er, had a bug on you," I lied lamely.

"Well thanks for getting rid of it for me," he said quietly before clearing his throat. "Wanna watch a movie tonight? Get a pizza?" he asked, thankfully changing the subject from the weird chest touching I'd just done.

I smiled at the thought. *Heck yeah! I love movie night.* We hadn't had one in over a month because I'd been in England visiting my stepdad's relatives. "Yeah, definitely. You bring the ice cream and I'll supply the popcorn," I suggested, grinning. That was the usual deal.

"I have Paranormal Activity 3. I bought it yesterday."

"You did? Why did you buy that? You hate ghost movies," I replied, confused.

He shrugged. "I knew you wanted to see it."

I sighed happily. I loved my best friend to pieces; he was so sweet and thoughtful all the time. "Hell yeah, as long as you don't make fun of me if I jump or scream or anything," I bargained, eyeing him suspiciously.

"Hey, when have I ever made fun of you for jumping at a scary movie?" he asked, faking hurt and squeezing my shoulder.

"Er, let me think. When we watched The Exorcist, or White Noise. Oh, what about the time we watched Shutter. You laughed at me for days about that!" I pouted.

He burst out laughing. "Oh yeah! Man, that one was so funny. You should have seen your face. *'Holy freaking shit, Clay! I'm so scared! Check the closet!'* that was hilarious," he said, laughing his head off, doing a terrible impression of my voice as he quoted my fright word for word. I slapped his bare chest harder than I thought, making a loud slapping noise. "Ouch, Riley Bear, that hurt," he joked, rubbing his chest but still laughing.

"Oh poor baby, did a big bad girl hurt you?" I teased in a baby voice as I reached out and rubbed his chest where I'd slapped him. His skin felt so soft and warm under my hand that I didn't want to pull it away. I was enjoying it way too much. I forced my hand away and bit my lip, wondering what on earth was wrong with me today. We were back at the locker rooms then; I smiled as I made my way to the girls changing room. "I'll take this home and wash it for you," I suggested, untying the knot at the back of his t-shirt that I was wearing

I started to walk away, but he grabbed my hand, making me turn to look at him. "The answer is no, Riley. I wasn't joking." He smirked at me and then turned and walked away, leaving me standing there confused.

He wasn't joking about what? The movie? Not teasing me? I rolled my eyes and headed into the showers not bothering to worry about it, Clay was just too confusing sometimes.

• • •

"HEY, RILEY, WOULD you like to try out for cheerleader? We have an opening," a pretty blonde girl chirped as I finished getting dressed.

"Um, no thanks. I'm not really cheer material." I smiled politely, shaking my head.

"Oh, well you know that cheerleaders get to date all the hottest guys. Clay's on the football team. If you wanted to date him you'd need to be a cheerleader for him to even notice you," she said a bit harshly.

I frowned at that statement. "I don't need to be a cheerleader for my best friend to notice me, trust me."

"Best friend, yeah right. I saw the way you two act. You branded him for goodness sake and he didn't even care. If one of us had done that he would have freaked," she snapped, sneering at me.

I just shrugged. "That was just a joke; I knew it would make him laugh." I pulled my hair back into a messy bun again.

Suddenly she gasped. "What the heck is that?" she asked, pointing to my neck.

I looked up into the mirror to see a large purple hickey on my neck. "Son of a bitch! This is going to take forever to go. I'm going to kill him," I whined, touching it roughly, as if poking it would make it disappear.

"Did Clay give you that?" the girl asked with wide eyes. I scrunched my nose up and nodded. *That ass is going to pay for this! I'm going to wait until he's asleep, and then jump on him tonight.*

"Wow, I've never seen him brand anyone before," the girl said quietly. "You must be an awesome screw," she mused, looking at me with wide eyes.

I looked at her, shocked. "He's my best friend! It was a joke that's all; I've never slept with him." Well, that statement wasn't strictly true, I'd *slept* with him plenty of times, but I'd never had sex with him. In fact, I'd never had sex with anyone. I'd never done more than kiss anyone actually.

The girl looked at me with a sceptical expression on her face; she clearly didn't believe a word I'd said. Then she turned and stormed off, looking like she was close to tears. I frowned, having no clue what I'd said wrong.

chapter

two

The rest of the day seemed to fly by. I had fun with Rachel during our other lesson together, and we exchanged numbers. I asked her about the girl from gym, and she said that apparently Jennifer dated Clay a few times - by that I took it that he'd slept with her a few times - and that she wanted to be with him, but he refused to be exclusive. I wasn't surprised by that revelation at all, that was typical Clay, no commitments.

When I got home I told my mom and stepdad, David, that Clay was coming over tonight and that we were going to order pizza. They were fine with it, as always. Clay practically lived at our house. He would stay over at our house every Wednesday, Saturday and Sunday. He always had done ever since we were little kids.

After showering and changing into my pink Betty Boop pyjama shorts and tank top, Clay knocked on my bedroom door. "Hey, Riley Bear," he greeted, walking in as if he owned the place as usual, dumping his stuff on the chair. "Ice cream is in the freezer, as promised. I got cookies and cream and strawberry sorbet because I know you can't ever make up your mind which you prefer."

I smiled excitedly and placed my cell phone in his hand. "You order pizza," I chirped, gripping his other hand and pulling him from my room and down to the kitchen while he dialled and placed our order.

After stuffing some popcorn in the microwave, I sat on the kitchen counter and he stood with his back to me, leaning against the counter between my legs. I wrapped my arms around his neck and rested my chin on his shoulder, pressing my chest into his back. He was rubbing my shins with his thumbs as we both watched the microwave go round. I sighed happily. I'd missed this so much.

"Hey, Clay. I missed you!" my mom cheered, coming into the kitchen and pulling him into a hug.

"Yeah you too, Sandra," he replied, giving her his charming smile. He held out a hand to my stepfather. "David, how was your trip?"

David shook Clay's hand with a warm smile. "Great, son, it was great. Shame to come back, but to be honest I don't think I could have stood for anymore of Riley's whining!" he joked, jabbing me in the ribs playfully. I just rolled my eyes, tipping our popcorn into a bowl. My mom just giggled like a school girl.

"Whining? What about?" Clay asked, obviously confused, looking at me quizzically.

David laughed. "You for goodness sake. *'I miss Clay! When are we going home, I want to see Clay! Why won't my cell phone work, I want to text Clay'*," David said, mimicking a girly voice, laughing. Clay just laughed too and put his arm around my shoulder.

"Shut up, David! I wasn't whining. I just missed my best friend that's all. A month is a long time you know!" I countered, throwing a bit of hot popcorn at him. He caught it and ate it, still laughing to himself. In reality, I knew I'd been a pain but, in my defence, a month was an extremely long time to go without one of Clay's hugs.

"Well, have a lovely night. We're now off out for dinner," Mom said, giving us both a kiss on the cheek.

Just then the doorbell rang. "Pizza's here!" David shouted from the hallway. I ran towards the front door, grabbing my purse as I went past. "No need, I've got it," David said as he passed me the pizza and kissed my forehead.

I smiled gratefully. As stepfathers went, I knew I got a great one. He loved my mom and me like crazy. I was only seven when they got together; he raised me and treated me like I was his own. David was the only dad I had ever known. My own father was no more than a sperm donor who wasn't interested in being in my life and had skipped town when he found out my mom was pregnant with me. My mom and David had tried for a baby but then they found out that David couldn't have kids. He spoilt me like crazy.

Once my parents had left, Clay and I took the food and popcorn up to my room as usual. After stuffing ourselves with pizza, we caught up on everything that we had missed for the last month. We finally put the DVD on at about nine thirty. Clay changed into his pyjamas - which essentially meant that he just took off his jeans and t-shirt because he always slept in just his boxers - and jumped into the bed next to me.

The movie was scary, really scary. At one point I had my face pressed so hard against his chest that my nose was going numb. He already had his arm around me, so he brought up his other arm to hold the back of my head, tangling his fingers in my hair.

Finally, the movie was over. I looked up at him expecting the laughter that always came after we watched a scary movie. But he didn't laugh; instead, he just looked at me, staring at every part of my face. My breathing started to speed up because something just seemed different, I couldn't put my finger on it, but for some reason I was suddenly noticing how handsome he was. How his skin felt against mine. How his hand tightened in the back of my hair making my stomach flutter. The air seemed charged with something, getting thicker somehow, making my breathing shallower.

What the hell is wrong with me? I know I haven't seen him for a month, but jeez, this is freaking crazy!

Suddenly he snapped out of it as if he came out of some sort of trance. "I'll get the ice cream," he muttered, jumping off the bed, stopping the movie before heading out of the room.

I sat up, rubbing a hand over my face, slightly dazed as to what was going on. *What on earth is wrong with me today?*

He smiled as he walked back into the room a couple of minutes later. "So, what'll it be, Riley Bear?" he asked, holding out the two cartons to me. I forced a smile, deciding to ignore the confusion that seemed to be settling over me. He obviously hadn't felt anything because he was behaving normally, so maybe I was just tired or something.

"Hmm, I'll go for the strawberry sorbet," I chose, taking it and digging in.

He plopped down next to me, talking animatedly about his football practice. "So, I've got something that I wanted to ask you," he said, suddenly looking serious. I immediately tensed up; Clay was never serious. I raised one eyebrow, waiting for him to continue. He cleared his throat. "I was wondering if... well... now that you come to my school, I thought... well I wondered if maybe you would wear my number?" he asked, stumbling over his words as he looked at his ice cream.

"Wear your number, what are you talking about? What number?" I asked, frowning and taking my opportunity to steal some of the ice cream from his pot.

He just laughed and reached over, taking my half eaten tub of ice cream and handing me his. "I don't know why I even make you choose, you always end up eating mine too," he teased, chuckling again. I just smiled guiltily and dug into the cookies and cream. "So yeah, what I was saying. You know I'm running back for the football team, right? Well, now that you come to my school you'll be expected to attend the games. Everyone goes, and there's always a party after." He winced, rubbing the back of his neck.

"Okay, I'd love to watch you play. I've never seen you play properly before, only in the park," I replied, smiling.

He just nodded. "Yeah, so, well, the guys have this thing where you have to give your away shirt to your girlfriend to wear to, you know, show support," he mumbled. "But I've never had a girlfriend. So I was wondering if you would wear it for me and be my number one fan, cheer me on?" he asked, frowning, clearly uncomfortable.

I felt the proud smile stretch across his face. "Of course I will, silly! I'm already your number one fan," I stated, digging him in the ribs with my elbow.

He looked up at me and beamed. "Thanks."

I yawned; I still hadn't caught up from my lack of sleep last night. We hadn't arrived back home until late and even then I'd had trouble getting to sleep because of nerves about starting the new school.

"You're tired. I'll get the light," Clay said, taking the almost finished ice creams and dumping them in the trashcan. I turned on the bedside light as he flicked off the ceiling lights. I watched him walk back to the bed and climb in beside me. He truly was beautiful, both inside and outside. I had missed him so much. I shifted over so he could get in and he wrapped his arms around me as usual and pulled me to his chest. We were both lying on our sides facing each other, our bodies touching. He was just staring at me again.

"What's wrong?" I asked quietly. There was something he wanted to tell me, I could tell, I knew him so well.

"About that bet earlier," he whispered, moving his face a little closer to mine.

My heart sped up. *Shit, I forgot about the bet! He doesn't really want me to kiss him, does he?* I could feel his warm, sweet breath blowing across my face.

"Yeah?" I croaked, nervously. What was I supposed to do if he kissed me? It was a bet, we never backed out of a bet, and he'd won fair and square. If the outcome had been different then he would have kissed whomever I had chosen.

"I want to claim my prize," he whispered, rolling forward slightly so that I was now half underneath him, his chest pressed against mine, pinning me to the bed.

"Clay, what the?" I gasped, but he was already inching his head towards me. I froze; I didn't know what to do, so I did nothing.

Gently his lips grazed across mine, so lightly that I could barely feel it. He pulled back to look at me again. "Can I kiss you?" he whispered huskily, his voice sounded so sexy I whimpered.

"For the bet?" I asked, still confused. *Why would he even want to kiss me in the first place?* He nodded, looking a little sad for some reason. "Umm... okay."

As soon as the words left my mouth, he brought his lips to mine, kissing me tenderly, passionately. And my days it felt incredible. His soft lips fitted mine perfectly, setting my body on fire. He traced his tongue along my bottom lip so I opened my mouth, eager for more. I felt his tongue slip in and massage mine gently and slowly. The taste of him was amazing, and I couldn't help but moan into his mouth. I'd never been kissed like this in my life. I'd kissed a few guys, but this, this was something else entirely.

I brought my arms up and wrapped them around his neck, tangling my hands into his hair, trying to get him closer to me. He made a small moaning sound in the back of his throat that made my body start tingling. He pulled away, only to kiss along my jaw line and down my neck, making me moan this time. He made his way back to my mouth again; I kissed him hungrily, as if I could devour his soul. I felt his hand snake up my leg to rest on my hip, before gently slipping under my pyjama top, his fingers tracing across my stomach and sides. My whole body was tingling with a burning desire that I barely even understood.

As his fingers bit into my hip, it suddenly dawned on me what I was doing. *I'm making out with Clay. He has his hand under my top. It's Clay, my best friend. What the heck am I doing? I don't even like him in that way, do I?* I reluctantly pulled my hands out of his hair. I put them on his chest and gave him a small shove.

He immediately pulled back to look at me for a couple of seconds before taking a deep breath and sitting up. "I'm sorry, Riley. I'm so sorry." He groaned, putting his hands up to cover his face. He looked extremely upset. I reached out to pull his hands away from his face. I didn't like it when he hid his emotions from me, we talked about everything, we had no secrets. I needed to know what this was all about.

"Clay, what was that? Why did you do that? I mean, not that it wasn't good because it was... but, I mean... what?" I stammered, confused and embarrassed. I could feel the blush burning my cheeks, and was silently grateful that there was only the bedside light on so it wouldn't be too noticeable.

He gulped. "I don't know. I shouldn't have done that. I'm so sorry, please forgive me," he begged, looking at me with pure horror across his face.

Wait, why does he look so horrified? Oh my God, am I a bad kisser? Am I that repulsive to him that he is horrified that he's just kissed me? Immediately I was terrified that this was going to ruin our friendship.

"Clay, don't worry about it. But it shouldn't have happened, let's just leave it at that, shall we? I mean, I don't want things to change between us, do you? You're my best friend in the whole world, I couldn't lose you," I said, starting to tear up.

He pulled me close to him and let me cry on his chest. "I couldn't lose you either, Riley Bear," he whispered, kissing the top of my head.

I pulled back to look at him, my best friend, my angel, the guy I needed to have in my life forever. "Let's just pretend that this didn't happen then, okay?" I suggested hopefully.

He wiped my face and smiled a small, sad smile. "Okay, Riley Bear." He moved and settled down onto his back, pulling me close to his side with his arm round the crook of my neck. He leant over and turned the light off.

I buried my face in his chest and breathed in his beautiful smell, trying to calm myself. I had hormones running all over my body. Part of my mind was screaming at me to grab him and kiss him again, to run my hands over his perfect body, to take off his clothes and run my tongue over every inch of him. But the other part, the sensible part, was telling me to close my eyes and go to sleep and in the morning forget that this even happened. Finally, after what seemed like forever fighting my body's urges, I drifted off to sleep in his arms, listening to his heartbeat.

• • •

WHEN I OPENED MY sleepy eyes in the morning, the first thing I saw was him staring at me. He looked tired. I traced the dark circle under his eye with my finger. "Did you not sleep well?" I asked, trying my hardest to ignore the part of me that was telling me to jump on him and kiss him again. I genuinely had no idea what had come over me, but instead of just seeing Clay as my best friend and the goofy kid that I used to build mud pies with, I could suddenly see the attraction that he held for other girls.

He smiled weakly, but it didn't reach his eyes. "Not really. I was a little worried."

"Worried? That movie scared you, didn't it," I teased, laughing hysterically.

He laughed and tickled me, making me squirm. "No, Riley Bear, it didn't scare me. You were the one whimpering and talking in your sleep all night," he replied, suddenly looking sad again.

"Whimpering and talking?" I asked, confused. I thought back to the dream I kept having last night. It was about Clay, he'd said that he couldn't be my friend anymore, then he'd turned and ran off, and no matter how fast I ran after him, I just couldn't catch up. I shook my head, trying to clear it.

Clay brushed my hair away from my face softly. "You kept saying that everything was ruined. You kept calling for me, and crying," he whispered, pulling his arm tighter around me. I couldn't speak. "Have I ruined everything, Riley? Please tell me that we can forget what happened last night, please," he begged, looking me straight in the eye.

I nodded and tried to smile. I would forget it, I would make myself. I loved Clay too much to let him walk out of my life. "Of course we can. Why don't you go back to sleep? We can skip the run today and have an extra hour in bed," I suggested, putting my head back on his chest. I heard him sigh in contentment, and I looked up to see he had his eyes closed, and a smile was tugging at the corners of his mouth.

• • •

THE NEXT COUPLE OF days were a little strained. Clay didn't touch me much, didn't put his arm around my shoulder or hold my hand like normal. It was weird, and I missed his contact so much. I didn't want to say anything about it, so I just went with it. By Friday I couldn't take it anymore, the loss of contact was really starting to get to me. I was walking to class with Rachel, I hadn't spoken to her about what had happened between me and Clay, but she had noticed that we seemed to be acting a little different around each other. I saw him walking towards me with Tom, so I stepped in his path so he had to stop.

"Hey, Riley Bear. Everything okay?" he asked, with a big grin. I nodded and wrapped my arms around him, hugging him tightly. He didn't respond at first, he just stood there, then slowly he wrapped his arms around me and buried his face in my hair. "Riley, what's up?" he asked breathlessly, pulling back to look at me. "If someone's upset you I swear to God I'll-" he started, but I put my finger on his lips to stop him.

"No one's upset me. I've just missed you these last couple of days, that's all," I explained, kissing his cheek and pulling away.

He smiled weakly; he obviously knew what I was talking about. "I missed you too."

"Come on, Riley, we'll be late for class!" Rachel shouted, making me jump.

Clay smiled. "Get going then. I'll see you after school," he instructed, stepping to the side to let me pass. I stuck my tongue out at him as I started to walk off. Just as I got past him, he swatted my behind playfully. I sighed happily and walked off without saying a word. Hopefully that would be the end of that.

That night was his game night. He was driving, and afterwards he was taking me to my first party since starting the school. I was a little nervous about it, but Clay said that he would look after me. Rachel had told me that apparently these parties could get a little wild.

"So, you still gonna wear my number?" Clay asked, grabbing my hand to help me out of his car once we pulled into the school parking lot. He didn't let go as we walked to the school heading towards the boys' locker room. I smiled happily. Everything seemed to be back to normal between us since this afternoon.

"I sure am, if you want me to," I replied, biting my lip.

He grinned. "Of course I do. You're my best friend, Riley Bear."

My heart dropped a little, but I didn't know why. I *was* his best friend, nothing more. So why did I want to be all of a sudden? Why couldn't I stop thinking about that kiss and how his lips fitted so perfectly against mine?

He pulled me into the boys' locker room with him. "Hey, she can't come in here!" someone shouted as I was dragged inside.

My eyes went wide; there were half naked boys everywhere. "Hmm, nice view," I mumbled, smirking. I glanced around the room, raking my eyes slowly over each of the boys in turn.

Clay laughed and put his hand over my eyes, putting an abrupt end to my ogling. "Come on, pervert, let's get that shirt for you and then you can go!" he said, laughing, leading me forwards. I could hear whistles and comments that made me smile. Clay muttered something like 'shut the heck up' and then he put something in my hands. Still covering my eyes, he pushed me forwards again.

Once we were outside the door, I giggled. "Mmm, thanks for that," I chirped, waggling my eyebrows at him jokingly.

He rolled his eyes with an easy smile. "Want me to walk you to the field?" he offered, slinging an arm around my shoulder.

I shook my head and laughed at his sweetness. He had always been like this to me, ever since we were kids he'd walk me to places because he was worried about me getting hurt. "I think I can make it."

He chuckled too. "Okay. I'll see you after." He smiled and headed back into the locker room. As soon as the door opened, I could hear his teammates ribbing him about me. I just smiled and looked down at what I was holding. It was a huge maroon football shirt. I turned it round to look at the writing on the back. 'PRESTON 12'. I smiled and slipped it on over my tight black top and light blue skinny jeans. I walked out to the field with a big grin and sat with Rachel, watching the game and fooling around.

"Hi," a male voice said next to me after a little while.

"Er, hi yourself," I replied, turning to look at him. He was tall, really tall, probably about 6 foot 3, he was well built but not overly muscled. He had shaggy black hair that swept over his forehead and bright blue eyes. There was a little scar running through his left eyebrow which had a little silver piercing next to it, he also had a lip ring at the corner of his bottom lip. The black t-shirt he wore clung to his body, he'd paired it with low slung jeans and biker boots that he wore undone. He was so handsome that he looked like he had just walked out of a modelling shoot. I suddenly realised I was staring and looked away quickly, turning my attention back to the field where the game was still going on.

"So, you're dating Clay Preston?" the guy asked.

Why on earth does everyone think that? I turned back to him. "What makes you say that?" I asked, confused. I didn't recognise this guy from school. If I had seen him before, I definitely would have remembered his handsome face.

"Well, you're wearing his number. That's kinda a girlfriend's job," he countered, smirking. I looked down at myself, spotting Clay's away shirt that I was wearing. I had totally forgotten that I was wearing it.

"Er, no actually. We're friends that's all. We're not dating," I corrected, looking back to the field.

"Well, that's great. I'm Blake," he said with an easy smile. I bit my lip as I discreetly checked him out again.

"Riley," I replied, trying to ignore the butterflies I had in my stomach as I pretended to be interested in the game again. I could feel him staring at me.

"So, you go to South Shore?" he asked, nodding his head towards the field.

I nodded. "Yeah, but you don't do you?" I already knew the answer to that question though; he certainly hadn't been here this week. I noticed that all the girls - and even some of the moms - were staring at him with lustful expressions on their faces.

"Nope," he answered, popping the p. When he didn't elaborate I turned away from him and smiled to myself. *Okay, well if he wants to play, then we'll play.*

"Come on, Clay!" I shouted, standing up and clapping.

I saw Clay turn to smile at me so I gave him a wink and sat back down. Blake turned back to me again. "Not dating, huh?" he asked, smirking again.

"Nope," I answered, popping the p like he had done to me.

He laughed. "So, Riley, you doing anything after the game?" he asked with a flirtatious smile that made my butterflies take off again.

"Yep." I fought a smile at his annoyed expression.

"What are you doing?" he asked, moving closer to me so that the sides of our bodies were touching.

"Going to a party with Clay." I shrugged.

He drew in a deep breath. "Okay well, I guess I'll just have to take someone else out for dinner then." He pouted and sighed dramatically as he slid further away up the bench.

I winked teasingly. "Yeah, you will."

He laughed and shook his head, looking slightly bemused; he obviously wasn't used to having to work for a date by the look of him. That was when Rachel came running back with our fries and cokes. She looked at Blake sitting next to me, and her mouth dropped open.

"Holy freaking shit! You're Blake Chambers!" she practically shouted, squeezing herself between us, almost sitting on his lap.

"Yes I am," he replied, smirking at her. That was obviously the reaction he wanted from me; she was almost drooling on him. I took my fries and started eating, trying to get into the football game but failing miserably. I didn't have a clue what was going on. The scoreboard said we were winning, but that was all I knew. Suddenly, everyone jumped up booing and shouting. I looked round at everyone, confused, wondering what I'd missed. Blake was grinning at me.

"What happened?" I asked, confused.

He shook his head, laughing quietly. "Foul ball," he explained. "Don't you know anything about football?" he asked, smirking again.

I shrugged, raising my eyebrows. "I know we're playing in blue today." He just laughed his head off; he had a really nice laugh.

• • •

THE GAME ENDED, and we'd won. Clay and Ben were carried off the field by the rest of the team for setting up and scoring the final touchdown that had secured the victory. "I'll see you at the party," Rachel said, getting up.

"Okay," I replied absentmindedly, playing with my cell phone, reading a text from my mom about her and David not being home tonight because they were staying at a hotel. Apparently, David was surprising her for their half year anniversary, but I already knew that anyway, he'd told me last week. I didn't notice that Blake had moved up next to me again. The bleachers were almost empty now, but I still had to wait for Clay.

"What party are you going to?" he purred in my ear, making me shiver.

"Um, I really don't know who's it is. I only started at this school this week; I have no idea who anyone is." I shrugged.

"So I can't persuade you to go out to dinner with me tonight?" he asked, giving me an adorable puppy dog face. I looked into his light blue eyes and drew in a shaky breath because he was making me slightly nervous. I never usually got nervous around guys, but this one made my palms get a little sweaty.

"Nope, sorry," I replied, trying to sound like he wasn't having an effect on me. He reached out and snatched my cell phone out of my hands, punching something in. "Hey!" I cried as I tried to get it back from him.

He just laughed as he held it out of reach. "How about tomorrow night?" he asked.

I smiled; tomorrow was movie night. "Can't. Busy," I stated matter-of-factly,

"Day after?" he offered, raising his pierced eyebrow.

"Busy," I replied, laughing now.

He sighed, shaking his head. "I won't give up you know. I always get what I want," he warned, looking me straight in the eyes. My stomach twisted in knots at his confidence. I would bet that that statement was true too. While he looked like that, I bet he had girls falling at his feet daily.

"That's your choice," I replied with a sly smile, looking at him through my eyelashes, trying to be seductive. He drew in a deep breath through his nose and let it out as a sigh.

Just then Clay walked up the stairs towards me. He was glaring at Blake. I had no idea why he would be shooting him that look at all, Clay usually liked everyone. I jumped up and ran to him, throwing my arms around him, kissing him on the cheek. "That was great! Well done," I chirped enthusiastically.

He laughed. "Yeah right, Riley Bear. Tell me one play that I did, and then I'll believe that you understood what was going on," he teased, tickling me.

I chewed on my lip, desperately trying to come up with something. He really did know me too well. "Well, there was a foul ball. And your touchdown at the end was superb," I replied, shooting a glance at Blake who laughed and shook his head at my pathetic attempts at a cover-up.

"She was watching, Don't worry, she didn't miss your skills there, Preston," Blake mused as he started to walk past us. "Oh, I almost forgot. Here's your phone, Riley. Give me a call if you change your mind," he added, winking at me. I smiled as he purposefully rubbed his finger across mine when I took the phone.

"I won't change my mind, so don't hold your breath," I replied, smirking. Blake just laughed and walked off. I couldn't help myself; I watched his butt as he walked away. I turned back to see Clay looking at me angrily. "What?" I asked innocently, blushing because he'd caught me staring at a guy's behind.

"He's too old for you," he said simply, putting his arm around me and leading me in the opposite direction to where Blake went.

"Too old for me? Do you know him then?" I questioned.

"Yeah I know him. He used to go here but he left two years ago. I was on the football team with him for a while. His name's Blake Chambers," he replied. I frowned at the barely disguised anger that I heard in his voice.

"Okay and you don't like him, right?" I asked, squeezing myself closer to him.

"Not really. He's a total player. I think he'd slept with all the girls at school before he left." He shook his head in disapproval.

"Hmm, sounds like someone else I know," I joked, tapping my chin.

He laughed. "I am nothing like him; I think he literally slept with *all* of the girls in school. There were even rumours that he slept with one of the teachers. And I say again; he's too old for you," he said sternly, looking at me warningly. I nodded and smiled as if I understood, just to put an end to the conversation.

• • •

THE PARTY WAS AS wild just as Rachel said it would be. There were all sorts of alcohol, body shots, drinking games, loud thumping music. I even spotted a couple of guys from school selling drugs, but I stayed well clear of them.

I was on my fifth shot when Rachel dragged me to dance. "So, you met Blake Chambers," she gushed excitedly.

"Oh hell yeah I met him, and I would definitely like to meet more of him." I sloshed back my vodka, shuddering at the slight burn of my throat.

She sighed dreamily. "He is so hot."

I nodded in agreement. "Definitely hot. But he's a total player though I heard," I replied, dancing to the beat of the music. Someone started to grind against my back; I turned around to see a blond boy trying to dry hump me from behind. "Do you mind?" I growled, putting a hand on his chest and pushing him away.

"No, baby, I don't mind at all." He laughed, moving back to me again.

I grabbed hold of his crotch, squeezing hard. "If you want to keep these, I suggest you get them the hell away from me," I spat venomously, squeezing a little harder, making him let out a little squeak and squirm under my grasp.

"Okay, okay, jeez. Sorry!" He held up his hands in defeat so I let go. He winced before cupping his crotch and walking away with a subtle limp.

I turned back to Rachel who was practically on the floor laughing. "What?" I asked, giggling even though I had no idea why.

Oh crap, I think I may be a little tipsy! I blinked a couple of times, looking around at the now extremely busy room.

"You are sooooo badass," she hissed in my ear, still laughing hysterically.

"Yeah, Clay taught me." I shrugged. "Let's get another drink and go outside for some air, okay?" I grabbed her hand, not waiting for an answer, and pulled her to the kitchen; we downed a shot and grabbed another to take outside.

Clay caught hold of my hand at the door. "Just like I showed you, huh?" he said, smiling proudly. I just nodded and kissed his cheek as Rachel and I staggered out of the door, giggling.

We sat on the swing set in the yard. "So how old is Blake anyway?" I asked Rachel who was leaning so far back on her swing she looked like she would fall off.

"Er, I think he left two years ago. So that would make him twenty I guess?" she replied, making it sound more like a question.

"Clay and him didn't really seem to like each other." I winced, thinking about the tension that I'd felt radiating off Clay earlier when they met.

"I think they played together on the football team when Blake was still at school. Blake played running back position too, and I think that Coach was riding them both pretty hard, making them compete for the spot. I don't think they ever got on because of that," she slurred, hiccupping at the end.

Clay came out then, strutting across the grass to us. "Hey, Riley Bear, you ready to call it a night?" he asked, pushing me gently on the swing from the front. I smiled happily. He used to push me on the swings all the time. He'd even built me a swing once for my birthday using a piece of rope and a large stick, and hung it from the old oak tree in my backyard. He had fallen out of the tree trying to tie the rope and broke his arm. As soon as his plaster cast was taken off he'd gone straight back into the tree and finished tying it. It still hung in my garden. "Rachel, you want a ride home?" he asked, shaking his keys at her to get her attention off of his body.

She giggled. "Hmm, do I want to ride with Clay Preston?" she purred suggestively, narrowing her eyes, looking him up and down.

I giggled, and Clay rolled his eyes. "Come on you two drunken girls, get in the car," he instructed, reaching out a hand for me. I took his hand and danced to the car drunkenly. We dropped Rachel at her house first, and Clay walked her to the door. The next thing I knew someone was pulling on my jeans, trying to get them down.

"Hey!" I squeaked, pushing the hands away from my half off jeans and trying to sit up. *Wait, what the hell? Am I going to be raped?* I started screaming and panicking.

A hand clamped over my mouth. "Riley! Riley Bear, it's just me! Jeez, calm down," Clay said loudly, pushing me back down. I opened my eyes and saw his beautiful green eyes inches from mine. I started to cry tears of relief. *Oh thank God it's just Clay!* I threw my arms around his neck and hugged him tight.

"It's okay. Shh, sorry. You fell asleep in the car. I was just putting you to bed, that's all," he murmured in my ear, smoothing down my hair. I looked around curiously. I was in my room, in my bed, he had already taken off my boots. Realisation dawned on me; he must have carried me from the car and was trying not to wake me. *Bless him, that's adorable!*

I giggled, feeling stupid. "I'm sorry." My heartbeat started to slow as he rubbed my hair. "You scared the crap out of me," I admitted, pushing my jeans further down but I was obviously drunk because they didn't actually move anywhere. He laughed and pulled them off for me, then stripped out of his clothes and climbed in bed with me.

He settled down on his side, facing me, but didn't touch me. This was the first time we'd been in a bed together since he'd kissed me, and he looked really unsure of what to do. My eyes were starting to droop again so I knew it wouldn't be long before I was asleep. I pushed hard on his chest to get him to roll onto his back and lifted his arm around me as I nuzzled onto his chest. I heard him laugh quietly, and I fell asleep listening to the sound of his heartbeat.

chapter three

The following week passed in a blur. Clay and I were completely back to normal, there was no awkwardness at all, which was great. I loved my new school. Rachel and I had become close friends, and I started hanging around with her group of friends too. Everyone was nice to me at school because I was friends with Mr Popular. Clay was his usual charming and protective self around me; I had a feeling he was warning the guys away, but I was still getting hit on a lot. I turned them all down nicely.

Today was Friday again. I was perched on the bleachers with Rachel and Jeff, wearing Clay's shirt again and we were happily tucking into hotdogs. I was really trying to watch the game this time. Clay had been trying to teach me some of the rules ready to watch, but everything was going so fast that I couldn't actually keep up.

"Hey, you never called." The bench bounced a little as someone sat next to me. I recognised his voice immediately - Blake. I tried not to look at him; I didn't want to have to look at his hotness again. I needed to remember that he was too old for me. *Him being too old for me doesn't mean I can't do a little flirting though...*

I turned to face him and gulped as I looked at his face. His blue eyes were shining with amusement as he cocked his head to the side.

Oh dear lord, he is even hotter than I remembered!

"Hmm, I had better things to do," I replied, waving my hand dismissively.

"Better things? What can be better than going out on a date with me?" His brow furrowed, as if he was a little confused that I'd rejected him again. I smiled to myself; he clearly wasn't used to rejection, that much was obvious from his lost expression. Not that I was surprised though, with the way he looked he probably had girls falling at his feet every day.

"Washing my hair. Walking the dog. Cleaning the house. You know, that kind of thing," I teased, shrugging.

"Well you don't know what you're missing out on," he said, smiling cockily.

"Hmm, I could probably guess actually. There would be some crappy food and maybe a crappy movie, where you would insist on sitting in the back so we could make out. And then, depending on how well the date went, there may be a little action in the car as you dropped me off. Am I close?" I asked, raising an eyebrow.

He laughed and shrugged. "Pretty close," he admitted, shaking his head in amusement. He leant in closer to me; his breath blew across my cheek making my skin prickle. "You know, I really like a challenge," he whispered in my ear sending shivers down my spine again.

"Well then you're definitely in the right place. I can be quite challenging," I whispered back, winking playfully.

"Hmm, I can see that." He slung an arm around my shoulder casually. I elbowed him in the side quickly and stood up, not wanting to take the flirting to anything physical.

"Come on, Tom, move your skinny ass! That ball's not gonna catch itself!" I shouted, giggling as he waved and shook his head at me. I really liked Tom, we teased each other constantly. He was a really lovely guy.

As I sat back down I was careful to put a little space between my body and Blake's. But that didn't seem to matter though because he moved up next to me again as soon as I was on the bench.

"You busy tonight?" he asked. I nodded slowly, fighting a smile. "And tomorrow?" he asked. I nodded again. "And I suppose the day after that?" He sighed dramatically. I nodded again and hid a smile at his playful annoyance. I could tell that he was actually quite enjoying the chase, especially if this was his first one like I imagined that it was.

"I'm not giving up. I'll come here every week and ask you out until you say yes," he vowed, running a lazy finger up my leg.

"Blake, honestly, you're wasting your time. I mean, do you even remember my name?" I asked, looking at him sceptically.

He nodded his head and looked a little hurt. "Of course I do, Riley. I haven't been able to stop thinking about you since last Friday." He frowned, as if he was admitting a weakness.

I smiled a little inside. That was really sweet. Then I remembered what people said about him, that he was a player, and he just wanted in my pants, nothing else. "Look, Blake, I don't know how old you think I am, but I'm only sixteen," I admitted, shaking my head.

He gasped, his eyes widening from shock. "Oh shit! Really? I thought you were eighteen. You're so close with Preston. I know he's a senior, so I thought you were too," he said, shaking his head slowly, looking at the floor.

"So, like I said, you're wasting your time," I repeated, shrugging and turning back to the game. I expected that to be the end of the conversation. It wasn't.

"So, you just turned sixteen, or..." he trailed off, looking at me hopefully.

"Er, no. I'll be seventeen next month, on the twenty-fifth," I answered, confused.

His face brightened immediately. "Okay, well then you're only a year off," he said, winking at me.

What the hell does he mean by that? A year off of what? I gave him a quizzical look, waiting for an explanation, but he just laughed. "A year off of what?" I asked, raising my eyebrows.

"You know what I'm gonna call you from now on?" he asked, ignoring my question. I smiled, wondering what on earth this was going to be about. "Jailbait," he smirked.

I laughed at that and shook my head. "Jailbait?"

"Yep. Because if you keep looking so damn hot you're probably gonna get me thrown in there." He wasn't smiling anymore, in fact, he looked a little sad.

I frowned. "You'd better stop talking to me then," I suggested, watching the game again, but I couldn't get my mind off of his sad expression.

"Yeah, maybe I should," I thought I heard him mumble as he stood up and walked away. Again, my eyes were instinctively drawn to his ass as he walked away.

• • •

A MONTH LATER IT was my birthday. I really hated birthdays, not the getting older part or anything, but I didn't like the whole fuss that came with it - the singing, the cake, everyone knowing. I hated being the centre of attention and birthdays made sure you were exactly that. Today was going to be a bad day. I rolled over, just about to get out of the bed, but Clay wrapped his arms tighter round me pulling me back to him.

"Happy Birthday, Riley Bear," he chirped in my ear. I smiled and he reached over the side of the bed and came back with a small rectangular present.

He had a huge grin so I leant over and kissed him on the cheek. "Thank you, Clay. But you shouldn't have bought me anything," I insisted, taking the present he was offering.

He rolled his eyes. "I know, I know, you don't like birthdays. But I like buying for your birthday, so suck it up." He laughed. I laughed too and tore off the gift wrap to reveal a rectangular red velvet jewellery box.

I looked at Clay. "Tell me you didn't spend a lot of money," I pleaded.

He sighed dramatically. "I didn't spend a lot of money. Just open it."

I took a deep breath and opened the box. Inside was a beautiful gold bracelet. Hanging near the clasp there was a small gold heart with what looked like a little diamond set in it. I couldn't speak. It was so beautiful, it was just perfect. I felt my eyes filling with tears.

"Oh shit! You don't like it? I can change it. Don't cry, Riley Bear," he groaned, pulling me to him and rubbing my back.

I pulled back and looked at him. "Of course I like it. I love it! Thank you, Clay, it's beautiful. It's just so perfect, so, *me*. Thank you," I said, kissing him on the cheek.

He laughed and rubbed the back of his neck. "Okay, great. I thought you'd like it. I saw it and I just had to get it for you. I actually bought it about three months ago, I wanted to give it to you then," he replied, blushing a little.

I smiled and pulled the bracelet out of the box holding it out to him. "Will you put it on for me?" I asked, grinning happily. Hopefully my thoughts about this being a bad day were going to be totally wrong, because my birthday was off to a fantastic start so far.

He put the bracelet on me, his fingers lingering around my wrists. I could feel heat coursing up my arm as my breathing sped up. I looked at him; he had his jaw clenched tight in concentration. I held my breath and looked away from his beautiful face to try and stop my hormones from going crazy.

Why can't I just stop lusting after my best friend? Things had been strained recently, not awkward or anything, but I just couldn't stop looking at Clay in ways that I really shouldn't look at him in. I also kept getting jealous whenever he would kiss other girls in front of me. I really needed to get a grip of myself; we were friends, nothing more than that.

He clipped it on and then moved away from me quickly as if I burnt him. "I'm gonna go make you some breakfast," he stated, climbing out of the bed, not looking at me.

"Why don't we go out for breakfast? I'm in the mood for a chocolate doughnut." I smiled as he turned his nose up in disgust.

"Jelly doughnut!" he countered, smirking at me. This was an old argument that no one ever won, so I just laughed. "And, seeing as it's your birthday, I'm buying," he added as I got up to shower.

• • •

AFTER A LONG AND hard day of lessons, I walked out of the school only to see a large group of girls all standing around gossiping near the door.

"I can't believe it! He is sooooo hot!"

"I think I've died and gone to heaven."

"Mmm, he is yummy."

I rolled my eyes and tried not to make any sort of scoffing noise because they were obviously fawning over a boy. They were all staring in the same direction. Out of interest, I flicked my eyes that way too. I assumed that Clay or one of his friends were standing there, because they usually warranted the same kind of reaction from their little fan girls at the school. But instead of Clay or one of his friends, I saw Blake leaning against his car. He was wearing a white t-shirt, black leather jacket, low slung jeans and his black boots again. I felt just like one of the little girls that were going gaga over him seconds earlier. He looked so hot that my mouth actually started to water.

I shook my head at myself and walked out to go and find Clay. He was at a long football practice tonight so I had over an hour to wait for him.

As I crossed the parking lot and headed towards the field, Blake shouted me. "Hey, Jailbait!" he greeted, jogging to catch up with me.

I turned and smiled. "Hey, what are you doing here?" I asked politely, whist trying to discreetly check him out again. I could see the planes of his chest and abs through his t-shirt. The wind blew his spicy, manly scent towards me, making my stomach flutter. His hair ruffled up in the breeze so he raked a hand through it, somehow making it even more stylishly messy.

"I wanted to wish you happy birthday," he said simply, smiling his sexy smile.

"You what? How did you know it was my birthday? We've only met twice." I looked around quickly to make sure no one heard that it was my birthday today. No one was close enough to hear our conversation though, so I breathed a sigh of relief.

"You told me last time I saw you," he explained. He shoved a hand into his jeans pocket and pulled out a small red material bag with black swirls on it.

"You remembered that? From a month ago?" I asked, my mouth hanging open in shock.

He laughed. "I can remember things you know. I'm not just a pretty face," he replied sarcastically, winking at me.

"And who said you had a pretty face?" I asked, narrowing my eyes trying to hide my smile.

He laughed. "Here, I got you this." He held out the little bag to me.

I gasped at his thoughtfulness. "You got me a present?" I asked, stepping closer to him to take it. He nodded and watched me as I opened the string at the top of the material bag, and then tipped it up into my hand. A little red metal rose fell out onto my palm. It was really cute. It had a string on one end; I turned it over to look at the back.

"It's a charm for your cell. I know it's a bit lame, but girls like that kind of thing, right? And I knew you didn't have one, so..." he trailed off, seeming uncomfortable as he shifted on his feet.

I smiled gratefully. I couldn't help but think that him being all sweet was a direct contrast to the rumours that I'd heard about him around school. "It's great. Thank you, Blake."

"Here, hand me your cell," he instructed, holding out his hand for it. I gave it to him and he took the little charm too, threading the string through the hole at the top of my phone, looping it. He passed it back to me, and I smiled at how cute the little charm looked with my red cell phone. It suited it perfectly. "Maybe now when you use your cell it'll remind you of me and maybe you'll call me," he suggested, tipping his head to the side.

I smiled again and stepped closer to give him a hug. I wrapped my arms around him a little awkwardly, and he did the same. "Thanks," I whispered.

I felt him shudder against me. "Careful there, Jailbait," he joked, pulling away a bit sheepishly. I laughed and rolled my eyes playfully. "So, what are you doing for your birthday tonight?" he asked, looking at his feet.

"Not much really. Clay's coming over and I think my mom and stepdad will probably bring out a cake or something." I scrunched up my nose up in disgust.

"You don't want Clay coming over, or you don't like cake?" he asked, laughing.

"Oh come on, who doesn't like cake?" I replied, smiling.

"Oh, so you don't want Clay over," he countered, waggling his eyebrows.

I slapped his arm. "Shut up! I just don't like the whole birthday, cake and singing thing."

"Why not?" he asked, looking genuinely curious. I sighed; I really didn't want to talk about the whole being the centre of attention thing, so I just shrugged instead.

"Thanks for the charm, Blake, that was really nice of you. I should go though," I said, turning to walk to the field again.

He grabbed my hand to stop me walking. "You need a ride home?" he offered.

"No thanks. Clay's driving me; I just need to wait for his practice to finish." I shrugged, turning to leave again.

"What, you have to wait until four thirty?" he asked, with wide eyes whilst looking at his watch.

"Actually, five. They're going over some new plays or something, for some big quarterfinal or something or other." I shrugged, putting my hands up in a 'I haven't got a clue' gesture.

He laughed. "You really don't know anything about football, do you?" he teased, grabbing my hand and pulling me towards his car.

What the heck is he doing now? Is this boy crazy? "What are you doing Blake? I said I don't need a ride home," I mused as he opened his passenger door for me.

"Okay, that's fine. But I can take you out for an hour and a half then drop you back at school before practice finishes," he countered, smirking as he took my bag out of my hand and threw it on the backseat.

I knew I shouldn't go with him, I hardly knew him, and he had a bad reputation. But he honestly seemed so sweet and not like what I'd heard about him from Clay.

He must have sensed my indecision. "I promise I won't try anything on you, Jailbait. Scouts honour. I just want to buy you a milkshake for your birthday." He motioned for me to get in the car, a dazzling smile stretched across his full lips. I took a deep breath and got into the car. He shut the door with a chuckle - he obviously liked getting his own way.

He drove us in silence. His car was nice, I had no idea about cars so I didn't know what sort it was, but it was clean and smelled like leather and his aftershave. I actually felt quite relaxed considering that I was alone in a car with an older guy that I knew hardly anything about. I tried not to let my mind register what a terrible idea this was. I tried not to think about the fact that I had just gotten into his car and no one knew where I was or that I was with him.

After a few minutes he pulled into the parking lot for a little diner and stopped the car. We got out and headed up to the diner. He pushed the door open and held it there, motioning for me to go first.

"Wow, very gentlemanly," I complimented, actually impressed that he had done it.

"I can be a gentleman when I want to be. I just don't want to be that often," he replied, grinning cheekily. I rolled my eyes at him and sat in one of the booths.

He sat opposite me as the waitress came over and gave him an exceptionally seductive smile. "Well hello. What can I do for you?" she asked, looking at him through her eyelashes.

"Hey. I'll have a chocolate shake with extra ice cream. Jailbait?" He looked at me, raising his eyebrows, waiting for me to order too.

The waitress dragged her eyes away from Blake just long enough to sneer at me. "Er, I'll have a strawberry shake, please." I shrugged, trying not to show how uncomfortable I felt under her intense gaze. The woman actually looked like she wanted to stab me or something.

"Put extra ice cream in hers too would ya?" Blake requested before turning back to me and smiling. "Trust me on this one." He winked at me, grinning. The woman smiled at him again, but he was too busy reaching across the table to notice.

He took my hand, and I just sat there in shock. *This guy is way too old for me, and he's incredibly hot - so what on earth is he holding my hand for?* I pulled my hand back putting it in my lap; he looked a little hurt but smiled to cover it up.

"So what did you get for your birthday?" he asked.

"Well, aside from a new charm for my cell, my mom and David got me a new iPod. And Clay got me this bracelet," I replied, jiggling my wrist to make it shine when it caught the sun. He reached out and took hold of my wrist, gently bringing it to him so he could look at it.

"It's pretty," he muttered, taking hold of my hand again. I tried to pull away again, but he frowned and gripped my hand a little tighter. "Please?" he said quietly.

I looked into his eyes and could feel myself being drawn in. I stopped struggling and let him hold my hand. It actually felt nice, though very different from when Clay held my hand. When Clay and I held hands it was just natural, normal, like breathing. But this felt nice in a different way; his hand was warm and slightly rough to the touch.

The waitress came over and placed our drinks down, giving me another dirty look as she walked away. I took a big swig of my milkshake and moaned in appreciation. It melted on my tongue, the extra ice cream making it thick and creamy. "Wow, I think that's the best milkshake I've ever had," I admitted, taking another pull on the straw.

He nodded. "Yeah, I thought you'd like it."

"So how old are you exactly, Blake?" I asked, grabbing a spoon so I could eat the ice cream that was floating at the top of my milkshake.

"I turned twenty-one just over two months ago," he answered, frowning, looking a little upset about something.

"So what's with the face? You don't like being twenty-one?" I asked, giggling. Maybe he thought he was getting old or something.

"I don't mind the age. It's just that I waited a long time to find someone that I liked and when I finally do she's so much freaking younger than me it's not even legal!" he huffed, stabbing his straw into his milkshake forcefully.

I smiled but quickly hid it. *He likes me?* The thought made my stomach flutter with excitement, but the thing is, there was nothing we could do about it. If I had sex with him then he could be charged with statutory rape due to my age.

"Oh, you like someone? Do I know her?" I teased.

"It's not a joke, Riley," he snapped, shaking his head. *Oops, okay temper!* "Sorry, I didn't mean to snap at you like that. It's just so frustrating," he apologised, squeezing my hand gently.

It was quiet for a minute; I didn't know what to say, so we both just stared at the table. "So tell me some more about you," he suggested, looking up with an easy smile.

"What do you want to know?" I asked, sipping my milkshake again. I was secretly glad for the conversation because I hated uneasy silences.

"Well, what kind of music do you like? What do you like to do in your spare time? What's your favourite colour? That kind of thing," he suggested, waving his free hand around.

"Well, I like R&B stuff mostly. I like to dance and go to the movies. And, I know it sounds boring, but I love to read. My favourite colour is pink," I said smiling, answering all of his questions in turn. "What about you? Are you in college or something or do you work?" I asked,

"At the moment I'm working at Old Joes over on East Street. It's a scrap yard, but I don't really want to be doing that so I'm always looking for something else." He shrugged.

We chatted for about an hour and then he paid for our drinks. When we were ready to leave, he took my hand and helped me out of the booth in another gentlemanly gesture - which gained me another glare from the waitress. She stepped in front of him and put her hand on his chest. "So, can I get your number?" she purred sexily, trailing her finger down his abs.

He laughed and raised our intertwined hands. "Seriously? You think you have a chance when I'm holding her hand?" he asked, shaking his head and pulling me to the exit. I was stunned. I almost choked on my laughter, quickly putting my hand over my mouth and turning it into a cough. But I'd done it too late; she'd seen me laugh. She gave me a death glare before stomping off. He didn't seem fazed in the slightest, just pulled me out of the door and over to his car, opening the passenger side for me.

"Jeez, did you have to be so rude? I thought she was gonna stab me or something," I scolded, laughing and shaking my head.

He chuckled. "I wasn't rude! What was I supposed to say? You would rather I gave her my number to be polite?" he replied, grinning at me cockily.

"No. But you could have just said no thanks or something; you didn't need to bring me into it." I slapped him playfully on the arm which just made him laugh again.

We arrived at school with five minutes to spare; he pulled into the almost empty parking lot. "So, do you think I could get your number?" he asked, seeming a little nervous about it. He looked really sweet and vulnerable, not like what I had been told about him at all. He hadn't even tried to kiss me, and he turned the waitress down not even paying one ounce of attention to her.

"Blake, what's the point? This can't go anywhere," I countered, shrugging.

He sighed. "Please can I have your number? Let's just see, please? A date that's all. I really like you," he said, scratching absentmindedly at his jaw.

I chewed on my lip and thought it through. *I guess it can't do that much harm. He's only asking for a date, it doesn't mean I have to sleep with him.* My mind flicked to Clay, he would go crazy if I went out with Blake. I forced all thoughts of Clay out of my mind. Why was I thinking about him again anyway? He was just my best friend; I didn't need his permission to go on a date with a guy.

"Jailbait?" Blake prompted, snapping me out of my mental debate.

"Er, yeah okay, I guess," I agreed, taking the cell phone that he was now holding out to me and punching in my number. He had a huge smile on his face, showing all of his perfectly straight white teeth. I couldn't help but smile back. This had been fun so the date would go okay too. Or maybe he wouldn't even call me in the first place; maybe he would drive away and just delete my number. Maybe he was asking just to see if he could get it, like a challenge or something. "I'd better go, Clay will be out soon," I said, climbing out of the car.

"Okay. I'll call you," he vowed as I shut the door.

It had turned cold so I pulled my jacket tighter around me as I walked to the field. Suddenly, my cell phone started ringing in my pocket. I looked at the screen seeing that it said Blake on it. I frowned, confused as to how I got his number, then I remembered that he'd stored it in there the first night I met him, at the game.

"Hello?"

"Just checking you gave me the right number," he replied and laughed before hanging up. I laughed too as I snapped the phone shut. I looked at the little rose charm and smiled as I put it back in my pocket.

"Hey, Riley Bear!" Clay called as I reached the field. He jogged over to me and went to throw an arm around my shoulder so I quickly jumped away.

"No way, look at the state of you," I cried, horrified, looking at him distastefully. He was covered in mud, sweat, and grass. He looked down at himself and laughed, suddenly his head snapped up to look at me with an evil glint in his eye. I gasped, immediately knowing he was going to cover me in something nasty. I turned and ran as fast as I could. I could hear him chasing behind me, laughing. Within a few feet he grabbed me from behind and rubbed his face in my hair. "Ew! Clay!" I whined, giggling.

He just laughed and threw his arm over my shoulder, leading us off of the field. "Sorry you had to wait for me. It's lucky you waited inside though, it's getting cold out here," he mused, pulling me closer to his side.

I opened my mouth to tell him I'd been with Blake, but nothing came out. *Oh just man up and tell him, Riley!* I took a deep breath, knowing he wasn't going to like the fact that I'd just spent an hour with the guy he told me to stay away from.

"So what movie do you wanna watch tonight?" he asked just as I was about to speak.

"Um, I don't mind. How about New Moon?" I offered.

He groaned. "Jeez the shifter again? Haven't you seen enough of him already?" he whined.

I grinned and shook my head forcefully. "No way. You can never get enough

Taylor Lautner in your life," I replied, smiling as I pushed him towards the locker rooms to shower.

• • •

JUST AS I THOUGHT they would, my mom and David pulled out a cake after dinner, and they sang happy birthday to me. I looked over at Clay, he wasn't singing because he knew that I hated it. He never sang happy birthday to me. But he did sit there with a huge smirk on his face while I grimaced and wriggled, uncomfortable with the attention. They even made me blow out the candles like a five year old.

After, we watched New Moon again and Clay, sweet boy that he was, didn't complain once - even though I'd made him watch it about six times already. Just as we settled into bed to go to sleep, my cell phone beeped. I looked at the screen: 1 new message from Blake. I pressed read:

'Hey, just wanted to say goodnight. Maybe I could take you for a crappy dinner and a crappy movie tomorrow? Blake ;)'

I laughed because he'd used my words that I'd once said to him. "What's so funny?" Clay asked, putting his arms behind his head, settling himself into my bed like he owned the place.

"Er, nothing, it's just Rachel that's all," I answered, unsure why I was lying to him. I snapped my phone shut and laid next to him as usual.

chapter four

"Crap, it's him! So, what do you think? Should I go?" I asked Rachel as I looked at my cell phone that was flashing in my hand.

She looked at me like I was stupid. "Why the hell are you asking me? It's Blake Chambers for goodness sake! Of course you should go!" she replied, rolling her eyes at me. I sighed; I just didn't know what to do. Blake had text me early this morning asking if I would go out tonight at seven, my phone was currently ringing in my hand, and I was just staring at it still undecided.

I took a big breath and answered the phone. "Umm, hey," I said quietly.

"Hey, Jailbait. You okay? You took a long time to answer," he replied, sounding a little nervous.

"Yeah, I was just talking to my friend. I didn't feel the phone go off, that's all," I lied, grimacing at Rachel who was staring at my phone like a lovesick puppy.

"So, did you get my message this morning?" he asked.

"Mmm hmm," I mumbled, looking pleadingly at Rachel for something to say. She was frantically nodding her head with wide eyes mouthing 'say yes' over and over.

"Okay, well, do you want to go?" he asked after a few seconds of silence.

I looked at Rachel one last time. "Say yes!" she stage whispered at me.

"Yes," I agreed quietly. I heard a muffled, "Yessssssssss!" from the phone that I assume I wasn't meant to hear. "Kinda excited there are ya?" I joked, smiling in spite of myself.

He cleared his throat. "Oh, yeah sorry, you weren't meant to hear that," he replied sheepishly. "So where do you live?" I could hear him rustling paper around in the background.

"I live on Cotton Road, near the pond. It's number seventeen. You know where that is?" I asked. I hoped he did because I was useless with directions.

"You live on Cotton Road? No wonder you're so close to Clay. That's where he lives, isn't it?" he asked, sounding a little surprised.

"Yeah, he lives next door actually," I answered.

"Okay, well I know where it is, I've been to Clay's before. So, I'll pick you up at seven then?" he suggested, sounding really excited.

"Sure, see you then." I snapped the phone shut and breathed out a sigh of relief that it was over. Not that talking to him was hard, because it was actually quite easy, but the whole decision thing was a pain in the butt.

Rachel was practically bouncing on the spot with excitement. "Great, that's done. So the next question is, do you tell Clay?" Rachel said, grinning. I groaned. I couldn't lie to my best friend, but at the same time I didn't want to have to tell him either, he would be seriously pissed about it. I shrugged in response to her question. "Okay, I have a solution. How about we just avoid him altogether? That way you don't have to lie to him or tell the truth. There's only one period left and you don't have it with him. Just text him and tell him that I'm taking you home tonight so you don't need a ride," Rachel suggested.

I felt the smile creep onto my face. That was actually a pretty good idea. That way if the date ended up being a disaster then Clay didn't have to know. And, if it went well, then I could tell him about it tomorrow.

"Okay, good plan. We'll make an evil mastermind out of you yet," I chirped, hugging her tightly.

• • •

I WAS INCREDIBLY nervous. I had never been nervous about a date before, ever. I'd left my hair down and added some soft curls and a tiny bit of make-up, I never wore a lot so I didn't want to go too overboard. Rachel had come in after she dropped me home and had helped me pick out an outfit. I was now in light blue skinny jeans and a tight red V-neck top that showed a little cleavage but wasn't too slutty. I'd opted for red, open toed high heels that would probably kill me if I had to walk or dance in them, but he'd said dinner and a movie in the text so they would be sufficient for that.

I felt sick with nerves. I just kept staring at myself in the mirror and fussing with my hair, wondering what an incredibly hot guy like him would see in someone like me. In my opinion, I was just average. The only people that thought I was more than that were my parents, and probably Clay, but I was pretty sure they were all just biased.

I heard the doorbell ring. "Holy crap, he's early," I muttered looking at the clock that said five to seven. I bounded out of my room to get the door, only to hear voices coming from the hallway. I gasped because David was probably about to embarrass me by asking him a hundred questions, like he did to all of my dates. I stopped out of sight to listen.

"So, where are you taking my daughter tonight?" I heard David ask. I smiled a little at what he'd said; he had always called me his daughter.

"Er, I thought we would go to this little Italian restaurant that I know, and then go see a movie. Is that okay? I mean, does she have a curfew or anything?" Blake asked.

"Well, it is a school night. You do know she's only seventeen, don't you?" David asked. I winced at this conversation and pushed myself away from the wall, bounding down the stairs with my face flaming with embarrassment.

"David! He knows how old I am. Jeez, leave him alone would you?" I insisted, giving him a kiss on the cheek and grabbing my black leather jacket. I refused to look at Blake until my cheeks stopped burning, but I could feel his eyes on me.

"Well, like I was saying to Blake here, it's a school night, Riley, so your mom and I agree that you should be home by eleven," he stated, looking at me sternly.

I gave him my puppy dog face, pouting my lip. "But, David, we might not get time to see a movie if I have to be back by then," I whined, looking at him pleadingly.

"Oh. Well, all right eleven thirty. But not a minute past!" he conceded, shaking his head.

I laughed and kissed his cheek again. "Thanks." I smiled and turned to face Blake for the first time.

"I got you these," he said, handing me a dozen red roses.

I gasped a little shocked. That was a really sweet move; I would have never thought he would be sweet like that. The only person that had ever given me flowers was Clay.

"Wow, they're beautiful. Thanks," I gushed, not knowing what to say. My stepdad was standing there watching me with a one eyebrow raised. I felt my face heat up again.

"You're welcome," Blake replied, grinning.

"David, could you ask Mom to put these in some water for me?" I asked, holding out the flowers for him. He nodded in agreement as I took a step towards the door, pulling on my jacket. "I'll see you later."

"Goodbye, Sir," Blake said, holding out a hand to David.

He shook it firmly. "You look after her, you hear me?" he instructed sternly.

Blake nodded and smiled politely. "I will, Sir," he answered. He smiled at me as we walked to the car. "You look really beautiful," he complimented, looking me up and down slowly, making me feel a little self-conscious.

"You don't look bad yourself." That was the understatement of the year right there. He had on his biker boots, nicely ripped jeans, and a black shirt that he had left undone a little and had rolled the sleeves up to his elbows. His hair and face were gorgeous as usual.

I was so completely checking him out that I didn't even realise that we had got to the car already. He was standing there next to the open door, waiting for me to get in, and I was too busy staring at him.

I mentally slapped myself. I was being a real idiot right now, I needed to get a grip and calm down. "Er, sorry. I was just thinking whether I brought my cell phone or not," I lied, blushing and getting in the car.

"You have it?" he asked. I nodded and he smiled before closing the door and walking round to the driver's side. "You like Italian?" he asked once he was in his seat next to me.

I nodded and grinned. "Doesn't everyone?" I asked. He smiled as we pulled out of my drive.

• • •

THE RESTAURANT WAS nice. It was small, intimate, and perfect for a date. There were candles on each table making it quite romantic. "So, you have your dad completely wrapped around your little finger. Are you a daddy's girl?" he asked while we were eating.

"He's not actually my dad. He's my stepdad," I corrected. "But he's really great. He married my mom when I was seven so he's always been there really. I guess in a way I'm kind of a daddy's girl. He likes to spoil me and he gangs up on my mom with me." I laughed.

"He seems like a nice guy," Blake replied, smiling,

"Yeah, he's the best," I agreed. "That good?" I asked, pointing at his lasagne.

He nodded quickly. "Want some?" he offered, holding out a forkful to me.

"Wow, that's so romantic, Blake. You want to feed me?" I joked, trying not to laugh. He snorted and shook his head, putting the forkful in his mouth instead. "Hey, I was gonna eat that, I was kidding!" I cried, grinning.

He chuckled and got another forkful, holding it out to me. I put my hand over his and brought the fork to my mouth and took the food off the fork slower than normal, trying to make it look seductive. I think it had the desired effect because he drew in a jagged breath through his teeth and let it out in a little moan.

The taste of it made my mouth water, and caused a little moan to escape my lips. It was incredible. He really knew some good places to eat! *I bet that's because he's been on a lot of dates because he's a player.* I forced myself to stop thinking about him that way, I shouldn't keep thinking about him with other girls. So far the date had gone great, so I was going to give him the benefit of the doubt about his romantic history.

"Wow. That's really good," I gushed, after I had finished chewing. I'd have to bring Clay here. Lasagne was his favourite, and my chicken pasta was tasty too, so he wouldn't even mind swapping. Clay always did that. He always ordered something that I'd like so that we could swap half way through.

Wait, why the heck am I thinking about Clay again? Riley, you're on a date with a super-hot guy, stop thinking about your best friend! Stupid, stupid, stupid!

"Yeah. Me and my sister come here a lot to eat," Blake replied, digging in again, seeming totally oblivious that I was thinking about another boy while I was sat with him.

"How old is your sister? Are you close then?" I asked.

"She's twenty-six. And yeah, we're pretty close. I live with her actually. My parents died when I was thirteen, Michelle was nineteen so she became my legal guardian after that. She's really great, you'll like her," he explained with a fond smile.

I frowned. I really hadn't seen that coming. He'd lost his parents? That was so sad. "I'm sorry about your mom and dad. But your sister sounds great for taking you on like that and still being a kid herself," I praised. I was kind of in awe of this girl who was only two years older than me when she had to start raising a grieving hormonal teenage brother.

"Michelle's great. She works here actually. Not tonight though, it's her night off." He grinned. I breathed a sigh of relief when he said the last part. I didn't really want to be meeting his family on a first date.

"And what does your sister think of you dating a minor?" I asked, smirking at him. *There is no way he's told his sister about me. Ha! Let's see what lie he'll come up with.*

He shrugged casually. "Well, at first she thought I was crazy, but now she just said 'what will be, will be', whatever that means." He shrugged, looking unconcerned. He actually looked like he was telling the truth – either that or he was a remarkably good liar.

"Hey guys, you all done here?" the waiter asked, taking our empty plates. "Can I get you any desserts or coffees?"

Blake turned to me and smiled. "Jailbait?" He cocked his head to the side looking extremely cute as he waited for me to make the decision.

"Umm, no thanks," I said, smiling at the waiter.

"Okay, just the check then, please," Blake told him. When he walked off with the plates, Blake looked at me curiously. "You don't want a dessert? I thought all girls liked dessert," he said, frowning and leaning in towards me over the table.

"No, I like chocolate and popcorn," I countered, waggling my eyebrows, making him laugh.

We decided to watch a comedy film in the end, and he bought popcorn and chocolate. In fact, he hadn't let me pay for anything all night long. He'd said that I could pay next time and gave me a sly wink, saying that then I would need to come out with him again.

On the way to our screen, we walked past a group of boys who were all standing around the foyer, waiting for their screen to be cleaned; they all turned to me and started whistling and playful making cat calls. I felt Blake stiffen next to me and he grabbed my hand, pulling me away from them, to his other side protectively, whilst shooting them death glares.

I giggled. "Wow, possessive much?" I teased, grabbing a handful of popcorn. He just continued to glare at them until we were at the door to our screen.

"So, where do you want to sit?" he asked once we were safely inside.

"What? You don't want to sit at the back?" I asked, faking shock.

He laughed. "I would definitely like to sit at the back. I'm asking you where you want to sit," he replied, gently squeezing my hand that he was holding.

I giggled and pulled him forwards. "Let's go for the middle," I suggested.

He sighed and nodded, following behind me. "Whatever you say, Jailbait."

I sat about three quarters of the way down. I didn't go too close to the back so that he would get any funny ideas - not that I didn't want to make out with him though, because I certainly did. This date was actually going great, and I was surprised at what a nice guy he was, well, so far anyway. I tried to keep in mind that he was a player but it was hard when he was being so sweet.

As the movie started he put his arm over the back of my chair casually as if he thought nothing of it. It was quite sweet actually. His hand was only a few centimetres away from my shoulder so I reached out and tangled my fingers with his, pulling his arm around my shoulder instead of being on the chair. From the corner of my eye I saw him look at me and smile, so I just kept looking at the screen. The movie was funny, and we both laughed at the same parts, which was good.

Once it had finished we walked slowly back to the car, holding hands. My shoes were really starting to hurt me now; I silently cursed Rachel.

"You okay?" he asked, when I stopped to take the damn things off.

"Yeah, my shoes are hurting me that's all. They're new; I should have worn them in," I moaned, tugging the other one off.

"You can't walk barefoot; there could be glass or something." He frowned and shook his head forcefully.

I laughed and started to walk again. "Blake, jeez! It'll be fine."

"No way!" He caught my hand, pulling me to a stop as he squatted down in front of me.

"What are you doing, checking for glass?" I asked, laughing at him.

"I'm not letting you walk with no shoes so I'll carry you," he replied. I could almost hear him roll his eyes at me. I sighed dramatically, faking exasperation, when in reality, that was actually really sweet.

"I'm heavy," I warned as I wrapped my arms around his neck and my legs around his waist.

He just laughed. "Heavy? Yeah right, I think I can handle it," he scoffed, standing up, wrapping his arms around my thighs. It actually felt quite weird to have another guy do this sort of thing. I was so used to Clay that even Blake's body felt a little wrong between my legs.

I rolled my eyes at myself. *There I go, thinking about Clay again!*

• • •

WHEN WE PULLED into my drive he smiled happily. "There, I got you home in plenty of time," he boasted, nodding at the clock on his dashboard. It was 11:16.

I laughed. "Well, thanks for tonight. I had fun." I smiled a little nervously, not really knowing what to say. I wasn't exactly experienced with boys, so I felt a little awkward.

"I did too," he replied, smiling his perfect smile, showing me all of his teeth. "I'll walk you to your door." He pushed his door open and jogged around to my side to open the door. As I went to step out he grabbed me around the waist and threw me over his shoulder, making me squeal from shock as my world turned upside down. He just laughed at my reaction. "Shh, you'll wake the neighbours. I don't want Clay to come and kick my ass," he joked as he carried me up the steps to my porch. He pulled me down into his arms before setting me gently onto my feet. "Next time we go out, wear more comfortable shoes," he instructed, nodding at my heels in my hand.

"Next time? Who said I want to go out with you again?" I asked, still slightly breathless from being carried.

He smiled and stepped closer to me, his eyes flicked down to my lips. I felt my eyes widen in shock as I realised he was going to kiss me. He was inching his head forwards slowly, obviously giving me the chance to move if I wanted to. I didn't. His lips touched mine gently for a couple of seconds. It felt a little weird because of his piercing, but it was still really nice. He made a small moaning sound and then pulled away slowly with a sigh, looking at me happily, smiling. I smiled too. The kiss was perfect, sweet and soft. It had definitely left me wanting more. I gulped and sighed a little.

"Okay, well maybe tomorrow night?" he asked, seeming a little nervous again.

I chewed on my lip. Tomorrow was Wednesday, a movie night.

"Um, I can't. I actually have plans with Clay tomorrow. It's kind of tradition, we always hang out on Wednesdays," I said apologetically. He just nodded without expression. "I'm free on Thursday though," I offered, raising an eyebrow.

Instantly, his face brightened. "Okay, great. Thursday then. I'll pick you up at seven again?" he suggested, beaming.

"Sure." I smiled because he looked so happy about it. He inched forward again and just as his lips brushed against mine, the front door opened. He jumped away from me quickly.

"Oh I thought I heard voices!" my mom chirped, standing there in her fluffy pink robe.

"Hi, Mom. Er, Mom, this is Blake. Blake, my mom, Sandra," I introduced, waving between them.

He reached out a hand and shook hers, smiling. "Nice to meet you."

"Mmm, you too," my mom replied, looking him over. She shot me a look and raised her eyebrows before smirking and going inside, closing the door behind her.

I laughed nervously. "Wow, that was awkward."

He grinned. "I'd better get going, you've got school tomorrow," he said sarcastically, obviously poking fun at my age.

"Ha ha. Go on then. I'll see you Thursday," I said, turning to go inside.

He grabbed my hand stopping me. I looked back at his gorgeous face wondering if he was going to try for the kiss that my mom interrupted. "Can't wait. Sleep well." He winked at me and turned to walk off to his car. I really couldn't help myself, I watched his butt again.

As soon as I closed the door, she was there, as I knew she would be. "Oh my gosh, he is so handsome!" my mom gushed, fanning her face, looking at me with wide eyes.

I giggled, flicking my eyes around the empty hallway. "Don't let David hear you say that," I joked.

"Oh he already told me he was a good-looking kid. Actually, he sent me out there so I could get a look," she admitted, laughing.

I gasped. "Are you serious? He sent you out to see a fit guy?" I said, shaking my head. My stepdad really was too funny sometimes.

She just laughed again. "Well, he seemed like a nice boy, despite the piercings. Did you have a good time tonight?" she asked, looking me up and down.

"Yeah actually I did. And he is a nice guy, from what I've seen so far," I confirmed, shrugging.

"So, you're going out with him again on Thursday..." she trailed off, biting her lip.

I gasped. "Were you listening?"

She shook her head in protest. "I wasn't listening; I just heard, that's all. So how was the kiss? Was it good? Did the piercing feel funny?" she asked. I just laughed; my mom had always been great and easy to talk to.

"It was really nice, Mom. Right then, I'm going to bed. G'night." I kissed her cheek before I headed towards the stairs.

"Riley?" she called when I was about two steps up.

"Mmm?" I mumbled, turning back.

"I know he's older than you and, therefore, probably more experienced. But that doesn't mean you have to rush into anything. However, if you do decide to take things further, please be safe. If you need to talk to me about anything, you know you can, don't you?" she asked, looking at me lovingly.

"I know that, Mom, and thanks." I smiled gratefully and turned heading up to bed. When I walked into my room, I immediately saw the vase of roses that my mom had put on my desk for me. I smiled and headed over to them, running my finger across the soft petals, before leaning in and breathing in their sweet scent. I sighed happily and grabbed my pyjamas, changing and slipping into bed.

I laid awake for a long time, just thinking about the kiss and how much I wanted to kiss him again, and again, and again. Suddenly, my phone beeped with a new message. Grabbing it off of the side, I opened it eagerly.

'I had a really great time tonight. Can't wait for Thursday. Sweet dreams, Jailbait'

I smiled and finally drifted to sleep with a smile on my face.

chapter five

"Hey," Clay chirped as I climbed into his car in the morning. "Hey, yourself," I replied, kissing his cheek. He smiled, and I felt my heart speed up because of how handsome it made him look. I really needed to stop looking at him like that, but ever since that kiss I just saw him differently. I gulped as I remembered the issue at hand - I needed to tell him about my date with Blake. "Er, Clay, I need to tell you something but I don't want you to get annoyed or yell at me or anything. Agreed?" I asked, nervously playing with my hands in my lap.

"Okay, I won't get mad, I promise. What's wrong?" he asked. I could hear the concern in his voice; he obviously already thought this was going to be something bad. He pulled into the school parking lot but we didn't move to get out. I didn't say anything, I couldn't think of how to phrase it. He was going to go crazy for sure. He'd already told me to stay away from Blake. "Riley?" he prompted, taking my hand and rubbing soothing circles in the back of it with his thumb.

I took a deep breath before speaking, "Okay, well, I went out with Blake Chambers last night. And, I'm... well, I'm seeing him again tomorrow." I quickly looked out of the windshield, not wanting to see his expression. He drew in a sharp breath through his teeth, and I grimaced, waiting for him to explode.

"You went out with him?" he whispered.

I frowned, a little taken aback. That really wasn't the reaction I expected. I looked over at him; he looked so sad that I almost cried. I moved over to sit on his lap and wrapped my arms around his neck, putting my forehead to his.

"I'm sorry. I know you don't like him, but he was actually really sweet to me," I assured him.

He had his eyes squeezed shut, and his hands were clenched into fists on the seat, his jaw clenched tight. He didn't say anything so I reached down and put his arms around my waist, just needing a little affection because his silence was killing me. He didn't unclench his fists, but he left his arms around me which I took as a good sign.

"It was fun. I had a nice time," I continued.

He snapped his eyes open and pulled his head back from mine, his expression turning angry. "Did you sleep with him, Riley?" he spat venomously.

I gasped in shock. *Did I sleep with him? Is he seriously asking me that?* "How in the hell can you ask me that? It was a first date for goodness sake, Clay! Is that what you really think of me? That I'm a slut?" I snapped, opening his door and climbing out, stomping off angrily. I was seriously angry with him. The damn boy slept with anything that moved, but yet he had the nerve to judge me?

I heard footsteps behind me before he grabbed my hand, pulling me to a stop. "I'm sorry. I shouldn't have asked that, I know you wouldn't have. It's just that he's such a player. That's all he wants you for," he said, frowning angrily.

"Oh, so the only thing I'm good for is sex, is it?" I shouted, shaking my head at him in disbelief. We were starting to draw a crowd now people were stopping to listen to us shout at each other.

"You know that's not what I think! But he will, trust me!" he shouted back, making me flinch from the anger in his voice.

"Clay, what the hell? Is it so hard to comprehend that someone might want to be with me, for me? You think I'm good for nothing else?" I asked, hurt that he could think of me that way.

"Riley, for goodness sake, of course not. You know I love you for you. How the hell could you say that? But he's different. He's so much older than you; he's only going to be after one thing." He pulled on my hand, trying to get me to move closer to him. I stood my ground and made him move to me. It was silly, but I refused to be the one to concede - I'd done nothing wrong. He stepped forward and wrapped his arms around me tightly, kissing my temple. "I'm sorry, Riley Bear, I am. I didn't mean it like that. I'm really sorry. I just don't like that guy. I don't trust him," he whispered in my ear. His hot breath blew down my neck making me shiver as tingles spread down my body.

"Well you don't have to like him, Clay. But you can put this grudge against him aside for me, can't you?" I asked quietly, wrapping my arms around him too and burying my face in his neck.

"Yeah I can do that for you, Riley. I'd do anything for you," he murmured, kissing my temple again and sighing.

"Shows over! Come on, everyone can get to class!" Tom shouted, waving his hands towards the school. I pulled back to look at Clay. He smiled a defeated smile at me; I smiled back and grabbed his hand, pulling him into the school.

• • •

THAT MORNING WAS weird. Everyone was asking me about Clay. They wanted to know how long we'd known each other, how we met - all sorts of strange things. More girls than usual were giving me death glares, and not one boy asked me out.

"Rachel, what's going on today? Why are the girls all acting like they want to kill me more than usual?" I asked, looking around the cafeteria receiving a room full of hateful glares.

"Clay declared his undying love for you in the parking lot, so they're all jealous. I heard the cheerleaders talking in the bathrooms; they're plotting ways they can get revenge on you. At this point I think they're actually talking about slipping some poison into your drink," she explained, giggling.

"WHAT?" I shrieked, looking around at everyone. "He did not declare his undying love for me! Jeez, we're friends! Why is everyone making such a big deal out of me and Clay?" I asked, shaking my head, grimacing.

"Me and you, what?" he suddenly asked, wrapping his arms around me from behind.

Rachel grinned. "All the girls are hating on Riley because you told her that you loved her and would do anything for her. Someone recorded it on their cell phone, so of course, the whole school has seen it," she said simply, shrugging her shoulders.

I gasped and Clay just laughed and gave me a squeeze. "Oh well, that's true. She knows that anyway," Clay said, kissing my neck and starting to suck on it.

I elbowed him in the stomach and pulled away, laughing. "Don't you dare mark me again, Clay Preston, or else!" I warned, trying to look threatening.

He just laughed again and rolled his eyes. "I'm so scared of you, Riley Bear. So scared," he said sarcastically, grabbing my hand and pulling me to his table.

"So, how long have you two really been together?" Terri, a slutty looking cheerleader, asked me with a fake smile but hate glaring out of her eyes.

"Oh for the love of all that's holy!" I cried, throwing my hands up in the air.

"Oh come on, muffin, they're only curious," Clay cooed, smirking at me as he kissed the back of my hand.

I elbowed him in the ribs harshly. "Will you stop?" I growled angrily, shaking my head at him. He had been impossible since I sat down, he'd been playing the loved up boyfriend routine all lunchtime, touching and kissing me, laughing and tickling me, making me squirm. He wasn't denying anything, he was making everything worse. Every time someone asked if he loved me, he just said yes.

"Stop what, sweet cheeks?" he asked innocently, winking at me.

"Clay, enough now. Seriously, you're starting to piss me off," I snapped, pulling my hand out of his.

"Ooh, lovers tiff?" Ben teased, smirking at me.

"So, are you two like gonna get married?" Tiffany asked, curling her hair around her finger, looking dreamily at Clay.

"Eventually. I'd marry her tomorrow if it were up to me," he replied, tucking my hair behind my ear. My mouth fell open. Seriously, I was three seconds from kicking his perfect ass if he didn't start denying these freaking rumours.

Just then my cell phone rang. I looked at the caller ID to see that it was Blake. I jumped up, grinning. "Excuse me," I chirped, climbing off the bench and walking away for a bit of privacy.

"Hi, Jailbait," he greeted when I answered.

"Hey, what are you doing calling me? Shouldn't you be at work?" I replied, trying to ignore the stares that were boring into me from the people on the table behind me.

"I am at work. I'm on a break right now so I thought I'd call and see how you slept," he said easily.

"I slept very well actually. How about you?"

"Honestly, not so good. I couldn't stop thinking about that kiss. It had me tossing and turning all night," he joked. I burst out laughing at his little innuendo.

"Oh really, it was that good for you, huh? Well then you just wait until you see what else I can do. I can really rock your world if a kiss can keep you up all night," I purred, trying to sound seductive.

He moaned, so I knew my flirting had obviously had the desired effect. "Jailbait, that's not fair," he whined.

"Well suck it up, Stud. You wanted to date a minor, so you can deal with the consequences," I joked, trying not to laugh.

He sighed. "You sure you can't make it tonight?" he asked hopefully.

"I'm sure. Clay and I have plans tonight. But he's seriously pissing me off at the moment so if he doesn't buck up his ideas, then I will be free," I said, shooting Clay a warning glance. He wasn't looking at me though, he was just staring down into his lap, frowning.

"Oh yeah, what's he doing?" Blake asked curiously.

I sighed, not wanting explain. "Nothing. It's just a joke that's gone too far, that's all. Listen, I'd better go. I'll see you tomorrow night." I snapped my phone shut and walked back to the bench. Everyone was staring at me with wide eyes.

I sat back down and took Clay's hand, squeezing it gently to get him to look at me. He looked at me with a fake smile and sad eyes. "Enough now, please?" I begged. He just nodded and squeezed my hand back.

"So, who was that on the phone?" Terri asked, smiling wickedly, obviously thinking I had been caught out at something.

"Blake Chambers," I answered, shrugging. All the girls at the table gasped and immediately started asking about him and going on about how hot he was. All talk of Clay and I was long gone, thank goodness.

I looked at Clay again. He looked so sad and hurt; I slung my arm around his waist and leant against him wanting to see him smile again.

"I'm sorry. I'll stop now," he muttered.

I turned and kissed him on his cheek, smiling gratefully. "I love you too, by the way," I whispered. He grinned and slung his arm around my shoulder, all awkwardness and annoyances were forgotten.

● ● ●

"SWEET OR SALTY?" Clay called from downstairs, shaking the two packets of popcorn.

"You choose I don't mind!" I shouted, staring at my wall of movies. I settled on Black Swan and stripped off my top and jeans, standing in my underwear. I leant over to grab my pyjamas when the door opened and Clay walked in.

"Oh crap, sorry!" he cried, blushing and turning around quickly.

"Are you blushing, Clay Preston? Seriously?" I teased, chuckling. "Honestly, it's okay. It's only like seeing me in a bikini. You've done that loads of times." I shook my head, giggling. He'd probably seen hundreds of girls in less clothing than I was wearing, but yet he still had a slight blush to his cheeks as he rubbed the back of his neck looking anywhere but me. "My pyjamas are on that side there. Would you pass them to me?" I asked, pointing at the drawers next to him. I turned back to the movie and skipped through the trailers.

As I turned back, Clay was closer than I thought, so I bumped into him, losing my balance. His hands shot out and grabbed my waist to steady me, and then he quickly whipped his hands away as if I had burnt him or something. My sides were tingling where his hands had touched. I blushed because of how close he was. His chest was pressed against mine. I looked up into his eyes; he seemed to be torn about something. He looked like he was trying to solve an extremely hard math problem. After an excruciatingly long couple of seconds, he closed his eyes and stepped away, holding out his hand to pass me my pyjamas. I got dressed quickly and climbed in the bed. I discreetly watched as he slipped his clothes off, standing there in just his black boxers, the muscles tensing in his back while he folded up his jeans.

He was so beautiful that it was a little hard to take in. I honestly had a feeling that God had outdone himself when he made Clay. I bit my lip to stifle the moan of need that I felt as I raked my eyes over his whole body, slowly, thinking of all the things I wanted to do to him. My whole body tingled with desire. I'd never felt an attraction like this for a boy, ever. But this was my best friend I was looking at, this seriously needed to stop. What was wrong with me lately? Suddenly he snapped off the light, putting an end to my ogling. I sighed, and scooted further down on the bed, getting comfortable.

He handed me a bowl of popcorn so I started eating to take my mind off of how close his hard sculptured body was to me. "You went for sweet then?" I smiled, popping another piece in my mouth.

"Yeah. I made you sweet, and I've got salty because I know you'll want to swap in a while so you can have both anyway," he replied, nudging me in the side.

I smiled because of how well he knew me. That was such a sweet thing to do – a typical Clay moment. He really was going to make a great boyfriend when he decided to finally choose someone. I pushed away the jealousy I felt at the thought of him actually being serious about someone. I had no right to be jealous, he wasn't mine. We were just friends, nothing more. I snuggled closer to his side and sighed happily when he put his arm around me as we watched the movie.

chapter

six

Clay insisted on being there when Blake picked me up the following night - much to my embarrassment. He stayed downstairs while I got ready; I didn't know what we were doing tonight so I went for a denim skirt that cut off at mid-thigh, and a fitted black button-down shirt with a red lacy bra underneath that you could see a little if you looked closely enough, which I assumed Blake would do. I went for ballet flats in case we were walking anywhere. For ease, I pulled my hair up into a twist at the back so that it was casual but also looked smart in case we went to a restaurant or something.

I was ready early so I went downstairs to wait with Clay. As I walked in his eyes went wide and his mouth popped open for a split second before he rearranged his expression and gulped.

"Do I look that bad? Should I change?" I asked, looking down at myself.

"No, you look beautiful, Riley. It's just, maybe you should put on a different shirt, you can see your bra in that one," he said, frowning and rubbing the back of his neck nervously.

I laughed. "That's the whole point. That's how you wear it. You've seen this before," I countered, shaking my head at him.

"Yeah well I wasn't trying to get into your pants like he will. He'll see that as an invitation!" he snapped, then immediately looked apologetic. "Sorry, I didn't mean that. I'm just a little worried, that's all," he said, slowly looking me over again.

After a couple of seconds he didn't speak, and I started to feel a little uncomfortable. Why on earth was he looking at me like that? His eyes were lingering over my breasts and legs. *Holy crap, is Clay lusting after me?* "Clay, are you checking me out?" I cried a little shocked. *Oh God, please say yes and kiss me again!*

He jumped about a mile in the air and looked around a little guiltily. "No," he answered loudly, shifting on his feet, clearly uncomfortable.

Wow, he really was checking me out. I guess that just proved how much of a player that he was if he would look at me the same way he looks at all his other girls.

I laughed nervously, not really knowing what to say. "Seriously, I was joking," I said quickly. He sighed and resumed rubbing his neck. "You're not going to embarrass me are you?" I asked, looking at him pleadingly.

"I just want to talk to him, that's all," he replied just as the doorbell rang.

"I'll get it," I chirped, turning to run into the hallway. But he grabbed my hand and pulled me behind him, laughed wickedly and ran to the door first.

"Better luck next time, little girl," he teased as he opened the door, still laughing.

"Hey, Clay. Long time no see," Blake greeted easily.

"I'll be right back," Clay muttered, pushing me backwards and stepping outside. As he started to shut the door behind him, I rammed my hand against the door stopping it from shutting in my face.

"Clay, are you serious?" I asked, shocked. Was he really going outside to speak to Blake in private? "What am I, like five? You can't threaten him in front of me?" I asked, slapping the back of his head lightly.

Blake chuckled. "It's okay. Let's let him get it off his chest," he suggested, winking at me playfully as he pulled the door closed. I just stood there shocked, my mouth hanging open like an idiot. As soon as the door closed the shock was gone so I quickly put my ear to the door, trying to listen to what they were talking about. The only thing I could hear was muffled voices, no distinct words. I sighed and went to sit on the stairs to wait.

After a couple of minutes Clay opened the door and walked back in, shaking his head and muttering under his breath. Blake looked annoyed too. "All done with the grown up boys talk?" I asked sarcastically. Blake chuckled as I shot a death glare at Clay.

"Yeah, all done. Have a good time," Clay replied, throwing his arm around my shoulders. He kissed my cheek and brought his face to my ear. "Any problems at all, you call me and I'll come and pick you up. I don't care what time it is or where you are. You understand?" he whispered fiercely.

I nodded in understanding. "Okay," I agreed. "I'll see you tomorrow, Clay." I turned, grabbing my jacket. When I looked up, I realised that Blake and Clay were glaring at each other. "Guys and testosterone, seriously, that is so annoying," I grumbled, grabbing Blake's hand and pulling him out of the door whilst rolling my eyes.

"You look great. Nice legs." Blake smirked as we walked to his car.

"Thanks, but if you're trying to impress me then you need to work on your compliments," I teased, giggling at his frown.

"Work on my complements? Okay, how about this..." He pushed me gently against the side of his car and put his hands on either side of my head, bringing his face close to mine. "You look so incredibly hot that you're making my mouth water," he said with an easy smile.

I giggled again. "A little better," I admitted.

"You're incredibly beautiful?" he countered, raising an eyebrow.

"Better."

"Okay, how about this then; you look so hot it would totally be worth the five years I would get if I had sex with you right now," he growled, pressing his lips to mine for the second time.

I giggled against his lips and pushed him back. "Really? No, that doesn't really work for me. Number one, who said I would have sex with you anyway? And two, Clay is watching and he's probably about three seconds from coming over and kicking your ass," I teased, opening the car door.

"Yeah well, that would be totally worth it too," he chuckled.

We drove to the shopping complex, chatting easily. I actually felt comfortable with him which was a good sign. "So what are we doing here?" I asked as we walked into the building. This was a weird place to take someone for a date.

He smiled sheepishly. "Well there's this little café in the back that does the best pie in the world," he explained, taking my hand and pulling me in the right direction.

"So you've done extensive pie research in other countries?" I teased.

He laughed. "You really are a funny girl." He shook his head, smiling at me

"So they tell me," I replied, rolling my eyes before giving him a cocky smile. "Try not to get me any evil death glares from psycho waitresses today okay?"

"I'll try my hardest, Jailbait," he replied, smirking at me.

Just then a waiter came over. "Hi, what can I get you?" he asked in a bored voice, not looking up from his pad.

"I'll have the cheeseburger but without mustard. And apple pie with ice cream for dessert," Blake answered before looking at me expectantly.

"And for you, miss?" the waiter asked, finally looking up at me. He was quite young, probably my age. He looked at me as I ordered my chicken burger and apple pie, his eyes not leaving me once. As his gaze drifted down to my cleavage, I shifted uncomfortably.

"Dude, are you fucking seriously staring at my girlfriends tits while I'm sitting right here?" Blake asked, standing up looking really angry.

"Er, no, I just, er..." the waiter stuttered, stepping back,

"Just go make the food before I break your fucking face," Blake almost growled, looking terrifying.

I flinched from the tone of his voice; Blake sure did have a possessive streak by the sound of it. My face flushed with embarrassment that he'd just said that. I couldn't help but feel bad for the poor waiter guy as he practically ran away from our table, bumping into the chair on another table where he was rushing.

"Blake, that was uncalled for and embarrassing," I whispered, scowling at him.

"What? Jeez, didn't you see him staring at you? I could almost see his hard on," he spat, scowling back at me. We sat in angry silence for a couple of minutes, and I was just wondering if I had made the wrong decision coming tonight when he reached over and took my hand. "Sorry, I didn't mean to embarrass you," he said, his voice sincere and apologetic.

"It's okay. But I can look after myself you know. You can't start a fight with people for looking for goodness sake; otherwise I would have to fight every girl on the planet for looking at your pretty face," I stated, shaking my head. He really had double standards. I hadn't exactly caused a scene when the girl had literally asked him out in front of me the other day at the diner.

"You would fight for me?" he asked, raising his eyebrows.

"No, I don't fight. I'd get Clay to do it," I joked, laughing.

"What is Clay, your little lap dog? You really have him well trained," he mocked, laughing and shaking his head obviously amused by his own put down.

"I really don't like people mocking other people," I growled angrily. "Clay's my best friend in the whole world, so just lay off him would you? What the heck is up with you two anyway?" I asked, frowning.

He recoiled, obviously a little taken aback by my scolding. "Well, when Clay tried out for the team, the coach put him as my second. I got injured and was out for a few weeks, and when I came back I had to share my place with Clay because he played so well while I was off. I don't do well with sharing, so I slept with the girl he was seeing," he explained, shrugging as if it was nothing.

I gasped, shocked at the revelation. No wonder Clay didn't like him.

"You what?" I cried angrily, sitting back in the booth to put some distance between us, shaking my head in disapproval.

"Hey, I'm not like that anymore. That was three years ago," he said quickly. "And he wasn't even serious about her anyway. He was just pissed because I got in her pants quicker than he did," he added, smiling proudly.

I felt my anger spike again at that statement. He was sitting there all proud of himself for using a girl, just to get payback on someone? He really wasn't what I was starting to think he was at all. I'd made a mistake in coming out with him, I could see that now. I should have listened to Clay in the first place.

I stood up. "Can you take me home, please? I think I've made a mistake in coming out with you," I said, grabbing my jacket and turning towards the door.

"What? No! Come on, Riley, please?" he begged, grabbing my arm and pushing me back into the booth roughly and then he slid in next to me so I couldn't get out.

"Just move," I spat venomously, trying to stand up again. He frowned and pushed down hard on my leg to stop me from moving anywhere.

"Just hear me out, please? I'm sorry," he begged, shooting me the puppy dog face.

I shook my head forcefully. "I just want to go home. Will you take me, or not?"

"No," he answered, looking a little smug. I reached into my pocket and pulled out my cell phone. "What are you doing?" he asked, frowning again.

"I'm calling Clay to come and get me." I snapped open my phone angrily. Before I could dial his number, Blake snatched the phone out of my hand and put it in his pocket. "What the hell? Give it back, Blake. I'm not kidding around," I cried, giving him my best death glare and holding out my hand for it.

"Riley, listen to me, I'm sorry. I shouldn't have said that to you. And I know I shouldn't have done that to Clay in the first place, but I was so angry at him. After my parents died the team was the only thing I had left in my life. Everything fell apart. Football was the only thing that kept me sane, and then Preston came along and ruined it. I was so angry that I just lashed out. I'm not like that anymore, I swear," he said sincerely, looking into my eyes with a begging expression. "Please?" His eyes dropped down to the table, his shoulders slumped forward. His whole posture looked sad and defeated as if he knew it was no use.

I sighed. How was I supposed to say no when he looked so remorseful and sad? *This boy has some serious issues!* "Okay fine. I suppose I can't go before I've tasted the world's best pie," I conceded, still a little angry with him but rolling my eyes because I couldn't seem to say no. His head snapped up and he beamed at me, a big grin spread across his face. He bent his face towards mine going in for a kiss.

"Cheeseburger?" An older lady asked, standing there with two plates of food. Obviously our previous waiter was too scared to come back to our table after what Blake had threatened.

"Wow, you've got great timing," Blake muttered, chuckling to himself as he smiled up at the lady. "The cheeseburger's mine, thanks." He shook his head in amusement as she put his plate down in front of him. I smiled because that was the second time he had tried to kiss me tonight and failed. I hid my grin by stealing one of his fries.

• • •

"SO, WHAT DO YOU want to do now?" he asked after we had finished eating.

"I don't know. What do you think?" I shrugged as we walked out of the café. I looked up and spotted an amusement arcade across the way. "Oh!" I was so excited that I almost jumped up and down. "How about that?" I suggested, pointing at it. I grabbed his hand, pulling him in there, not even waiting for him to answer. It was packed and really noisy.

"An amusement arcade?" he asked, grinning.

I nodded and dragged him to the change booth. "I love these places; I didn't even know there was one here," I replied, jamming a ten down excitedly for some change.

He rolled his eyes and handed me a pot to put the change in. When my pot was full of coins, I grabbed his hand and almost ran through the crowd to the slot machines. "Wow, excited much?" he teased, wrapping his arms around me from behind.

"Shh, can't talk, playing," I joked, pointing to my machine. He chuckled and held me tighter.

After about two minutes I'd used up all of my money. I was seriously terrible at these machines and always pumped them like they were going out of fashion. My money never lasted very long, but it was so much fun that I just didn't care. I turned towards him, about to suggest that we go and find somewhere else to go before I wasted all of my allowance, when I spotted something over his shoulder. "Oh my God! They've got air hockey," I cried excitedly.

He laughed at me, shaking his head. "You're really easy to please. Listen, go wait by the table and make sure no one gets it. I'll get some more change," he instructed, giving me a little push in the right direction.

I stood by the hockey table and waited for him. After a minute a sharp slap stung my butt. I gasped as I turned; opening my mouth to make some comment about being a minor, but it wasn't Blake that was standing there too close to me. I stepped back, frowning a little. There were three guys standing there, about my age, all tall, and looking at me like I was something to eat. I gulped, silently wishing I'd listened to Clay and changed.

"Hello, beautiful," one of them purred, walking to stand beside me. He raised his hand and brushed it against the side of my face, his eyes playful.

I slapped his hand away angrily. "Get the hell off me," I growled. I flicked my eyes over to the change desk to see Blake was still in line waiting to be served. I frowned and headed in his direction. As I stepped past one of the guys, he grabbed my arm roughly, pulling me to a stop.

"Don't walk away, we just want to have a little fun that's all," one of the others sneered, looking me over hungrily, making me feel a little sick. "You like to have fun?" the other one asked, licking his lips. The one that was holding my arm started pulling me towards the door. I felt my heart start to race in my chest as I started to panic. I opened my mouth to scream for help, but his hand covered it quickly, muffling my panic. It was so busy no one paid the slightest bit of attention to the girl being guided out of the side entrance to the arcade. People were too engrossed in their own games, spending their own money.

Just as I was forced through the door, I heard an angry voice from behind me. "What the fuck are you doing? You better let her go now before I beat the shit out of you," Blake growled from behind me. They guys turned to look at him, so I whipped my head around too, feeling my panic start to fade because someone was going to help me. Blake was glaring. He actually looked pretty terrifying as he straightened himself up to his full height, his posture alert and tense.

"Easy there, buddy. We were just talking to the girl here," the one holding me said, pulling me against his chest.

"I said let her go now! If you have hurt her I swear to God I'll kill you," Blake spat, taking a step forward, his jaw clenched tight with anger.

"I haven't hurt you, have I?" the guy teased, pressing his lips to my ear making me flinch away from the contact. I shook my head and looked at Blake helplessly as the guy's grip tightened on my upper arm.

Blake suddenly took another step forward and one of the other guys stepped towards him at the same time, closing the distance. Without missing a beat, Blake ducked down slightly and punched the guy straight in the chest. The guy immediately staggered back, holding his chest, wheezing.

"Let her go, now!" Blake ordered again, taking another step forward. The other guy stepped up and tried to punch him, but he missed, his fist flailing wildly. These three obviously weren't used to actually picking on someone of their own size. Blake grabbed hold of the guy's hair and brought his knee up at the same time as bringing the guy's head down, smashing his face hard into his knee. He pushed the almost unconscious guy to the floor and turned his attention back to me again.

"You have one last chance to let her go. And I'm warning you, if you have hurt even one hair on her head I will rip your fucking head off," he said through his teeth. The guy pushed me towards Blake, holding his hands up in surrender, sneering. Blake shoved me behind his body and carried on stalking forward. He'd obviously decided that he didn't want to let this guy off without causing him some pain too.

"Hey, what's going on here? Hey, stop! Everyone get down on your stomachs, hands above your heads!" a male voice commanded. I turned to see two police officers with their guns out, pointing them at Blake and the only other guy that was on his feet. Blake took a deep breath and hissed it out through his teeth; he closed his eyes and laid on his stomach on the floor.

The officers came up and put cuffs on all four of the guys, their guns still drawn. "Wait, what are you doing that to him for? It wasn't his fault! He was helping me," I said quickly when I realised they were taking Blake too.

"Miss, we'll have this straightened out by morning. But your boyfriend was fighting in a public place, I don't care who started it," the officer said nastily as he started to drag them off towards the exit.

"No!" I protested, starting to cry.

"Hey wait, you can't leave my girlfriend here on her own. Please?" Blake cried, looking desperately at one of the officers.

The cop looked back at me, probably weighing his options. Finally, he sighed deeply. "Fine. Miss, you can come with us to the station while we sort this out," he agreed, waving a hand for me to come along too.

I begged them the whole way to the station, but they just wouldn't listen to me. They weren't interested in why they were fighting; apparently it wasn't their job to investigate. There was trouble and the perpetrators were arrested, that was all they seemed to care about. I was sitting up front with one cop while the other was sitting in the back of the van with the three guys and Blake. After we got there one guy led me to the reception where I was told to wait and that someone would come and take a witness statement.

My first thought was to call Clay, but part of me didn't want to tell him. He already hated Blake so this was going to make everything worse. My only other option was David, but I knew he would probably kill me if he knew I was here. He would never let me out with Blake again, even if this mess wasn't his fault. I pulled out my cell phone and looked at it for a minute, trying to decide. In the end, I knew I needed Clay's help. The police officer at the desk had said that I needed an adult present to make my statement. Clay was over eighteen so he would be able to do that for me. And apart from the logical reason of wanting to call Clay instead of David, I also just needed him here with me.

I took a deep breath and dialled his number. He answered on the first ring – it was almost like he was sitting there waiting for me to call. In truth, I knew he probably was. "Riley! What's happened? What's wrong?" he asked, no hello or anything.

"Clay, I need your help. Calm down, I'm fine. Just listen to me, okay?" I pleaded, knowing he wasn't going to like this at all.

He took a shaky breath. "What's up?" he asked, concern colouring his voice.

"Blake's been arrested, and I'm-" I started, but he exploded, cutting me off. "WHAT THE FUCK ARE YOU TALKING ABOUT? ARRESTED? WHERE THE HELL ARE YOU?" he almost screamed. I had to hold the phone further away from my ear, wincing as his volume hurt my head.

"Calm the heck down and listen!" I said quickly before he had the chance to rant some more at me. "Some guys grabbed me and tried to force me to go with them. Blake saw and he saved me. But he ended up fighting in the shopping complex and then the cops came and arrested him. But he didn't do anything. Well, actually he did, he kneed one guy in the face and punched another in the chest, but he was just defending me, I swear. But they won't listen to me, Clay! They haven't even taken my statement," I explained, bursting into tears again.

"Okay, Riley Bear, it's okay. Don't worry. I'll come down there and talk to them. Where are you? Downtown?" he asked, concerned again.

"Yeah, on thirteenth," I sniffed.

"Okay. I'll be there in about fifteen minutes." I could hear the sound of his car starting up so I knew he was on his way already.

Clay ran in a few minutes later and I wrapped my arms tightly around his neck, probably nearly choking him, but he didn't complain he just rubbed my back while I sobbed onto his shirt. When I had calmed enough he pulled back to look at me, putting his forehead to mine and cupping my face in his hands.

"Okay, Riley, tell me the truth before I go over there and speak to the clerk, did Blake start this fight?" he asked, searching my eyes with his.

I sniffed loudly. "I promise he didn't. They grabbed me and he stopped them. But when the cops came he was fighting, so they won't listen to me," I explained, hoping he understood me even though my body was hitching with sobs and my voice was croaky. He smiled sadly and wiped my tears away with his thumbs.

"Okay, Riley Bear, wait over there," he instructed, pointing to the chairs by the window.

He walked over to the desk and spoke quickly with the desk clerk. I couldn't hear what he was saying, but he was waving his arms around and talking quite animatedly, gesturing to me a couple of times. About a minute later the desk clerk shook her head and picked up her desk phone, putting it to her ear. Clay stood there in silence, waiting. After another couple of minutes another officer in plain clothes walked out and spoke to Clay and shook his hand. Clay nodded his head in my direction and they both started walking over to me.

I stood up as they approached. "Miss Tanner, we're ready to take your witness statement now. Mr Preston has consented to be your adult," he said, nodding to a door I didn't even realise was behind me.

We went in and sat down while the officer turned on a little tape recorder and they started the interview. It took about thirty minutes in total. I had to keep going over and over everything. But after that he just told us to wait back in the reception again.

"How in the hell did you do that, Clay? I've been asking and asking since I got here but they wouldn't even talk to me," I said, resting my head on his shoulder. My eyes were heavy because it was so late; my head hurt with a stress headache and my chest was tight because of all of the crying I'd done in the last couple of hours.

"You just have to know the right things to say that's all. I told them that if they didn't come and take your statement soon, that we would be calling the press office to report how they treat people who should have been treated like a hero and a victim," he explained, shrugging as if it was no big deal.

I leant in and kissed his cheek, feeling a surge of love wash over me for my best friend. He'd come to my aid in the middle of the night, no questions asked, and had just fixed everything for me. I really didn't feel like I deserved this boy in my life, he was just too special for words sometimes. I smiled weakly at him. "Thank you for doing this for me," was the only thing I could say. I had no words to tell him how I felt about it; my brain was just too tired to comprehend it all. He smiled back and wrapped his arms around me tighter.

After another half an hour Blake walked into the reception, frowning. When he saw me, he smiled. I jumped up and threw my arms around his neck, crying again. Immediately I was internally scolding myself for all the crying I'd done tonight. I was guessing I looked a right state right now, all red and blotchy and covered in snot.

As I pulled away, he laughed. "Yep, that hug was worth getting arrested for," he said with an easy grin.

"Are you okay? Is your hand okay?" I asked, taking his hand and looking at it curiously as I stroked his knuckles. It must have been sore where he punched that guy.

"I'm fine. I was worried about you though," he replied, putting a finger under my chin and lifting my face. He wiped my tears away with the cuff of his jacket and sighed deeply.

Clay walked up and did something that I had never expected to see - he held his hand out for Blake to shake. Even Blake looked totally shocked at the gesture. "Thanks for looking out for Riley. I owe you for that," Clay said, shrugging.

"You don't owe me, man, it's fine," Blake replied, shaking Clay's offered hand. They both looked so uncomfortable that I couldn't help but laugh at the situation. You could practically cut the tense atmosphere with a knife, but I appreciated the effort they both were going to. They both looked at me like I was crazy. Clay rolled his eyes at me; he already knew I was crazy anyway.

"So come on I'll drive you to the shopping complex to get your car," Clay suggested as he walked off through the doors without waiting for us. Blake smiled down at me and took my hand. We walked to the car in silence. I sat in the back trying desperately not to fall asleep.

"I think I should take Riley home. It's almost one in the morning. If she comes home at this time of night with you her parents will go crazy," Clay said, frowning. I gulped as I thought about it. I knew one thing for sure: if I turned up past curfew with Blake, I would never get to go out with him again.

"No, it's fine, I'll take her," Blake refused.

I winced as I interjected quickly, "Actually, Blake, I think Clay's right. My parents are going to be really pissed that I'm out past curfew. It will be a lot easier if Clay drives me, honestly." He looked at me over his shoulder for a couple of seconds, and then nodded in agreement. We drove the rest of the journey in awkward silence.

Clay pulled up next to Blake's car, and I got out with him. "Well that was interesting," I joked with a smile.

"I'm sorry that I got arrested and ruined our date." He looked at the floor, awkwardly kicking at the dirt with one foot. I smiled as I wrapped my arms around his neck and kissed him. After a couple of seconds I ran my tongue along his bottom lip, when I got to his lip ring I sucked it into my mouth, rolling my tongue over it. He moaned and wrapped his hand around the back of my neck, opening his mouth and slipping his tongue in massaging mine. His kissing was forceful, demanding and sexy as hell, but I couldn't help comparing it to the kiss that I'd shared with Clay. I must admit that while this kiss was great, my body wasn't alight like it was when I had kissed my best friend.

I pulled away with a blush to realise that Clay must have seen that. I had no idea why I was so embarrassed though – I'd seen him make out with lots of girls; it wasn't as if I needed to feel awkward about kissing Blake in front of him. But I did for some reason.

"Thank you for what you did," I whispered, pecking his lips again.

"Well thank you for what you just did," he replied, his voice husky and low.

I grinned and rolled my eyes at him. "I'd better go home. My parents are already going to be worrying about me," I said, pulling away and walking back to Clay's car.

"Hey, Jailbait, you going to the game tomorrow?" Blake called as I was just about to open the door.

I nodded. "Provided I'm not grounded."

He grinned. "Okay. Well I'll see you there. If you're not grounded of course," he said, getting in his car. I sighed deeply, knowing what had to happen now. Now it was time to face the music.

chapter

seven

"Where the heck have you been, young lady?" my mom screeched as soon as I walked through the door.

"Er, well, I..." I mumbled, scrambling to think of something that would make her face turn back to the normal shade instead of beet red.

Clay wrapped his arm around my shoulder. "It was my fault. I'm sorry, Sandra. I met Riley out and we went on to a party my friend was having. We didn't realise the time otherwise we would have been back sooner," he said, giving them his adorable puppy dog face. He was so good at lying, if I hadn't seen the tiny twitch to his eye even I would think he was telling the truth.

"Oh, well that's different then. We thought you were out with Blake tonight, Riley," David chimed in, looking at me expectantly, obviously still a little angry, but he clearly believed Clay's story.

"I was, but then I went onto the party with Clay." I looked at my feet as I spoke; I wasn't a convincing liar, unlike my best friend. Lucky for me they were both tired so they gave up quickly.

"Okay well we're going to bed. Goodnight, kids," Mom said as her and David walked up the stairs.

"Goodnight," we both called at the same time.

I yawned and stretched, my eyes becoming heavy all of a sudden. "Thank you, Clay." I turned and smiled at him. I really didn't deserve him sometimes. He was the best friend a girl could wish for.

"Anytime, Riley Bear. I'd better get going," he replied, nodding towards the door.

"Stay with me, please?" I begged. I didn't want to be on my own, I had a feeling that if I was, I'd have nightmares about the guys at the amusement arcade.

He looked at me for a few seconds then nodded. "Okay." He locked the front door and followed me up to my room.

I was so tired that I couldn't even be bothered to put on my pyjamas, so I just stripped out of my top and skirt as I walked, dropping them on the floor. I climbed into bed in my underwear. He took a deep breath as I shrugged out of my clothes, but I was too tired to care.

"Riley, where are your pyjamas?" he asked quietly as he stripped off his clothes. He shuffled on his feet, flicking his eyes around my room, clearly uncomfortable as he tried not to look at me.

"Too tired," I muttered, almost asleep already.

He sighed and had the pained look on his face again; he just stood there for a couple of seconds before climbing in the bed next to me in his boxers, pulling me to him. I was conscious of his hands on my almost naked body, but instead of being uncomfortable, I liked it way too much. I could feel his skin against mine making me tingle. I kissed his chest tenderly, and then buried my face in his neck and instantly fell asleep.

Clay was kissing me, kissing down my neck as he stripped off my bra and panties. His hands were running over my body slowly, making me burn in need. I pulled off his boxers and saw he was already aroused. I moaned at the sight of him. I pulled him back to me. "You sure?" he asked as he hovered over me. I nodded and kissed him again as he pushed himself inside me. I let out a load moan at the feel of it. He made love to me with a slow and steady rhythm making me moan and call his name. Each thrust made me feel like he was pushing me towards something glorious. I was almost there, I could feel it building. He thrust again...

I jerked awake with a gasp. "Holy shit!" I hissed as I burst out laughing. *Crap, I was just dreaming about having sex with Clay!* I buried my face in the quilt, giggling and trying to slow my breathing that was coming out in pants. *Damn it, why did I have to wake up then? I only needed another couple of seconds.*

I rolled over to cuddle Clay, but he wasn't there. I sat up, squinting through the darkness trying to see him. The only light was a green haze coming from my alarm clock.

"Clay?" I whispered, reaching out my hand to the shape I could see lying still and as far away from me as possible in the bed.

"Er, yeah?" he asked huskily. I blushed as the sound of his voice brought back memories of the dream. I giggled again but tried to hide it.

"Why are you all the way over there?" I asked, scooting over to him.

He held out both hands, putting them on my hips to keep me an arm's length away. "Er, Riley, don't." He sounded extremely uncomfortable.

I was getting worried now. Something sounded wrong. "What is it, Clay?" I asked, concerned.

"Nothing. I just, I... er, you were er, and I..." he stuttered and then sighed.

"What?" I repeated, still trying to get to him. He was holding my hips securely away from him. "Clay! What is it?" I asked, no longer struggling.

He sighed. "You were dreaming about me, Riley, and it sort of had an effect on me," he explained uncomfortably.

I gasped as my whole face heated up. I was silently glad it was dark in the room. *Had I been talking in my sleep again? He knew I was having sex with him in my dream and it turned him on?* Suddenly I burst out laughing. I couldn't stop, I was in hysterics. Clay started laughing too which just made me laugh harder.

"I'm sorry! I didn't mean to, but I just gave you my virginity in my dream," I choked out, laughing so hard that I was crying.

"Well thanks for that. It sounded like I was good," he replied, chuckling. I nodded in confirmation, laughing still.

I moved his hands off of my hips and scooted to him so that we were face to face. I could feel his erection pushing against my lower abdomen. I bit my lip, the desire I felt in my dream was back with a vengeance. I was still giggling.

"I'm sorry; I can't believe that. That's so embarrassing." I buried my face in his chest, blushing and cringing. If that had happened in front of anyone else I would probably never be able to look them in the eye again, but this was Clay, *my* Clay. We never let anything come between us for long.

"Don't worry about it. I'm embarrassed too; I couldn't help my body's reaction though. I mean, what guy can hear this without it having an effect on him? '*Oh, Clay, harder. Oh God, Clay!*'" he said, doing a high pitched girly voice, making me blush and giggle again. I slapped his stomach playfully, but as I drew my hand back it accidentally brushed against his crotch. I snapped my hand away quickly as his muscles seemed to tighten on his body.

"Oops, sorry!" I gasped, blushing again. "Jesus, Clay, are they all that big?" I asked my eyes wide, honestly a little scared. I'd never had any experience with that kind of thing. Kissing and cuddling was about as far as my expertise went in that department.

He laughed and moved his hips backwards on the bed so we weren't touching there anymore. "I don't know, Riley. I guess so, but I try not to look too much," he replied with a small chuckle, still sounding uncomfortable.

"I'm really sorry about that. But if it makes you feel better I was really enjoying myself. I just woke up about a second too soon though." I sighed and closed my eyes, shaking my head remembering the feeling building up inside. That was my first ever dirty dream, and it had to happen when I was in bed with the guy I was dreaming about. Life certainly can be cruel sometimes.

Clay laughed so I wormed my way back to him, cuddling him tightly. He sighed as he ran his hands down my sides; stopping when he got to my panties. Then, slowly, his finger traced along the edge of them, across my ass, heading towards my core. I stopped breathing; my heart was beating way too fast. His breathing was coming out in ragged gasps.

"I could help you finish if you want," he purred huskily as he rubbed me gently through my panties. Pleasure shot through my body, not like in the dream but a hundred times better because it was real. I couldn't speak, I just moaned quietly. I felt him move his hand to the edge of my panties and slip his hand inside them, his fingers slowly working themselves towards my centre. I stiffened and grabbed his wrist. He stopped immediately.

"What the hell are you doing?" I asked breathlessly.

He leant forward and kissed the side of my neck. "I want to hear how the dream ended," he growled seductively. His breath blew against the overheated skin at my neck, making me gasp and squirm.

"Clay," I said, but it actually sounded more like I moaned his name. He moaned quietly too and the sound made me ache for him. He kissed my neck again, gently biting on the skin. I didn't feel like I was in control of my body anymore. I reached my hands out and tangled them in his hair, pulling his face to mine roughly. He kissed me tenderly and licked along my lip wanting to deepen the kiss. I opened my mouth, eager for his taste again. His tongue slipped in and just like before, it was amazing, tender, slow and perfect.

My whole body was burning in need for him. He pulled away and kissed down my neck unclasping my bra at the same time and pulling it off. That was where I came back to reality. *What on earth am I doing right now? There is no way I'm going to have sex with my best friend. This is wrong.* But at the same time that the thought formed in my head, everything in my body was protesting that it was, in fact, right.

"Clay, I can't! I'm not going to have sex with you." I said the words but my goodness I didn't mean them. I was still panting as my body ached like nothing I had ever felt before.

"I know. Just let me help you finish, please?" he begged, kissing down to my stomach. *I can't, can I? But oh God I want him to.* "Please?" he whispered against my panties making me shiver with desire.

He hooked his fingers in the sides and pulled them down slowly, giving me time to stop him. I didn't stop him, I couldn't, I wanted him so badly. He worked them all the way off and eased my legs apart gently. I had no idea why I was letting him do this. I had never even let a boy touch me intimately, yet here I was getting naked with my best friend. The difference with those other boys that I'd dated was that I trusted Clay with my life. He ran his tongue along the inside of my thigh causing me to moan loudly.

He chuckled. "Shh, Riley Bear. Your parents."

I held my breath. Clay crawled up the bed, settling himself against my side as he kissed me again. His beautiful taste seemed to scramble all of my senses and make me lose all coherent thoughts. My mind was a mess; I was just starting to conclude that this was a dream when his fingers brushed between the apex of my legs. Shockwaves radiated through my whole body so I knew I was awake. I gasped and bit his bottom lip by accident which just seemed to make him clutch me closer to him. The feel of it was unbelievable. The way he moved his fingers was both skilful but teasing at the same time. I kissed him harder, clamping myself to him, wanting to be closer as every nerve ending in my body seemed as if it was on fire.

My hand acted of its own accord, tracing down his hard body and slipping inside his boxers. He gasped as I touched him tentatively. He broke the kiss and put his forehead to mine, his breathing speeding up as I let my fingers explore new territories on his body. "Damn, Riley, what are you doing?" he asked breathily. His nose skimmed up the side of mine, his eyes seemed to burn with a passion that made my toes curl.

I shrugged, grinning nervously. Actually, I had no idea what I was doing – hopefully this was right. I wrapped my free hand around the back of his head and guided his lips back to mine, eager for his taste again as our hands continued the slow exploration of the other's body. He moaned into my mouth. The sound sent my heart flying in my chest. Being with Clay like this felt so incredibly right. It was beautiful, intimate, and made even more special because of the fact that he was my best friend in the world and someone who I trusted wholeheartedly.

Out of nowhere my body seemed like it shattered into a thousand pieces as pleasure shot to every part of my body. Clay kissed me, swallowing my moans as if he wanted to keep them all to himself. I felt his body tense against mine as he let out a low groan at the same time. Our hot breaths tangled together as my heartbeat drummed wildly in my ears. He put his forehead to mine and closed his eyes, a small smile tugged at the corners of his mouth before he kissed me softly.

"Mmm, I liked the ending," he said, before kissing me again.

I giggled against his lips. "Not as much as I did." I chewed on my lip as my body slowly calmed down and I came back to reality.

He grinned and pulled my hand out of his boxers, rolling onto his back and pulling me tightly to his side. "That was incredible. You've done that to a guy before, right?" he whispered, tracing one finger over my cheek, his eyes raking over every inch of my face.

I shook my head, wriggling to get closer to him, and setting my head on his chest. "Nope."

He laughed quietly. "Seriously? Damn," he mused. I smiled against his skin, letting his scent fill my lungs. "Go back to sleep," he whispered, shifting and kissing the top of my head. I closed my eyes and sighed contentedly as I listened to his heart still racing in his chest as I fell back into a satisfied sleep.

• • •

I WOKE UP IN the morning and rolled over to hug him, but I immediately noticed that I was alone in the bed. I frowned in confusion, my eyes flicking around my room, searching for him. I was alone.

Realisation suddenly dawned on me. He'd used me and left before I even woke up. *Well that's great, just freaking fabulous! He really is a player. I can't believe he did that to me, that he used me and then just disappeared in the morning! I really am an idiot.* I slapped myself on the forehead with my palm and then rolled over, burying my face into the pillow and screamed as loud as I could. When I was out of breath, I rolled back over again, glaring angrily at the ceiling.

My mind was spinning. *What on earth am I going to say to him? This is going to be so awkward today, and I'm going to lose him!* I started to cry. The thought of Clay not being in my life was awful. I couldn't let that happen, I couldn't be without him. I laid there, my eyes closed, my whole body tight with stress. I couldn't think of a single thing that would make this better today. How was I going to face him after this? Knowing that I was just one of the sluts that he used for his own pleasure.

"Good morning, sleeping beauty."

I snapped my eyes open and sat up as Clay walked into the room with a towel wrapped around his waist, rubbing another through his damp blond hair roughly. He looked so handsome that my mouth started to water. I wiped my tears and wrapped the sheets tightly around myself.

"Er, hey," I replied, blushing.

He looked at me and frowned. "Have you been crying?" he asked, coming over to the bed.

I quickly jumped out of the other side pulling the sheets with me. "No," I lied looking around the room wildly for something to put on.

"Are you sure? Is everything okay?" he asked. I nodded and spotted a long t-shirt on the floor; I bent and grabbed it, and with a huge amount of difficulty, managed to get it on whilst still covering myself with the sheet.

When I looked back to him, he seemed really sad for some reason. "I'm going to take a shower," I squeaked, blushing again and almost running out of the room.

"Okay well, I'd better go home and change for school. I'll... er... pick you up at the usual time." He rubbed at the back of his neck like he always did when he was nervous.

"Okay," I muttered as I slammed the door shut and ran for the bathroom.

Tears were flowing uncontrollably down my face. I cried in the shower until I felt sick. Everything was ruined. Our whole relationship was now spoiled and dirty. I'd lost him. He was my best friend in the world, but we wouldn't be able to get past this. It was just going to get worse and worse until we couldn't even look at each other anymore. I was so stupid for letting that happen last night. I should have listened to my head that was telling me not to do it. But I guess it was too late now, we couldn't take it back.

When I was done in the shower, I cautiously stepped back in my bedroom, looking around to see if he was still there. The room was empty though so I breathed a sigh of relief. I dressed quickly and dried my hair, pulling it back into a messy bun. I winced at my reflection in the mirror. I looked terrible this morning. I had bags under my eyes from having about three hours sleep last night, and my eyes were also puffy and red from crying. I applied a bit of concealer and mascara to try and disguise it. It worked a little, but I still looked tired.

"Riley, Clay's outside," Mom shouted from downstairs.

I frowned and took a couple of deep breaths before pulling on some converse and running downstairs.

"Riley, about last night," my mom started, her eyes narrowing as they locked onto mine.

I felt my whole face flush with embarrassment. Had they heard what Clay and I had done? Did they know? What on earth was I going to say?

"I don't appreciate you coming home at that time, young lady. Your stepfather and I were worried about you. You should have called us! Thank goodness you were with Clay," she continued.

I felt my ridged body relax as I breathed a sigh of relief. I had seriously thought she knew what happened in my bed with my best friend. "I know, Mom. I'm sorry. It won't happen again," I promised. There was no way that I would spend the night at the police station again waiting for Blake. *Holy crap, Blake!* What on earth was I going to do about Blake? I was supposed to be meeting him tonight at the football game and I'd done that with Clay last night. Was I turning into a slut?

"Okay, Riley. Come on, you'd better get going, Clay's waiting for you," Mom instructed, giving me a little push towards the door. I nodded and headed out of the house, fingering my schoolbag nervously as I walked to his waiting car. I was mentally planning what I was going to say, picking through options and dismissing them quickly. I couldn't exactly say: 'Hey, Clay. So, about last night, I know you played me so let's just try to be friends still?' That wasn't exactly going to work.

I took a deep breath and climbed into the passenger side, giving him a big fake smile. He smiled back, but it didn't reach his beautiful eyes. He looked really sad about something, but he was clearly trying to hide it.

"Hey, I thought you wouldn't get time to eat so I brought you this," he said, holding out a piece of toast with chocolate spread and a carton of orange juice. His hand brushed mine as I took it and I blushed as my blood seemed to fizzle in my veins.

"Thanks, Clay." I munched on the toast quietly, trying not to cry. Again I mentally scolded myself for doing that last night. He was being his sweet and adorable self this morning, bringing me my favourite breakfast even though he didn't like the smell of chocolate spread. He was being thoughtful even though he played and used me last night. It kind of broke my heart even more.

I sighed, and I saw him look at me from the corner of my eye. "Riley, about last night," he started.

I took a deep breath and shrugged dismissively. I silently prayed that my voice wouldn't break as I spoke. "It's okay. Let's just pretend it didn't happen, all right? I don't want anything to change between us; please can we just forget it?" I suggested quickly before he could say something we would both regret. He snapped his eyes to me and let out a sigh before frowning and looking back out of the windshield.

"That's what you want?" he asked quietly.

"Yeah, I do. I don't want to lose you. Please, let's forget it and pretend that it never happened. Be friends?" I begged. I knew it would be hard pretending that it never happened, because if this awkward situation had taught me just one thing – it showed me how crazy I was about him. I had no idea when it happened, but somehow that month apart had made me realise just how much I needed him in my life.

"Okay, Riley Bear. Let's forget it," he agreed, nodding. His hands tightened on the steering wheel tightly as he pretended to be engrossed in the traffic as he drove us to school. I smiled weakly. Maybe this could work out. Maybe we really could pretend like it never happened. I prayed with all of my heart that it did because I just couldn't bear to think about my life without him in it.

chapter eight

I avoided Clay all day, it was hard work, but we needed a few days to get over this little blip. I was so tired because of getting in so late the night before. Every time I closed my eyes I saw his face, I imagined he was kissing me, remembering the feel of his hands on me, the taste of his tongue on mine. I couldn't avoid the ride home with him though, so I waited by his car at the end of the day. He came up looking a bit sheepish and gave me an uncomfortable hug that lasted for a split second before he pulled away.

"Hey, Riley Bear."

"Hi. You have a good day?" I asked, getting in.

"Yeah. You?"

"Yep," I agreed, frowning at this awkward situation. It was like there was a ginormous elephant in the car and no one wanted to acknowledge it. "Rachel's picking me up for the game tonight so I won't need a ride," I added, trying to keep the conversation going.

"Oh, okay. You still want my number?" he asked quietly, looking at little unsure of himself.

I grinned. "Sure I do. I'm still your number one fan." That would never change. He beamed and nodded happily making my heart melt and my body tingle. I gave him a quick kiss on the cheek as I jumped out of the car when we got home. "Well, good luck for the game. I'll see you after, okay?" I waved goodbye as I ran through the gap in the fence between our two houses.

"See ya, Riley Bear," he called, watching me leave.

I smiled to myself. *Okay that wasn't too bad. Maybe we can actually make this work. I really hope we can.*

•••

I WAS SAT IN THE bleachers cheering along with everyone else. I didn't know what I was cheering for, but I was still doing it anyway. Suddenly, an arm snaked around my waist making me jump and squeal from fright. I looked up to see Blake standing there, looking as hot as ever. He was smiling at me and looked extremely happy. My thoughts flashed to Clay, but I quickly pushed them away and smiled back.

"Hey, Jailbait. How are you today? You look tired," he mused, grinning cockily.

I rolled my eyes. "Wow, Blake, you certainly know how to make a girl feel special."

He grinned and pulled me closer to him, his side pressing against mine. "I missed you."

I gulped. He'd missed me? A wave of guilt rushed over me because I suddenly felt like I'd cheated on him by doing that with Clay last night. Technically I hadn't cheated though because we weren't actually together.

"I'm growing on you, huh?" I teased.

"Yeah, like mould," he joked, tickling me in the ribs making me giggle and squirm away. His hand took mine, rubbing my knuckles with his thumb as we watched the game with him explaining some of the plays to me. He gave up after a little while, laughing when I still just didn't get it. "You know for a smart girl you can be a bit of a dumbass," he joked, digging me in the ribs with one finger.

"Takes one to know one," I replied, winking at him.

Okay this was easy, he was easy to be with, and he was hot. So he didn't give me the chills when he touched me, so he didn't set my body on fire when he kissed me like Clay did. But Clay wasn't interested in having a girlfriend so I needed to do something to get him off my mind, and Blake was definitely a good guy at heart.

"So, what are you doing after the game?" he asked, leaning in close to my ear.

"I'm going to a party with Clay and Rachel." I shrugged. I frowned, knowing that I would probably spend the night avoiding Clay, but that wasn't a total lie.

"Think I could come?" he asked, putting his arm around my waist as the game finished.

"I'm not sure. I guess so," I agreed uncomfortably. It wasn't my party but I was sure they wouldn't mind another person tagging along.

"Okay. I could drive if you know where it is."

I shook my head and laughed. "I have no idea where it is."

Rachel leant over then. "Are you talking about Matt's party?" she asked. I nodded. "You can follow me, I know where it is," she offered, smiling.

Blake started chatting to her then while still holding my hand. I looked out across the field and saw Clay take off his shirt, spinning it above his head in celebration. I watched as his muscles moved, taking in the way his chest rose as he breathed, and his big grin. I imagined running my fingers through his hair and running my tongue down his abs.

Something squeezed my hand jerking me out of my little fantasy. I looked up, Blake was watching me strangely; it was almost as if he was waiting for something. *Oh crap, has he been talking to me?* "I'm sorry, what?" I asked, smiling apologetically.

He laughed. "I said are you waiting for Clay or do you want to ride with me?" he asked, smiling.

I thought about it quickly. It would be so much easier if I rode with Blake - but I told Clay already that I'd ride with him.

"Er, I already told Clay I'd wait and ride with him," I replied uncomfortably. He nodded in agreement, not seeming too bothered. We chatted some more about random things, and after a little while, Clay came up the stairs. He was back to scowling at Blake again. It looked like all truces drawn last night, were forgotten.

"Hey, Clay. Great job," I chirped as I jumped into his arms, wrapping my arms and legs around him like normal. As soon as I did it, I wished I hadn't. Our faces were inches apart, and our bodies pressed together in places that I shouldn't be thinking about touching, but I was, I was thinking about last night. My heart stopped and then took off in a sprint. He looked uncomfortable too.

"Thanks, Riley Bear." He smiled awkwardly, setting me down on my feet again.

I looked up to see Blake giving Clay a look that may just have been able to kill him on the spot. He looked jealous as hell. He reached out and grabbed my hand, yanking me towards him and away from Clay roughly so that I lost my balance and slammed into his side.

Clay glared at him venomously. "What the fuck? You could have hurt her!" Clay shouted angrily as he stepped forwards.

"Keep your fucking hands off my girlfriend!" Blake spat, stepping forward as well.

I looked between the two, not knowing what to say or do.

"Girlfriend? You've been on like two dates!" Clay growled, taking my hand and pulling me back to him gently.

I winced at the look on his face. *Are they going to start fighting?* I started to panic, I reached out and put my hand on Clay's chest and pushed him back a couple of steps, stepping forwards with him, just needing to put some space between them.

"Chill out, both of you! What's wrong with you? You're like a couple of kids," I scolded, looking between the two of them. Blake was glaring at my hand on Clay's chest. Clay actually looked like he was gloating a little. I frowned. What would he have to gloat about? Then I realised that by separating them, I'd moved away from Blake with Clay. I guess it did kind of look like I was choosing a side.

"Seriously, stop arguing! Clay, Blake's coming to the party tonight at Matt's. Blake, you're gonna follow Rachel so I'll see you there, okay?" I instructed, looking back at him with a small smile. He was still staring daggers at Clay. "Blake? I'll see you there, okay?" I repeated when he didn't answer.

He shook his head slightly and looked at me. "Yeah, okay. See you in a bit," he agreed, turning and walking off, his shoulders still tense.

I turned back to Clay. He was watching Blake leave, a smug expression plastered on his face. "Clay, please, you promised you would try and let this grudge against him go for me," I said quietly, looking at my feet.

He pulled me into a hug and kissed the top of my head making me shiver. "I have let it go, but he grabbed you and pulled you for goodness sake. He could have hurt you," he replied, his voice still tight with anger.

I moved back to look at his face. "He didn't hurt me, Clay. Come on, you were glaring at him as you walked up the stairs," I countered, frowning.

He sighed deeply. "Riley, I don't like him; he's not good enough for you." He looked at me almost pleadingly as he spoke.

"He's not good enough for me? Then who is?" I asked. *Please say you, please say you.*

"No one. No one's good enough for you," he whispered, kissing my forehead and putting his arm around my shoulder.

No one? Oh come on that's not fair! "No one is good enough for me? So I can't be with anyone?" I asked sarcastically, pushing him away so I could wipe a tear that fell. I had no idea why I was so upset. Was I honestly expecting him to say he wanted to be with me? Why was I so disappointed that he didn't? I knew he wouldn't.

"Of course you can, Riley Bear, you could have anyone you want," he replied quietly.

"What if I want Blake?" I asked, watching his face for his reaction. He stiffened and grimaced before he rearranged his face into a small smile.

"I'm sorry, Riley. I promise I won't do it again. But if he hurts you, I swear to God, I'll kill him," he said sternly.

"And I love you for it, Clay, I do, but what if he doesn't hurt me?" I asked, taking his hand, interlacing our fingers.

"Then I'll be very happy for you if he makes you happy," he said quietly. "Come on, let's get to this party." He tugged on my hand gently, nodding towards the parking lot.

• • •

AS WE ARRIVED AT the party, I saw Blake standing outside waiting for me. Clay took my hand as we walked to the house and I could see Blake staring at our hands, an angry frown on his face.

"Clay, I'll see you in a bit, I just want to talk with Blake," I said at the door.

"Okay." He kissed my temple and shot another smug look at Blake as he walked off. Blake watched him go angrily, his jaw tight.

"Blake, I need to talk to you. Wanna walk with me?" I asked.

"Sure, Jailbait," he agreed, taking my hand.

I walked a few yards away from the house and sat on the grass. He sat next to me quietly, obviously waiting for me to speak first. I took a deep breath and decided just to say what was on my mind. "I've already spoken to Clay so I just wanted to talk to you as well. I need to make a few things clear," I said, looking at him intently.

He nodded, looking a little unsure. "Okay."

"Clay's my best friend. I've spoken to him about this problem between the two of you, and he's promised to let it go. But I need you to know that Clay is always going be in my life. I don't want to have to choose between you two. You have no need to be jealous of him, but if you do make me choose, it won't be you," I said, looking at him sternly. I needed him to know this, it was important that he knew where he stood. We'd only been on two dates, I hardly even knew him. If this conflict continued, then I would stand with my best friend, no question. He needed to know that. "And I'm not your girlfriend," I added.

While I said my little prepared speech he was staring at the floor, frowning angrily. When I finished talking, he sighed deeply. "Do you want to be?" he asked, looking up and smiling at me sweetly.

I frowned, a little taken aback. *He's gone from frowning to smiling in a matter of seconds. Is this boy bipolar?* "Blake, I like you. You're really sweet, and my goodness you're hot," I replied, laughing. He smiled cockily. "But if you're going to be jealous and possessive, then no I don't," I continued. That wiped the smile of his face.

He frowned. "Look, I know that you're close friends, I get that, and that's fine. But I won't have my girlfriend wrapping her legs around some other guy, holding his hand and kissing him," he growled, glaring at me angrily, tightening his hands into fists.

"Then the answer's no." I shrugged, standing up and quickly walking into the house leaving him sitting on the grass. I wouldn't change my relationship with Clay, not for anybody.

• • •

A COUPLE OF HOURS later I was dancing with Rachel. I'd had way too much to drink already, my head was buzzing. An arm went around my waist resting on my stomach pulling me back into a hard body; the other arm came up holding a cup in front of my face.

"Vodka jelly?" Clay offered, handing me the wobbly green slush. I giggled and took it, chugging it down immediately. It was weird and burnt the back of my throat as I swallowed. I winced at the disgusting taste; it was like lemons or lime.

"Ew! Clay, that's gross. Was that lime?" I asked, shuddering. I hated lime jelly, but it was his favourite.

"Yeah." He chuckled in my ear his lips brushing against it as he spoke.

Another song started, he was still holding me close to his body. "I love this song!" I cried happily. The beat took over and I started dancing properly, swaying my hips and getting really into it. He was moving with me so I started sexily grinding into him. I bit my lip as I rubbed against him. His hot breath blew down my neck making my skin prickle. His other hand moved to the outside of my thigh. I could feel the tingles spreading from his hand shooting all around my body.

I'd had enough drink to give me the confidence to turn around and face him; I intertwined our legs and continued to grind into him. I didn't care if people were watching; I couldn't see anyone but him. My body was starting to burn as I looked into his beautiful green eyes. His hand moved to my ass as I wrapped my arms around his neck. He was a really good dancer, and this felt sexy as hell to be dancing like this with him. He bent his head and kissed the side of my neck, just once, then pulled back to look at me. Lust was written clear across his face. I wanted him so badly that my whole body was aching for him.

"You wanna go home?" he whispered in my ear.

No, I want you right here. I almost said it but managed to stop myself in time. Suddenly I realised when he'd said. He was asking me to go home with him. What exactly did that mean? Did he feel the same way as me, or did he mean that he'd had enough of this party and just wanted to go home? Either way dancing like this with my best friend needed to stop. I bit my lip and nodded. He smiled his beautiful smile and took hold of my hips, turning me around, guiding me forwards out of the door. He was pressed close to my back as we both headed out of the house, his arm wrapped around me, his thumb stroking my stomach.

He opened the car door for me so I got in, smiling and trying not to blush. We didn't speak all the way home. As soon as he pulled in to my driveway he leant over and kissed me, tracing his tongue along my lip. I opened my mouth feeling his tongue slip in and massage mine, making me moan into his mouth because of his taste. He reached over and took hold of my waist, pulling me to his lap. My hands automatically twisted into his hair, pulling him closer, deepening the kiss. I heard the car door open, and I was jostled slightly as he climbed out. He didn't set me down; instead he guided my legs around his waist as he gripped under my ass, supporting my weight. He kicked the door shut before carrying me towards the house, never once breaking the kiss.

Oh God, Clay, hurry up!

My body was screaming for him. He pushed me against the front door, kissing me deeply. After a minute or so we were still there making out. I whimpered because I just wanted to get inside already. Why were we still outside anyway?

"Clay, let's go upstairs," I breathed as he kissed down my neck.

He laughed. "I'm waiting for you to unlock the door, Riley," he teased, still chuckling.

"Oh." I giggled and fumbled in my pocket for the key. I couldn't find it though so he laughed and set me on my feet gently.

"Here, let me," he suggested, pulling my hand from my jeans pocket. He smiled at me as he slipped his hand in instead. I felt his hand go around the key almost instantly, but instead of bringing his hand out, he pushed his hand further into my pocket and pressed his fingers between my legs, massaging gently. I gasped from both the shock and the sensation of it. He used my distraction to his advantage and kissed me again. Finally, when I could barely stand anymore, he pulled his hand out and unlocked the door.

Bending slightly, he gripped his hands on my ass again and picked me back up. I smiled and pressed my lips to his as he carried me through the house towards my bedroom. Luckily at this time of night no one was up. He went straight to my room and laid me on the bed, climbing on top of me with a moan. His eyes were dancing with excitement as he brought his head down to kiss me again. I dug my fingers into his back gently.

"Riley," he breathed, making me so hot that I could easily have burst into flames. I rolled him onto his back and sat up, straddling him. I could feel how aroused he was, and my whole body was practically vibrating with excitement because of it. I smiled at his body's reaction to mine, and he smiled back. "Riley, you are so beautiful," he murmured, lifting his head to kiss me again as he rolled me so I was underneath him. "I love you," he whispered suddenly.

My heart stopped at those words. He loves me? Then it dawned on me that he meant like friends. Of course he loved me, I was his best friend, he had to love me, it was a rule of some sorts. He didn't love me in that way. But I didn't care. He was perfect and even if I could only have him for tonight, I wanted him.

I kissed him back hungrily. "I love you too, Clay," I said honestly. His face lit up and he continued to kiss my face and neck, his hands urgently roaming my body as if he wanted to touch every part of me. "Clay, have sex with me," I begged. I'd never felt so close to anyone in my life, but I still wanted more.

He pulled his head up to mine and looked into my eyes as he frowned. "Riley, no. Not like this. It's your first time, it should be special," he protested huskily whilst still letting his hands explore my body.

Suddenly, he sucked hard on the base of my throat. "Did you just brand me?" I asked, giggling.

He chuckled. "Just marking-" he started, but I interrupted him.

"Making your territory, I know," I interjected.

"Exactly." He laughed and sucked the same spot again. I rolled him underneath me and started to suck on his neck in return. "Do a good one, I want it to last," he instructed. I could tell by the tone of his voice that he was smiling. I giggled and sucked harder then pulled back to look at it.

"Perfect," I announced proudly, looking at the red hickey on his neck.

"Yeah, you are," he agreed, running his hands up my back.

Where I was on top, straddling him, we were touching together intimately, even through his jeans and mine I could feel how excited he was. I was aching for him. The need was almost painful. "Have sex with me," I repeated, already gripping the bottom of his t-shirt and pushing it up his chest.

He frowned, shaking his head adamantly. "No, Riley," he protested, rolling me under him again.

A wave of humiliation washed over me at his rejection. I couldn't help my reaction, I burst into tears. I knew I would only get him for the night, but he wouldn't even do it. I felt so stupid, awful, used and ugly.

I pushed his chest angrily, trying to get him off of me. "I think you should go," I croaked, still crying.

"What? Why? Because I won't have sex with you?" he asked. I nodded in confirmation and he frowned, looking even more confused. "You're telling me to leave because I won't take advantage of you while you've been drinking and with your parents down the hall?" he asked incredulously.

"Clay, seriously, please go," I begged, sobbing and pushing his chest again to get some personal space.

He shook his head fiercely. "I don't understand. Please tell me what I really did wrong," he begged, pinning my hands down above my head and looking into my eyes.

"You don't want me, so please just go. You're making me feel worse," I choked out, crying harder.

He gasped. "You think I don't want you? That's what this is about?" He almost looked angry as he said it.

"I just offered myself to you and you turned me down! I know I only get this one night, but you don't even want me. You'll screw anything that moves, but not me!" I wailed. He groaned and raised my arms, wrapping them around his neck, pulling us both up into a sitting position, holding me on his lap like a child.

"Riley Bear, of course I want you, you're the most beautiful thing I've ever seen in my life. But it's your first time. It should be special, in some posh hotel or something. Not after having too many drinks at a party and having to be quiet in your bedroom because your parents are down the hall," he cooed, kissing my tears away and smoothing my hair back. He smiled at me tenderly.

I kissed him with everything I had, squeezing myself to him tightly. He moaned in the back of his throat and kissed me back passionately. It was so easy to believe when he was kissing me that I was the only girl for him, that he loved me like I loved him, that he wanted and needed me too. I let myself believe it; I tightened my grip on his hair and tugged on it lightly making him moan again. He was an incredible kisser, the way he moved his mouth in sync with mine made the hair on the back of my neck prickle. My mind dimly registered that he was probably an expert kisser because he was a player. He had probably kissed hundreds of girls just like this and made each one of them feel like they were the only girl in the world. The thought brought a lump to my throat so I quickly pushed it away. I didn't care about those other girls. Tonight he was mine, and I was going to enjoy it.

He laid us back down and I ran my hands down his chest still kissing him passionately. He kissed me back hungrily. It was a serious kiss, he truly meant this one. His tongue explored every inch of my mouth. By the time he broke it, I was almost dizzy, and we were both panting hard.

"I love you, Riley Jane Tanner," he said, looking into my eyes. I was still out of breath so I couldn't say anything back; instead I just smiled, feeling my insides dancing with happiness. "This might take a while, but I want to kiss every square inch of your body," he murmured, trailing little kisses across my forehead, over my eyelids, nose, and cheeks. I giggled as he gently nibbled my earlobe, pulling at my clothes to get them off the same as I did to his. I felt a blush creep onto my face because I was naked in front of him again, but that embarrassment quickly disappeared when I looked into his eyes.

His hand had made its way back down between my legs, and he was rubbing me gently making me moan as he was still planting little kisses around my neck and shoulders. My body was throbbing with pleasure I was moaning and panting.

By the time he'd kissed his way down to my chest, I climaxed, crying out his name. He smiled down at me, his eyes twinkling with amusement.

"Thanks," I breathed, running my hands through his hair.

"Riley, I'm nowhere near done," he told me and went back to his little kissing task. I must admit he was quite methodical, I don't think he missed an inch. After he'd finished kissing down my body, I had my turn, finally getting the chance to do what I was thinking about earlier. I ran my tongue over every part of his chest while my hands explored his toned body.

When we were both panting and sweating I slumped back down next to him, and he pulled me into his arms. I giggled at his face; he was gazing at me like I was some kind of goddess or something. "That was freaking incredible, Riley, I'm not kidding. I mean, holy shit, are you sure you've never done any of this before?" he asked, breathing hard.

"Hmm, well there was that one time when..." I trailed off teasingly. He narrowed his eyes at me, tickling me, making me giggle and squirm.

"Quick, let's get some sleep before I make you do that to me again. You're gonna need your sleep anyway, because tomorrow I need to do your back," he purred, giving me a wicked grin. I smiled. *Does that mean that I get more than one night?* I didn't want to get my hopes up, I had already had two perfect nights with him, I wasn't going to be greedy. "I'm gonna get the light," he whispered, climbing out of bed.

I moved and climbed under the covers and then I felt him slip in next to me. I kissed him once more and rolled onto my side again feeling the heat of his body press against my back. His arms wrapped around me and pulled my back hard against his chest as his legs tangled with mine. I sighed in contentment. If I had died right then, I would have been the happiest girl in the world.

chapter nine

I woke in the morning and immediately remembered last night. I smiled and giggled quietly. My muscles were aching a little, but it actually felt nice, like a little reminder of him. I rolled over to see that his side of the bed was empty again; my heart stopped until I noticed that on his pillow lay a folded piece of paper and a yellow tulip. I sat up and smiled running my finger over the waxy petals. Yellow tulips were my favourite flowers; his mom grew them in their backyard. My heart skipped a beat when I thought of him going over to his yard to pick me the flower, and then sneaking back into my house. I chewed on my lip as I picked up the note he'd left.

> Riley,
> I've gone to help Matt clean up after the party. His house was a bit of a mess apparently. Give me a call when you wake up, we need to talk about us being friends and what happened last night.
> Clay

My heart stopped again as it felt like someone had dumped a bucket of cold water over me, washing away the happiness I'd felt seconds before. *We need to talk about last night and us being friends. What on earth does that mean?* I gulped as my tired brain slowly worked it all out. Clay was regretting it. I knew what he was going to say to me: that he didn't like me in that way, that he didn't want a girlfriend, and it shouldn't happen again.

I couldn't breathe; I knew this was coming so why did it hurt so much? I shook my head trying to clear it. I could feel the sadness creeping in because, for just a little while, I'd let myself start to believe that he wanted me. I guess I'd gotten my hopes up. I just needed to stay calm, and then I would still be able to walk away with my best friend. But this kind of thing needed to stop happening, if it carried on then it would ruin our friendship and before long we wouldn't even be able to look at each other.

I climbed out of the bed stretching my body like a cat, my leg and hip muscles were tight but not painful. I walked into the bathroom and looked at myself in the mirror. My hair was sticking up in all directions and had a large knot in the back from our exertions last night. My lips were a little puffy from all of the kissing, and I had a huge hickey on my neck. I switched on the shower and stood under it for a long time, trying desperately not to get upset. Last night was incredible, and I wouldn't have changed it for the world. At least I got to keep those memories forever and still have my best friend.

Once my muscles were relaxed enough I got out and went back to my bedroom. I decided to call Clay and get this sorted quickly. As I picked up my cell phone I saw I had three new texts, all from Blake.

11:03 p.m. - *I'm really sorry Jailbait. I really like you and want to try. I promise I won't say anything about Clay. Please call me when you get this, your phone is turned off x x*

1:12 a.m. - *Please Riley, can you at least talk to me? I'm going crazy! Your phone is still off, or maybe you're avoiding me? Please call me*

10:12 a.m. - *Riley, I'm really sorry. Please call me. I can get over it I promise, I really think this could work between us x*

I frowned because of how into our non-existent relationship he was. I liked him but not in the way that I liked Clay. I sighed because I was thinking about Clay again; I seriously needed to stop doing that. I needed to move on so that things didn't get awkward between us. Maybe Blake could help me with that. I sighed and pulled on some clothes then sat back on the bed, just staring at my cell phone. My eyes were reading Clay's number over and over. I knew I needed to call him and get this sorted out quickly, but I wasn't sure if I had the courage to speak to him. What on earth was I supposed to say?

I took a deep breath and pressed call, closing my eyes and willing this to go well. "Hey, Riley Bear," he chirped when he answered. He sounded so happy that my heart gave a painful squeeze. I silently wondered how this had all happened. How had I allowed myself to fall in love with my best friend?

"Hi. How's the cleaning going?" I asked cautiously, not knowing how to start the awkward and painful conversation.

"Yeah good. We're nearly done now, it's a good job too because his mom's due back in an hour." He chuckled quietly; I could hear a trash bag rustling in the background so he was obviously still working.

I needed to get this done quickly, like pulling off a band aid. "Clay, about last night," I started, trying to sound confident even though I didn't miss the little shake to my voice as I spoke.

"Yeah," he replied. His voice was so husky and throaty that it made my stomach flutter. I looked up at the ceiling and tried to push away my feelings for him.

"It can't happen again, Clay." A tear slid down my cheek as my words were met with silence on the other end of the line. I pushed on with my prepared speech, wanting to get off of the phone so I could breathe again. "It's gonna ruin our friendship, and I won't allow that. I need you in my life, Clay, and if this keeps happening then it's gonna be too hard for us to stay friends." I wiped my face harshly, rubbing away the traitor tears. The pain that those words caused was unbearable. I clenched my fist as tightly as I could, trying to think of something else other than the pain that was threatening to crush me. "Clay, promise me this won't happen again. I couldn't stand to lose you, I just couldn't." I closed my eyes tightly, waiting for his reaction. He still hadn't said a word and I was starting to wonder what he was thinking.

He drew in a shaky breath. "Okay. I promise I won't do that again. It was my fault, I shouldn't have," he said finally. I could hear the pain in his voice, he was really regretting it.

"It's not anyone's fault, Clay, but you're my best friend in the world, and I want it to stay that way, okay?" I smiled weakly now. I could do this, I could get past this, and we would be fine. Our friendship would be just fine.

"Listen, Riley, I gotta go," he said quietly.

"Okay. Bye." I smiled to myself. That was done, we could still be friends. I didn't care how hard this was for me; I needed to have him with me so I'd do anything that it took. Even if it ended up ripping my heart out.

I hung up and settled back on my bed, looking at my ceiling, trying not to think about him in ways that I shouldn't. My cell phone rang and I answered it without looking at the caller ID, expecting it to be Rachel. She usually called the morning after a party to tell me all about any hook-ups from the night before.

"Hey, Rach," I greeted, smiling weakly. *Maybe some gossiping will bring me out of the depression that I can feel myself slipping into.*

"No, Jailbait, it's me," Blake said uncomfortably. I sat up quickly, wincing, and immediately scolding myself for not checking who was calling before answering. I wasn't mentally prepared for this at all. I had no idea what I was supposed to say to him.

I squirmed uncomfortably on the bed. "Oh, hi."

"Did you get my messages?"

"Umm, yeah. I just got them a couple of minutes ago," I replied nervously.

"Okay, well do you think I could come over so we can talk?" he asked. He sounded so hopeful that I squirmed even more.

I looked at the clock, it was just after midday. "Um... sure, okay. My parents are leaving at two, why don't you come over after that?" I bit my lip hoping he would say no. I just didn't want this, I wanted Clay not Blake.

My mom and David were driving to a friend's wedding this afternoon. They were making a weekend of it and staying in a hotel until Monday, so I had all weekend on my own. My parents had asked Clay to come and stay with me so I wasn't in the house on my own - that was going to be beyond awkward tonight. I sighed at the thought; I guess we'd just have to move past it.

"Yeah okay. I'll come over about half past two then," he said excitedly. "See ya."

"Mmm, bye." I closed my eyes again. I hated this situation but I guess I was stuck with it. I pushed myself up off of the bed and went downstairs to spend some time with my parents before they left. I tried my best to forget everything that happened last night.

• • •

AT EXACTLY TWO thirty, the doorbell rang. I answered it to see Blake standing there with a large grin and a bunch of flowers. I smiled because of his sweet gesture.

"Hey, Jailbait." He walked in a little awkwardly and handed me the flowers.

"Hey. Thanks, you shouldn't have." I smiled gratefully and pressed them to my nose, inhaling the sweet scent, before heading to the kitchen so I could put them in a vase.

"I wanted to. I needed to apologise for being an ass." His hand rubbed the small of my back gently as he smiled at me apologetically.

I forced a smile. Everything felt so totally wrong, but what I wanted couldn't happen. Clay and I couldn't happen. "Well you're forgiven."

He stepped forward then and kissed me, his lips pressing against mine almost insistently. I didn't kiss him back at first because I was too shocked. Clay's face flashed in my mind, but I pushed it away and kissed him back.

The kiss felt nice, but wrong. A small part of me was screaming that this wasn't how I was meant to be kissed. In my mind I was comparing the feel of this kiss to Clay's gentle and passionate kisses. I raised my arms and tangled my hands in his hair; his hands found my hips and he lifted me onto the kitchen counter, stepping forwards so his body was between my legs. He moaned as I sucked on his lip ring. I felt his hands sliding slowly up my thighs until he got to the top of my legs then moved them to the small of my back pulling me closer to him. He broke the kiss only to place little kisses down my neck. Just as I was starting to relax into the sensations, he stopped suddenly and pulled back.

"What the fuck is that?" he hissed, frowning, looking at my neck angrily.

My eyes widened as I remembered about the huge hickey I had on my neck. "That's nothing, just a joke. Clay did it for a laugh. It's kinda his thing, he's done it since we were kids," I explained, shifting uncomfortably on the counter.

"He gave you a hickey for a joke?" he asked, shaking his head in disbelief and slamming his hands down on the counter either side of me angrily. I jumped and looked at him shocked. *Man, he really has a short fuse!*

"Blake, it was a joke last night at the party that's all. Nothing was meant by it. We're just friends." I said the last part slowly, emphasising each word.

He bit his lip, seeming torn. I could see the jealousy and anger clear on his face, but he was obviously trying hard not to let it out.

I carried on talking, trying to make it better, "Listen, Clay and I have an extremely close friendship; I've known him since I was a baby. You have nothing to be jealous of at all," I lied. "If you want to try to make this work then you're going to need to get used to it. Clay is always going to be there," I said sternly.

Half of me was praying that he would just turn and walk out. I didn't like doing this, it made me feel cheap and used to be with someone when I wasn't into it. But another part of me wanted him to tell me that it was okay. Part of me wanted him to make me forget Clay, to make me want to be with him and stop me hurting and wanting my best friend, when he didn't want me in return. I had a feeling that if I tried hard enough I could easily fall for Blake. He was sweet, hot, funny, and easy to be with. I bit my lip and waited for him to speak. The ball was in his court now, and I didn't know what I wanted him to say more.

"It's just weird, that's all. I'm not used to having to share a girl's attention, but then again, I'm not used to wanting to be with a girl other than for sex," he admitted, rubbing his jaw nervously. He stepped forward again. The selfish part of me that wanted to feel better, rejoiced. "I really like you, Riley, but we're gonna have a lot of problems; your age for one thing. It's actually not legal for me to do anything with you until you're eighteen."

I pulled his face to mine and kissed him again. He responded immediately, making a small moan in the back of his throat as he pulled me closer to him again. His hands moved up, gripping my waist and pressing against me tightly as he kissed me deeply.

"This sort of thing isn't allowed then?" I asked as he peppered little kisses down my neck, licking my skin.

I felt him sigh, his breath blowing across my shoulders. "This is allowed, but I can't actually go all the way with you. I'm allowed to do everything else though," he purred, looking at me with a wicked grin.

I gulped nervously. I wasn't expecting things to move on that fast. "What about Clay?" I asked, trying to change the subject. The look in his eye told me that he wanted to jump there and then. That look scared me a little; I wasn't ready for things to move that quickly with him. Clay, on the other hand, I would go all the way with... I immediately mentally scolded myself for thinking about my unobtainable best friend again. I needed to stop torturing myself about it. Clay didn't want me that way, so I needed to stop wishing for it.

Blake sighed, looking slightly angry again. "I told you, I'll just have to deal with it." He bent his head forward, heading to kiss me again.

I held my breath trying to process his words. By 'deal with it' was he saying that he wanted to have a relationship, or that he just wanted to use me for a one night stand? Raising one of my hands, I put it on his chest and pushed him back. He frowned as I climbed off of the counter. "We're not done talking," I stated, walking into the lounge and plopping onto the couch. He followed me in there and sat down next to me, looking confused.

"Well what else is there to talk about?" he asked, moving closer to me and nuzzling my neck.

"Well, I won't be used. I'm not going to sleep with you. If you want to be with me, then we agree to take things slow," I explained, looking at him seriously. He looked a little taken aback but nodded slowly. "I'm assuming that you being a player means that you've never been in a real relationship before?" I asked, smiling at the thought. He was like some kind of emotional virgin.

"Er, yeah, I've never really had a girlfriend," he admitted, looking a little embarrassed about it.

I nodded again. "Okay. Well here's how it works then; you need to trust me. I won't let you cheat on me at all. If you want to be with other girls, then go be with them. If you want to be with me, then you commit to it."

A smile crept onto his face that made him look really cute. "I haven't even looked at another girl for the last six weeks," he boasted.

I couldn't help but giggle at that statement. *Does he really think that not sleeping with a girl for six weeks is going to impress me? He really has no idea about girls.* "Six weeks isn't a long time, Blake." I laughed.

"Hey, it is for me! I'm usually with a different girl every other night, but since I met you I just don't want anyone else. It might not sound like a big deal to you, but trust me, that has never happened to me before," he countered defensively.

I chewed on my lip. *I guess that is kind of sweet in a weird man-whore kind of way.* "Okay, I get it, you've refrained from sex for six weeks, I'm impressed." I rolled my eyes playfully. He laughed and leant in, kissing my neck again. "Still not done talking," I protested, pushing him away again.

"Jeez, what more is there?" he asked, throwing his hands up theatrically.

"I'm a virgin," I said quietly, trying not to blush.

His eyes widened as he looked at me shocked. "You're kidding me." There was a small smile tugging at the corners of his lips.

"Nope, not kidding," I confirmed. I looked at his face, trying to work out what was making him smile like that. He laughed quietly, shaking his head in amusement. I felt the scowl slip onto my face. Was he laughing at me or mocking me for not being experienced? "What's so funny?" I asked, annoyed. Without answering, he pushed me down onto the couch and settled himself on top of me, still chuckling as he kissed me again. I put both hands on his chest and pushed him back to get some personal space. "What's funny?" I repeated.

"I've never been with a virgin before," he explained, kissing down my neck.

I closed my eyes and tried not to wince at the thought of being with him physically, letting him do the things that Clay had done last night, go even further. The thought scared me. I wanted Clay so badly, I wanted him to be my first, and that feeling hadn't gone away at all. Hopefully, in time, that feeling would fade though. I would just have to keep trying to forget him and take things slow with Blake.

"Slow down. You're getting way ahead of yourself there," I instructed, but my authority wavered as he nibbled on my earlobe and I giggled like a little girl.

"Okay, well you're just going to have to tell me how fast you want to go. This virgin and minor thing is all new to me." He actually sounded quite excited about it all.

"Oh great, so now I'm some kind of project?" I asked, laughing. He laughed too and rolled off me onto his side so that we were facing each other. His arm wrapped around my waist as he smiled at me reassuringly. It felt nice, different, but still nice.

"You're not a project. I just don't want to do anything you don't want me to," he replied, running his hand up my side, smiling at me.

We chatted easily for a while. He was really easy to get along with and actually quite funny, but I just couldn't shake the feeling that this was wrong, that he was wrong for me. My body and soul ached for Clay to be here with me like this.

About an hour later we were making out on the couch, cuddling and flirting. At some point he'd taken his shirt off, and I was slowly trailing my hands down his chest - being careful not to go too far down to give him the wrong impression. This already felt like we were moving way too fast, but doing this was almost keeping my mind off of Clay. I say almost because I still couldn't help comparing everything to Clay, his body, his taste, how he moved his hands. Blake was a lot rougher than Clay, more forceful and demanding, not tender or loving.

He had a great body, not as muscular as Clay, but lean, sculptured and very hot. He had a tattoo on his arm of some sort of dragon thing, and he had one of his nipples pierced.

Neither of us heard the front door open, but I heard someone gasp. Blake jumped off of me quickly. I looked up to see Clay standing there, his hands clenched into tight fists, his eyes shooting hateful looks at Blake.

"What the hell are you doing, Riley?" he almost screamed. He wasn't looking at me; instead his murderous gaze was locked on Blake.

"Hey, man, I might be mistaken but I thought you lived next door," Blake said smugly, laughing as he pulled on his shirt. I pushed myself up from the sofa, my face blazing with embarrassment.

"Blake, I swear to God," Clay started to say as he stepped forwards menacingly. He actually looked like he wanted to beat the life out of Blake.

"Clay, I didn't hear you come in," I interjected weakly, trying to diffuse some of his anger.

His eyes snapped to me. "No of course you didn't, you were too busy getting it on with this piece of shit," he spat. His head nodded in Blake's direction, but his eyes didn't leave mine. I swallowed as I looked at his face. He looked hurt, and something else... jealous, maybe? But he wouldn't be jealous though, that was just a stupid thought. Clay never got jealous over girls; he just used them for his own pleasure, just like he'd used me last night.

I stepped forwards. "Clay, I wasn't getting it on with him. And for goodness sake, I thought you promised you would let this grudge go," I countered, waving a hand between the two of them.

He took a deep breath before he spoke. "Whatever. I just came back to tell you that I'm going out with Zoë tonight."

I flinched and tried to hide the jealousy that I felt because he was going to be with that skank and that she would definitely have her hands on him - and probably more than that too. Bile rose in my throat at the thought of them together.

"What time will you be back?" I asked weakly. My voice broke slightly as I looked at the most gorgeous face in the world.

His eyes flashed something like hurt or sorrow before he shook his head violently. "That's the point, I'm not coming back. I'll be staying at hers tonight."

My breath caught in my throat at his cold tone. *He isn't staying here with me tonight? He's going to leave me on my own so he can go sleep with some whore?* I never thought Clay would ever do that to me. He knew I'd be scared on my own, and Saturday night was always our night, always.

"Clay, my mom and David aren't here this weekend. You promised you'd stay so I won't be in the house on my own," I protested weakly, desperately trying not to cry while my heart was breaking. The only thought that was circling around my mind was this, *my best friend, the guy I was in love with, is choosing a meaningless one night stand with some other girl, over me.*

"I'm sure Blake will stay with you if you ask him," he replied. And with that he turned on his heel and stormed off.

I just stood there staring after him in a state of shock. He had never looked so angry with me before and I hated that look on his face. I felt sick. I barely registered the arm that looped around my waist, or the chest that I was now clamped against.

"I'll definitely stay if you ask me," Blake said. His eyes were shining with excitement.

I didn't want him to touch me at all. My world was falling apart; the pain in my chest felt like it was killing me. I needed to get him to leave; I wanted to be on my own because I didn't know how long I could keep the tears away.

"No thanks. That would definitely be too fast for me, but thanks for the offer," I declined, patting his chest. "Look, you should go. Rachel's coming over in a bit and we're gonna watch a movie so I need to get changed and stuff," I lied. I went on tiptoes and kissed his cheek, before taking his hand and leading him to the door.

He looked a little sad as he agreed and kissed me goodbye, telling me he'd call me tomorrow. He made me promise that if I changed my mind and needed him tonight that I'd call him so he could come over. I smiled at him gratefully, secretly knowing there would be no chance that I'd call him. If I did that he'd expect physical contact, and I really just wasn't ready for anything heavy with him right now. I closed the door behind him and leant against it, taking deep breaths. As soon as I heard his car drive away I couldn't hold the sadness at bay anymore. My heart broke into a million pieces as I slid to the floor, crying helplessly.

chapter
ten

I felt awful, like I was dying. I made myself get up and go to bed. It was only half past four, but I needed to curl up in my bed. I grabbed the pillow Clay always used and buried my face into it, breathing in his smell, trying to calm myself.

I must have fallen asleep because I woke as two arms wrapped around me and moved me over into a hard chest. A hand smoothed the hair from my face and soft lips pressed against my cheek.

I looked up into two familiar green eyes, and I felt like I was home. Everything was okay now because Clay was here with me. Nothing else mattered. "I'm sorry, Riley Bear," he whispered, putting his forehead to mine and holding my cheek. I closed my eyes enjoying his closeness. "I'm an asshole, I know, and I'm so sorry. I love you."

I couldn't speak so I did the only thing I wanted to do in the world other than hold him tight - I kissed him. He responded immediately, kissing me back with so much passion that it took my breath away.

He pulled out of the kiss too soon and I whimpered at the loss of contact. Tears started to form in my eyes because he'd just rejected me again. "I need to say something," he said, stroking my face lightly with the back of his fingers. I closed my eyes not really wanting to hear it. "This doesn't mean the same for me as it does for you," he said quietly.

I frowned. I knew that. Did he think that I didn't know that already? I wanted him with every bone in my body, but he was just getting a quick thrill. I knew there was a difference in our feelings.

"I know that, Clay." I left my eyes closed, not daring to look at him because I knew I would cry. "I know that this is something fun for you," I admitted, pressing my lips to his again softly. *Now that we've admitted it maybe we can still do this and be friends at the same time - like friends with benefits.*

He pulled away looking at me intently, a slightly confused expression on his face. "No, Riley, it's not fun for me."

I gasped, horrified. *It isn't even fun? What the hell? Did I do something wrong? He said that I was good at it; he must have lied to me.* My breathing sped up as I started to panic. Heat flooded my face as I wished the earth would open up and swallow me to hide my embarrassment.

"Riley! Riley, that's not what I meant, jeez. Of course it's fun for me in that way, but what I meant was; I don't want you to just be something fun. I love you. I want to be with you, but I'll be here for whatever you need. If you need a friend, then I'll be your friend. If you need someone to hold you, then I'll be that too. Whatever you want, I'll do anything," he said quietly, rubbing my cheek tenderly.

I still couldn't breathe. My heart was beating so fast I thought it would kill me. *Clay wants me? Am I dreaming?* I felt like I was still sleeping and that I was trapped in some dream. If it was a dream, then it was certainly the best dream I'd ever had in my life. Silently, I wished I'd never wake up. I looked up at him hopefully. The warmth that was spreading from his fingers to my cheek was melting my heart.

"Clay," I whispered. How was I supposed to respond to that? He'd just told me that he loved me and that he'd do anything for me - what could I possibly say back to that? I had no words to describe my feelings; everything was just a jumbled mess of unspoken words in my head.

"It's okay, Riley Bear. I know things are gonna be difficult from now on, now that you know how I feel, but I promise I won't stand in the way of you and Blake. I'm sorry for what I said and for walking off like that. I was hurting. I wasn't going to meet Zoë; I just said that because I was lashing out. I promise we can make this work. It'll hurt like hell, but I can put my feelings for you aside and be your friend, I promise. I just needed you to know, finally," he said.

I looked at him, shocked. That was easily the longest speech I had ever heard him make. I smiled at him and he smiled back, kissing my forehead and laying his head back with a contented sigh. He was probably just pleased that he had finally told me the truth and got it off of his chest.

Did he seriously think that I didn't want him though? Was he actually crazy? Every girl I knew wanted to be with Clay. He was the most perfect boy in the world.

I sat up quickly and looked down at his beautiful face. "I love you too, Clay."

He nodded and smiled his beautiful smile. "I know that. But I just needed you to know finally, that I'm in love with you. I've been in love with you as long as I can remember."

I bent my head and kissed him gently on the lips; my heart hammered in my chest as the happiness threatened to overflow inside me. "Clay, I'm in love with you too," I said quietly, looking into his eyes.

His eyes lit up and his face went from complete shock into the biggest smile I had ever seen him do. I couldn't help but smile in response. "You love me?" he asked excitedly. I laughed and nodded in confirmation. He grabbed my face. "You're being serious, Riley? You love me?" I could hear a hint of desperation in his voice as he looked at me hopefully.

I nodded again, watching as his face lit up into a huge smile. "Yes, Clay, I love you." I grinned at his ecstatic expression; he looked like a kid that had just been given a brand new bike.

He kissed me passionately, tenderly, making a moaning sound in the back of his throat that made my whole body burn. He grabbed hold of me and rolled over so I was under him, running his hands through my hair, still beaming at me. "I wish you'd told me this a couple of days ago, I've been going through hell I swear. I was so happy when I woke up next to you after that first night, then when I came back from the shower you looked so horrified. I thought maybe you'd been crying," he said, shaking his head at the memory, looking hurt.

"I had been crying," I admitted, trailing my hands down his back feeling his muscles move as he tensed.

"Why?" he asked, kissing my cheek.

"I thought you'd left me, I thought that you played me and that everything was ruined."

He frowned. "That's why you said we had to forget it?" he asked quietly, still stroking my hair.

I nodded. "I thought you regretted it. You're a player, Clay; you've never even had a girlfriend. I thought I needed to straighten it out before things got awkward. I thought you'd used me," I explained, hooking my thumbs in his belt loops spreading my fingers out over his ass.

He bent his head, trailing little kisses from the corner of my mouth across my cheek to my ear. "I've told you hundreds of times why I've never had a girlfriend," he whispered, nibbling on my earlobe. I frowned at that. He'd told me? I couldn't remember.

"Why?" I asked confused.

He laughed. "Riley Bear, you're the only one for me. I don't want a girlfriend if it's not you," he said simply. *Oh God yeah! He always says that, that because I wasn't interested in him was why he was a player, and never wanted anything serious. He always told me that I was the only girl for him.*

I thought back to all the times he'd told me that he loved me or that he would do anything for me. All the times he made me things, little surprises, picking me flowers, everything he did for me. I'd always just laughed at him thinking he was joking, but that was him telling me how he felt. *Oh man, I've been so stupid!*

Happiness burst inside me as his words washed over me. "So what you're saying is that you want me to be your girlfriend?" I asked, giving him a flirtatious smile.

"No, Riley Bear. What I'm saying is that I want you to be my everything, my soul mate, my girlfriend, my whole world," he said, kissing me lightly. I blushed and giggled like a little kid. He smiled at me sheepishly. "Okay was that too much?"

"Maybe a little," I admitted, pulling his face to mine and kissing him passionately. "I have one thing I would definitely like you to be," I purred, rolling so I was on top of him again.

"Anything," he murmured, running his hands down my back, across my ass and down my thighs, making me moan breathlessly.

"My first," I whispered in his ear seductively.

He gasped and rolled over again so he was on top and kissed me. The kiss was amazing, it made my whole body tingle, it made me lose myself in the glory of it. By the time he pulled away to kiss my neck, I was giddy with desire. I pulled at his jeans trying to get them off as quickly as possible; he was doing the same to my clothes. I was already down to my panties and bra before he pulled away.

"Crap! We can't, I don't have anything," he groaned, slapping his forehead. The disappointment I felt was overwhelming, it was almost painful.

I looked at his face to see he felt the same as me; suddenly he brightened and kissed me again. I smiled against his lips because he must have thought of a solution, maybe he'd remembered a spare condom in his pocket or something. The nervous excitement was starting to build back up again.

Oh my God, I'm about to have sex with Clay! I was still pulling at his jeans pushing them all the way off when he took hold of my hand, pulling it away and interlacing our fingers.

"Riley, I don't have one," he repeated, rolling off of me again, still beaming at me.

"Then what do you look so happy for? I thought you just remembered you had one in your wallet or something," I said, pouting.

He laughed and ran his thumb across my bottom lip as he spoke. "I'm happy because we don't have to rush anything. We have forever for me to be with you, we don't have to do this tonight. It's not a 'tonight only' offer is it?" he asked with a teasing smile. I rolled him under me. He was only in his boxers I still had on my bra and panties; I sat up and gave him an evil smile.

"Well to be honest I'm not sure if I'm still gonna want you tomorrow," I joked, pretending to think about it whilst running my hands down his chest.

"Oh, really? Well then maybe I'd better make the most of you tonight then."

He shot me a wicked smile and sat up quickly, tickling me, making me laugh and squirm around on his lap.

I pushed him off and jumped up, still giggling as I ran for the door. I heard him jump off the bed behind me; I ran as fast as I could downstairs but it was no use, he was gaining on me. I made it to the kitchen before he grabbed my waist and span me around, picking me up by my hips and wrapping my legs around his waist.

"Hmm, now what's a fitting payback for running away from me?" he teased, narrowing his eyes at me and pretending to think as he walked forwards. "I know." He took one more step and pressed my back against the fridge. I screamed as the cold door touched my skin and jerked into him further as I dug my fingers into his shoulder and yelped from the shock.

He laughed and moved backwards, kissing me passionately, running his hands up my back, warming it up again. "I love you, Riley, so much," he cooed. "We don't need to rush this. I want to be with you, I want to make love to you, jeez I want to make love to you so much," he put his forehead to mine before continuing, "but we have all the time in the world."

I kissed him again and my stomach suddenly growled loudly, ruining the moment.

He laughed and pulled away. "It's a movie night, how about I order us a pizza while you choose a DVD?" he suggested, setting me down gently. I nodded in agreement and turned go back upstairs. I knew he was watching me so I purposefully swayed my ass seductively as I walked. I heard him moan, and I bit my lip trying not to laugh. "Choose something that's gonna scare you, I like having you cling to me," he called after me, laughing wickedly to himself.

When I got to my room I spotted his t-shirt strewn casually on the floor where we'd carelessly discarded it earlier. I smiled as I slipped it on, surrounding myself with Clay's beautiful scent. As I walked over to the shelf containing my DVD's, I caught a glimpse of myself in the mirror. I gasped, my eyes widening in shock, I looked awful. My face was puffy and red from crying, my mascara had smudged under my eyes so I looked like a panda, and my hair was all messy. I groaned. What was Clay thinking? He could do so much better than me!

I quickly grabbed a brush and started to brush out the knots and tangles from my hair; then I grabbed my face wipes and wiped my smudged make-up off. Grabbing my make-up bag, I started to apply some concealer to the red blotches. I had just finished applying mascara to one eye and was about to start the other when Clay cleared his throat from the doorway.

I jumped and looked at him. "Why are you doing that?" he asked, amusement colouring his voice.

"Isn't it obvious? I look a complete mess from all the crying," I answered, turning back to the mirror.

He walked in and grabbed my face wipes from the side, turning me around to face him; he pulled one out and wiped my freshly applied make-up off my face gently. "You are the most beautiful girl in the world, Riley, you don't need any of that," he said, throwing the wipe in the trashcan and kissing me tenderly.

My heart melted into a puddle because of how romantic that was. "I just wanted to look nice for you," I admitted, chewing on my lip, blushing.

"I'm sorry, but you'll never look nice," he replied, grabbing my hand and pulling me over to the hundreds of movies I have.

"I won't?" I asked, lagging behind him on purpose so I could watch his butt.

"Nope, never. You are too perfect to ever just look 'nice'. And do you mind not staring at my ass?" he replied, chuckling.

I reached out a hand and slapped it playfully. "I thought it was my ass now," I countered, sticking out my tongue.

He moaned breathily and pulled me forward. "Come on, Riley Bear, choose a movie. The pizza will be here soon." He wrapped his arms around my waist and rested his chin on my shoulder. At random I chose iRobot, it wasn't exactly a scary movie like he asked, but it was the first one I saw and I didn't plan on watching much of it anyway.

The doorbell rang so I skipped off to answer it while he pulled on his jeans. "Wait, you're only in a t-shirt!" Clay called as I made my way to the door. I didn't particularly care though, I was too hungry. I opened the door to a guy from our school. I tried to think of his name, my best guess was Steven and that he was a senior the same as Clay.

"Er, hi. I have your large pizza, half margarita, half super loaded and your chocolate fudge cake and banoffi pie," he greeted, looking me up and down slowly, his gaze lingering on my bare legs.

I heard a sound from beside me so I knew that Clay was there. I held up one finger to him, signalling for him to wait. "Hi. It's Steven, isn't it? You go to South Shore, right?" I asked with a bright smile, leaning against the doorframe and crossing one ankle over the other.

"That's right. And you're Riley Tanner," he replied nodding. A cocky grin stretched across his face as he looked at me.

I smiled. "I just wanted to ask you, is there some reason why none of the guys ask me out at school?" I asked, biting my lip and looking at him through my eyelashes. I heard Clay shuffle so I held up a hand to him again. Just as I knew he would, he did as I asked, he didn't move or say anything.

"Actually, everyone knows you're Clay Preston's girl. He's like seriously in love with you, it's totally obvious. So I think they just stay away because of that," Steven replied, shrugging casually.

Clay Preston's girl? "Really? Everyone knows that?" I asked a little shocked. *Did everyone know it but me?*

He nodded. "Yeah. But if you ever want to step away from the whole stereotypical jock I would definitely take you out," he offered, looking down at my legs again.

"I'll keep that in mind, Steven. Now, how much do I owe you for the pizza?" I asked, trying out my flirty voice on him.

He licked his lips and looked at his receipt. "Well it says here fifteen fifty, but let's just call it like ten bucks, and I'll tell them I dropped the desserts," he said, winking at me conspiratorially.

"Well thanks, Steven, that's really sweet," I replied, flirting like mad. I put my hand on Clay's chest behind the door so he knew I hadn't forgotten him.

"Sweet is my middle name," Steven said in his cocky voice.

I giggled playfully. "Wow, your parents must be hippies or something. Who names their kid that?" I joked, turning to grab my purse. He laughed. Clay reached out and handed me a ten, I winked at him and he shook his head at me rolling his eyes, a smile playing at the edge of his mouth. I turned back to the door and handed over the money.

"So are you having a sleep over or something?" Steven asked as he slipped the money in his pocket.

"Definitely having a sleep over, but I'm hoping there won't be much sleeping going on," I replied, winking and taking the food. "See you at school," I added as I stepped back into the house and pushed the door shut with my hip.

"That was shameless, Riley Bear," Clay scolded playfully as he took the boxes from my hands with one hand and grabbed me with the other, pulling me in for a long kiss.

"Shameless slutty behaviour, check. Discounted food, check," I countered, smirking, making him laugh. As I walked towards the stairs, I shrugged out of his t-shirt and hung it over the banister, walking up the stairs in my underwear, knowing he was watching.

"Damn it, woman, you are so hot," he breathed as he ran to catch up.

• • •

"SO WHICH DESSERT do you want?" I asked, looking between the two cartons. I really had no preference, they were both my favourites. Clay just raised an eyebrow at me as if this were a silly question. "You ordered one of each so we could swap halfway through because you knew I wouldn't be able to make up my mind," I guessed, rolling my eyes. He just nodded so I grabbed the one nearest to me which happened to be the chocolate fudge cake. "How do you know me so well, Clay? I mean, seriously, you're like the sweetest boy in the world." I shook my head in awe.

"I pay attention to you, Riley, a lot of attention," he replied, grinning wickedly. "So how's that one?" he asked, nodding at my cake.

"It's pretty good; you know what would make this taste ten times better though?" I asked, getting a big blob of the chocolate sauce and icing on my finger.

"No, what?" he asked. He hadn't noticed as he was too busy stuffing his face with the other dessert.

"This." I reached over and wiped the chocolate across his abs, giggling to myself.

Clay jumped and looked down at it in shock. "That's supposed to make it taste better?" he asked, looking at me confused.

I bit my lip and nodded in confirmation. "Uh huh." I leant in and pushed him onto his back, bending my head and licking the chocolate off of his stomach. His whole body tensed as he sucked in a breath through his teeth. *Wow this was an excellent idea, and sweet Jesus it does taste ten times better too!*

"Riley, you're really good at all of this for a virgin. That was seriously hot," he said breathlessly, raising his head so he could watch me spread some more on him before licking it off again. I still couldn't get used to the idea that this boy was mine, that he loved me and wanted me. "Mmm, I want to try it," he said suddenly, pushing my shoulders so I had to roll onto my back. He unclasped my bra and wiped banoffi pie over my stomach, drawing it in a heart shape. It was so cold that I burst into a fit of giggles, but the giggling stopped as soon as his hot tongue touched my skin, leaving a wet trail in its wake. I gasped and closed my eyes, just enjoying the attention from my boyfriend.

After all the dessert was used up we were just having a passionate make out session. I was still in my panties, and he was in his boxers. We made no moves to take them off; we had all night so there was no rush.

He kissed across to my ear and laughed. "What?" I asked, my voice sounding husky from all the kissing.

"You have cream in your hair," he replied, grinning. I smiled too as another idea formed in my head that he was sure to like.

I put my hands on his chest and pushed him off me. I stood up and took a couple of steps away before slipping off my panties throwing them at him. He looked a little shocked as they hit him in the chest and fell into his lap. I turned around and walked off.

"Where are you going?" he questioned.

I smiled over my shoulder seductively. "I'm going to take a shower and wash this out of my hair. Want to come and help me?" I invited, raising my eyebrows.

He closed his eyes and moaned breathily then opened them back up to look at me with a hungry, lustful expression clear across his face. I giggled and walked off in the direction of my bathroom knowing that he would follow.

• • •

I HAD THE BEST SHOWER I had ever had in my life. We washed each other, and he even conditioned my hair, he combed it through and everything. After nearly an hour we both booked a bit prune-like so we decided to get out. I wrapped my hair in a towel and reached to get another for my body, but Clay beat me to it. He then proceeded to dry every inch of my body thoroughly. I just watched him the whole time. I watched as the water dripped from his hair and trailed its way down his body before it soaked into the towel he had wrapped around his waist. I envied that drip of water I really did.

"There you go, Miss Tanner, I think you are officially free from traces of banoffi pie." He stood up and kissed me softly. I giggled as he trailed his hands down my sides making me shiver.

"Hmm, I'm pretty tired, I think I'm gonna go to sleep now. Unless you can think of anything else we can do, Clay?" I trailed my finger down his chest and hooked it in the towel at his waist, tugging gently making it fall to the floor. "Oops, silly me," I mused, raking my eyes over his body.

"You're a freaking pervert, Riley, my eyes are up here," he joked, laughing and pointing to his face.

"I've been looking at your eyes for years, Clay; I'm just trying to give the rest of you a chance to catch up." I winked at him, wriggling closer to him, feeling his body heat seep into my skin.

He grinned and grabbed my waist, lifting me easily, throwing me over his shoulder and slapping my ass gently. From this angle I had a perfect view of his toned back and pert little behind. He carried me to the bedroom and threw me gently on the bed.

"Let's watch the movie," he suggested, putting the DVD in and pressing play, he switched off the light and got into the bed naked. I saw the opening credits, but that was about it before he turned to me with an expression so lustful that it sent shockwaves through my body. "Are you sure you're not gonna freak out in the morning and tell me you just want to be friends? Because I really don't think I can take that again," he said, his eyes tight with tension.

I cupped his face and looked into his eyes. "I'm sure." There was no way in this world that I was going to change my mind, but part of me was terrified, thinking what if we did this and it didn't work out? Would we be able to stay friends then? But I just didn't think that there was any way either of us could *not* try; it was definitely worth the risk because what if it did work out and we got to have this forever?

"Will you be my girlfriend?" he asked quietly, playing with my fingers anxiously. I smiled; they were the sweetest words in the world as they came out of his sexy mouth.

I nodded. "Yes." I actually felt so happy I could burst into song. "So I get to be your first something too," I mused, tracing my finger along his jaw, feeling the slight stubble from the day's growth.

"You're my first a lot of things, Riley Bear," he corrected, with a knowing smile.

"Yeah, like what?" I asked curiously. *He's a total player who's slept with more girls than he can remember. What can I possibly be the first of?*

"You were my first crush, first love, first girl I ever gave flowers to, well, actually you're the only girl I've ever given flowers to. First girl I ever kissed," he said.

He was about to continue, but I interrupted, "First kiss? What are you talking about?"

He laughed. "When we went to Mrs Polinski's wedding and you were bridesmaid. Don't you remember? They made us kiss for a photo while we stood under that flower arch thing."

I laughed at the memory of it. Mrs Polinski was one of our neighbours. She didn't have much family, so she'd asked me to be her bridesmaid and Clay was pageboy. I'd been six, and Clay had been seven. The wedding photographer had thought we were cute and made us pose in front of the happy couple and kiss. I'd forgotten all about that.

"And you were chewing bubblegum so the photographer told you off for chewing and made us do it again," I replied, smiling as that replayed in my head. I had gotten so angry at him that day because he was chewing and ruined the photos so we had to take them again.

He grinned sheepishly. "Yep, so like I said first kiss. First time anyone's ever smeared food on me and licked it off." He licked his lips subconsciously as he looked at my body, a little twinkle to his eye that made me grin like a fool. "First shower with a girl, which was so incredibly hot, by the way, that I get chills just thinking about it," he continued, kissing my neck. "My first and actually the only person I've ever given a hickey to or received one from. The list goes on and on. And I want you to be my only for all of those too. I don't ever want anyone else." He wrapped his arms around me, pulling me close and burying his face in my hair, inhaling deeply. I felt was so safe and warm and happy that it was a little overwhelming. I stifled a yawn, and he laughed. "Wow, I wore you out, huh?" he teased.

"Yep, boyfriend, you did," I mumbled sleepily, patting his chest and smiling at the word boyfriend. He kissed my forehead and I was vaguely aware that he switched the movie off before I fell asleep.

chapter eleven

When I woke in the morning, Clay was spooning me from behind with his arms wrapped around me in a vice grip. I knew he wasn't awake yet, I could hear his deep breathing in my ear. I loved the sound of his breathing when he was asleep. When I was a kid and he would stay over, I would lie awake for ages just listening to the calming sound of his rhythmic breathing.

I smiled happily as I remembered last night when he told me he loved me, and all the things that we did, the thought of them had my body already tingling in anticipation of those things that would happen again and hopefully would be happening a lot from now on. I thought about having sex with Clay, what it would be like, whether it would hurt. I decided that I needed to get on the pill and fast because I wanted him so badly that it would only be a matter of time.

I briefly panicked that he might have changed his mind during the night, but I pushed the thought away quickly, he wouldn't have changed his mind, that was just me starting to second guess him like I did the last two times when I said I just wanted to be friends. I knew better now, he was in love with me, and I was in love with him.

I wondered what would have happened if he had told me this a year ago or two years ago, before I realised I was in love with him, would it have ruined everything then? If I hadn't gone away and visited family for a month and missed him so much, would I have ever realised my feelings for him? I sighed, genuinely not knowing the answer to that one.

His arm was resting under my neck and bent across my body, trapping me against him in a little protective cage. I smiled to myself and kissed his arm that my head was resting on. Unconsciously, he pulled his arms tighter around me, the small move made my heart melt. He'd always been cuddly when he slept over; even when we were kids he'd always lie right next to me and hold my hand while we slept. Maybe that should have given me some clue as to his feelings for me. I shook my head at how clueless I was about it. He had been in love with me for years, and we'd wasted so much time.

Careful not to wake him, I turned over in his arms. He was still sound asleep and looked like an angel, so peaceful and beautiful. I drank him in greedily, the shape of his eyebrows, his straight nose and square jaw, his perfect kissable mouth. His lips actually looked so inviting that, before I knew what I was doing, I'd leant forward and kissed him gently. He stirred in his sleep so I quickly laid back down, closed my eyes and faked sleep.

I felt the bed move slightly, and his weight shifted so I knew he was awake. I didn't move as I fought the smile that was trying to break out on my face. I heard him sigh and then he traced his fingers from my temple to my jaw slowly. "You are so beautiful, Riley. I love you so much," he whispered, before kissing my forehead tenderly. I couldn't do it anymore, I wanted to tell him I loved him too, but first I wanted to have a little fun with him...

I cracked open my eyes to see him lying there staring at me with a contented smile on his face. "Hi," I croaked, surprised by how husky my voice sounded.

He smiled his heartbreaking smile. "Hi."

Okay time to make him squirm. "Clay, listen, about last night, I think we should just be friends," I said, trying not to smile.

He didn't fall for it though, he laughed and rolled so that I was underneath him and pinned my wrists down either side of my head. "No way, Riley Bear, you agreed to be my girlfriend, now you have to deal with it." He bent his head and kissed me hungrily as his hands slid from my wrists up to my hands, holding tightly.

I moaned into his mouth. His kisses never ceased to amaze me, impossibly every one felt better than the one before. I couldn't move my hands because he was still pinning them down so I raised my legs and wrapped them tightly around his waist pulling him closer to me. Loving the feel of his weight as it pressed me down into the mattress. He kissed me so passionately my body was burning with need and excitement.

He broke the kiss and smiled down at me, finally releasing my hands.

I sighed, looking at every inch of his handsome face. I wanted to take things further with him; the feel of his body on mine was making me needy and anxious. "I want you so much, Clay," I admitted, running my hand down his chest and stopping as I got to his abs, tracing them with my fingertips.

He smiled, rubbing his nose against mine. "Let's just wait and make it special, okay? This will have to do for now," he said huskily as he slid one hand down between my legs and started rubbing me lightly. I moaned loudly and he watched me with his eyes shining with excitement. My body felt as if it were in heaven. I was tantalisingly close to my climax when my cell phone rang on the bedside unit. I jumped, letting out a little squeal from the shock because it was right next to my head. Clay laughed quietly and pulled away from me. "It's okay answer it," he instructed, nodding at it as it continued to vibrate and flash.

Shook my head, pouting. "I don't want to answer it; I want you to finish what you're doing."

Clay grinned and brought his lips to mine, kissing me softly for a second. "Answer it, it might be important, I promise I'll finish this after."

I huffed and pouted, grabbing the phone and answering it without looking at the screen. *This had better be important!* "Hello?" Even I could hear the annoyed tone to my voice because of the bad timing.

"Hi, Jailbait," Blake chirped.

My eyes flew open wide in shock. *Holy crap!* "Er hi, Blake," I replied, looking away from Clay who stiffened and suddenly looked tense.

"So how'd you sleep last night? You never called."

I glanced at Clay who now for some reason looked as if he was trying not to laugh. *What's he grinning like that for?* I gave him my best quizzical expression, but he just shook his head slowly as a wicked grin stretched across his face.

"Er, I slept great actually, Blake, how about you?" *Wow, this is awkward!*

Before I could even process it, Clay slipped his hand back between my legs. I bit my lip to stop the sound that tried to escape, and squeezed my legs shut, clamping his hand there so he couldn't move it. I glared at him warningly.

"I slept okay, I was thinking about you a lot though," Blake answered. I turned my attention back to the phone in confusion. *What is he talking about?* Clay somehow still managed to get his fingers to move gently. I gasped.

"Oh," was all I could manage to say to Blake.

Clay was now kissing across my stomach and had used his other hand to unclamp my legs so he had better access. "So you were all right on your own last night then? I was really hoping to be able to come over and help you housesit," Blake teased. The suggestion in his voice wasn't hard to miss. Clay was kissing around my neck as he continued to rub me gently down below. I gasped as my body bumped up a gear. "What? What's wrong?" Blake asked worriedly.

I clamped my hand over the phone as I moaned.

"Nothing, I just er..." Suddenly my body kicked up another gear as Clay sucked on the side of my neck, covering my body with his as he carried on his beautifully torturous assault with his fingers. I closed my eyes, my mind going a little numb because of the sensations. I was definitely going to lose control soon. Clay was doing this on purpose, but I was enjoying it too much to protest.

"What? You what?" Blake prompted when I didn't continue with my sentence.

"I just saw a spi... spi-der!" I replied, almost shouting the last word as I bumped up another gear. Clay chuckled quietly against my neck so I squirmed, trying to get away but he just pinned me down with his weight, his eyes sparkling mischievously.

"You saw a spider?" Blake asked incredulously.

I nodded. "Yeah, yeah a spider and I'm going to kill it when I get off the phone," I replied breathlessly. Clay just laughed again as he trailed his other hand across my stomach tickling me as he continued to work his hand between my legs.

"Riley? You there? I said can I come over?" Blake snapped.

Oh crap, had he been talking to me? "It's not really a good time." I clamped my hand back over the phone as another little moan left my lips. *Seriously how is Blake not hearing this? I am going to kill Clay I swear, he's doing this on purpose! Bastard.* Suddenly I felt that rush of sensation pushing me on and I knew I needed to get off of the phone quickly. "I've got to go, there's someone at the door," I lied, snapping the phone shut just in time to moan Clay's name and dig my fingers into his back as my body shook and little stars danced behind my eyelids.

Clay laughed, full on laughed. He kissed my cheek and pulled back, grinning. The enjoyment was clear on his face, he looked extremely proud of himself.

I raised my hands to his chest to push him off of me, but he just pinned them back to the bed, laughing wickedly. "You jerk! I can't believe you did that!" I cried angrily, but my voice had lost a lot of its authority due to me hardly being able to breathe.

He gave me his adorable puppy dog face that usually got him out of trouble with me when we argued. "I love you, Riley," he vowed, kissing me passionately and showing me how much that sentence was true.

Okay now that's just not fair! How the hell can I stay mad at him when he is kissing me like that? He's such a cheater!

He pulled away with a cheeky grin and I couldn't help but smile back. "So I'm forgiven?" he asked, playing with a stray bit of my hair, smoothing it back from my face gently.

I nodded and rolled my eyes. "Yes, but you're still a jerk."

"Yeah but you still love me," he countered cockily.

I sighed and knew there was no way I could even pretend that I didn't, it was probably clear on my face anyway. "Yeah I do," I agreed, running my hands down his back to squeeze his ass. *Jeez that ass!* My mouth was watered at the thought of it alone.

The phone rang again, and this time I jumped off of the bed to get it. "Hi, Blake," I answered, quickly pulling on my bathrobe.

"Who was at the door?" he asked. I frowned. *Door? What's he talking about?*

"What door?" I asked, before slapping myself on the forehead as I realised.

Dammit! That's what I said 'there's someone at the door'. Clay laughed so I made a shush action with my finger. "The door, right, er, it was... it was Clay," I said, sitting on the desk chair.

"Clay? So what you two made up now?" He didn't sound particularly happy about it.

"Yeah, we made up now," I confirmed, glancing over to Clay who was pulling on his boxers and looking around for his jeans from yesterday.

"So can I come over?" Blake asked, still sounding pissed off.

"Er, Blake, that's not really a good idea, I've got some things to do." I squirmed on the seat as Clay stood there watching me. I didn't really want to have this conversation with Blake while he was standing there, it made it more difficult.

Blake huffed. "What things? Can I help?"

I knew I needed to bite the bullet and get it over with. I mentally crossed my fingers that he'd take it all right. "No. Listen I just don't want this okay. I'm really sorry, I am, but it's just not gonna work out between us," I said quietly.

I hated to feel like this. I'd ended a few relationships before, never serious ones, but I still hated to say the words. But Blake and I weren't even together. We'd talked about being together but never actually agreed anything; we'd only been on two dates.

"What the fuck do you mean not gonna work out?" he practically shouted. I flinched a little from the tone of his voice and turned my head so that Clay wouldn't know he was shouting, I had a feeling he'd go crazy, he already had a problem with him.

"Blake, I'm sorry but we never actually started anything so..." I trailed off not really knowing how to finish the last part.

"Screw that! We never started anything, I like you, I told you!" He was full on shouting now. He actually sounded scary, and I was glad we were doing this over the phone.

"I know and I said I was sorry, but at least you can go back to screwing random girls every night without the threat of jail hanging over your head," I consoled, trying to cheer him up a bit.

"I don't want to screw random girls! Fucking hell, Riley, are you not listening?" he screamed.

I flinched again. "Blake, seriously calm down, we went on like two dates. I'm sorry, but it's not gonna work. I have to go." I hung up the phone quickly, frowning at the wall. He'd taken that a lot harder than I imagined.

I took a deep breath before turning my attention to Clay, noticing how mad he looked. "Was he giving you a hard time?" he asked through his teeth.

I shook my head quickly. "No, he was just upset that's all." My phone buzzed in my hand, and I looked at the caller ID. Blake again. I winced and rejected it before switching the phone off completely and smiling up at Clay, pretending nothing had happened. "So what shall we do today?" I asked, getting up off the chair and wrapping my arms around him.

"Well we haven't been on an official date yet," he teased, smirking.

A date? Wow, a date with Clay Preston, every girl's dream.

I felt the moronic grin slip onto my face. "Okay, why don't you go home and change and pick me up in an hour," I suggested, pushing him towards my bedroom door.

"What? Why? I've got clothes here, why can't I just wait here for you?" he asked, frowning because I was making him leave.

"Because boys pick girls up for dates. Now go!" I instructed, pointing at my bedroom door sternly.

He laughed. "Mmm, I like masterful Riley," he said, pecking me on the cheek giving me a sly wink before he strutted confidently out of my room.

Once he left I showered and then pulled on a pair of black skinny jeans, pairing it with a loose fitting blue gypsy top. I added my usual tiny bit of make-up and some perfume that Clay had bought for me. I smiled when I sprayed it on. I'd smelt it on someone once, but they couldn't remember the name of it, Clay had gone out that afternoon and smelt hundreds of perfumes in the store before he found the right one and bought me a bottle as a surprise. I wondered now how I'd ever missed that he was in love with me. Thinking back, things like that made it glaringly obvious. I grinned to myself because such a sweet boy was in love with me. He'd asked me to be his girlfriend. The thought made my insides melt into a puddle.

• • •

AFTER ABOUT THREE quarters of an hour I was downstairs waiting for him when the doorbell rang. I jumped up excitedly. *My first date with Clay!* I practically skipped to the door and threw it open with a big smile on my face, only to see that it wasn't Clay, it was Blake. His eyes were narrowed, his jaw clenched tight as he glared at me angrily.

Oh no! "Hi, Blake, what are you doing here?" I asked quietly, looking up the driveway to see if Clay was anywhere near. I had a feeling that if the two of them were together there would be a problem.

"I needed to talk to you," he replied, staring at me intently.

I gulped. "Okay, come in." I stepped to the side and held the door open in invitation. He walked past me, and I closed the door quickly. I needed to get him out by the time Clay came to pick me up so that they wouldn't start arguing again. "Blake, I'm sorry, honestly I am, but I just don't think that-" I started, but he spun around and pinned me against the wall so fast that it knocked the wind out of me. I gasped from the shock and looked at his face with wide eyes. He looked so angry that it made me shrink back against the wall, trying in vain to make myself smaller somehow.

"Shut up, Riley, for fuck sake!" he shouted in my face.

Holy shit! What the hell is wrong with him? I could smell the alcohol on his breath. Was he drunk? I'd only spoken to him like an hour ago. I looked around wildly for something, anything, I actually didn't know what.

His hand slammed down against the wall near my head making me squeak from fright. "Why? Tell me why! Yesterday we were talking about going out then today, you want nothing to do with me?" he shouted in my face again. The venom in his voice made my stomach ache.

Okay, do not mention Clay!

I gulped, scrambling to come up with a reason that had nothing to do with my best friend. "It's the age thing. I feel rushed. I'm just not ready for an older boyfriend right now, that's all. I'm sorry," I lied breathlessly. My heart was beating so loud and fast that he could probably hear it too.

He looked at me for a few seconds before he spoke. "I want to be with you, I've not felt like this before." He seemed to be calming down a bit now.

"I'm sorry, Blake, really I am." I smiled weakly, hoping that was it and that he would just leave.

Instead of leaving though, like I'd hoped, he moved forward crushing my body against the wall as he kissed me roughly. He kissed me so hard that my lips were crushed against my teeth. I whimpered and tried to turn my head to the side, but he gripped my chin stopping me from moving. He forced my mouth open and pushed his tongue in. I squeezed my eyes shut as I brought my hands to his chest to try to push him away from me. I shoved as hard as I could, but he didn't budge. He pulled his head back and pushed his body up against mine, crushing me against the wall.

"Blake, don't, please," I begged, shoving on his chest again, trying to push him off me.

He grabbed my wrists in his hands and slammed them against the wall. Pain shot up my right wrist, and I let out a piercing scream before I could stop myself. "Shit! Ow please you're hurting me!" I cried breathlessly. I was crying now, but I could see his face soften.

"I... I'm sorry, Jailbait, I didn't mean to. Are you okay?" he asked quietly, kissing away my tears.

I turned my head. "Please don't," I whimpered, trying to squirm away from him again.

"Fuck it, Riley! Why did you make me do that? I don't want to hurt you." He stepped back, running his hands through his black hair roughly.

"Please just go, please. My... my parents are upstairs," I lied weakly, trying to get him to leave.

His head snapped up to look at me, his eyes turning hard again. "No, your parents are away all weekend, we're alone. Why are you lying!" He sneered at me angrily, stepping closer to me again.

"I'm scared! You're scaring me." I sobbed.

He stopped where he was. "I'm scaring you?" he asked quietly, his gaze dropping to the floor.

I nodded, cradling my arm to my chest, trying desperately to ignore the blinding pain that was making me feel sick. "Yes."

"I'm sorry, Jailbait, I'll go, I'm really sorry, but you wouldn't answer your cell, and I started thinking all these crazy things about you and Preston alone in the house. I just needed to see you." He wiped my face gently with the back of his hand, brushing my tears away.

I couldn't concentrate on anything other than the pain. He smiled weakly, his face was inches from mine, and he was moving in to kiss me again. I swallowed loudly. "Please, Blake, you need to go, I'll... I'll talk to you later okay." I faked a smile hoping he would buy it.

He sighed, kissed me on the cheek and smiled. "Okay, I'll talk to later then. Just make sure you answer your fucking phone when I call, okay?" he snapped. He took my hands in his making the pain double and shoot up my wrist again. I flinched and bit my lip so I didn't cry out. I tasted blood in my mouth where I bit down so hard. I nodded in agreement. At this point I would agree to anything just to get him out of the house.

He smiled and turned, stalking out of the door without another word. For a few seconds I stayed where I was, pressed tightly against the wall, too afraid to move. But once he was out of sight I ran to the door and closed it. I slumped down on the floor leaning my forehead against the wall, sobbing, cradling my wrist until I heard my favourite voice in the world.

"What are you doing here?" I heard Clay say outside.

"Just seeing my girlfriend. You need to stay the hell away from her, Preston," Blake threatened.

"Girlfriend?" Clay scoffed. "Fuck you, asshole. Go spread your STD's around some more." Clay's voice sounded closer to the door this time.

I was shaking now, my whole body felt cold. "Preston, you better shut your fucking mouth, or I swear I'm gonna shut it for you," Blake snapped.

I heard Clay laugh. "Yeah, because that worked out so well for you last time," he mocked. His voice was right outside the door now, and I willed him to come in.

"Screw you, Preston."

A car door slammed, and an engine started up. I expected Clay just to come in as usual, but he didn't, instead he knocked on the door. Weakly, I pushed myself up off of the floor, wiping my face with my good hand and taking a deep breath to try and get some control over myself. I had no idea how I was going to explain this to Clay.

As I opened the door, a bunch of yellow tulips were held out to me. "Hey, Riley Bear, I got you these." My lip trembled because of the safeness that I felt just because he was here. He looked up at me and suddenly dropped the flowers, scooping me up into his arms. "What the hell? Are you okay? Did he hurt you? Shit, Riley, what happened?" he asked. I could hear the worry and anger in his voice.

I put my head on his shoulder and cradled my arm protectively, sobbing on his shoulder. I couldn't speak. He carried me over to the sofa and sat down, settling me onto his lap, rocking me back and forth, stroking my hair.

"What happened? Did he hurt you?" he asked tenderly. I nodded and held out my wrist. Clay took hold of it gently looking at it as he sucked in a breath through his teeth. I swallowed my sob as I looked down at it too, it looked swollen and red.

Clay muttered something under his breath that sounded like "I'm gonna kill him" or something along those lines. Gently he moved me off of his lap, sitting me on the couch, and then he walked off in the direction of the kitchen. I heard him banging around in there and then moments later he came back with a bag of frozen peas. He scooped me back up onto his lap and held the peas to my wrist.

"What happened?" he asked quietly, kissing my forehead.

"He just showed up. I... I thought it was you, then he just went crazy, shouting and... and..." I couldn't finish because my sobs had started again at the thought of him kissing me and how helpless I had felt when he trapped me against the wall.

He wiped my tears away gently. "It's okay, Riley Bear, I'm here now. It's okay," he murmured over and over until I calmed down.

I pressed my face into the side of his neck, hoping his smell would soothe me as I told him the rest of what had happened. "He was so angry. He said he wanted to be with me, he was shouting at me and then he kissed me." Clay sucked in a big breath when I said the last bit. "I tried to push him off, honest I did, Clay, but he grabbed my arms and slammed my wrist on the wall." I sat up a little, trying to look into his eyes. I needed to know that was okay, that we were okay. He frowned and looked at my wrist with a tight jaw. "I tried to push him off I promise." I touched his face with my other hand. "Please say that's okay," I begged quietly.

His eyes snapped up to mine. "Okay? Hell no it's not okay! He kissed you against your will, he fucking hurt you! That's nowhere near okay!" he spat angrily.

"I'm so sorry, please forgive me," I mumbled, crying again.

"Forgive *you*? What the hell are you talking about? Why would I need to forgive you, Riley Bear, you've done nothing wrong," he murmured, stroking my hair again lovingly, pressing his forehead to mine. "Come on let's get you to the hospital and get this wrist checked out."

I smiled gratefully as he stood and helped me to my feet, wrapping his arm around me tightly and holding the peas to my wrist. "Wow, this is gonna be a good first date, Clay," I joked, trying to ease the tension I could feel radiating off of him.

He laughed humourlessly. "As long as I'm with you, I don't care what we do," he replied. "And, by the way, you look beautiful." He bent and kissed me softly. I kissed him back, moving to get closer, but my wrist throbbed making me yelp into his mouth. He pulled back quickly, wincing as he looked down at my arm. "I think this might be broken," he said quietly, bending his head so he could kiss it.

I nodded in agreement. "I think so too." He led me out of the house grabbing my purse and locking the door behind us.

• • •

WE SPENT NEARLY five hours at the hospital before we finally we arrived back home. I had a cast on my wrist. Clay was right; I had fractured it, and would have to wear a cast for the next six weeks. When we arrived back to my house, Clay was fussing over me like crazy, being his usual sweet, attentive self, getting me pillows and drinks, making me dinner. He even offered to come to the bathroom with me in case I needed help, I'd declined, laughing at him, but as it turned out I couldn't do my jeans back up after with one hand so I had to ask him to do it - much to his amusement.

I'd told Clay everything Blake had said, and when I told him that I'd said I would talk to him later in a bid to get him out of the house, he'd stiffened and gone quiet. I didn't know what he was thinking about, he wouldn't tell me so I'd just changed the subject.

I made a statement to the police, but they said that there was not much they could do about it. There were no witnesses so it would be my word against his. Apparently the fact that I had invited him into the house from the street would look bad on my part. Blake did have previous history so they were going to go and talk to him and tell him to back off, that was all the help they could offer.

We were now lying on the sofa together watching some crappy reality TV show. Bored out of my brain, I rolled over in his arms and kissed him lightly. He responded immediately, tangling his hand into the back of my hair as he kissed me back. When he pulled out of the kiss he smiled, but it didn't quite reach his eyes. His whole body was still tight with stress, like it had been all day. I sighed deeply, wishing I could make him feel better.

"Clay, what's going to cheer you up? How I can I get that thundercloud from above your head?" I joked, snuggling closer to him and revelling in the warmth that his body provided.

He laughed, seeming a little confused. "Thundercloud?"

I nodded. "Yeah, you've been in a foul mood all day and so angry it wouldn't surprise me if you've given yourself an ulcer," I confirmed, before adding, "but you've hidden it very well."

"I hid it well? Then how did you know I've been angry?" he asked, his jaw tensing again. I pointed to it and smiled.

"That right there is your first give away, the clenched jaw. The second is your eyes, they get all tight when you're angry, and the third is your hands. I'm not sure if you realise but you've had a permanent fist since you came over here this morning," I explained, bending my head and kissing the corner of his mouth as his lips pressed together in a thin line.

He sighed deeply. "I'm sorry, Riley, have I been an ass?" he asked, taking my face into his hands gently.

I shook my head. *Seriously, Clay, an ass? That would never happen.*

"You've never been an ass, never, you're too freaking sweet and romantic and thoughtful to ever be an ass," I replied honestly. He smiled and I stifled a yawn, hiding it behind my hand. "Want to go to bed?"

He smiled and nodded, kissing me softly as he climbed over me and got to his feet. As I went to sit up, he shook his head and slipped his hands under my body, lifting me bridal style and carrying me upstairs to my bedroom.

I smiled and pressed my face against the side of his neck, loving how romantic he was being. When he set me gently on the bed I wrapped my good arm tightly around his neck, pulling him down on top of me. His mouth slanted over mine in a kiss that made my toes curl and my stomach flutter with both nerves and desire. When my hands went to the bottom of his shirt, he pulled away and shook his head, frowning.

"I don't want to hurt you, so why don't we not do anything tonight? You should rest and get some sleep," he suggested, kissing each of my fingers on my injured hand.

I whimpered with disappointment. "Clay, are you kidding me?" *He doesn't even want to make out or fool around for a little while? My arm will be fine during that.*

I pulled his head back down to mine, kissing him again. He moaned against my lips. "Riley Bear, we don't have to rush anything I told you, let's just get some sleep okay. We've got a big day tomorrow." He smirked at me, settling himself on the bed next to me, stroking the fingers on my bad hand.

Big day, what is he talking about? "What's happening tomorrow?"

He smiled proudly. "I have to introduce you to my friends as the love of my life, mind you, they already know that, but they don't know I finally told you," he explained, bending his head and nuzzling against my neck.

I gasped in shock as I processed his words. Everyone really knew but me! "Your friends all knew!" I questioned, frowning.

He nodded. "Yeah I told them about you years ago. I think everyone knew I was in love with you apart from you."

I groaned. I wasn't looking forward to tomorrow; the girls there were going to hate me even more for this.

"What?" he asked, looking at me softly as he rested his arm across my stomach.

I shrugged. "I'm just not so excited about everybody knowing that's all."

He frowned, suddenly looking a bit worried. "Why not?"

I sighed, pouting. "All the girls are gonna hate me, Clay. They already hate me for just being your friend. Now that you're off the market I'm probably gonna get killed or something," I said dramatically.

He laughed and traced my pouty lip with his thumb. "Don't worry, I'll protect you from those nasty girls," he teased. Another yawn crept up on me, and this time I couldn't even try to disguise it. He smiled at me knowingly. "Tired?"

I nodded. "Can you help me with my clothes?" I felt a little helpless; I already knew I'd have trouble with the buttons on my jeans.

He laughed softly and nodded. Taking hold of my top and pulling it carefully over my head. I winced as he pulled it off of my injured arm. The pain meds were starting to wear off a little now so it was beginning to ache again. He stripped off of the rest of my clothes too, leaving me in just my underwear. A cheeky smile stretched across his face as he kissed me quickly before stepping off the bed and shedding his clothes too.

I let my eyes rake over him as he slowly peeled them off. It was kind of like watching a live strip show, and I couldn't help how my hormones spiked at the sight of his flawless body. *My goodness he is so beautiful.* But Clay was so much more than just good looks, he was the kindest, sweetest, funniest, most considerate and generous boy in the world... and he was mine. I sighed happily.

When he was down to his boxers he climbed back in bed with me, wrapping his arms tightly around me. I snuggled into his chest, enjoying the way his skin felt like silk against mine. He sighed sadly so I looked up to see him frowning.

"What's wrong?" I ran one finger along the line of his jaw.

"Your parents will be home tomorrow, which means that we won't be able to do this much." He sighed again, rubbing his hand up and down my back. "I wish it was just you and me, or that I could stay here with you all the time."

I smiled at the thought. "Hmm, that would be nice," I agreed. "But at least you still get to stay over here a couple of days a week."

He shook his head and slung one leg over mine, trapping me against him. "Riley Bear, once we tell our parents that we're together they won't let me sleep in here with you anymore, I guarantee it."

I frowned. I loved Clay sleeping in here with me; I didn't want to lose that. "They will, it'll be fine," I assured him, but in the back of my mind I knew he was right. Once my parents found out we were dating, there would be new rules imposed, my guess would be that sleeping in the same bed would be a huge no no.

He chuckled. "We'll see."

I rested my head on his chest as my mind started whirling. I'd been thinking about Clay and our relationship all day, and I was starting to make myself a little uneasy about it. I knew I needed to talk to Clay about it otherwise it would eat away at me and make me nervous and insecure. I gulped, feeling my face already flooding with heat. "Can I ask you something? It's kinda embarrassing."

He smiled, looking at me quizzically, obviously having no clue of the awkward conversation I was about to start. "You can ask me anything, Riley Bear." His fingers brushed across my hot cheek softly.

"Okay well," I took a deep breath, hoping my voice didn't shake with nerves, "I was thinking about sex."

A smile twitched at the corners of his mouth. "Oh were you now?"

I nodded, chewing on my bottom lip. "I was thinking that you're, er... and I'm er..." I sighed and closed my eyes, hoping that not seeing him would make this easier to say. "Is that actually gonna fit inside me?" I asked, hating myself for asking the question.

He chuckled quietly, his hand cupping the side of my face. "Yeah, Riley, it'll fit don't worry," he whispered, kissing my cheek.

I winced at the thought and looked up at him. "Is it gonna hurt me?"

He sighed sadly and nodded. "Yeah, it will the first time, but we'll take it slow. I don't want to hurt you," he replied, smoothing my hair down and looking me in the eyes. I could see all of his love for me shining through.

I smiled. "I know you don't. Will it hurt you?" I asked, frowning again.

"No, why would it hurt me?"

"Well, I thought there was some kind of barrier you had to break the first time you have sex. I just wondered if it would hurt you when you do it." I chewed on my lip, feeling stupid and wishing I hadn't asked.

"I don't know, Riley, I don't think so. But I don't care if it does; I'd much rather it hurt me than you."

I smiled because of how sweet that sounded. "Will you help me? I mean, I have no idea what to do, Clay. What if I'm terrible at it and I disappoint you?" I panicked, starting to get myself worked up. This was what I'd been stressing about all day. Clay had been with *lots* of girls, all of which would have more experience than me and would know how to please a man... what if I was a let down?

He frowned, taking my face in his hands, looking at me fiercely. "Riley Jane Tanner, I love you more than anything, you would never be a disappointment to me!" he assured me. "Of course I'll help you, but judging by the things we've done so far, I don't think you'll need my help," he added with a small chuckle.

I smiled weakly. "But you've had sex with so many girls, Clay, how can I compare to that?"

"Riley, I have had sex with a lot of girls, you're right, but I don't ever want to have sex with you," he replied, kissing me tenderly. "I only ever want to make love to you. That's how you compare."

"Aww, that's so sweet," I mused, feeling my heart stutter in my chest.

He smiled and rolled on top of me carefully, kissing me again. He kissed me until I forgot the reason for my worrying; it all seemed silly when he was kissing me so lovingly. "I love you," he murmured, looking so happy my heart missed a beat.

"I love you too," I vowed.

He grinned his boyish smile and cuddled me tightly to his chest. "Goodnight, Riley Bear." I sighed contentedly and closed my eyes, safe in the knowledge that my best friend and guy that I was hopelessly in love with, would hold me all night long.

~ Clay ~

I HELD HER TIGHTLY in my arms waiting until she was in a deep sleep. Her broken arm was laid protectively across my chest so that she didn't roll on it and hurt herself or anything. I couldn't calm myself down. I felt sick. I was so angry that I could barely breathe. I'd felt like this all day, and it was eating me up inside.

Just after midnight she was breathing heavily so I gently pushed her off of me, setting a pillow in my place and resting her arm on it instead. I slipped out of the bed and pulled on my jeans. She stirred in her sleep as I moved around the room. *Crap, please don't wake up, Riley!* She didn't so I grabbed her cell phone off of the bedside cabinet and slipped out of the room, heading downstairs as I switched it on.

It immediately started buzzing as text messages started coming through. I gulped and looked at who they were from: six new messages, all from Blake. I sat down on the sofa, gritting my teeth, resisting the urge to smash something or jump in the car and go and rip his head off because he'd hurt her.

I looked over the texts quickly. They were sent at various points throughout the day. They were all the same sort of thing, he was sorry, he missed her, and he couldn't wait to see her. I took a deep breath trying to calm my frayed nerves. I didn't want Riley to know I'd done this so I couldn't start shouting because it would wake her up.

When I was as chilled as I was going to get, I pressed call and waited until he answered. Each ring was winding me up a little more. If he didn't answer the phone, I was going round there to do this in person. On the eighth ring, he answered, his voice groggy, like I'd woken him up.

"Hey, Jailbait." The sound of his voice almost sent me over the edge so I squeezed my eyes shut tightly.

"It's not, Riley, it's Clay," I growled. *Wow, staying calm is harder than I thought.*

"What the hell are you doing with my girl's phone, Preston?" he shouted.

"I'm just calling to tell you to stay the hell away from Riley. If you ever even look at her again I'm going to rip your head off," I warned.

He made an angry scoffing noise. "Screw that, she's my girlfriend, and you need to leave her alone. I won't have you doing all that friends shit with my girl," he shouted angrily.

I jumped off the sofa at the word girlfriend. "You fucking broke her arm, asshole! If you come near her again you're going to wish that they threw your ass in jail by the time I'm finished with you," I retorted, gripping a hand in my hair, trying to keep my voice down in case I woke her.

"It was an accident. The police can't do anything, they just said to back off," he replied, sounding a little smug.

I could feel the rage building up inside me. I forced myself to stay on the spot as my body wanted so badly to jump in the car and go and finish this. "I'm fucking telling you now, I don't give a shit what the police said, you come near her again and I swear I'll kill you," I spat down the phone angrily.

"I can't say away from her, I'm crazy about her, she's mine."

"No she's not! And you need to back the hell off! We're together now, and I won't let you hurt her, so you'll stay the fuck away if you know what's good for you." I squeezed my eyes shut again, trying to block out the images of her crying in pain earlier.

"Together? You fucking can't be together, she's mine!" Blake roared angrily.

I smiled gloatingly. "Trust me, we're together. I don't want you anywhere near her. You even think about calling or texting her again, and I swear you'll regret it," I promised.

He laughed mockingly. "Thanks for the warning there, Preston." I could almost hear the sneer in his voice.

"I promise, Chambers, I will bury you," I said slowly, forcing the words to come out at a reasonable level. I snapped Riley's phone shut, ending the conversation. I couldn't talk to him anymore, I knew that if I heard one more word in his smug voice I wouldn't be able to stop myself from going there, and that certainly wouldn't help the situation if I got myself arrested for murder.

I turned her phone back off and headed back up the stairs to her room. Riley was lying in the exact place I'd left her, her beautiful body sprawled out on the bed. *Jeez, she's so perfect.* I never thought I'd ever be with her, I'd wanted her for so long, but she'd never even looked at me that way. It had been killing me all these years to have her so close and love her like I did. Seeing her go on dates and stuff with other guys was painful. I had always been content just to be in her life, I was happy being her best friend as long as I got to be around her. But that month away was pure torture. Every day I woke up and felt sick because she wasn't here and because I couldn't talk to her. That was what made me try to make her see me as something more than just her best friend.

I smiled as I slipped off my jeans and crawled into the bed, lifting her broken arm and moving the pillow out of the way. I pulled her to me and held her cast protectively against my chest. In her sleep she nuzzled into my neck, snuggling closer to me. I turned my head and kissed the top of her head. I still couldn't comprehend the fact that she loved me, that she wanted me the same as I wanted her. I honestly felt like the luckiest guy in the world. I felt happier than I had ever felt in my life. I would never let anything hurt her ever again.

"I love you, Riley Bear," I whispered, closing my eyes and willing myself to sleep so that I could forget that asshole for a few hours. Riley was right, I was definitely going to give myself an ulcer if I didn't stop thinking about it.

chapter
twelve

~ Riley ~

I got up early in the morning and threw on his shirt, leaving him in the bed to sleep. I sighed contently as I made my way downstairs. I picked up the phone and dialled the doctors' clinic, arranging an appointment for four o'clock. I needed to get on the pill fast, it wasn't going to be long before I convinced Clay to sleep with me, not that he would need much convincing, but he obviously wanted to make it memorable. I wasn't sure when this would be possible though. He was right, it would be more difficult for us to be together once my parents found out. I highly doubted that they would let him sleep in with me as usual once they found out we were a couple.

I was starving hungry so I thought I would surprise him with breakfast in bed. Clay loved pancakes so I grabbed all the ingredients from the cupboards and started making them. It was difficult only having one working hand, especially breaking the eggs, but somehow I managed. Once I'd made an enormous stack of chocolate chip pancakes and two glasses of orange juice I plopped it all onto a tray and struggled to pick it up.

Hmm, maybe I hadn't thought this through properly! How am I supposed to carry a tray with only one hand? I laughed and shook my head at myself. Out of nowhere, two arms shot around my waist. I squealed and jumped a mile into the air, almost spilling the food everywhere. I turned quickly only to see Clay standing there in his boxers with an amused look on his face.

"What are you laughing at, my beautiful girlfriend?" he asked, kissing my neck.

I slapped his chest, pouting. "I thought you were asleep. I was making you breakfast in bed. Now you've ruined my surprise."

He smiled and bent forward, biting my pouty lip gently, causing me to giggle like a little girl. "I'm sorry, Riley Bear, how about I go back to bed and pretend I'm asleep?" he offered, pulling away from me and turning around.

I laughed and grabbed his hand before he could escape. "Actually, I was having a bit of trouble anyway," I admitted, frowning at my useless cast.

"What's the problem, beautiful girl?" he asked tenderly, slipping his arm around my shoulder.

I laughed and pointed at the tray with my bad hand. "I can't carry the stupid tray with one hand."

He didn't laugh like I expected him too; instead he looked angry but quickly rearranged his expression into a fake smile. "I'll get it." He picked it up easily and nodded his head towards the stairs motioning for me to go first.

• • •

AN HOUR LATER I was finally ready to leave. Clay had been ready for almost forty five minutes. "Stupid boys having it easy," I mumbled. It took me longer to get dressed than normal with my cast. I had, however, remembered to put on easy to pull up pants so I could go to the bathroom on my own at least. I'd opted for green combat style pants that had a popper instead of a button, and a simple black V-neck shirt. I couldn't manage to do my sneakers so I slipped them on and left them undone, knowing I would need to ask Clay to do them up for me.

Eventually I made my way downstairs to see him watching sports channel. I cleared my throat behind him making him jump. "Hey, you look amazing," he complimented, turning the TV off and grabbing my waist pulling me in for a kiss. He pulled back and looked at me from my head to my toes, and then started to laugh. Without me even asking he bent down and laced up my shoes for me. I smiled at how sweet he always was.

"Are you ready to go?" he asked as he stood up and pulled me back in for a hug.

"Er, Clay, I'm gonna have to drive myself today, I have somewhere to be after school." I chewed on my lip hoping he wouldn't ask me to elaborate.

He frowned, shaking his head. "No way, I'm not letting you drive yourself today; this is the first day of school that I have you as a girlfriend! I want to show you off," he whined, kissing my neck. I giggled as he nibbled my earlobe.

"I'll meet you there; I have an appointment at four."

He pulled back and raised one eyebrow quizzically. "What sort of appointment?"

I squirmed on the spot. I didn't want him to know. Being the respectable boyfriend that he was I knew that he would insist on coming with me, but he really needed to go to his football practice. If he knew I was going to see a doctor about contraception then he would blow off his practice so he could accompany me, that much I was certain of.

"None of your bees wax, Clay Preston," I replied playfully, smirking at him and knowing that he hated secrets.

His frown deepened. "I can drive you to your appointment," he countered, looking at me hopefully. He bent his head again, sucking on the side of my neck, no doubt darkening his hickey from the other day.

"You can't. You have practice."

"Shit," he grumbled under his breath. He pulled back and looked at me then, his green eyes boring holes into mine. "Okay, well how about this; we take your car to school then you can go to your appointment while I'm at practice, then you can pick me up after."

I shook my head in rejection. "I can't, Clay. The place I'm going usually runs late with its appointments, what if there's a hold up and I'm not back before practice finishes?" *Ha, I win!*

He shrugged easily. "Then I'll wait for you." He handed me my car keys with a satisfied smile as if it was decided.

I sighed in defeat. "Okay fine, but don't blame me if I'm late back." I slapped his butt with my good hand as I sidestepped him so I could grab my schoolbag from the hall.

"So what's the appointment?" he asked again, giving me his adorable puppy dog face. I frowned and quickly looked away, if I stared at that face for too long I would crack and tell him.

I didn't answer as I carried on walking towards the front door, ready to go. He let me get about three steps away before his arms snaked around my waist, and he pulled my back against his chest. I felt a little thrill go through me from the contact and how nice it felt to have his arms around me, this time in a non-friend way. His breath blew across my shoulder, making my skin prickle. I still wasn't used to him creating these feelings in me; I'd spent so long just being his friend that feeling like this for him was kind of alien to me. I had a feeling I would fast get addicted to it though.

"What's the appointment, Riley Bear?" he repeated. His voice was soft and pleading as his thumb stroked over my stomach. "Please tell me, I thought we agreed when we were little never to keep secrets from each other," he persuaded.

I sighed, knowing he was right. I remembered making that pinky-swear with him. "I have a doctor's appointment," I grudgingly admitted, turning in his arms so I could wrap one arm around his neck.

He gasped, his eyes widening in panic as he looked down at me worriedly. "Oh shit! Are you okay? Does your arm hurt? What can I do? You want to go back to the hospital?" he asked, looking around frantically. I had no idea he was looking for though, I didn't think he did either.

I went up on tiptoes quickly and kissed him softly to banish his freak out. "Clay, I'm going to the doctors to go on the pill," I explained because he was obviously panicking that this was about my arm.

His body relaxed instantly. "Are you sure you're all right? I mean your arm..." He looked down at my cast and winced.

I smiled and kissed him again. "I'm going to go on the pill, that's the appointment. Now stop stressing, jeez you've always been such a worrier," I scolded playfully as I rolled my eyes.

"Only about you," he replied, kissing me again.

I smiled against his lips and pulled back out of his arms. "Right, so it's agreed then, we'll take my car and I'll pick you up like you said."

He shook his head. "No, I'll come with you. This is about me too you know, we should go together," he protested.

I knew this would happen! "No," I refused. "And anyway, how do you know it's about you? I'm not letting all my other boyfriends come so why should you get preferential treatment?" I teased.

"Because you love me more than the others."

"Hmm, well that's true I guess, just don't tell them I said that," I replied, playing along. He laughed and wrapped his arms around me, obviously thinking he had won. "But you're still not coming, Clay," I said sternly. He gave me the puppy dog face again and I almost caved in. Almost, but not quite. "No! You have practice so I'm going on my own. That's the end of it." I kissed his nose and turned, heading for the door again.

He sighed dramatically and I heard him following along behind me towards the front hallway. As I picked up my schoolbag he cleared his throat theatrically. I looked up to see him with one raised eyebrow, holding out his hand for my bag. I sighed and handed it to him grabbing his hand after and dragging him out of the house to my car.

"You drive," I instructed, tossing him my keys to him as I walked to the passenger side. He nodded and slipped into the driver's seat, grinning happily and practically bouncing in his seat. "Why the excitement, Clay?"

He grinned over at me. "I can't wait for everyone to know that you're mine."

I smiled at his enthusiasm, while I secretly dreaded it because I already knew what the girls' reactions would be. They already hated me for just being his friend; I was almost scared to see what they thought of me now that I was actually dating him.

When we got to school and he'd parked the car, Clay made me wait in my seat while he ran round to get my door. "Thanks," I muttered, blushing and waiting for the gossiping to start again about us.

He held out a hand to help me out of the car. I smiled and slipped my hand into his, looking around shyly. As he shut my door, he pushed me gently against the car, pressing every inch of his body to mine as his mouth claimed mine in a scorching hot kiss that made my insides tremble. In the back of my mind I thought I could hear gasps and excited chattering, but all I could focus on was Clay and the way his kiss seemed to melt my insides.

When he broke the kiss he put his forehead against mine, breathing deeply as a smile tugged at the corners of his mouth. I grinned and brushed my nose along his jaw line. "Mmm, how about we skip school today and you take me back to bed?" I whispered jokingly. He let out a low groan and moved quickly, pulling open my door as he nodded in agreement. I giggled and shook my head because I was joking and he obviously wasn't. The lustful look on his face plainly told me that he wanted to go home again so we could fool around.

I put my hands on his chest and pushed him away from me as I rolled my eyes in mock disapproval. "Come on let's get this over and done with."

He just moved back to me quickly, pressing his body against mine. "I just need a minute," he said shyly, trying to tell me something with his eyes. I frowned, confused, until I glanced down to see that the kiss had gotten Clay a little excited downstairs so he obviously needed time to calm down again.

I giggled, my cheeks immediately flaming with heat because I'd caused that. But at the same time I actually loved that us kissing could get him that excited, it made me feel extremely wanted and special. "You really are insatiable, Clay," I teased as I ducked under his arm that was trapping me against the car; I caught his hand and gave him a little tug as I started to walk. He groaned and caught up to me quickly, walking close to my back and using my body as a shield as he held on to my hips tightly in place against him.

His friends were all sitting around on the hood of the same BMW that they always seemed to congregate at in the morning. I made my way over to them with Clay still hiding behind me. As I stopped at the edge of their group I discreetly ground my ass against him, which made him hiss through his teeth and his fingers bite into my hips. "Stop that, Riley," he whispered in my ear, holding me firmly in front of him. I had no idea why he was still holding me so tightly; me standing this close to him didn't seem to help the 'situation' at all, if anything it was making it worse judging by the feel of him pressed so tightly against my back. I stifled a giggle as I shifted from one foot to the other on purpose, brushing against him again. "Riley," he warned. I laughed and bit my lip.

"Hey, man, what's up?" Tom greeted, holding up a hand and slapping Clay a high-five. I looked over my shoulder and raised a sneaky eyebrow at Clay. I knew exactly what was up.

"Hey, guys, let me introduce you to my girlfriend," Clay said proudly, kissing my temple.

Tom's eyes widened. "Girlfriend? Are you serious?"

"Yep, totally serious. I told her finally," Clay replied, holding me tightly against him and beaming proudly. The three boys' eyes shot to me so I nodded in confirmation. Smiles stretched across their faces as Tom cheered and Ben patted Clay on the back in congratulations. From the corner of my eye I saw that some cheerleaders had started to make their way over to us. Zoë was leading the pack, her eyes set on Clay as she smiled a predatory smile. I groaned. *Great, here comes the disapproval and hateful glares!*

Clay nodded. "I finally told her I loved her on Saturday night. Guess it was about time I grew some balls and admitted it," Clay joked. He turned me gently, and his lips covered mine, kissing me passionately. I kissed him back immediately. When he pulled away he was grinning happily as he trailed the back of his knuckles over my cheek. My gaze flicked to the cheerleaders again, only to see that most of them looked like they were trying to shoot lasers out of their eyes and turn me into a pile of dust on the floor. I shrank back into Clay and squirmed uncomfortably. *Will I ever get used to people looking at me like that? I don't think so...*

Clay's friends were all beaming at us both so I knew they were obviously pleased about it. I needed to get away quickly though before he announced it to everyone else. I hated being the centre of attention so today was going to be an exceptionally long day indeed.

"Er, Clay, I'm gonna go find Rachel." *Hopefully she won't look at me like she hates me!*

He nodded, tightening his arm around my waist. "Okay, girlfriend," he agreed, smiling. "I'll see you in first period." He kissed me again until I was breathless and then let me go, his eyes alight with happiness. As I turned to walk off he slapped my ass and whistled at me. I rolled my eyes at him and skipped off to find Rachel. I'd text her last night to tell her to meet me at my locker and that I had something to tell her.

When I got there, she was waiting for me with a big grin. "I know, I know, I've heard. You and the extremely hot Clay Preston were seen approximately seventeen minutes ago making out in the parking lot. Now is that true or false?" she asked with a huge smile.

I nodded in confirmation, grinning like the cat that got the cream. "Yep, true," I confirmed. Suddenly she gasped, her eyes widening in shock. *Okay, it's not that hard to believe, is it?*

"What the hell have you done to your arm?" she cried loudly, drawing weird looks from the people that were standing around in the hallway.

"Oh I er..." *What on earth should I say to her? I can't tell her about Blake, what if someone hears and it goes round the whole damn school!* "I fell, no big deal," I lied sheepishly.

She giggled suddenly. "Were you drunk?"

Ooh, that's an easy out! "Yep wasted," I lied. She rolled her eyes as she linked her arm through mine, trotting off down the hallway and dragging me with her. As we walked to classes I tried my best to ignore the whispers as people walked past me. News of me and Clay was obviously spreading fast.

• • •

THE REST OF THE morning was pretty much the same. Rachel asked for every detail about how we got together, what we had done, had we had sex, was he a good kisser, everything. I answered almost everything with 'no comment' much to her annoyance.

At lunchtime, we were all sitting at the usual lunch table. "I think we need to have a road trip," Ben suddenly suggested. Everyone was immediately agreeing and deciding where to go, when, and who would want to go. Within minutes, it was decided that we would go to Vegas this weekend. Ben was going to get fake IDs for anyone that needed them. We were all to arrange with our parents tonight to see if the trip was even possible.

Clay grabbed hold of me excitedly. "Vegas, Riley Bear, that means slot machines!" he chirped, grinning. I could feel the excitement trying to bubble up inside me, but I forced it back down again. There was no way that my parents were going to let me go on a road trip to Vegas.

I smiled sadly. "My mom and David won't let me go, so I'm not gonna get excited about it."

He just shook his head, frowning. "You don't know that, they might be all right with it because you're going with me," he said, smiling proudly.

I shrugged. My parents had always loved Clay, but I still didn't think they would let me go. "We'll see, I'll ask them," I agreed.

"It'll be fine," Clay assured me.

I nodded just to placate him but actually didn't believe it in the slightest. I knew he would be allowed to go because his parents were a lot more laid back than mine were. I frowned as I thought about spending a whole weekend without him. That would suck under normal circumstances, but was made even worse by the fact that we'd just gotten together.

He cocked his head to the side, looking at me curiously. "What's wrong? I can tell you're thinking about something."

I forced a smile because I didn't want him to feel guilty about going away when I wasn't allowed to, that wouldn't be fair of me. "Nothing, I just don't think my parents will go for it, so I'm gonna miss you that's all." I leant in and kissed his lips softly, pressing my side against his tighter.

He looked a little confused. "What do you mean? Why would you miss me?" he questioned, wrapping his arm around me tightly.

"Because I love you, silly. Won't you miss me?" I asked, feeling a little hurt.

He shook his head. "Riley Bear, I think you're confused about something." He shifted in his seat, grabbing my hips and pulling me onto his lap so I was straddling him. "I'm not going if you can't go," he finished, smiling at me as if I'd said something stupid.

I gasped, shocked. *He wouldn't go? That's just stupid! I'm not letting him miss out on the fun if I can't go, that's not fair at all.* "Clay, if I can't go you're still going," I said firmly.

He sighed. "Whatever, it doesn't matter right now anyway. Let's just see what our parents say first." His hand gripped the back of my head, guiding my mouth to his as he kissed me deeply. I smiled against his mouth and decided he was right, maybe they would let me go; I guess I'd see when I asked them. There was no point in worrying about it unnecessarily.

• • •

AFTER SCHOOL I WENT to the clinic and amazingly, got in only five minutes late. I had to answer tons of questions about my sexual activity. The doctor seemed very impressed that I was going on the pill before having sex and congratulated me on being responsible. Together we decided that I should go for the contraceptive injection. It was a quick injection in the bottom, and it lasted for a full twelve weeks. She even said that after three or four shots that it would actually make my periods stop all together. I was certainly pleased about that part.

She did it there and then and apparently it only took a couple of days to get into my system. She gave me a leaflet about it, apparently there weren't very many symptoms I needed to worry about, maybe stomach cramps today or tomorrow as it worked its way around my system, but that was about all.

I went to pick up Clay, and surprisingly, I was on time. I pulled into the parking lot just as he was walking out of the locker rooms. I got out of the car and leaned against it, waiting for him to come to me. He spotted me and broke into a jog, wrapping me in his arms as he got to me. I grinned happily, and he kissed me hungrily, pulling back and looking at me like I was the most precious thing in the world.

"I missed you," he whispered, planting another kiss on my forehead.

I chuckled wickedly. "You missed me? It's only been an hour," I joked, running my hands through his hair. In reality I knew exactly how he felt because I'd missed him like crazy too.

"Yeah, but I've hardly seen you all day," he explained. "I've missed *this*," he added, pulling me closer to him and crushing me against his chest.

I sighed contentedly. I'd missed being in his arms too; it felt so nice just to be held by him like this. "Let's go home so we can cuddle up on my bed," I suggested, already loving the thought of that. He made a little groan and nodded, pulling open my door for me and waiting until I'd gotten in before closing the door and heading around to the other side.

"So how did you get on at your appointment, Riley Bear?" he asked, holding my hand as he drove us towards our street.

"Good. I decided to go for the injection so I don't have to do anything at all apart from go back for another one every three months," I replied, smiling, happy with my choice of contraception. The doctor had concluded that this was the best one for me to go for; apparently a lot of girls my age that went to parties ended up pregnant because they were sick with a hangover in the morning and their pills were brought out of their system.

"Injection? Seriously, they do that?" he asked, shocked.

I nodded. "Yep, right in my butt cheek. I'm probably gonna get a bruise or something," I said, faking hurt.

He squeezed my hand, smirking at me cockily. "I can kiss it better for you if you like," he offered.

I laughed and nodded, deciding to try my hand at flirting. "I was hoping you would say that." My flirting attempt was obviously a decent one because he sucked in a deep breath through his teeth and let it out as a sigh as he looked at me excitedly. We pulled into my drive then so I unbuckled my belt, noticing that my parents' car was sitting in their usual spot. "Wanna know the best thing?" I asked Clay.

"Yeah, of course," he replied. "I wish you'd have let me come with you, I wanted to be there for you." He squeezed my hand again as he said it so I knew his words were true.

I smiled. "I know, and I love you for it, Clay, but you had practice. She would have made you wait in the waiting room anyway so there wouldn't have been much point even if you had come with me." I brought his hand up to my mouth, kissing his knuckles softly.

He sighed. "Yeah okay. So what's the best thing?" he asked curiously.

I smiled and climbed out of the car, heading up to my front door and then stopping to wait for him. Once he got to my side I leant into him and smiled seductively, putting my hands on his chest as I brought my mouth up to his ear. "It only takes a couple of days to get into my system and then you won't ever need to wear a condom again," I whispered, grazing his earlobe with my teeth.

He moaned breathlessly. "A couple of days?" he repeated. I nodded, kissing his cheek and giggling at his lustful expression on his face. *He obviously likes that little fact!*

Before he could say anything else, I gripped his hand and dragged him into my house with me. I could hear chatter in the lounge so we both headed in there. "Hey, Mom. Hi, David," I chirped, skipping happily into the room and pulling them both into a hug.

My mom gasped, her eyes widening in horror as she looked at me. "Oh God, Riley, what's happened to your arm?" she cried. Her eyes were already filling with tears as she reached out and touched my plaster cast.

Oh crap, I forgot all about my arm! "Oh, er, well I..." *Okay, how do I tell my parents this?*

Clay stepped forwards, his arm snaking around my shoulder. "We had a problem while you were away, maybe you should sit down," he said confidently. I smiled at him gratefully because he always took care of things for me; he always knew when I needed help without me even needing to ask. I loved that about him. He sat down on the sofa and pulled me down close to his side, looking expectantly at my shocked parents.

They both sat down on the opposite sofa, looking at Clay worriedly. I sat there while he explained the whole thing to them, Blake, what the police had said, the hospital, everything. As Clay spoke, David was getting madder and madder; I could see it building like a storm on his face. Before Clay had even finished, David jumped out of his chair, his face a shade of red that I'd never seen on him before. "That fucking asshole! I spoke to him; I thought he was a decent kid! Just wait until I see him, I'm gonna fucking kill him," he spat.

My mouth popped open in shock. In all the years that I had known him, that was the first time I had ever heard my stepdad cuss. It sounded so weird, and so menacing because I could tell that he meant it, the anger behind his tone made that perfectly clear.

Clay stood up and put his hand on my dad's shoulder reassuringly. "Don't worry about it, David. He won't hurt her again I promise," he said sincerely. I winced at the threat in Clay's voice, I knew that if Blake ever came near me again, Clay would have trouble controlling his temper and I prayed that would never happen. I never wanted to think of Clay getting hurt, ever.

My mom shifted nervously on her seat. Just from the anxious look on her face I could see that she could feel the tension in the air too. "So, aside from the whole hot guy that turns out to be a psycho, and the broken arm, did we miss anything else?" she asked, raising one eyebrow at me and then flicked her eyes to Clay and then back to me again.

I gulped, knowing that she had somehow figured out that Clay and I were together. *Honestly, does nothing get past this woman? She's like a freaking ninja!*

Clay grinned and looked down at me before touching the side of my face lightly. The gesture was small, but it made my heart ache in my chest. But I knew I couldn't tell my mom about us, not yet.

I shook my head quickly, shooting Clay a quick warning look. "No, Mom, nothing else," I lied. Clay's face fell, and I wanted to blurt out the truth, announce to the world that he loved me, but I knew that if I did that then my chances of being allowed to Vegas with him were pretty much non-existent. I cleared my throat, trying to ignore the hurt expression on his face. "Mom, do you think I would be able to go to Vegas this weekend with some of the guys from school? All my new friends are going, and I thought it would be really great to get to know them better," I asked. "Clay will be there too of course," I added, knowing that was the sweetener and my only chance at getting a yes.

Clay visibly relaxed as he sat back down next to me. Hopefully he now understood why I hadn't told them about us.

My mom made a scoffing noise in her throat as she shook her head adamantly. "Vegas? No way. I'm sorry, but no," she refused. There was not even an ounce of indecision in her voice.

I frowned. My last shot was a crafty one, but it was the only chance I had. It was now time to play up to the soft stepfather who liked to give his daughter anything she asked for. I looked at David and gave him my best puppy dog face. "It's just that I don't know any of them properly, and I've been finding it a bit hard to fit in and make new friends because of starting a new school. When they asked me to go I just thought that I'd be able to feel part of the group a little more, instead of just being the new girl."

David squirmed under my pleading expression, clearly uncomfortable. "Sandra, they're too young to get in any trouble there. She'd love Vegas, the lights, the ambiance," he said, looking at my mom and smiling hopefully.

I knew it was bad to use the old heart strings, but this was Vegas we were talking about here, and a whole weekend alone with Clay. Mom sighed because as usual my dad and I were ganging up on her. "You are going, Clay?" she asked, looking at Clay questionably.

Clay grinned, looking like he was having a hard time not laughing at my little speech. "Well I haven't spoken to my parents yet, but I think they'll say yes," he replied. I knew he was right, his parents trusted him completely because he was a completely trustworthy person.

My mom groaned and looked at David who gave her a small encouraging nod. "Okay. *If* Clay's going then you can go, Riley, but only if Clay's going," she agreed somewhat reluctantly.

I squealed from excitement, jumping up and kissing them both on the cheek. "Thank you! You're the best parents, ever!"

Clay grinned but shook his head discouragingly. "Don't get too excited yet, I might not be allowed," he warned, but just by the happy tone of his voice I could tell that he thought the same as me and that we would definitely be going. "I'd better go ask permission then I guess," he added, winking at me.

David stepped forward. "Clay, thank you for looking after Riley this weekend, you really are a good kid," he said, holding out his hand towards

Clay. Clay grinned and shook my dad's hand in a very grownup and respectable gesture that actually made my heart stutter in my chest. I loved that my dad thought so much of my boyfriend, it made my insides all warm and fuzzy.

• • •

CLAY WENT HOME then to speak to his parents, but called me ten minutes later only to tell me that his parents had agreed to the trip. He told me that he'd already text Ben and asked him to get me a fake ID.

After dinner I was stretched out on my bed, lying on my stomach as I did my homework. A small knock at my bedroom door made me look up just in time to see Clay walk in with a big grin on his face.

"Hi," I chirped because I wasn't expecting to see him for another hour or so.

He smiled and closed the door behind him. "Hey you," he replied as he walked over to the bed. "So, let's see this sore spot you want me to kiss," he suggested, sitting on the edge of the bed and stroking one hand over my ass.

I giggled and pushed his hand away. "Pervert," I scolded playfully. I picked up my leaflet that I'd been given from the doctor and held it out to him. "I have homework to do, so you can amuse yourself with this while you wait," I said, turning back to my English essay.

He didn't even complain as he settled himself down on the bed next to me, opening the leaflet and reading it intently. While I scribbled my essay, he read the whole thing from cover to cover. When he was done, he rolled onto his side and silently played with a lock of my hair while I finished my assignment. When I was finally finished half an hour later, I rolled onto my side facing him. I smiled at him gratefully. I felt like the luckiest girl in the world because my boyfriend had just laid their patiently while I finished my essay. He really was adorable.

I kissed him softly before pulling back and sighing contentedly. He smiled and rested his head on his arm as he smoothed my hair down for me, tucking a stray piece behind my ear. "You know, I was a little worried when you didn't tell your parents about us," he said quietly. "I was worried that you were ashamed of me or something. But then I realised that if they knew, they wouldn't let me take you to Vegas. That is the only reason you didn't tell them, isn't it?" he asked, looking a little worried about my answer.

I wrapped my arms around his neck and carefully rolled onto my back, pulling him on top of me. "Of course it's the only reason. I wanted to tell them, but like you said before, once they know then things will change. There's no way they would let me go away with my boyfriend, but they'd let me go away with my best friend," I explained. I kissed his chin, nibbling gently.

His face lightened as he seemed to breathe a sigh of relief. "Okay, good."

He kissed me then, pressing himself to me tightly. I wriggled under him as his hand ran down my side, snaking under my shirt and tickling across my stomach. My whole body was yearning for more as I gripped my good hand into the back of his hair. "I am *so* looking forward to this weekend," he whispered, kissing me again.

Hell yeah, me too! I now have a whole weekend with Clay in a hotel room, and I plan on not wasting a single second of it! The kiss deepened, getting hotter and hotter until I could barely even think straight. Needing to feel his skin against mine, I pulled his t-shirt off over his head and ran my hands over his sculpted body. Clay responded immediately, pushing my shirt off over my head and pressing himself to me tighter.

Just as his hands started to roam my body, there was a knock at the door. I gasped, and Clay jerked away from me, throwing my shirt in my face as he made a dive for his that was on the floor.

When everything was normal, I quickly laid back down on my stomach and tried to look innocent. "Er, yeah, come in," I called, flicking open my maths book and picking up a pen, pretending we were doing nothing out of the ordinary.

My mom stepped in, smiling knowingly. I felt the blush creep onto my cheeks, and Clay laughed but tried to hide it by turning it into a cough. "Finally, huh?" was all she said as she looked between the two of us expectantly.

I swallowed nervously. "Finally?" I repeated, faking confusion even though it was glaringly obvious what she was asking. *Okay, this is starting to freak me out. Why is she not telling us this is stupid, and shouting at Clay to get off of my bed?*

She nodded. "Yeah, finally. I just wanted to say that I think it's terrific, and I'm really pleased for the two of you." She winked at me, grinning like a proud mother hen.

Okay it's time for the bad acting to make another appearance... "Mom, seriously, I don't know what you're talking about," I lied. "Clay's just helping me with my homework and then we're gonna watch a movie." I glanced at Clay who actually looked a cross between amused and confused. *Hmm, that's actually an extremely good look for him... Okay, focus on the Mom situation, Riley!* I forced my eyes away from Clay and looked back in time to see my mom roll her eyes at me.

"Right," she retorted sarcastically, shaking her head. Her eyes fell on something on the bed, and she stepped forward to pick it up. I noticed a split second too late that it was the leaflet I'd given to Clay. *Oh no!* She scanned the front. "You're on the pill, Riley?" she asked.

Okay game over, no more lies. "Yeah, Mom, I went today." I sat up, and Clay did the same, but I refused to look at him, I kept my gaze on my mom's face, wincing and waiting for her to freak out. Instead of shouting though, she actually started to tear up. "Mom, you okay?" I asked quietly. She sat on the bed in front of me and pulled me into a hug. *What the... why on earth is crying and hugging me?*

She sniffed loudly. "I always thought I would come with you for this kind of thing. I was waiting until you were ready and then you know, I thought you would come to me to talk about it. I wouldn't have been mad," she said in a small voice.

I gulped. I really wasn't expecting this reaction. She was sad that I hadn't talked to her about it, but not mad that I'd gone and got myself on contraception? "I know that you wouldn't be mad," I replied. That wasn't strictly true, I was expecting her to be a little mad, but I was going to talk to her about it eventually. "But I didn't need anyone with me, I was fine," I added, trying to reassure her. I glanced over at Clay who now looked terribly uncomfortable and confused - and this too was a good look for him.

My mom pulled back to look at me. "I am so proud of you, this is really responsible," she praised, cupping my cheek with one hand and reaching out to squeeze Clay's hand. "You too, Clay." She smiled warmly, and I got even more confused. "I think it's best that we not tell your stepfather about this until after Vegas. I don't think he'd like the idea of you two together alone like that," she suggested, shaking her head and frowning thoughtfully. "Oh but, Clay, you should tell your parents. Linda will be so pleased."

I smiled uncomfortably. *Okay, now I've slipped into crazyville or something surely. My mom knows we're together and doesn't care, well, actually she does care, she's pleased about it?*

"Mom, how did you even know?" I asked, shaking my head in awe. She had some incredible spider senses or something!

"How did I know? Well, I've always known how Clay felt about you," she said, chuckling and winking at him conspiratorially. "It was so obvious. Sorry, Clay honey, but it really was." Clay rolled his eyes, smiling but nodded sheepishly at the same time. "But you had no idea," she added, turning back to me. "I told you time and time again you two would end up together, but you always just laughed. As soon as I saw you walk in the door together I could tell by the way you were looking at each other." She stood up and smiled. "Well, I'll let you two get back to whatever you were doing before I interrupted." She headed to the door, and I suppressed a giggle. When Clay turned to look at me my mom pointed at him behind his back, fanned her face and mouthed, "So hot," to me. I burst out laughing as I nodded in agreement. "Clay, will you be staying over tonight?" she asked at the door.

His mouth popped open in shock as he looked at her. "Oh, er, would that be all right with you now that... you know?" he replied, looking at her hopefully.

She smiled and nodded. "Of course it is, honey. Just don't forget to tell your mom about you two, she really will be pleased." She grinned and stepped out of the room, closing the door behind her.

As soon as we were alone, Clay and I looked at each other and burst out laughing. "Okay, was not expecting that," I admitted, shaking my head in awe of my mother. I really was one lucky girl.

Clay grinned and moved closer to me, his eyes sparkling with mischievousness. "Hmm, so where were we before we were interrupted?" he asked, raising one eyebrow.

I grinned and instantly pulled my top over my head, reaching out and doing the same to his. After tossing them both on the floor, I wrapped my arms around his neck and laid back down, pulling him on top of me again. "Right about here I think," I stated, giggling.

He laughed and went straight back to kissing me as if he hadn't kissed me for weeks. His hand worked the buttons on my pants, pushing them down over my hips so he could slip his hand around the back to grope my ass.

I gasped as I remembered what I had in my pocket. "Oh! Wait, Clay, wait," I whispered, reaching into my pants pocket. Excitement was bubbling up inside me at the thought of what was about to happen. I dug in my pocket but couldn't get them out because my stupid cast restricted my finger movements.

Clay smiled and pulled my hand out. "Let me get that." He pushed his hand into my pocket, and a frown slipped onto his face as he pulled the foil packets from my pocket. He sat up on the bed, looking at them for a few seconds, unmoving. It was a strip of condoms. The doctor had given them to me to 'use in the meantime' she had said. I smiled and sat up too, kissing him urgently, eager to take things further with him. He kissed me back, but he didn't seem as into it as before.

"What's wrong?" I asked quietly. He was still just holding the condoms, staring at me weirdly.

He frowned, his whole posture screamed uncomfortable and nervous. "Nothing's wrong, it's just, I don't want to do this now. I thought we agreed I could make it special for you."

I smiled because of how adorable he was. "It will be special. It'll be our first time," I countered, kissing him again. He kissed me back, but I had a feeling it was only so that he didn't hurt my feelings.

He broke the kiss and stroked the side of my face with one finger. "I know that it'll be special for that reason, but I just don't want us to look back on this in ten years' time and wish that your parents weren't down the hall." He looked at me pleadingly, his green eyes willing me to understand. I sighed. I knew he was right, but the thought of having him now and not having to wait was almost too tempting.

"Fine," I grumbled, "but soon I'm gonna have you begging for me."

He laughed, slipping the strip of foil packets into his jeans pocket. "No doubt about it, Riley Bear," he agreed. He leant forward and kissed me, nibbling on my bottom lip as he moved closer, making me lay down with him hovering above me. "But I'm not opposed to a little foreplay," he whispered, kissing across my face and down my neck.

I gasped and dug my fingers into his back. "How about a lot of foreplay?" I bargained breathlessly.

He chuckled, his hands going to the clasp of my bra. "Deal."

chapter thirteen

I woke in the morning to Clay sitting on the edge of the bed with a tray in his hands. I smiled at him; he was dressed and ready for school already. "Hey you," I croaked, rubbing my sleepy eyes and stretching my tight muscles.

"Hey, my beautiful girl. I made you breakfast in bed today." He shot me a heart stopping smile, and I felt my insides dance with happiness. *He made me breakfast in bed? This boy is too sweet!* He handed me the tray and smiled sheepishly. "I couldn't make pancakes like you made for me, so I had to go for something easier."

I looked at the tray and grinned. There sat my favourite, chocolate spread on toast, and a bowl of fresh fruit salad. He had even picked me a yellow tulip from his backyard and had put it in a glass of water. I chewed on my lip as my heart sped up double time. *Is he really mine to keep? How can someone as amazing as Clay fall in love with me? He is so out of my league!*

"Thank you, Clay, this is incredible. I love you," I gushed.

He moved to sit next to me, wrapping his arm around my shoulders. "I love you more," he replied, kissing my cheek.

My stomach growled so I picked up a piece of toast and started munching on it, when all of a sudden a thought occurred to me and I froze mid-chew. Clay hated chocolate spread; he couldn't even stand the smell of it. Did this mean he wasn't going to come anywhere near me today? I looked at him horrified at the thought.

He stiffened, looking concerned. "Did I make it wrong?" he asked, unconsciously crinkling his nose in disgust as he looked at it.

I shook my head and swallowed my mouthful. "No, it's great, but I wish you hadn't made this, now you're not gonna be able to kiss me," I whined, pouting.

He laughed and leant closer to me, kissing me tenderly. When he pulled back he dipped his finger in the chocolate spread and ate it, making a face. "I would eat a whole jar of that disgusting stuff for you. There is nothing in the world that could stop me from kissing you, Riley Bear," he cooed.

I sighed contentedly as my insides melted into a puddle at his sweetness.

• • •

AT SCHOOL THAT DAY everyone was buzzing about our trip to Vegas. Everyone had checked with their parents and was allowed to go, so in total there would be ten of us. Me and Clay, Rachel and Jeff, Ben, Tom and Craig, Claire who was Ben's girlfriend, and Jenna and Beth who were both really nice.

Ben had brought his camera and was going to get some fake IDs made for Jenna, me and Rachel who were the only ones who didn't have one. I was practically bouncing off of the walls as we spoke about it and planned it out. The trip was going to be awesome. Tom was apparently borrowing a thirteen seater minibus from his brother's friend, and we were planning on leaving early Saturday morning. The drive would take around six hours.

On the way to class after lunch my cell phone beeped. I pulled it out of my pocket to see that I had a new message. I opened it to see it was from Blake. I gasped and instantly recoiled, wondering what he was going to want. Why was he even contacting me in the first place after what he'd done to my arm? Clay was a little way in front, talking to his friends so I quickly read it:

'Jailbait, I've really missed you. I'm so sorry about what happened the other day. Please let me make it up to you. I promise it will never happen again, B x x'

I QUICKLY DELETED the message in case Clay saw it. I knew he'd go crazy if he knew that Blake had contacted me, he already wanted to beat the life out of him as it was so I didn't want to add any more fuel to the fire.

Clay turned just as I slipped my cell phone back into my pocket. "Hey, Riley Bear, come on I'll walk you to class." He slung his arm around my shoulder, guiding me away from everyone else and towards the study hall. I was supposed to be in gym with him but because of my arm I was excused to study for an hour instead. I nodded and pressed into him tightly as we walked; revelling in the safeness that he gave me. When we got there he kissed me outside the door, sending tingles down my spine. When he pulled away he had the familiar pained expression on his face - which I now realised was because he wanted to do more than what he was doing.

His look made my stomach get fluttery; I grabbed his hand and pulled him into the nearest bathroom not interested in study hall in the slightest. We could skip and just make out for an hour instead. Clay burst out laughing as I locked the bathroom door behind us. "What the hell are you doing, Riley Bear?" he asked, grinning and looking under the stalls to make sure we were alone.

I pulled him to me and kissed him hungrily, just needing to taste him and feel close to him. He made a moan in the back of his throat and pushed me against the wall kissing me deeply. He pulled away when I was almost dizzy and started kissing down my neck slowly making my whole body burn. I gasped, so turned on that I could barely remember my own name.

That was when fate had to intervene and ruin our make out session though. The fire bell started ringing shrilly from the corridor. "Noooooooo!" Clay whined, putting his head on my shoulder and sighing dejectedly. I laughed as he pulled away from me, pouting as he unlocked the bathroom door.

"We'll pick up from here later," I suggested, grinning as his face brightened. He slipped his hand into mine and pulled me into the hallway where the ringing got louder. We mingled in with the crowd and made our way to the parking lot, pretending we had been there the whole time.

"Where the hell were you two?" Tom asked with a huge smirk on his face. I blushed, and Clay wrapped his arms around me tightly so I could bury my face against his chest and hide.

"We got lost," Clay joked, chuckling. All the boys were laughing too, and then Vegas talk resumed while we waited.

After about twenty minutes we were allowed back in the building, apparently someone had been messing around melting a pen on a bunsen burner in science so it was a false alarm. I kissed Clay on the cheek not risking anything else and made my way to class again.

· · ·

AFTER SCHOOL I stayed in the study hall to finish my maths homework while Clay had practice. When I knew he would be finishing I made my way out to his car to meet him.

He grabbed me from behind and pressed himself close into me, running his hand down my thighs. "You finished early," I muttered, leaning back into him. He felt a little strange against my back, not as comfortable as normal. I frowned and turned to see if he was okay. I gasped in shock at what I saw. Instead of Clay standing there touching me, it was Blake. I staggered back a couple of steps, and he followed me with a smile.

"Hi, Jailbait," he chirped, leaning in to kiss me.

I turned my head at the last second so he kissed my cheek instead. He pulled back, glaring at me angrily and I flinched.

"W-what are you doing h-here?" I stuttered, feeling sick and looking wildly around for Clay. He was due out of practice any minute. The parking lot was empty though, there was no help.

"I came to see my girlfriend, silly," Blake replied, reaching for my hand. I jerked my hand away quickly before he could touch me.

Girlfriend? Is he seriously saying that after what he did to me? "Blake, I'm not your girlfriend. I'm with Clay," I retorted, shaking my head. As soon as I said it I wished I hadn't. His ice blue eyes seemed to blaze with fury. I barely had time to see his arm move before he slapped me across the cheek, making my head whip to the side as pain exploded in my head making my vision blurry.

"You fucking whore. I *knew* you were seeing him! You said you were just friends for fuck sake," he roared. His hand curled around my upper arm, his fingernails digging into my skin. I was shaking now, I wanted to run, but my feet wouldn't move.

"I... I... didn't, we... we only just got together... I wasn't," I protested, but another blow struck my face making me dizzy and confused. This time I stumbled, unable to stay on my feet. I put out my hands to break my fall and pain shot up my broken wrist again making me scream and clench my teeth as I fought against the urge to vomit.

"You're going to break up with him. Now!" he barked angrily, pulling me up off of the floor by my good arm. His tight grip made me wince as tears fell from my eyes.

Just then there was a blur and Blake fell to the floor, dragging me back down with him, scraping my knee on the concrete. I looked up through my tears to see Clay; he grabbed me, picking me up off of the floor and pushed me gently towards Tom who held me tightly. Ben and Craig both moved to Clay's back ready to help him if he needed it, he didn't. Clay jumped down and started punching Blake.

"I told you to fucking leave her alone!" he was shouting as he threw punch after punch. I couldn't stop crying. Blake's face was covered in blood, and he had his arms over his face as a shield. Clay stood up and kicked him hard in the stomach. "If I ever see you near her again I swear to God I will beat you until you're dead. Do you hear me, Chambers?" he shouted, kicking him again and again. Blake winced and nodded, coughing and spluttering. Craig and Ben suddenly grabbed Clay, dragging him away while he was still thrashing around trying to beat the life out of Blake.

"Enough, Clay," I heard Ben say fiercely. Clay took a deep breath and nodded in agreement. The second they let him go, he came over to me, taking me into his arms and pulling me to his car. He climbed into the passenger seat, pulling me onto his lap as he looked at me worriedly, rubbing my back softly as I sobbed onto his shoulder.

"It's all right, Riley. It's all right, beautiful girl," he murmured, kissing my hair. He pushed on my shoulders gently, making me pull back. I looked up into his angry and concerned face. I sniffed loudly, trying to get control of my emotions. Clay rubbed his hands gently over my face, wincing as I flinched when he touched my sore cheek. "Are you okay?" he asked quietly, looking at me concerned. I wasn't sure of that answer. I wriggled my fingers on my injured arm, making pain shoot up it again. I yelped, and he took hold of my hand. "It's hurting again?" he asked, clenching his jaw tightly. I nodded, and he hissed through his teeth. "Okay, Riley Bear, let's go back to the hospital and get it checked out," he suggested, shifting me onto my seat and climbing out before buckling my seatbelt for me. I watched as he ran round to the driver's side and climbed in, starting the engine and pulling out quickly as he buckled his belt at the same time.

· · ·

IT TURNED OUT THAT nothing else had broken in my arm but that the break had moved slightly so they had to redo my cast. The police came to take a statement again. Apparently because there were witnesses this time they would be able to arrest Blake because most of the boys from the team had seen him slap me the second time. The police warned Clay about fighting, but because of the circumstances they let him off without a caution thankfully. Clay had called my parents but had told them that there was no need to come to the hospital and that he would drive me home as soon as I was discharged.

After a couple of hours we pulled into my driveway, and I sagged in relief. My whole body felt exhausted and being pumped of pain meds was making me sleepy too. Clay and I hadn't spoken much while at the hospital. To be honest, he was too angry, and whenever I'd tried to talk to him his answers were just one syllable or a grunt or something. I had a feeling he was regretting not taking his opportunity to kill Blake when he had it.

Clay helped me inside where I was immediately attacked by my parents who pulled me into hugs and kisses. Mom was crying and hanging all over me as she gushed about how awful it was to see her baby in pain. I frowned as David pulled Clay to one side, I couldn't hear what they were saying, but it looked like David was pleased with Clay, probably for beating the crap out of Blake no doubt.

When they'd finished with whatever talk they were having, Clay stepped back to my side and looked at my mom hopefully. "Is it okay if I stay again tonight? I know it's not my night, but I just want to make sure Riley's okay," he asked. I could tell from his expression that even if they said no that he would be sneaking in through my window anyway.

"Of course, son, you can always stay here, you know that," David replied, patting him on the back affectionately. Clay smiled and hugged me tightly, kissing my forehead. I closed my eyes, enjoying his closeness but when I tried to open them again it was incredibly hard. I really needed sleep.

"I'm really tired, I'm gonna go to bed. Clay, you should go and speak to your parents and tell them you're staying here again," I instructed, nodding towards the front door.

He nodded in agreement. "Yeah. I'll be back in a little while." He smiled and turned, jogging out of the door to go and speak to his parents. I smiled weakly at my parents and made my way upstairs, shrugging out of my clothes awkwardly and putting on a pair of pyjamas. I climbed carefully into the bed, cradling my aching arm to my chest and fell asleep almost instantly.

• • •

AS I SLOWLY STARTED to drift into consciousness I smiled because Clay's smell was all around me. It was so comforting that I snuggled closer to him, smiling as his arms tightened around me, clamping me to him. I hadn't even heard him come to bed last night because I was so out of it. I cracked my eyes open and sighed contentedly as his handsome face came into focus. Unable to resist, I bent my head and kissed him softly.

He stirred and woke up immediately, giving me a sad smile. "Hey, Riley Bear." His fingers traced across my cheek with a sombre expression.

"Morning." I bent forward and kissed him again gratefully. "Thank you, Clay, I realised last night that I never thanked you for what you did," I said, looking deep into his beautiful green eyes.

"You don't need to thank me." He pulled me tighter against him, rubbing my back gently.

I snuggled into his chest and fought the urge to cry again. I didn't want to keep dwelling on it, but every time I thought about Blake I started to feel scared and vulnerable. Yesterday had terrified me, and I didn't ever want to feel like that again. "I love you, Clay. I'm really sorry for all this trouble." A tear escaped down my face even though I was trying my best to keep them at bay.

Clay groaned, leaning in and kissing my tear away. "Please don't be upset, I can't stand to see you cry." He smiled sadly as he wiped my face tenderly. "I love you too, by the way." He bent his head and kissed my cheek softly, looking crestfallen.

I sniffed and forced a smile. "I'm gonna go take a shower, will you come help me?" I asked, not trying to be seductive but actually asking for help, I wouldn't be able to wash my hair properly with one hand.

"Sure," he agreed, getting out of the bed and pulling me up too, leading me to the bathroom. After taking a look in the mirror, I realised why Clay had been stroking my face and looking sad. I had a reddish purple tinge to one cheek; it wasn't too bad, it just looked a little flushed unless you looked closely.

• • •

EVERYONE WAS LOOKING at me weirdly and whispering at school all day. I hid whenever I could, not lingering in the hallways between classes, and spending longer than necessary in the bathroom. The police rang at lunchtime to say that they had cautioned Blake, but they had to let him go. Clay hadn't been impressed about that news, but there was nothing else they could do. They did say that if Blake contacted me again in a threatening manner that I could get a restraining order against him, but I didn't think that I would need to after the mess that Clay made of his face the previous day.

Clay was extremely protective all day long. He'd told his friends everything that had happened so someone was always walking with me. It was annoying at first having Ben or Tom lingering behind me like watchdogs whenever Clay wasn't around, but I could understand that Clay was worried about me so I let it go. Knowing I had someone with me obviously made him feel better, so I could put up with it for his sake. After school, Clay met me after my final class and escorted me to the field so I could watch his practice - and so he could keep his eyes on me, but he never actually said that.

As he led me to the benches that ran along the side of the field, and told me not to go anywhere, I smiled and looked at him quizzically. "You're not always going to be this overprotective, are you?" I joked, squeezing his waist.

He smiled sheepishly. "I don't know what you're talking about, Riley Bear," he replied, shrugging innocently.

I chuckled and rolled my eyes. "Of course you don't, boyfriend."

He gave me a gorgeous smile and sat me on the benches before running across the field to his team. The whole hour Clay didn't really take his eyes off of me and kept scanning the area looking for Blake. He got in a lot of trouble from his coach for not paying attention, and got taken out a lot by his teammates because he was too distracted to defend himself.

As soon as the whistle blew he ran over to me as fast as he could, his eyes still scanning the area. I laughed and shook my head in disapproval. "You need to stop! He's not gonna come back after yesterday," I insisted, going up on tiptoes and kissing his lips. He bent his knees and wrapped his arms around me, picking me up, using one hand to wrap my legs around his waist. "Ew, Clay, you're all sweaty and dirty," I whined, pouting.

He laughed wickedly. "Hmm, now say that in a more breathy voice," he flirted, smiling.

Ben cleared his throat next to us. "Now, now, enough of that, no one wants to hear you two flirting," he joked. I laughed and gently slapped the back of this head in reprimand. "Hey! Clay, keep your girlfriend in check," he joked, rubbing his head dramatically, making everybody laugh.

• • •

CLAY REMAINED ON high alert for the rest of the week at school. He'd also, somehow, managed to convince our parents to let him stay with me all week at our house too. On Friday, instead of sitting in my usual spot in the bleachers with Rachel, Clay was making me watch the game from the front line, near the players' entryway so he could get to me easily in case Blake showed up. At half time I got a text. Expecting it to be Clay texting me from his locker room, I smiled and opened it.

'Jailbait, why are you not sitting in your usual place? I see you're still wearing Preston's shirt, I thought we agreed you would tell him it's over. Do it now, Riley. I'll see you after the game. B x'

My heart stopped as my blood seemed to turn to ice in my veins. *He knows I'm wearing Clay's shirt... he can see me?* I looked round to where I normally sat in the bleachers, and sure enough, Blake was sat there looking at me angrily. He had a cut over the bridge of his nose and a black eye. Bile rose in my throat as my hands started to shake. I couldn't look away from him as he smiled at me - and it was a real smile too, like he truly meant it.

I stood up slowly and, at the same time, he stood up too, mirroring my movement. *Oh God... I need to get to Clay.* Without taking my eyes off of Blake, I squeezed past the people sat in my row. When I finally got to the end of the aisle, I bolted for the players' entryway. I couldn't breathe as I imagined him grabbing me, hitting me, looking at me with those angry eyes again. I ran down the tunnel towards the locker room as fast as my legs would take me. When I got to the end I threw the door open and stumbled in. The players were all sitting around, having a drink as the coach shouted about things that had gone wrong in the first half. I burst into the room crying hysterically.

"What the hell are you doing here?" the coach reprimanded, turning to me and frowning angrily.

Clay jumped up and ran to me, pulling me away from the door and pushing me behind him as he opened the door quickly, looking out into the hallway with a murderous expression on his face. I grabbed his hand, pulling him back to me, wrapping myself round him to stop him from going out after Blake.

"Stupid fucking asshole! I'll kill him. Riley, let me go!" he shouted, gently trying to take my arms from around his waist. "Tom, take her," he ordered, finally prying me off of him and bursting through the doors.

I shook my head in protest, watching as the door slammed closed behind him. "Clay! Don't, please don't," I screamed, trying to get out the door so I could go after him, but Tom wrapped his arms around me tightly. I looked round at the teacher. "Please stop him! He could get hurt," I begged, crying hysterically.

Without asking for an explanation, the coach burst out of the room, along with half of the team. Tom pulled me over to the bench and made me sit down. I was crying on his shoulder when Clay ran back into the room a few minutes later.

I jumped up he shook his head. "He wasn't there, Riley Bear," he said, wrapping his arms around me tightly. "It's okay, everything's okay I promise," he murmured, stroking my hair.

The coach came back in, followed by the rest of the team. "Somebody needs to tell me what the hell is going on, right now!" Coach ranted, looking at Clay expectantly. A little timer beeped on the side. The coach slammed his hand down on it, silencing it immediately. He shook his head. "Christ! We need to go back on." He waved his hand towards the door, looking around at the players that were all milling around unsure what to do. "Go, get out there!" he ordered.

The players all started filing out, but Clay didn't move. "You need to take me off, I can't leave Riley," he said sternly.

The coach groaned and threw his hands up in exasperation. "I can't just take you off for God's sake." He shook his head and took a deep breath. "Look, Clay, is this serious? Do you need help?" he questioned, quieter now, looking at Clay with obvious concern.

"Yes, it's serious. I need to call the police before I kill someone," Clay answered, tightening his arms around me.

The coach nodded, his eyes tight with worry. "Calm down. I'm gonna go restart the game, and then I'll be back so we can sort this out. Give me ten minutes tops," he instructed as he exited the locker rooms and went back to the field.

Clay cocked his head, looking me right in the eyes. "Did he hurt you?"

I sniffed and wiped my face, drying my tears. "No, he didn't hurt me. He was sat in the bleachers where I usually sit. He sent me a text." I passed him my phone in explanation. He read the message and I could see him trying to hold in his anger. Seconds later he called the police and arranged for them to come over to my house in an hour.

We explained everything to the police and set up a restraining order against Blake; if he came within a hundred yards of me again he would instantly be arrested and held this time. Clay was far from pleased about it, he wanted something to be done about it now, but apparently they needed to build a case first to take to court if he carried on. The Vegas trip was still going ahead as planned though, for that I was grateful. We'd arranged with Ben to pick us up in the morning at eight o'clock in the minivan. That meant we would arrive at the hotel we'd booked at about four in the afternoon if we stopped a couple of times along the way.

• • •

IN THE MORNING David pulled me aside while Clay loaded the van with our luggage. "Riley, I know you won't actually get to bet in the casinos or anything because you're not old enough, but here," he said, handing me an envelope.

I opened it to see it was filled with money. "David, what?" I gasped, shocked.

He chuckled. "There's a thousand bucks in there for you to have fun with okay. Let's call it an early Christmas present, but don't tell Mom all right?" he said, grinning.

Oh my God, is he serious?

"David, seriously?" I asked, still too shocked to form a longer sentence. He nodded, and I pulled him into a big hug, laughing as I kissed his cheek. "You're the best stepdad in the world. You know that, don't you?" I hugged him tightly.

He grinned. "I do now you've told me," he replied, kissing my forehead.

I chuckled sheepishly. "Well I'm really sorry I've never told you that before, but I mean it honestly."

"I know you do, kiddo, and you're the best stepdaughter in the world, and I'm sorry I've never told you before." He quickly took the envelope from my hands and pushed it into my jacket pocket as my mom walked into the room.

"Hey what's going on in here?" she asked, pulling me into another hug. As if on cue Clay walked in the front door and announced that he'd put all of our luggage into the minivan and that we were ready to go. I was practically jumping up and down with excitement.

"Okay well I'll see you guys on Monday afternoon," I said, kissing my parents again quickly.

David turned to Clay. "I know I don't have to ask you this, but take care of her for me, okay?" he requested, shaking Clay's hand

Clay just smiled and pulled me into a hug. "Always," he confirmed, pulling me towards the door.

As soon as we stepped into the van I got so excited I couldn't sit still. A *whole weekend of Clay, slot machines, hotel rooms, and no parents. This trip is going to be awesome!*

The drive was incredibly long. We tried to amuse ourselves with singing and games, but in the end the boys ended up chatting about football and the girls were sitting in the back gossiping about clothes and the boys.

"So I'm definitely gonna try for Tom this weekend," Rachel whispered, nodding.

I giggled and shook my head at her. What I'd learnt about Rachel was that she liked sex, a lot. But she couldn't commit to anything so she didn't want a boyfriend. For this reason she was popular amongst the guys, but she wasn't a slut. She was also well liked by the girls at school too because she was actually a lovely person, as opposed to girls like Zoë who gave it away trying to get a boy because of how he looked or his status.

"Gonna try for Tom? Surely you don't have to try very hard, I mean, he looks at you *all* the time. Haven't you two hooked up three times already?" I asked, rolling my eyes at her.

She nodded in confirmation. "Hmm yeah, I don't usually go back for seconds but he does this amazing thing with his hands... it's wow, it really is awesome." She sighed dreamily and looked at the back of Tom's head with a lustful expression.

Some of the girls laughed, but Claire leant forward in her seat, looking at Rachel hopefully. "Do you think you could get him to teach Ben?" she whispered, looking excited.

Rachel grinned. "I could ask him if you want," she offered. "What about you, Riley, does Clay need any help in that department?" she asked, waggling her eyebrows. I burst into hysterics; the idea of Clay needing help with anything like that really was laughable.

I shook my head. "No definitely not, but thanks for the offer," I replied, once I could talk again. They all looked at me in awe as I sat back smugly.

chapter fourteen

Finally, after almost eight hours, we arrived in Vegas and parked up at our hotel. The drive was long, and my butt was numb by the time I climbed out of the back of the minivan. Clay and I checked in and were given room number 401. I heard some of the other guys saying they were all near ours too. Once everyone had their room keys, we went our separate ways to go unpack and change for the evenings activities. The plan was to meet at half past six for dinner, and then we'd hit a club after. I had my fake ID which said I was twenty-one so getting into places shouldn't be a problem.

Clay and I took the elevator to the fourth floor, and for some reason, I started to get nervous. My hands were starting to sweat, and butterflies started to swoop around in my stomach. What was about to happen made my insides squirm with apprehension and excitement; I wasn't sure which sensation was the strongest if I was honest. Clay and I were about to have sex. I was finally going to lose my virginity, and to the most perfect boy in the world. The minute I started thinking about it my body started burning in need. Finally, after what felt like the slowest elevator ride ever, we got to our floor. I glanced at Clay and noticed that he actually looked nervous too, which made me feel marginally better.

After a short walk down a nice hallway, he opened the door to our room and gestured for me to go in first. The room was gorgeous. It had a king size four poster bed with red sheets. I actually blushed when I looked at it, thinking about what would be going on in it soon. The furniture in the room was made of dark wood; there was a large flat screen TV, and dressing table. I gasped as I looked around. The place was incredible.

I opened the only other door in the room, to see the bathroom. It was exquisite. It had a huge freestanding bath in the centre of the room, and a walk in shower spacious enough for two, twin sinks with fluffy white towels hanging underneath. Hooked on the wall there were even fluffy white bathrobes with the hotel's logo on the pocket.

"Clay, this must have cost you a fortune." I gasped, looking back at him.

"Totally worth it." He smiled and wrapped his arms around me, kissing me deeply, lifting me off of my feet and moving us over to the bed. As he pressed me into the mattress, settling himself on top of me, I moaned in appreciation. Even the mattress was soft and luxurious.

Clay broke the kiss and just looked at me as if he could see right down to my soul; as if I was some huge prize he had won and always wanted. I ran my hands through his hair and pulled him back to me. *Okay, this is it, time to lose my virginity.* I was so excited that my whole body was throbbing already at the thought, but he pulled out of the kiss too soon leaving me almost desperate and unsatisfied.

"We only have an hour before we need to meet everyone for dinner so why don't we get ready?" he suggested, pulling away to sit up next to me on the bed.

I groaned. "Seriously? We're in a posh hotel, with a big comfy bed, and yet you're gonna make me wait some more? What are you a masochist?" I whined, giving him my puppy dog face that usually worked.

"Oh no! Not the begging face, please," he said, laughing and tickling me until I couldn't breathe. "Come on, Riley Bear, I just don't want to have to rush anything, I want us to be able to take our time." He pulled me up to sitting and kissed my fingers on my bad hand.

I sighed in defeat and made my way to the bathroom, grabbing my bag as I went. He got up to follow me in there, probably so he could get in the shower with me, but I held my hand up to stop him. "Oh no you don't. You can wait out here, build some more anticipation. In fact, I think you should get dressed in Tom's room and then wait in the lobby for me," I instructed, giving him my stern face so he knew I was serious.

He groaned as I shut and locked the bathroom door. "That's so not fair, Riley Bear," he called through the door.

I giggled and turned on the shower, smiling to myself. "I'll see you downstairs at half past six," I called back. He groaned again, and a couple of minutes later I heard him leave the room.

I showered and dried my hair, adding soft curls with the built in curler and straightener in the bathroom. I added a little more make-up than usual, going for some light golden eye shadow, black mascara, and light pink lip gloss instead of clear. I figured I should make a little extra effort, after all I was supposed to be four years older than I was.

I slipped on my brand new 'losing my virginity' strapless lacy black bra and matching thong. Then I tugged on my little black dress over the top. It was tight around the bust and waist, which actually made my boobs look at least two sizes bigger than normal, then it flowed out around my hips to about mid-thigh. I pulled on a long necklace and slipped on my killer black high heels that made my legs look longer.

I looked in the mirror and even I thought I looked hot. After grabbing my little gold clutch purse, I was ready to go. A quick glance at the clock showed I had four minutes to spare. *Perfect*. I made my way to the elevator. When I got out at the lobby Clay was standing there waiting for me, he looked so handsome I could cry. He actually looked like he had just got done shooting for a fashion magazine or something.

His blond hair was his usual style of perfect, messy waves, he had on a black shirt that he wore undone a little so you could see some of his amazing chest, and he had rolled the sleeves up to his elbows showing his tanned and muscled forearms. He wore this with light blue American Eagle jeans that made his ass look edible. My mouth started to water, and my body tingle. I wanted nothing more than to drag him back to our room and rip that sexy outfit off of him. Going out in Vegas didn't interest me anymore after seeing him look like that.

When he saw me his eyes widened and his mouth fell open. I smiled inwardly. *Okay that's definitely the effect I was going for!* I turned and gave a little twirl, making sure my dress flew out seductively so he got a clear view of my thighs.

"You like?" I asked, biting my lip. He walked quickly up to me and wrapped his arms around me pressing me against the wall and kissing me deeply. When he pulled back we were both breathless.

"I don't like, I love," he corrected, putting his forehead to mine.

"Okay come on let's eat, I'm starved," Craig begged, waving his hands to the door.

Clay's hand slipped into mine as we walked out of the hotel. "You are so stunningly beautiful, Riley, that it's just not fair," he said, with his familiar pained expression as we walked along towards the restaurant. He was running his eyes down my body slowly like he wanted to rip the dress off me right here in the street. I moaned internally at the thought. *Jeez, this is going to be a long night.* Everything was so beautiful with the lights and noise; I didn't know what to look at first. This was my first time to Vegas, and I loved it already.

After we'd eaten we went to a club called Nero. It was great. The music was banging, and I'd already had a lot to drink so my head was buzzing along to the beat. Clay and I were dancing and laughing, all in all I was having an incredible night. I'd been hit on a few times, but Clay let me deal with it as usual, he wasn't actually the possessive type. He knew he could trust me, which I loved, but he also kept a close eye on me subtly for trouble. He really was the perfect boyfriend.

"Guys, let's go back to the hotel bar, they have a karaoke contest tonight," Ben suggested when we were all sitting down together. We all agreed to continue drinking in the hotel instead. It was only a block away from the club, but I was wasted and walking in zigzags as we made our way back there. I'd already taken my shoes off and was swinging them around singing Lady Gaga at the top of my lungs with the other girls. The boys were equally as drunk, though slightly less vocal.

We finally made it to the hotel, and after about four more shots, were playing truth or dare. Rachel had to flash her boobs; I admitted that I was a virgin but that I didn't plan on being one tomorrow - which made all the boys slap Clay on the back. Jenna had to drink a shot whist doing a handstand, which actually didn't work out well for her at all; she'd ended up with more in her eyes than in her mouth.

Clay was giggling like a little schoolgirl at some random joke that Tom was telling. Him and Tom were laughing so hard that Tom fell off of his chair.

Clay suddenly pulled me onto his lap. "I've got a great idea," he whispered seductively in my ear sending shivers down my spine. *Oh God, please say you want to take me to bed right now!* I turned and kissed him with everything I had.

"What's your great idea?" I asked, licking the side of his neck.

He giggled drunkenly and raised one eyebrow at me. "Mmm, well we are in Vegas, let's get married," he stated, giving me a smile that melted my heart.

Married to Clay? Oh hell yeah I'll do that! That was easily the best idea he'd ever had in his life. "Okay." I nodded in acceptance and grinned at him excitedly.

A heartbreaking smile split his face. "Come on then." He stood up, lifting me to my feet easily.

"Where are you two going?" Rachel asked, but it was barely understandable through the slurring. I giggled, practically bursting with excitement as I jumped on the spot like a little kid.

"To get married," Clay answered, taking my hand and marching off towards the exit, pulling me along behind him. I heard collective gasps, some cheers and lots of laughter as I stumbled along behind my soon to be husband.

Clay led me down the street and into a little jewellery store that for some reason was still open at one in the morning. We were laughing like little kids. "Hi, can I help you?" a woman in her early twenties asked. Her eyes raked over Clay appreciatively which just made me laugh even harder. *Yeah right, woman, I don't like your chances!*

Clay picked me up carefully, setting me on the stool that was in front of the counter. "Yep," he replied, popping the p, making us both laugh again. "We need an engagement ring and two wedding rings." He kissed me so fiercely that he nearly pushed me off the stool I was perched on. I grabbed hold of his neck, giggling.

Minutes later and the lady brought out a tray of engagement rings, setting them on the counter in front of us. I let Clay choose, I didn't care what it looked like as long as it came from him. Next he chose two wedding rings and then paid on his credit card. Clay's family had a lot of money; his dad was a big time plastic surgeon; therefore, Clay had a very healthy credit limit.

After we'd paid we walked out of the shop to see all eight of our friends standing there laughing and joking around. Jenna had a bottle of Jack Daniels so I grabbed it and took a hefty swig, wincing as the liquid burnt my throat on its way down.

"Come on then, Riley Bear, let's go get married," Clay chirped excitedly. I swayed along behind him to a little wedding chapel. I wanted Elvis to do it, but they didn't have him so we settled for a normal, boring minister instead.

"You really gonna get married?" Tom asked, laughing his ass off.

I nodded. "Yep! Let's get this done so I can go back to my room and screw the life out of my husband," I suggested, kissing Clay deeply and crushing myself against him tightly. I pulled back when I suddenly realised that I needed a bridesmaid if I was getting married. "Rach, you want to be my bridesmaid?" I asked her hopefully.

She squealed and nodded eagerly. "Hells yeah I do," she agreed, jumping up and down. "Oh crud, what's the rhyme? Wait, wait, you need some stuff for good luck. Oh what is it?" she mused, frowning, holding my hand. "Oh! Something bold, something new, something borrowed, something true," she sang, looking extremely pleased with herself for remembering.

"Something bold?" Jenna repeated. "Like what, like bold colours or something?" she asked confused.

I just waved my hand in a whatever gesture and went back to kissing Clay. *God he really is an incredible kisser, I can't wait to make love to him.*

"I can't wait to make love to you either," he whispered in my ear, biting my earlobe. I blushed and giggled. *Did I say that out loud?* I could hear the others all talking and laughing.

"Okay, Riley, we got it, that old lady told us," Rachel said, pointing to a middle aged lady behind the counter who looked extremely annoyed at being called old. I giggled and smiled apologetically at her as Clay walked off to sort out some licence or something that we needed before we could get married. Rachel grinned excitedly. "So the rhyme is something old and something new, something borrowed, and something blue. Well you can borrow my bangle it was my grandmothers, that'll cover old *and* borrowed. Something new can be your dress, that's new, right? So we just need something blue..." She looked around, frowning. Suddenly she gasped and ran over to the table where they had a fake flower arrangement. She grabbed a little plastic blue flower and shoved it roughly down my cleavage. "There, perfect. I am the perfect bridesmaid!" she declared proudly. "Clay, who did you choose for your best man? Because you know the bridesmaid and the best man have to have sex, right? It's tradition," she asked Clay, nodding her head in the direction of Tom obviously giving him pleading eyes.

Everybody laughed, and Clay nodded. "Yeah I was gonna ask Tom anyway," he replied, throwing the two blue ring boxes at Tom with a wink.

Clay pulled the third box out of his pocket and got down on one knee in front of me, opening a red velvet box.

"Riley Jane Tanner, I have loved you for as long as I can remember and I will love you forever. I promise to do my best to make you happy every day of my life. Will you marry me?" he asked, looking me straight in the eyes the whole time. *Boy would I! Jeez, I wish we were married already so I could be back in that hotel room now consummating it.*

I nodded, smiling ecstatically. "Yes."

He jumped to his feet, lifting me up and spinning us around in a circle before plopping me back down and slipping the ring onto my finger. I didn't even get a chance to look at it because the lady called us through to the chapel because the minister was ready for us.

The chapel was fairly small and intimate. It was completely white inside with little white chairs. A white carpet formed the aisle that led up the middle. Clay and Tom walked up to the front while Rachel and I stayed behind. Everyone else went to take seats, giggling and chatting. The music started so Rachel slowly staggered up the aisle, I couldn't help but laugh as she shot Tom a wink that said he was in for a good night.

When she got to the end, it was my turn. I kept my eyes firmly on Clay as I walked up the aisle, just marvelling over how perfect he was. I was having trouble walking in my shoes so I stopped halfway up to slip them off. "Jenna!" I called as I threw them to her, making everyone laugh. Clay grinned and motioned with his head for me to go to him so I skipped the rest of the way and slapped his ass as I stood next to him. The minister didn't look impressed.

The ceremony passed as a blur, and to be honest I wasn't listening to much of what she said, I was lost in Clay's beautiful green eyes, eyes that I hoped my children would have when we decided to have kids. He nudged me when it was time to say my lines, excitement and happiness clear in his eyes making my heart beat way too fast.

I repeated the lines after the Minster. "I, Riley Jane Tanner, take you, Clay Richard Preston, to be my lawful wedded husband. To have and to hold, for richer, for poorer, in sickness and in health, as long as we both shall live," I said clearly. When Clay said his lines to me he was beaming with pride and joy.

The best bit by a clear mile was 'you may now kiss the bride'. I threw myself at him with so much force that I nearly knocked him over. We were both panting by the time we pulled away. Everyone was clapping, cheering, and taking photos on their camera phones. I heard Ben say that he'd got video. We signed the register and staggered back to the hotel, laughing hysterically.

"Celebration drinks! Newlyweds over here," Ben shouted as we entered the bar, pointing to me and Clay. I giggled as everyone in the bar clapped and cheered as Clay kissed me deeply.

"Ooh, newlyweds! Come up here," the host of the karaoke competition instructed, pointing to the stage where he was standing. I giggled and hid behind Clay who shook his head, laughing, mouthing 'No' to the man. "Come on, I'm not taking no for an answer. Newlyweds up here now or I'll have security come and bring you up," the host man shouted again.

Ben and Tom were pushing us towards the stage. "No! I don't want to," I protested, laughing.

Clay turned and picked me up, throwing me over his shoulder but carefully holding my dress down so that it covered my ass from view. He carried me onto the stage, laughing his head off before plopping me down in front of the host and wrapping his arms around me tightly.

"So you two have just gotten married? Mr and Mrs..." the man prompted, trailing off, smiling.

"Preston," Clay said, squeezing my waist with a big grin.

"So, Mr and Mrs Preston, we're gonna let you have your first dance," he said, winking at me. "What's your song?" he asked, turning to the computer. I looked at Clay, stumped. We didn't have a song.

"James Morrison, 'You Make It Real'," Clay answered immediately. I gasped. *Holy crap, he's right, that is our song! He always makes me dance with him when that song comes on, and he even has it as his ringtone on his cell for me.* I swallowed a sob at how sweet he is as the man tapped on the computer and the song started. Clay laughed and pulled me into his arms as we slow danced to it. People were oohing and ahhing at us, but I couldn't focus on anything other than Clay's eyes which were radiating love and passion. When the song ended he kissed me, lifting me up off the floor so he didn't have to bend. Everyone clapped.

"So would you like to take the newlywed challenge?" the man suddenly asked, thrusting the microphone in my face.

I looked at him confused. "What sort of challenge?" I asked quietly, not willing to commit to anything.

He smiled wickedly. "Well you've had your first official dance, now it's time for the unofficial first dance. If you do it here on stage you win four bottles of champagne," he explained.

Our friends were all jumping up and down, howling and chanting '*do it! do it!'* loudly. "Unofficial first dance, what does that entail?" I asked sceptically. I could hear Clay laughing behind me so I turned and slapped his chest playfully.

"Well it's a lap dance," the host replied, winking at me playfully.

Oh my God, is he serious? "I'm not giving you a lap dance for four bottles of champagne! I just got married, are you crazy?" I cried, outraged, making everyone burst out laughing. Clay was almost on the floor laughing.

"Not for me! For your husband," the host cried in hysterics.

I blushed at my stupidity. *Holy crap, well that's embarrassing.* "Oh! Well if he wants one I will," I agreed, giggling and looking at Clay questionably.

He looked more than up for it and nodded eagerly. "Heck yeah," he growled, his eyes flashing with excitement.

The host disappeared and came back with a chair which he set in the centre of the stage. He tapped on the computer and a couple of seconds later a song I had never even heard of came on. I giggled and blushed.

He host smiled wickedly at Clay. "You're not allowed to touch her, that's the only rule; otherwise you lose the challenge and forfeit the champagne," he clarified, slapping Clay on the shoulder giving him a good luck smile. I pushed Clay roughly into the chair gave him my best sexy smile and began giving him a lap dance, grinding on him and rubbing my hands on my thighs seductively.

I heard him groan, and he quickly sat on his hands to take away the temptation as I ground hard on the now prominent bulge in his jeans, breathing deeply in his ear. I bent over so my ass was near his face and rubbing my hands down his legs seductively. His face told me he was thoroughly enjoying it, and to be honest, I was too. I was so drunk that I forgot everyone else was there and was quite happy grinding against him, getting myself off in the middle of the bar. Luckily the song ended, and everyone was cheering otherwise I probably would have carried on until we both finished.

When I went to get up Clay jumped up quickly and pulled me to him, holding me firmly in front of him, using me a shield again no doubt. I grinned and discreetly rubbed against him on purpose, making him moan breathily in my ear.

The host laughed as he came over to us. "Well you definitely won the challenge. I don't think we've ever had a couple get so into it before, you're a lucky man," he congratulated, slapping Clay on the back, chuckling. "Sam, four bottles of champagne for this couple for the newlywed challenge!" he shouted to the barman who nodded in acknowledgement, laughing to himself.

I blushed as I made my way off the stage with Clay clinging to me like his life depended on it. Our friends were all hooting and laughing by the time we got over to them.

"I got that on video. Man, that was the hottest damn thing I've ever seen," Craig said, winking at me.

"Yeah, I'm gonna need a copy of that," Clay said, laughing and squeezing my ass and pulling me onto his lap as the barman brought our champagne over. I sat there, deliriously happy, drinking champagne, chatting and laughing for about another hour before I fell asleep with my head in the crook of Clay's neck.

chapter fifteen

Death. A slow, painful death was what it felt like as sleep slowly ebbed away. My head was pounding, and my stomach churning so that I felt like I was moving even though I wasn't. *I am never drinking again!* I squeezed my eyes shut and groaned, which made Clay's arms tighten around me. I pouted and turned my head carefully in his direction. The room span as I moved so I silently prayed I wouldn't be sick. When I opened my eyes the room was so bright that I squeezed them shut again. *Ah! How much did I drink last night?* I rolled over and pressed my hands to my temples as my head seemed to give another painful squeeze. Clay chuckled quietly next to me, but I couldn't look at him, I was concentrating on not spilling my guts over the exquisite satin sheets on the bed.

"Good morning, my beautiful girl. Are you suffering today?" His hand rubbed up my back soothingly.

The sound of his voice was so loud that it made my ears ring. "Shh, baby, please," I whined, groaning again and burying my face in a pillow.

He laughed quietly and climbed out of the bed, coming back a few seconds later. "Here," he whispered, tapping my shoulder to get my attention. I rolled over and saw him standing there with two pills and a glass of water. I smiled gratefully, and he dropped the pills in my hand. The water burnt my dry throat as I chugged it down greedily.

I suddenly noticed that Clay was still dressed in his clothes from last night. A quick glance down at myself confirmed that I was still in last night's attire too. Relief washed over me because that meant we hadn't had sex. I was worried that we had and I didn't remember it. That would have been heartbreaking if I couldn't remember my first time. I smiled excitedly because I still had that to look forward to.

Clay smoothed my hair away from my face with a smile as he sat on the bed next to me. "You feeling okay?"

I frowned. *No way, I'm not feeling okay at all. I have the hangover from hell.* "Not really, you?" I asked, scooting forward and burying my face into his chest.

"My head hurts a bit but not as bad as yours by the look of it." He chuckled and wrapped his arms around me, lying on his back and pulling me down next to him.

We just lay there in silence as I willed the pain in my head to subside. My face felt itchy and tight so I rubbed at it roughly. Something hard brushed against my nose as I did so. I frowned and looked down at my hand, shocked to see two rings on my finger. A beautiful gold diamond ring, and a plain gold band next to it. *What the hell? Why am I wearing two rings? Who's are they?* Suddenly everything came flooding back, the jewellery store, the wedding chapel...

Oh my God, we got married! I started to panic. *Shit, we got married? I'm only seventeen! Not that the thought of being married to Clay scares me, but we're so young, and still in school for goodness sake. And my parents, oh dear lord, they're gonna go crazy! What If Clay is regretting this and thinks that I wanted to trap him or something, he could break up with me.* My breathing was coming out too fast as the thoughts flew through my mind.

Suddenly Clay rolled on top of me and kissed me deeply, nibbling on my lip gently. I kissed him back, my mind still racing with unanswered thoughts and questions. *We're married... does he know? He was just as drunk as I was last night, he probably doesn't even remember. How on earth am I going to tell him this?*

I put my hands on his chest and pushed him back, needing to talk to him. "Clay, last night we-" I started, but he shook his head and jumped in before I could finish what I was about to say.

"No, don't worry, we didn't have sex. You were so drunk that you fell asleep down in the bar. I had to carry you up here," he interjected. He kissed me again before I could clarify what I was trying to say. His hand cupped my cheek as he sucked my bottom lip into his mouth wanting to deepen the kiss. I knew I had to stop him before he distracted me too much, and I forgot what I was trying to say.

I pushed him completely off me and sat up needing personal space. "Clay, seriously, we need to talk." I massaged my temples wondering if it was possible to actually die from a hangover. The sitting up movement had made my head pound again.

He sat up next to me, looking at me curiously. "What's up, Riley Bear?" he asked, rubbing my back gently.

I looked at him and winced. He had no idea what I was going to say, he clearly didn't know we were married, that much was obvious by the quizzical expression. I took a deep breath. *How do I say this? Direct approach is best, I think.*

"Clay, look." I raised my left hand and chewed on my lip, waiting for his reaction. He frowned and looked at it for a few seconds, clearly not understanding, and then his eyes widened and his mouth popped open in shock.

"Oh, shit! That's right, we got married!" He gasped. I nodded but didn't say anything. I just watched as a slow smile spread across his face.

All right, what the hell is he smiling about? Does that mean he's not angry? Oh God, please don't let him break up with me! He looked down at his hand, and I followed his movement, seeing that a little gold band sat on his finger too. He started to laugh, and I started to worry about his sanity. There was nothing even remotely funny about this situation. We were teenagers. We were two drunk teenagers who got married in Vegas. I could see nothing amusing about that at all.

Suddenly he pushed me back onto the bed and hovered above me, his eyes alight with amusement and a loving smile on his full lips. "Well then I should have said; good morning, Mrs Preston," he said, kissing me passionately. I kissed him back until we were both gasping for breath and he pulled away. We just looked at each other not speaking. My mind was whirling again. *Okay, so how does this whole divorce thing work, and how could we find out? We'll need to find a lawyer or something. Do we need to do that before we leave Vegas?*

"What are you thinking about, Riley Bear?" he asked, smoothing my frown lines away with his finger.

I swallowed loudly, my mouth suddenly dry as a desert. "I was just wondering what we have to do, you know, how do we get divorced?" I admitted, running my hand up his back, still thinking.

He recoiled, looking at me like I'd suggested we drown a kitten. "Divorced?"

I nodded, wondering what his shocked reaction was for. "Well yeah, I mean, we got drunk and got married in Vegas, we've only technically been together for a week." I laughed quietly, chewing on my lip.

Clay didn't laugh though; he just sat up and turned away from me. "Right," he muttered.

What did I say? Is he upset? "Clay?" I sat up and touched his back, wondering why he was acting strange all of a sudden.

"No you're right. It's fine." He still wasn't looking at me.

I pushed myself up and manoeuvred so that I sat myself in his lap. "Talk to me, what's wrong?" I asked, gripping my hands in the back of his hair. When his eyes met mine the sadness that I saw there made my heart ache.

"Is the idea of being married to me really that bad?" he whispered.

He thinks this is about him? I shook my head quickly. "Of course not, don't be silly!" I rejected. "It's just because we're so young. We were drunk, I barely even remember it. Besides, you didn't really want to marry me, did you?"

He laughed sadly. "Riley, I've been waiting to marry you again since I was eight years old." He smiled, but it didn't quite meet his eyes.

Again? "Huh, what do you mean, marry me again?" I asked, confused.

He laughed. "We got married once before, don't you remember? I was eight, and you were seven. You made me marry you in your pink Wendy house with your dolls as witnesses," he reminded. I burst out laughing at the memory that rolled over me. *How the hell could I forget that? He'd held my hand all day and kept calling me his wife.* "I love you more than anything in the world, Riley. I want to be married to you. I hoped we'd get married someday, it just happened to be sooner than I thought it would." He laughed sheepishly, his hand tracing my back slowly.

I gasped. *Is he saying he wants to stay married?* "Clay, what are you talking about? You don't want to get divorced?"

He shook his head. "No I don't," he confirmed. "But if that's what you want, then we will. I just wish you'd give me a chance. I love you; I want you to be my wife." He bent his head forward, planting a soft kiss on the tip of my nose.

Thankfully, the painkillers had finally started to kick in and so my headache was beginning to dull which allowed me to think a little clearer. I didn't speak because I literally had no idea what to say. There I was, worried he would want to break up with me, and he was actually pleased about it.

I gulped as the silence stretched on way too long for my sanity. "But how? How can we stay married? We're both still in school, we live with our parents for goodness sake, Clay, we can't," I finally said, shaking my head.

He sighed and looked right into my eyes as he spoke, "Riley, do you love me?"

That's such a silly question! "Of course I do."

He smiled at my answer. "Do you think you're ever going to want someone else?" he asked. I shook my head fiercely. *There is no way I would want anyone else, I love Clay with all my heart.* His smile grew more pronounced. "Do you want to be married to me one day? Have a nice house? Kids?"

I thought about it. Did I want to wake up next to Clay forever? Have little mini Clays running around? I smiled, the answer was hell yeah I did. "Yeah I do, but we're so young."

"Our age doesn't matter. I'll be leaving school soon. I've already been offered my apprenticeship, and in two years I'll be a fully trained engineer. I'll earn good money. I'll be able to take care of you," he persuaded, looking at me pleadingly.

I stroked his face softly as I frowned. "I don't care if we have money, Clay." *Does he think I want him for the life he could give me?*

"I didn't mean it that way, Riley Bear. I meant that once I start my job I'll be able to afford to get a place of our own. We could move out, live together. You'd be able to go to USC like you always wanted, and we could get a place close so that we could both travel and then come back together at night. I promise I'd be the best husband in the world." He shot me the adorable puppy dog face that he was so good at, the one that I had a serious problem saying no to.

I thought about it, imagined us being married, having our own place and being a proper couple. The thought of it all sent a little shiver of longing through my system. Looking at Clay while he gave me the begging eyes, it all seemed so easy. *Mrs Clay Preston, it certainly does have a lovely ring to it...*

"Give me a chance, please," he begged.

I grinned as excitement seemed to bubble up inside me. Having Clay as a husband sounded like a dream come true to me. So what if we were young, we loved each other enough to make it work. I'd known him my whole life so it wasn't as if I didn't know him well enough.

"Mrs Preston?" I whispered.

He grinned, nodding as his eyes sparkled with hopefulness. "Mrs Riley Jane Preston," he confirmed, cocking his head to the side as he pulled me closer to him.

I shook my head, frowning playfully. "Who said I would take your name? Clay Tanner sounds good," I countered, trying to look serious.

He laughed. "If you really wanted me to take your name then I would, but I know you've always hated Tanner anyway." He winked at me, and I smiled. He was right; I did hate my surname because it was passed down to me from my real dad, the sperm donor. After mom and David got married they'd wanted to change my name, but weren't allowed to because they needed my biological dad's permission, and he was nowhere to be found. Having the surname Tanner just served to remind me that I sprang from an idiot's loins.

"True," I agreed.

"So you'll give me a chance? You'll stay married to me?" he pressed. His beautiful green eyes were dancing with excitement. I nodded in confirmation, and he let out an excited whooping noise before kissing me passionately. My insides started to dance with excitement too. I'd never really thought about marriage before, but now that it had happened I was so happy about it that my skin was prickling with sensation.

"On one condition," I bartered, raising my eyebrow at him.

He smiled, nodding eagerly. "Anything."

"*You* have to tell our parents." I shuddered. *That is not going to be an easy task so there is no way I'm doing that!*

He grimaced but reluctantly nodded. "Okay, deal."

A thought occurred to me then. "You know what I just realised?" I asked, giggling.

"What's that, my beautiful wife?" Clay replied, smirking as he said the words.

I leant in closer to him and smiled as I looked at him through my eyelashes.

"Well, we waited until after we were married to have sex." I ran my hand over his chest, my fingers fiddling with the buttons of his shirt teasingly.

Clay laughed. "You're right. Wow, that's really responsible of us," he mused, kissing me softly. I tugged on his buttons eagerly, knowing that there was nothing that was going to stop us from becoming one this time. I smirked proudly as I pushed his shirt down over his shoulders, marvelling over his body. *My husband's body... Dang, I'm a lucky girl!*

He made a little moan in the back of his throat as his hands slid down my back, slipping under the bottom of my dress and pulling me closer to him. "Mmm, Riley Bear, how about I order us some room service?" *Rejected again!* I frowned and pressed my face into the crook of his neck. *Does he just not want to sleep with me? Why is he always putting this off?* "What do you want to eat?" he asked, easing me off of his lap and getting to his feet. Looking at him standing there in just his jeans, I bit my lip as my mouth started to water. "Take that look off your face, Riley, you can't eat me." He laughed.

I sighed dramatically and climbed off the bed, unzipping my dress and letting it slide to the floor. I heard him gasp, and his lustful expression seemed to come back with a vengeance. I gave him a twirl, raising one eyebrow in invitation. "Like my losing my virginity lingerie?" I flirted. *Surely now I'm offering myself to him in just my underwear he'll forget about the food...*

He nodded, turning away and picking up a menu from the side. "Mmm, I love it, but I really think we should eat something. A good fried breakfast will get rid of your hangover," he replied. His muscles seemed to be tighter than usual, his posture tense and alert as he picked up the phone to call and place the order.

I frowned inwardly. *Is there something wrong with my body? Why doesn't he want me in that way?* "Will you order coffee too?" I asked, going to the bathroom. I needed a minute to think about what had just happened and process it. My confidence was bottoming out, and I wanted to be away from him for a while to figure it out.

I stalked into the bathroom, slamming the door behind me, making sure to lock it. I looked into the mirror and sighed. Maybe I wasn't pretty enough; maybe I just didn't excite him in that way. Thinking about it was making my head hurt again so I groaned and pulled my hair into a loose ponytail and washed my face. I'd speak to Rachel about it and see what she thought. Maybe I was doing something wrong; maybe I wasn't being seductive enough for Clay. Rachel would know what to do.

When I could put it off no longer, I pulled on one of the fluffy bathrobes and unlocked the door. As I walked back into the room, Clay looked up and me and smiled. His smile made my heart accelerate, and a little dreamy sigh leave my lips. I didn't know what to say but thankfully a knock at the door deemed speech unnecessary anyway.

It was room service. The food gave us a little break, and we made easy conversation about the casinos, and whether or not Rachel and Tom would have hooked up last night or not. When we'd finished eating, Clay stood up, nodding towards the bathroom. "Want to take a bath with me?" he asked, bending down and kissing my forehead gently. I hid my confusion by putting on a fake smile. I nodded in agreement even though I was bewildered as to what that meant - if he didn't like my body then why would he want to take a bath with me? He grinned and headed into the bathroom turning on the water while I sat there chewing on my lip. He came out a couple of minutes later. "You go get in the bath. I'll be there in a few minutes, I just need to text the guys and sort out what time they want to meet up and stuff." He gave me a little push towards the door.

Still confused, I headed to the bathroom, pushing off my robe and underwear and slipping into the bubble bath that he'd made. I kept my ears trained, listening for him talking or anything in the bedroom. I could hear him moving around but couldn't quite work out anything he was doing. I laid back into the water, soaking in the hot water, being careful not to get my cast wet. After a few minutes Clay came in, shucking his clothes instantly and climbing in behind me. His arms wrapped around me as I settled myself back against his chest. He picked up a washcloth and squeezed on some of the hotel's soap, starting to wash my body with it as he peppered little kisses on the back of my neck.

Closing my eyes I just enjoyed the intimacy of the moment. He was wrapped around me completely, and I could feel that he was enjoying himself too. His excitement was evident as it pressed against the small of my back.

I moaned and pushed myself up to my knees, turning to face him. He moaned quietly as he looked at me though heavily lidded eyes. I kissed him, hard, letting all of my frustration and need leak into it so that he would know exactly how much I wanted him. The kiss was so hot that it made me shiver with excitement.

"Make love to me, please," I begged. I needed him. I needed to feel closer to him than I had done with any other person; I needed to give myself to him completely in a way I would never give myself to anyone else, ever.

He didn't say anything, he just took a hold of my hips, pulling me closer to him as he stood up, lifting me with him easily. I squealed as I wrapped my legs around his waist, holding on tightly as I looped my arms around his neck. He kissed me as he walked over to the wall, grabbing one of the robes and wrapping it around my back. I smiled against his lips because he was always thoughtful, knowing Clay he probably didn't want me to get cold or something. By the time he got to the bathroom door, I was giddy with desire. Every part of my body was screaming for him.

When he opened the door and stepped into the bedroom, I gasped. It was dark in the room because the drapes were shut, but there were hundreds of little tea light candles placed randomly over every surface, casting romantic shadows everywhere. Red rose petals were sprinkled over the floor, the bed and furniture. It was so romantic and perfect that I started to cry as my heart ached in my chest. *This is why he stopped earlier and suggested we have food first? Because he wanted to do this?*

"When did you do this?" I asked breathlessly.

He smiled sheepishly. "I didn't need to text the guys, that was just an excuse to get a minute alone." He kissed me softly as he walked over to the bed, setting me down and climbing on top of me, looking down at me with lustful eyes. "I love you, Riley Preston," he whispered. I grinned at my new name, it sounded a little weird and would take some getting used to, but I loved it, especially in his sexy voice.

I smiled up at him, knowing that this moment was perfect. The candles, the weight of him as he pressed me down into the mattress, the way his eyes shone with joy, all of it made me realise just how much I loved him. He was my everything.

"I love you too," I replied, pulling him closer to me kissing him with every ounce of passion that was burning inside me.

This was it; this was the moment that we would finally be together. I thought I would be nervous, but I wasn't. I wanted this more than anything; I wanted *him* more than anything. I loved him with all of my heart and I knew that he felt the same.

• • •

OUR BODIES WERE slick with sweat by the time we were finished. I was well and truly spent, and if I was honest, a little sore too. "I love you," Clay said breathlessly, kissing my nose.

I grinned and closed my eyes. "I love you too," I told him honestly, and I did, I loved him more than anything and I was glad we were married because I had the most thoughtful loving husband in the world.

He rolled off me, pulling me to his chest as he breathed deeply into the top of my hair. I sighed in happiness. That had been beautiful, more painful than I imagined it to be, but still so special that it made my heart soar. He had been so gentle, so soft and patient. His hands and mouth had worshipped my body as he made love to me, whispering words of love and showering me with tender kisses. I couldn't imagine my first time being any better than that. I felt so close to him now that it was almost as if we were one. I smiled and kissed his chest. *My husband's chest.* That thought was definitely getting easier and easier every time.

A candle flickered next to the bed, catching my attention. I chewed on my lip because he'd gone to so much trouble just to make our first time so special. "I can't believe you did all this, it's so romantic, Clay, thank you," I mumbled, waving my hand at all the candles and rose petals that he had scattered around.

He bent and kissed my forehead. "You're welcome. I told you I wanted to make it special."

"It was definitely special," I confirmed.

He grinned. "Yeah it was, and I am the luckiest husband in the world."

"You like saying that word, huh," I teased.

He smiled, trailing little kisses along my face. He took my left hand in his, bringing it to his face and kissing the rings that sat on my finger. "I love saying that word," he murmured. When he looked into my eyes I could see all the love for me shining through them. I snuggled against him, loving how warm he was. We lapsed into a contented silence for a few minutes. He just lay at my side, playing with my rings, twirling them around my finger.

"Are you okay? I know that hurt you," he said finally.

I knew I needed to tell him the truth, he would know if I was lying anyway. "I'm fine, honestly. It hurt at first, but it got better," I promised. The pain hadn't lasted forever; his kissing and gentle movements had soon chased that hurt away. "Did it hurt you?" We'd talked about that before, and I was genuinely curious as to the answer.

He laughed, shaking his head. "No, Riley Bear, it didn't."

"Really? Well don't boys get it easy," I joked, rolling my eyes.

He grinned smugly, bending his head and kissing me until I could barely even remember my own name.

"I love you," he breathed, running his fingers through my tangled hair, smoothing it down for me. My eyelids were getting heavier and heavier so I nodded and snuggled closer to him. His lips grazed my shoulder as he pulled the sheets up around us, tangling his legs in with mine.

• • •

I WOKE AN HOUR later, with my body wrapped tightly in Clay's. I was a little achy, my muscles a little tight, but it was a pleasant feeling. A little reminder of Clay and what we'd done. I smiled happily and raised my head to see Clay's angelic face inches from mine. He looked so beautiful I couldn't help the smile that spread across my face. *This boy is my husband. I get to keep him forever.* I felt like the luckiest girl in the world.

"What are you looking at me for, Riley Bear?" he muttered, with his eyes still closed.

I giggled at being caught. "Wow, you really do know me well, how am I ever supposed to get one over on you?" I asked, grinning.

His arms tightened on me as he pressed his forehead to mine. "You don't need to get one over on me; I'll give you whatever you want."

"Mmm, you know what I want!" I flirted, inching closer to him and rubbing my nose up the side of his.

"What?" he responded. A smile tugged at the corner of his lips as he rubbed his hands over my back, probably thinking I was going to say him.

"Slot machines!" I cried excitedly, jumping out of the bed and laughing as his eyes popped open in shock.

He laughed and dragged a hand through his messy hair. "You and those damn slot machines," he joked, rolling his eyes playfully.

I raised one eyebrow. "David gave me a thousand bucks; want to help me spend it?" I asked, literally jumping up and down excitedly.

"A thousand bucks? Wow, Riley, we'll be back up here in thirty minutes the way you pump those machines," he joked.

I jumped back on the bed, pushing on his shoulders, making him fall back onto the mattress. I bent my head and blew as raspberry on his stomach as I tickled his side. He laughed but easily pushed me off, pinning me to the bed. "I think I'll have to hold your money for you. I'll give you maybe two hundred bucks an hour, then that way you won't run out too quickly," he suggested, tickling my sides, making me squirm. He kissed me for a minute and then pulled away, sitting up before helping me up. "Come on then, Mrs Preston, let's go spend some money." He rubbed his hands together excitedly, grinning.

chapter
sixteen

W e got dressed slowly. Clay helped me with my jeans, taking his time, seeming to make sure that he touched every part of my hips and stomach while he did so. I couldn't help but smile at the love and affection that I could see shining from his eyes as his fingers brushed over my skin, as if he'd wanted to touch every part of me again. After pulling my hair into a ponytail, we left to go downstairs to the casino. Clay phoned Tom when we were in the lobby to see where they were, and was told that they were already gambling, so we headed in to meet them.

The casino was already alive with activity even though it was only afternoon. The noises of the machines, the lights, the excited people milling around, all of it made my palms sweaty with excitement.

Ben spotted us first. "Hey, if it isn't the newlyweds! No regrets this morning? You two do remember you got married, right?" he teased, laughing.

Clay grabbed my hand and brought it to his mouth, kissing my rings gently. "Yep we remember, and nope no regrets," he confirmed, wrapping his arm around my waist and pulling me to his side as he grinned down at me. "I'm gonna get some chips and play some cards. Want me to get you some change for the slots, Riley Bear?"

"Sure, thanks." I pulled out the envelope full of cash and held it out to him.

Clay just shook his head, pushing it back into my pocket. "Don't worry, Mrs Preston, I've got money." He bent his head and planted a tender kiss on my forehead before he turned and walked away towards the exchange booth, with Tom following along behind him.

Craig stepped forward, grinning at me. "I can't believe you two last night. And that dance on stage was awesome, Riley."

Dance? "What dance?" I asked, confused.

He burst out laughing, and so did the girls that were standing there. "What dance, are you kidding me?" Craig asked incredulously. I shook my head, frowning and thinking back to last night. I remembered getting married, and then we started drinking again in the bar, and then I woke up in bed. I certainly didn't remember dancing.

"No, what dance?" *He's trying to trick you, Riley, don't fall for it.*

Craig smirked at me, chuckling under his breath as he pulled out his cell phone, fiddling with it. A few seconds later he passed it to me, nodding down at it. I frowned, taking it out of his hand and looking down at the screen. On it there was a girl in a black dress doing an extremely sexy lap dance to someone who was sat on a chair. She walked around behind him, and I gasped when I saw that the boy was Clay. *Oh my God! Is that me?* I blushed, horrified, but then I saw the look on Clay's face on the video, he was clearly loving it which seemed to make it all right somehow. I started to giggle quietly before it turned in to a full on laugh. I looked at Craig and the girls who were laughing too.

"That's awkward," I muttered, wincing.

Craig raised one eyebrow at me, grinning. "That was seriously hot. If you ever want to spread those around, I'll take one."

I playfully slapped him on the chest and waved my left hand in front of his face, fluttering my fingers. "Less of the flirting, I'm a married woman you know." I grinned at my own words. The more I thought about being married to Clay, the more I fell in love with the idea. From the corner of my eye, I spotted Clay walking back to us. I held out the phone to him and watched as his eyes widened, his whole body seeming to stiffen.

"Holy crap, I forgot about that! Damn, Riley, that was so hot," he breathed, pulling me to his side. He held out the phone to Craig and smirked at him. "I definitely want a copy of that."

I smiled, going up on tiptoes as I pressed my mouth to his ear. "You don't need a copy of that, Clay; you ever want to see that again all you have to do is ask. As your wife it's now my job to make you happy. So maybe next time I'll do it without the dress," I whispered. I felt his body tense, and he moaned quietly, closing his eyes, seeming to hold his breath. "Come on, husband, let's go spend some money," I chirped, patting his behind playfully and taking the pot of change that he got for me. I looked down into it and squealed happily. *Jeez, there must be like fifty bucks worth of quarters in this pot! This is going to be fun!*

He walked me to the slot machines where Rachel was already feeding the slots like her life depended on it. He kissed my forehead, smiling, before heading off towards the blackjack tables.

Rachel watched him leave with a smirk on her face before turning to me and raising one eyebrow. "So you two finally did it last night then?"

"This morning, actually," I corrected. "Apparently I fell asleep in the bar and didn't wake up till this morning." I shrugged, grabbing a handful of coins and pumping them into the machine one after the other.

"So..." she trailed off, looking at me with an expression that clearly meant 'spill all now'.

I giggled. "I'm not gonna give you any details, Rach, but I will say this, Clay is very talented." I winked at her, chewing on my lip as I remembered how beautiful it was.

Her mouth popped open. "Really? Damn, I knew I should have tried for him last year." She slapped her forehead in mock exasperation as she shook her head.

I laughed and threw a coin at her. "That's my husband you're talking about, girlie," I scolded, pretending to be annoyed.

She grinned, her gaze falling to my hand as she shook her head in awe. "I still can't believe you two got married last night. He is so sweet, Riley, and he loves you so much, and damn he is so hot! You're so lucky." She smiled, looking genuinely happy for me and I couldn't help but grin proudly.

"I know I am. So, what about you, any action with the best man?" I asked, waggling my eyebrows.

She nodded, sighing dreamily. "Oh yeah! And let me tell you, what Tom lacks in skill downstairs he more than makes up for with those sweet hands of his."

I burst out laughing, causing people around us to tut and give us funny looks so we quietened our voices, chatting about her night while we fed the slots.

Finally I ran out of money so I decided to go find Clay and see if he wanted to get something to eat, I was getting a little hungry. I called his cell to see where he was, and he informed me that he was still playing cards. He suggested that I meet him in the bar so that he could play another hand.

As I weaved through the casino and headed to the bar that he suggested, I spotted him sitting at a table with three other men. I waved, and he smiled. "I'll be done in a couple of minutes, then we'll go eat, okay?" he called to me as I walked past. I nodded and hopped up onto a stool at the bar, ordering a coffee. I didn't even get half way down before he walked up behind me and grabbed me. I squealed as he pulled me off of the stool, spinning me in a little circle.

"Wow, Riley, you were gone for over an hour and a half with that money, you really made that last. I was expecting that to be gone within thirty minutes," he teased.

I laughed thinking he was joking, but actually he looked serious.

I slapped his chest. "Hey, I'm not that bad," I pouted.

He laughed and leant forward, biting on my pouty lip, sucking it gently. I instantly forgot how hungry I was as I started to think about going upstairs and having him make love to me again. "You are that bad," he countered. "How much money do you think was in that tub?"

I shrugged. "I don't know, fifty dollars?" I guessed, smiling guiltily because he'd wasted his money on me. He just laughed, shaking his head and kissed my forehead. "How much?" I asked, when he didn't tell me.

"There was two hundred bucks in there, Riley," he answered, shrugging nonchalantly.

I gasped in shock. "You're fucking kidding me!" I shouted. Instantly I remembered where I was, and put my hand over my mouth because of my foul language.

Clay chuckled and put his hand over the top of mine, his eyes amused. "No I'm not *'fucking kidding you'*," he mocked, doing a lousy impression of my voice. "Anyway, did you have fun?" he asked, looking into my eyes. *Yeah of course I did, I love the slots.* I nodded in response because we both still had one hand covering my mouth. "Well good, that's all that counts. Besides, I did well at the blackjack table." He smirked at me cockily as he said the last bit.

Did well? He won some money? "You did?"

He was beaming; his eyes were dancing with excitement. "Yep, hold out your hand," he instructed, digging in his pocket for something. "I had to spend fifteen hundred bucks on my stake, but, what's mine is yours now, Mrs Preston." He dropped four little plastic poker chips into my hand. I pulled it back to look at them; I had no idea what they were. They had numbers across the middle. I shrugged and looked up at Clay who was watching me, obviously waiting for my reaction. He raised his eyebrows and nodded back down to the chips.

I looked at them again; there was a red and black one, a blue and black, a yellow and black one, and a green and black. I turned them and looked at them closer because there was obviously something I was missing. The blue one had $50,000 written on it. I gasped. *What the hell? No way!*

"Holy shit, Clay! You won fifty thousand dollars?" I almost screamed, looking at his face for confirmation. He clenched his jaw tightly and quickly looked around. *Oh whoops, okay I should not have shouted that in the middle of the bar! But is he seriously telling me that he won fifty thousand dollars, and only spent fifteen hundred?*

He shook his head and chuckled. "No, Riley." I let out my breath in a big gust. *I knew I had to be wrong. You can't win fifty thousand in an hour and a half.* Clay raised one finger, moving the chips around in my hand, separating them. He pointed to the blue one. "This one is worth fifty thousand," he said. My breath caught in my throat as my skin started to prickle with sensation. Before I had a chance to react he pointed to the yellow one. "This one's worth twenty thousand." *Holy shit, he won seventy thousand?* "The green one's two thousand." He grinned, watching my face as I struggled to comprehend what he was telling me. "And this one," he fingered the last one, "this red one's worth a hundred thousand," he concluded with a chuckle.

Oh dear God, I'm going to lose them. My hand is sweating, I'm going to drop his little chips, and he'll never forgive me. I closed my hand tightly around the chips in case I dropped them or something as my breath caught in my throat. *He won a hundred and seventy two thousand dollars? Is this some kind of bad joke? Is that even possible?* I couldn't breathe. My heart was beating fast, and I felt a little dizzy.

"Shit, Riley! Sit down, are you okay?" he asked, clearly panicked as he guided me to sit in a chair. "Can I get a glass of water for my wife, please?" he asked the barman quickly. He rubbed a hand across my forehead, pulling me into a hug. "It's okay, Riley. Shit, you're scaring me." He knelt in front of me, his eyes alight with concern. I couldn't speak so I just took his hand, pushing the chips into his palm and closing his fingers around them. Where I'd been holding them so tightly, my fingers were aching. "I told you, that's yours," Clay muttered, trying to give them back to me again. I shook my head and drank the glass of water that the barman was offering. Slowly I started to calm down, it was getting easier to breathe, and my head was losing some of the fog. Clay just sat in front of me his forehead touching mine rubbing my hands, looking at me worriedly.

"You won one hundred and seventy-two thousand dollars?" I whispered when I was in control again.

He nodded. "*We* won, it's yours too," he corrected, kissing my forehead gently.

I swallowed loudly. "Is this a joke, Clay, because if it is it's not funny." I narrowed my eyes at him. *If this is a joke then it is a pretty sick one.* He smiled at me happily, and I could tell by the excitement sparkling in his eyes that he wasn't actually joking. "You really did didn't you!"

He nodded and pulled me into a big hug, lifting me off of the chair and spinning me around in a little circle in celebration. "Now we can definitely get a place," he boasted, winking at me.

Oh God, Clay has just won $172,000 playing cards! He grabbed my hand and tried to put the chips back into my palm, but I just clenched my hand into a fist. "I don't want your money, Clay." I kissed him passionately. I wasn't interested in his money or his status or anything like that. For me, I loved every single thing about Clay Preston, the money was irrelevant. He kissed me back, wrapping me tightly in his arms and I felt completely whole, completely content, and the luckiest girl in the world just because this incredible boy loved me.

Clay pulled back and grinned at me, taking my hand and interlacing our fingers. "Shall we go eat, Mrs Preston?" he suggested, pushing the poker chips into his pocket as he nodded at the little restaurant behind us.

It wasn't too busy so we were seated immediately. Clay passed me a menu and smirked at me cockily. A couple of minutes later the waitress came over with her order pad. Clay grinned at me. "So what do you want to eat, Riley Bear? Steak? Lobster?"

I laughed and shook my head, closing my menu. "Cheeseburger and curly fries, extra tomato ketchup, and no salad, please," I told the waitress.

She nodded before smiling seductively at Clay, but it looked like he barely even noticed her because he was too busy rolling my rings around on my finger. "That sounds good. I'll have the same, but with some coleslaw on the side, please," he murmured, still seeming fascinated by my jewellery on my ring finger.

The waitress looked at his hands playing with my rings and then at me. She sighed in defeat, walking back to the kitchen to place our order. *Poor woman, I know how she feels; looking at him makes me feel like that too.*

Clay smiled over at me. "So I was thinking, when we get back we need to sort out money and stuff. Instead of opening a new account we could just add your name to mine," he said casually, as if this happened every day. I choked on my orange juice, making him look at me weirdly. "You all right, Riley Bear?"

"Clay, what are you talking about accounts? You mean like bank accounts?" I asked, shocked.

He nodded. "Well yeah, of course. We're married now, what's mine is yours. It's easier though if we just add you on, I could put the winnings straight in there now before we leave and then just add you on to my account," he suggested, shrugging. I stared at him with my mouth hanging open, unsure as to what I was supposed to say to that. "What?" He laughed, reaching over to my face and closing my mouth with one finger.

I shook my head in rejection, not having the right words to express my shock. "Just because we're married doesn't mean I want half of your money," I protested.

"I know that, but what I'm saying is, it doesn't matter if you want it or not, we're married now, so half of everything I have is rightfully yours. Hell, you can have everything, all I want is you." He shrugged nonchalantly, and I felt the smile tug at the corners of my mouth because of his sweet and romantic words.

"Clay, that's really sweet honestly, but I-" He put his hand over my mouth, silencing me before I could finish. His eyes were firm, his expression deadset.

"I'm not gonna argue with you about this," he stated. "You're my wife now. Husbands and wives share everything. I don't know what we're gonna do about the whole moving out thing until we've spoken to our parents, but that money will be perfect for a deposit on an apartment or something. It'll pay for your college fees, and there'll still be some left over for savings and stuff. When I finish senior year I'll be earning, and you'll still be a student, so whatever I earn will be yours too. There is nothing to talk about. End of discussion."

I sighed. I knew he was right. I had to finish my junior year, and then had another year left of high school after that. Then, if all went to plan I'd have another four years of college after too. I wouldn't have anything to give him or share with him for a while because of studying.

I nodded. "Okay," I reluctantly agreed. He grinned and at the same time the waitress brought our food over.

• • •

AFTER EATING WE played the slots again for a little while and I managed to spend all of David's money easily. Clay just watched me with an amused smile stretched across his face, his arms around my waist the whole time.

We all decided to take it easier than last night and only went out for a few drinks and a show before heading back to our rooms just before midnight. We had to leave at nine o'clock in the morning to make the long drive home, so no one wanted to do that with a raging hangover. Luckily all of our parents had consented to let us all have Monday off school so we could make the trip longer.

I was dreading going home for a few reasons. Blake and the police were one reason. Going back to school was another, because that would mean that I couldn't get to hang out with Clay as much. And the most obvious reason, the one that kept me awake for hours worrying about it - telling our parents that we had gotten married. Clay had promised he would do it, and whatever happened we would be together, but the thought of the anger or disapproval that we were going to get made me feel sick to my stomach.

I woke in the morning with Clay spooning me from behind, his arms so tight around me that I could barely move an inch.

I nuzzled into the crook of his arm that rested under my neck. "Clay?" I whispered.

"Mmm?" he mumbled sleepily. I'd kept him awake half the night because I couldn't sleep for worrying about going home, so I had made him distract me and give me other, more pleasant things to think about. I giggled at the thought. *No wonder he's still tired today...*

"I love you," I whispered to him, smiling.

He kissed the back of my head. "I love you too," he murmured, waking up now.

I snuggled back into him, brushing my naked body against his teasingly. "Want to make the most of the big four poster bed while we still have it?" I offered, chewing on my lip, hoping he'd say yes.

He groaned and bent forward, nibbling on my earlobe. "Jeez, Riley Bear, are you trying to kill me?"

I giggled and nodded. "Yep, then I get everything. Death by sex, I'm being kind though, it's a pretty good way to go," I joked.

He laughed, rolling me onto my back. "You're right that's a pretty good way to go." He kissed me until I was almost dizzy.

After he'd made love to me, we both laid there breathless, just looking at each other. I was so happy that my eyes were prickling with tears. *I can't believe I get to spend the rest of my life with this amazing boy.*

"That was…" he trailed off, still breathing hard as he swept my hair over my shoulder.

"Awesome?" I finished. He smiled and shook his head. "Incredible?" I tried again, smiling now too. He shook his head again, propping himself up on one elbow, beaming down at me. "Brilliant?"

"No, Mrs Preston, that was mind-blowing." He dipped his head, kissing my nose, my forehead, and my cheeks before making his way back to my mouth.

chapter
seventeen

By the time we were almost home, I felt sick with nerves. Clay had literally just disconnected a call to his parents, in which he'd asked them to meet us at my house so we could talk.

"So were they all right with that? Did they think something was wrong or..." I asked, wringing my hands together.

He took my hands in his and looked at me. "Breathe, Riley," he cooed. "Everything's going to be fine. And if it's not, well then we'll just check into a hotel or something until we find an apartment. Don't worry." He bent forward, kissing my forehead softly. All the girls were smiling at me sympathetically.

When we pulled up outside my house, Clay grabbed our bags from the back of the van. I stood there shaking and not wanting to go inside. The drive to get to Vegas had seemed to take forever, but the drive home to face this meeting had seemed to go by in the blink of an eye. Old Father Time was definitely playing tricks with my frayed nerves.

Rachel climbed out, pulling me into a hug. "Call me later. And if you need a place to stay you can stay at mine, I'm sure my mom won't mind. I don't think she'd let Clay stay, but he could probably stay with one of the guys."

I nodded numbly in response. Clay grabbed my hand and pulled me towards the house. I waved weakly at the guys as they pulled out of my drive, before turning to look at his handsome face making me feel better instantly.

"You ready, Mrs Preston?" he asked, wrapping his arm around me tightly.

I nodded. "As ready as I'll ever be," I confirmed. I wasn't going to feel any better the longer we left it, so we may as well get it over and done with. He smiled, and I took a deep breath as we stepped over the threshold into my house.

I could hear chattering coming from the direction of the lounge, so we headed in there. As we stepped into the room, they all looked up expectantly. My mom obviously thought we were going to announce that we were together because she had on her gloating 'I know something you don't know' face as she sat there, grinning smugly at us.

"Hey, guys, how was your trip?" David asked, jumping out of his seat and hugging me, and then holding out a hand to Clay who shook it firmly.

"It was really great," Clay replied. I stiffened as we hugged and exchanged pleasantries knowing that this was it, that he was about to tell them that we'd gotten married by accident. I had no idea how badly they were going to take it.

"So what's so important that we had to come over as soon as you get back?" Linda, Clay's mom asked, smirking at my mom. I glanced between the two of them quizzically. My mom had obviously let slip that we were together. I glanced up at Clay to see he was grinning like crazy. I frowned at his expression. *We're about to tell our parents that their teenage children got drunk and married in Vegas, and he's having a good time? He really is weird!* I couldn't control my body; I was sweating like a pig. I pulled Clay's arm off my waist and held his hand tightly, pulling it across my body so I could shrink behind his shoulder.

"Well, we have something to tell you, and we wanted to do it with everyone together, it'll be easier that way," Clay explained, still smiling happily. I held my breath waiting for him to say it. "Riley and I got married while we were in Vegas," he added simply.

I pressed myself closer to him and watched their reactions. Our moms both looked shocked, their eyes and mouths popping open. David looked confused, as if he hadn't understood what Clay had said. And Clay's dad, Richard, actually burst out laughing.

Okay I wasn't expecting that...

Everyone looked at him quizzically, but he just laughed harder and harder. David started to chuckle too. Richard shook his head and slapped his thigh as he continued to chuckle. "That's a good one, you almost got me there, I was like, what? Then I realised," he said, wiping a tear from his eye.

He thinks we're joking? I looked at my mom for help, only to see she was staring at our hands with the matching wedding rings. Clay shook his head. "It's not a joke, Dad, we really got married in Vegas," he said seriously. Richard stopped laughing immediately, and his face started to go red. I flicked my eyes to David who now looked murderously angry.

Before I could even flinch, David jumped out of the chair and grabbed Clay by his shirt, pulling him up to his feet, his face contorted with rage. I screamed from the shock and tried to get up, but Clay pushed me back down on the sofa, keeping his hand firmly on my shoulder so I couldn't stand. "You married my daughter in Vegas? Fucking hell, Clay, what the hell were you thinking? You two are just kids! She's a baby for goodness sake!" David shouted angrily, his fists tightening on Clay's shirt.

Clay didn't even flinch. "I know we're young, David, but I love your daughter more than anything."

Without warning David punched him full in the face almost knocking him over. I gasped, shocked that this had escalated that fast. Richard jumped up and grabbed David. "That's my son!" he ranted, shoving him away from Clay. Everyone was on their feet now, shouting at each other. David was trying to get to Clay, Richard was holding him back. Even our moms were shouting at their husbands, crying. Through my tears I looked at Clay worriedly. His lip was bleeding, and he looked angry. He grabbed my hand and forced me behind him as David broke free of Richard and lunged to grab my hand.

"You're not staying married to him, Riley! Get up to your room now! Tomorrow we go see a lawyer and get this mess sorted out," David ordered, pointing to the stairs and looking at me sternly.

I shook my head in rejection. "We're not getting divorced," I said quietly, gripping hold of the back of Clay's shirt. I felt his muscles tense as David tried to lunge for me again. Clay turned his body quickly so I was out of reach.

"Like hell you're not! You're getting divorced; we're not going to stand by while you two throw your lives away. You're not even dating, you're kids!" Richard shouted.

My mom and Linda exchanged a knowing look. "David, calm down, we need to talk about this," my mom implored, stepping to his side. "There has to be something that can be done without a divorce. Is the marriage even legal? Riley's not eighteen, and we didn't give permission. So maybe an annulment?" she suggested as if that would solve all of the problems.

Not legal? Oh God, are we not actually married? I felt sick with disappointment. I gulped and forced myself to stop thinking about it, there was no time for worrying about it now. If it wasn't legal then we'd deal with that later and get married again. "We're not getting an annulment either. Clay and I want to be married," I said confidently.

From the corner of my eye I saw Richard's hand move. Pain exploded across my face making me yelp as his palm connected with my cheek. Instantly Clay let out what sounded like a growl and grabbed his father, shoving him hard against the wall.

"You don't ever touch her! I don't care if you are my father, if you ever lay a finger on my wife again I *will* kill you," he barked. Richard cringed and nodded. Clay's jaw tightened as if he was trying to stay in control of himself. He turned round to face David, his eyes warning. "That goes for you too," he spat. He stalked over to my side, tenderly stroking the sore skin of my cheek. "I love Riley, and she loves me. We're staying married. It doesn't matter how old we are. I thought you'd be happy for us, but obviously I was wrong," he told them without taking his eyes off of me. "Come on, Riley Bear, let's go." He took my hand and guided me to turn, giving me a gentle push towards the door as he followed closely behind.

I was numb. Were we seriously about to leave home and cut off from our parents? I could barely comprehend what walking out of the house would mean. Suddenly Clay's hand was ripped from mine. I turned back quickly, only to see him on the floor. David was on top of him, his whole face angry as his fist connected with Clay's cheek. "You're not taking my daughter anywhere, you stupid little prick," he ranted as punched him again.

Clay threw him off easily without hurting him too much. I noticed that he hadn't made any moves to attack anyone other than the threat he made to Richard, he was firmly in control, unlike our parents. Clay pushed himself up, grabbing my hand and pulling me out of the house and over to his car. On the way past he grabbed our luggage that luckily had been left on the porch steps. He threw them into the back of the car angrily and then opened my door for me, making sure I was in safely before he walked around to the driver's side. Behind us my mom came bursting through the front door with Linda hot on her heels.

I opened my window so I could talk to them. "Wait! Where are you going? Don't just leave, please, we can talk about this. David will calm down eventually," my mom pleaded, stepping up to the window and wiping the tears from her face. Clay was in the car now, starting the engine. His whole posture was tense and alert.

"Mom, we can't talk to them while they're like that. Look what he did to Clay," I croaked, whimpering as I looked at Clay's rapidly bruising face and split lip.

My mom's chin trembled as she looked over at him. "I'm so sorry, Clay, I can't believe David would do that to you, he loves you."

"Sandra, it's fine. We need to go now though, I don't want Riley anywhere near them while they're like that, she could get hurt," Clay said angrily, looking back towards the house.

"But where will you go?" Linda asked weakly.

"We'll find a motel or something," Clay replied, sounding unsure.

"Do you need money?" Linda reached into her pocket, pulling out what looked like a hundred dollars and offering it to me through the window.

Clay shook his head. "No, we're fine, but thanks for the offer, Mom." He smiled sadly at her.

"Please don't go," she begged.

My mom reached through the window and gripped my left hand, looking at my rings. "They're beautiful, honey. Congratulations, both of you," she said, smiling despite the tears that glistened in her eyes.

I smiled gratefully. "Thanks, Mom. I'll call you." I hugged her awkwardly through the car window.

"Take care of her for me," my mom said to Clay over my shoulder.

He smiled at her. "I will, I promise."

She blew him a kiss. "I know you will. You're a good boy." She smiled at us both before stepping back to let Linda closer to the window.

Linda sniffed loudly. "Call me when you get to where you're going. Don't let them drive you away, please," she begged, hugging me.

"We'll call you tomorrow while they're at work maybe we could come over and pick up some of our clothes and stuff?" Clay asked hopefully. She nodded in agreement. Behind the car, the front door opened again, slamming against the side of the house noisily. David and Richard started making their way down the drive to the car, arguing between themselves.

"We need to go. Love you, Mom," Clay stated, putting the car in drive. Linda stepped backwards, and Clay pulled out of the drive. I turned in my seat to see our mom's hugging and crying, but they both were smiling weakly. David still looked angry as hell, and Richard just looked like he was still in shock. I waved a goodbye, and then burst into tears.

Clay drove us away and stopped after a few minutes, pulling up down a side road. He sighed and reached over, unbuckling my seatbelt. He gently pulled me onto his lap and put his forehead to mine. "I am so sorry, Riley Bear, I'm so sorry."

I looked at his beautiful face, wincing as I saw how sore it looked. His cheekbone had a red tinge to it, he had a cut on the bridge of his nose, purplish shadows were already forming under his eyes, and his lip was split. I touched his face while hissing through my teeth; he winced but smiled to cover it up.

"Oh God, Clay, are you okay?" I asked as a fresh round of tears started because he was in pain.

He pulled me into a hug. "I'm fine. I'm just so sorry that this happened," he replied sadly.

I pulled back to look at him, needing to ask him something. "Are you sorry you married me?"

He shook his head immediately. "I will never be sorry that I married you," he said sincerely. I breathed a sigh of relief and felt my body sag against his. "Are you sorry you married me?" he asked, looking worried about my answer.

"Well the wedding night was a bit of a let-down," I joked, chuckling wickedly.

He laughed, bending his head and kissing me, but he pulled back quickly touching his split lip. "Ow."

I put my forehead back to his, just looking into his eyes that I loved so much. "What are we gonna do, Clay?" I asked. Tears continued to trickle down my face slowly as I struggled to regain my composure. He kissed them away gently even though it probably hurt him to do it.

"Let's go find a motel or something for now. Tomorrow we'll go pick up our clothes and stuff, and then we can start apartment hunting," he said easily, as if this was something that happened every day.

I traced my finger over the bridge of his nose, across his cheek and along the line of his jaw. My love for him was overwhelming as I looked down at his face. He was my husband. It didn't matter about anything else; he would be the only thing that it would hurt me to lose.

I sighed. "Okay," I agreed. "Let's go check into a motel. But first we'd better stop and get some stuff for your face, because, baby, you look a mess," I teased, smiling sadly.

"Yeah but you still love me," he said confidently.

"Hmm, I don't know, your face was my favourite part." I narrowed my eyes playfully as I climbed back into my seat. He laughed and rolled his eyes, waiting until I had my belt back on before he started the car again.

We stopped at the nearest pharmacy and I jumped out buying cotton wool and antiseptic. After, we headed to the nearest motel. As we walked to the reception, the girl behind the counter was eyeing Clay appreciatively, even though he looked a little worse for wear. I couldn't exactly blame her though, because the cuts and bruises gave him a bad boy edge that really worked well on him.

"Hi, can we get a room?" Clay asked her.

"Sure. You want two singles?" she questioned, eyeing me with annoyance.

He laughed. "No I think my wife and I would like a double if you have one, but I'm pretty sure we could work a single too, right, beautiful girl?" he replied, winking at me. The girl shot me a dirty look as he paid for the room, but then went back to undressing him with her eyes right in front of me.

"He rocks those bruises, huh?" I mused as she looked him over again.

She shot me another dirty look and nodded. "He certainly does," she agreed. She smiled at Clay unashamedly. "Usually I don't go for married guys, but for you, I'll make an exception," she flirted.

I laughed incredulously. *Seriously, she's hitting on him with me standing right here? What a slut!* "Yeah okay, good luck with that one," I retorted, waving my hand dismissively.

Clay shook his head disbelievingly and wrapped his arm around my waist, pulling me to him and kissing me forcefully. The faint metallic taste told me that his lip had started to bleed again, but he didn't seem to care as he showed the girl that he wasn't interested in her.

She slapped the key on the counter to get our attention. "I gave you room four. It has a bath and a TV," she said, still smiling at Clay as if she had a chance.

"Thanks, but I don't think we'll be watching much TV tonight." Clay smirked at her as he took my hand and dragged me out of the reception. On the way to our room, I grabbed a bag of ice from the cooler so I could use it on his face. The room was basic, but at least it was clean and had a double bed, TV, fridge and air conditioning, it had its own bathroom with a bath and separate shower which was all we needed.

As soon as he shut the door, he grabbed me into another kiss, but I pushed him off quickly and shook my head. "Sit," I instructed, pulling out the dresser chair for him. He smiled and sat down obediently, watching as I ripped open the things we'd bought at the pharmacy. I set to work cleaning his cuts and then setting the ice to his face to try and keep some of the bruises away.

As I worked, he pulled me down on his lap. His fingers trailed up and down my thighs, distracting me from my task. I slapped his hands away playfully. "Will you stop, I'm trying to concentrate," I scolded, trying to sound stern. He smiled his cocky grin and moved his hands back to my legs again, squeezing my thigh. "Clay, stop! I need to clean your face up." I tried my best not to smile, but I was failing miserably.

His hand went to the back of my head, guiding my mouth to his and kissing me softly. I could taste the antiseptic on his mouth.

"I love you so much, Mrs Preston," he whispered, putting his forehead to mine and stroking my face.

"I love you too, Clay." I sighed, thinking about what my mom had said earlier. *Are we really not married properly?* That thought crushed me a little inside. I loved being married to him, committing to him and giving myself to him completely. "Clay, was it really not legal because I'm not eighteen?" I asked.

He frowned and shrugged. "I don't know. We'll have to look into it I guess. I hope it was," he said quietly. I really hoped it was too. I'd never really thought about being married to Clay, but now that I was I wanted it so badly I would do anything for it.

"If it's not legal then I'll just have to marry you again in a year," I suggested. That was the only solution; we would get married again on my birthday if it wasn't legal.

He sighed dramatically. "Oh well I guess I can cope with another wedding night, seeing as I let you down the first time," he teased. I laughed, and he grinned, tucking my hair behind my ear. "How about I order us a pizza?" he suggested. I nodded not even realising how hungry I was until he'd mentioned food.

chapter eighteen

After a restless night I woke up early. Rolling over tentatively I saw that Clay was still fast asleep next to me. I gulped as I looked at his face. It had gotten a lot worse overnight. He had two purple shadows under his eyes, and his cheek looked like he was blushing; the cuts over his nose and on his lip had healed but still looked sore and angry. I sighed and climbed out of the bed slowly, being careful not to wake him. After pulling on my clothes, I snuck out of the room and padded over to the benches that were on the grass out the front of the motel. I'd been thinking about this all night, I didn't want to move out and get a place if we didn't have to. I didn't want Clay to have to earn money to pay the bills if there was some way we could work this out with our parents.

My mom and David loved Clay dearly; it had just been a shock to them, that's all. Maybe now that it had sunk in a little more, we would be able to talk rationally about it all. I was hoping that if I called them maybe I could convince them to let Clay and I live there together. He practically lived at my house anyway so it would only be making it more official.

I dialled my house, silently praying that my mom would answer. I was still mad at David for hurting Clay but, over the course of the night, Clay had convinced me that I shouldn't hold a grudge, that he was only looking out for his daughter and that he hadn't meant it. Although I was still angry, I needed to get it sorted out quickly before Clay and I needed to rent a place. I didn't want to stay in a motel forever.

I held my breath while the phone rang; eventually David's familiar voice greeted me.

Please be okay! "Hi, it's me," I said weakly, closing my eyes, waiting for his reaction.

"Riley, where the hell are you, young lady? You get back here right now so we can sort this damn mess out," he growled.

I gulped. He hadn't calmed down at all. "David, there's nothing to sort out, Clay and I love each other, we want to be married." I tried out my most persuasive voice in a bid to calm him down. This act usually worked to his face, but I'd never tried it over the phone before.

"There sure as hell *is* something to sort out! You can't be married at seventeen for goodness sake. Get home, now," he ordered. I flinched from the hard, authoritative tone of his voice.

"No," I protested. "I just wondered if there was anything we could do to sort all of this out. Us stay married but come home?" I inquired hopefully, even though I knew it was pointless to ask.

He gasped. "Are you kidding? If you want to come home, then come home, but you do it alone. You understand what I'm saying?" he shouted. I could hear my mom crying in the background, telling him to calm down.

"David, please don't make me choose between you and Clay," I begged.

"I'm not allowing this, Riley. Come home now and stop being such a stubborn child."

I closed my eyes and swiped away the tear that fell. I loved David; I always thought of him as my dad, it was breaking my heart that he would make me do this. "I love Clay." I whispered.

"Then you're staying married, is that what you're saying?" he asked condescendingly.

"Yeah," I croaked.

"Well then I guess you've made your choice. When it all goes wrong your mother and I will be here to pick up the pieces, but I can't condone a teenage marriage. I love you, Riley." His voice broke through emotion as he spoke, and my heart hurt at the sound of it.

"I love you too," I whispered. I heard my mom wailing in the background, and he disconnected the call.

It felt like it was killing me, but I knew I'd made the right choice; I loved Clay with all of my heart. I wanted to be Mrs Preston. David was wrong; it wouldn't fall to pieces because Clay and I were meant to be together. In time he'd see that too.

I wiped my face and went to the nearest store to buy the classifieds, on my way back to the motel I stopped and bought doughnuts and coffees. Clay was still asleep as I slipped back into our motel room half an hour later. "Clay?" I whispered, sitting on the bed next to him. He grunted and moved to wrap his arms around me so I quickly moved the coffee and doughnuts out of the way as he threw his arm over my legs. "Clay?" I repeated a little louder.

He opened his eyes slowly and took in my already dressed form holding breakfast. "Hey you," he croaked sleepily

"Morning." I forced a smile, pretending I wasn't hurting inside. He smiled back and pushed himself up to sitting just as I held out one of the coffees to him. "I got you a jelly doughnut." I set the box on the bed, pulling a disgusted face and faking a shudder.

He laughed and picked one up, taking an enormous bite. "You're organised this morning. Why didn't you wake me? I would have come with you," he said, rubbing his hand up my leg lovingly.

I shrugged. "I wanted to get you breakfast in bed." I took a sip of my coffee and opened the paper, flicking through until I found the for rents section, then snuggled closer to him and laid it out across my legs so we could both read it.

"You bought a listings paper?" he asked, seeming proud of me.

I nodded. "Yeah," I confirmed. I knew I needed to tell him about calling home. "Clay, I rang David this morning, there isn't any way we can go home."

He sighed deeply. "I'm sorry, Riley Bear. He'll come around when he sees that this wasn't a mistake. When he sees how much we love each other everything will be fine," he assured me, rubbing my leg soothingly.

I kissed his lips softly and smiled. "Yeah I know. It's just sad that it had to happen this way. I figure that we'll have to skip school today and get everything sorted. I don't mind this place, but I don't want to stay here too long." I turned my nose up at the small, cramped room. Sooner or later we'd start tripping over ourselves in here.

I smiled and resigned myself to the fact that we would be renting an apartment. Part of me loved the idea of it, our first home, I just wished that Clay wouldn't have to pay for it and use his wages to pay the bills because I wouldn't be able to help being at school. At least we had the money from Vegas, that would pay for the deposit and rent. Clay didn't want to spend much of it though, he said he wanted to save it and use it to buy a place in a few years or at least use it as a deposit on our own place because it wouldn't stretch very far nowadays.

I climbed back on the bed with him, and we scanned through the paper. We found three apartments for rent in this area. Two of them were two bedroomed, and one was a one bed, they were all furnished which was perfect considering we had nothing. I called Rachel while Clay phoned the agents and arranged viewings of the apartments this afternoon.

"Hey, Rach," I greeted as she answered.

"Oh I've been so worried about you! How did it go?" she asked.

I took a deep breath before answering. "Not too good. We're in a motel and today we're going apartment hunting if that gives you your answer."

She gasped. "Oh no, I'm so sorry."

"Yeah don't worry about it. Listen, do you think you could get anything I miss from school today, and ask Tom to do the same for Clay?" I asked, stuffing the rest of my doughnut in my mouth,

"Yeah okay sure. Will you be in tomorrow?"

I thought about it and shrugged. "I don't know, depends on the apartment hunt I guess," I said honestly. "I better go. Thanks and I'll speak to you tomorrow," I mumbled, watching Clay as he stood up and headed to the bathroom butt naked. *Damn, my husband is yummy!*

"Yeah okay, see ya." She disconnected the call so I followed Clay into the bathroom wanting to ogle him some more.

He smiled and switched on the shower, stepping into the spray. "You just going to watch me or are you going to get in here and wash my back?" he teased. I giggled and chewed on my lip as I pulled my clothes off as quickly as I could with my plaster cast on my arm.

• • •

A COUPLE OF HOURS later we walked into the bank where Clay had his account. He grinned happily and led us over to the nearest free banking assistant. "Hi, I have an account with you, I've just got married recently so I wanted to add my wife onto my account, please," he said to the lady, smiling at me proudly as he held up our entwined hands as evidence of our wedding rings.

She smiled, seeming a little bemused. "You two are a little young to be married."

Clay shrugged, unconcerned. "Some people think so." His hand tightened on mine, his fingers stroking across the back of my knuckles.

The lady forced a tight smile, clearly sceptical that we were married so young. I shifted on my feet uncomfortably, not used to being under scrutiny from strangers. "Okay I'll need proof identity. A bank card and driving licence for both of you, and your marriage certificate."

Clay handed over all the relevant things, and she got to work updating Clay's account to add me on. All in all it took barely fifteen minutes. She informed us that we would need to come in again in a couple of days to collect my cards because we didn't have a permanent address. When the essential paperwork was done, we left the bank and headed to the nearest café, buying sandwiches. We ate in the park, both musing over the fact that we were potentially going to find our first home today. Clay seemed rather excited about the whole thing.

The first apartment was one of the two bedroomed ones that we had booked appointments for. We barely even made it through the door of the apartment before Clay laughed and turned around, walking out, telling the agent that it wasn't for us. The place was a health hazard, the walls cracked, and the ceilings yellow where the person who lived there before was a heavy smoker. I felt dirty even though I hadn't even looked around it properly. The next two bed apartment was just as bad. My hope of finding something was fading fast. It was going to take us forever to find a place, if this was the kind of thing we could afford. A frown covered Clay's forehead. He was obviously thinking the same as me.

All hope and excitement was practically gone as we followed the agent to the last apartment we had to view today. I knew that if this one was no good we would have to search a little further out. We wouldn't be able to go too far out though because Clay had already been offered his apprenticeship as an engineer for a really respected firm so he needed to be able to commute. The placement was his dream job, and he would be training on the job for the next couple of years.

When we pulled up at the next apartment, I was surprised at how pleasant it looked from the outside. The street was clean and the area nice. There were two allocated places to park and a little garden area that was shared with the three other apartments in the building. I glanced at Clay and raised one eyebrow. He smiled back, his eyes hopeful too.

As we climbed the stairs to the first floor, apartment 2A, I was trying not to get excited in case the inside didn't match the outside. As soon as the agent opened the door though, I felt the excitement swell. The hallway was nice, it was plain cream, and it had a hardwood floor with doors leading off to the bedroom, kitchen, bathroom, and lounge. Walking in I noticed that everything was cream and that the wood floor stretched through the whole apartment. Rugs placed strategically around gave the place a warm, cosy feel. The place was fully furnished so it had everything apart from bed sheets and towels. We could literally move straight in.

The agent was following us from room to room, pointing out sockets and aspect windows, whatever that meant. He said that the owner had purposefully left it neutral so that the tenant could redecorate to their tastes. When we got to the kitchen, I sighed contentedly. I could hear Clay chatting to the agent about the monthly bills, which apparently were included in the rent, but I was too busy looking through every cupboard and drawer in the kitchen, looking at all the saucepans, cutlery and plates that we would have. The place was perfect, and I could envision us living here happily. I looked at Clay, chewing on my lip, trying desperately not to jump up and down in excitement.

He grinned. "You like this one?" he asked with a hopeful hint to his voice. I nodded eagerly. He laughed and turned to the agent. "We'll take it." He extended his hand, relief seeming to wash over his face as they shook hands.

We couldn't sign the lease straight away; we had to wait an hour for him to draw up all of the papers, so we headed back to the motel. On the way there we decided it would be best to collect our clothes and stuff from our parents the following day. It was too late in the afternoon now, and our parents would be home from work soon. Personally I didn't want another run-in with David, and I knew Clay felt the same, so the longer we put that off the better. We booked another night in the motel so we weren't rushing around. The same receptionist flirted with Clay shamelessly as he paid for the room.

As soon as we walked through the door to our room I pushed him roughly, making him sit on the edge of the bed. "Whoa! Riley Bear, jeez, is somebody a little impatient?" he joked, smirking. I smiled seductively at him and turned on the TV to the music channel deciding to re-enact our unofficial first dance. I knew he'd like that. I started to peel off my clothes slowly, making his eyes go wide as he watched my every move. Merely seconds later he grabbed me, throwing me down on the bed roughly. I laughed breathlessly as I wrapped my arms and legs around him, pulling him to me. "You really are amazing you know," he whispered, trailing little kisses down my neck. I giggled uncontrollably as he 'marked his territory' on my neck as usual.

• • •

AN HOUR LATER WE walked into the agent's office and put down the deposit on the apartment, signing a six month lease. Once we were signed Clay grabbed me and lifted me off the floor, spinning us in a circle, laughing.

"I can't believe as of tomorrow we will officially be moved in to our own place," I squealed with excitement.

He kissed me, his arms tightening on my waist, clamping me against him, my feet still dangling inches from the floor. "How about we go out for dinner to celebrate?" he asked, finally setting me back on my feet.

I shrugged, grinning. "Sure, why not."

We walked to the nearest restaurant, hand in hand, chatting happily about what colours we would paint our place. I was even starting to get excited about grocery shopping because it would be *our* food, not family food. It was weird; everything felt different, menial tasks were now 'firsts'. I could barely wait.

Within ten minutes we were seated at a secluded table at the back of a quaint little restaurant and had already put in our order. Clay took my hand, interlacing our fingers as he smiled over at me. "We still need to go get our stuff so we'll have to choose a time when my dad and David will be at work so there's no more trouble. I hope they haven't burnt it or anything," he joked.

I rolled my eyes and shook my head. "Don't say that. You never know, you might be tempting fate."

Clay had a big grin on his face. He looked ecstatic. "We'll need to buy some bed sheets and towels and stuff tomorrow too."

Talk flowed easily as we ate. We made plans about what we would buy, what we already had, I gushed about the kitchen and the wooden floors. As we were halfway through dessert, my phone rang. I looked at the caller ID to see it was Blake. I stared at it in shock. With everything that had gone on in the last couple of days I had totally forgotten about him.

"You gonna answer that?" Clay asked, smiling at me. I gulped and shook my head. "What's wrong, Riley Bear?" He held out his hand for the phone.

I couldn't speak so I just handed it over, watching with wide eyes as he looked down at it. He gasped and flipped the phone open, putting it to his ear with a murderous expression on his face. "What the fuck are you doing calling her?" he spat down the phone. Almost immediately he gritted his teeth and snapped the phone shut, muttering expletives under his breath. He handed me back the phone. I just looked at him shocked. *Why the hell is Blake calling me? He really is crazy after everything that's happened.* "He hung up," Clay stated, clenching his jaw tightly. "We need to go back to the police." He took my hand, playing with my wedding ring absentmindedly.

I nodded in agreement. "Not today though, okay? I don't want anything else to happen today, it's been a long day. I can't take anymore, please, baby." I pouted, really not wanting to be dealing with police and interviews and statements tonight. I just wanted to curl up next to him and sleep.

He sighed. "Fine, but if he calls again we go straight to the police," he bargained.

I smiled, feeling my tummy flutter because of the protectiveness of him.

Suddenly my phone rang again. Clay snatched it up off of the table, his eyes flashing with anger. He looked at the caller ID and visibly calmed, handing it back to me. "It's your mom."

Oh God, what now? I answered it quickly, both nervous and excited to speak to her. I hadn't expected to hear from her after what David had said on the phone in the morning. "Hey."

"Hi, honey. How are you? Where are you? Are you and Clay all right? Are you at a hotel? I've been so worried," she babbled, her words all merging where she shot the questions out one after another.

I laughed, feeling warmth wash over me at the familiarity of her voice. "Slow down, Mom," I teased. "We're both fine. We're currently sitting having dinner in a restaurant. Are you okay? How's David? Has he calmed down since this morning?" I asked hopefully.

There was a long pause before she answered, and that pause told me everything I needed to know. He hadn't calmed down in the slightest. "David's so upset, honey. He's sorry about what he did to Clay, but he still won't accept it. I've been trying to reason with him but..." she trailed off uncomfortably. She didn't need to finish the sentence anyway, I knew it was useless.

I nodded, feeling my eyes prickle with tears. "There's not much we can do about that, I guess. He'll come around eventually." I hoped my words were true. I squeezed Clay's hand, willing myself not to cry.

"So how are you two getting on as a married couple?" Mom asked, forcing happiness.

I grinned at that. "Great, Mom. We found a place today, we're moving in tomorrow."

She gasped. "You found a place? What sort of place? Where? Oh my gosh, my little girl is a married woman who has her own place." She sounded like emotion was overwhelming her as she spoke.

I laughed at how strange that sounded. "It's on West Street. It's a one bed apartment, and it's just perfect, Mom. It's already furnished so we have hardly anything to buy," I enthused.

"Already furnished? That's great, Riley. What sort of thing do you still need to buy?" she asked.

"Well, linens aren't included so we need towels, bedding and kitchen towels, that kind of stuff."

"You sound so happy," she observed. "Is your place nice?"

I sighed contentedly. "Yeah, it's just perfect, you'd like it. Maybe you could come and look at it later in the week if you want," I suggested, looking at Clay who was smiling and nodding at me.

"I'd love to," my mom agreed. "I could bring Linda; I know she wants to see you too."

At the mention of Clay's mom, I felt my stomach drop. "Yeah how are they?" I asked uncomfortably. I had always liked Richard and Linda, but I didn't think that Clay would be as quick to forgive his father for slapping me as he was to forgive my stepfather for punching the crap out of his face.

"Linda's good, Riley, she's missing Clay. Richard's not too happy though. He thinks that you two have made a terrible mistake," she answered.

I drew in a shaky breath. That hurt to know that Richard didn't approve of our marriage either. "Well if Linda wants to come then you two are more than welcome anytime. Actually, I want to repaint a couple of the rooms in the apartment, so maybe at the weekend, if you're free, you could give us a hand," I suggested.

"I'd love to," she gushed. "I'm so proud of you. I know that it's weird me being proud of my seventeen year old daughter for getting married, but I always knew that you and Clay were meant to be together, I knew you would be married one day. He's such a good boy, and he loves you like crazy." She sounded so genuinely happy for use that it made the hair on my arms prickle.

I looked up at Clay and smiled. "Clay is a good boy, you're right," I said. He grinned over at me, eating the last of his dessert. "Mom, do you think it would

195 · Kirsty Moseley

be okay if Clay and I came over tomorrow and picked up my stuff so we can take it to our new place?" I asked, biting my lip nervously. I seriously needed clothes, I was wearing my last pair of clean panties today, and Clay was already going commando.

"Of course. David will be at work at the usual time, what time do you think you want to come?" she asked.

"About ten?" I suggested, looking at Clay for confirmation. He nodded easily.

"Okay great. I'm so excited to see you; I hate how we left everything. I'll see you tomorrow then," she said.

"Bye, Mom. Love you."

"Love you too." She disconnected, but not before I heard her start to cry. I sighed and tried to pretend like I hadn't heard it because I didn't want to get upset too. I would miss not seeing her everyday.

Clay called his mom and told her that we would go and pick up his stuff tomorrow after we had done mine. He seemed fairly happy when he got off the phone so she was obviously over the shock now too.

After dinner we went back to the motel. That night I was so excited about moving into our place that I could barely sleep. Clay, behaving as the dutiful husband, volunteered to keep me entertained until I fell asleep. After a couple of hours I was too exhausted to stay awake any longer and fell asleep in his arms.

chapter

nineteen

When I woke up in the morning Clay was already dressed. He woke me up by gently kissing my face. "Mmm, that's a nice wake up," I mumbled against his lips.

"Well I get to wake you up like that forever, Mrs Preston." He kissed me again softly before pulling away and smiling down at me. "I've run you a bath." He eased his arms under me and lifted me easily out of the bed making me laugh and wrap my arms around his neck. Luckily I was already naked so he carried me into the bathroom and plopped me into the warm water of the bath tub. "I'm gonna go and get some breakfast for us."

I sighed contentedly as he kissed my forehead and then turned and headed out of the room. *I'm a seriously lucky girl!* "Hey," I called just as he was at the bathroom door. He turned back to look at me, one eyebrow raised in question. "Feel like moving in with me today?" I asked, grinning wickedly.

"I'm not sure, it's a bit fast. I'll have to think about it," he teased, winking at me as he walked out.

• • •

WHEN WE PULLED up outside my mom's house, I looked up at it with a sinking feeling in my stomach. What happens if David decided to stay home from work today? What if my mom told him we were coming? What if he hurts Clay again? A million thoughts were passing through my brain at once so I didn't even realise that Clay was already out of the car and had opened my door for me and was now looking at me with concern clear across his face.

He took my hand and guided me out of the car, closing the door behind me. "Riley Bear, it'll be fine. We have to do this, unless you don't need your clothes?" he teased, raising an eyebrow cockily.

I pulled him close and put my mouth to his ear. "Well I do need them because I'm out of underwear, you wanna check?" I flirted, pulling his hand to round my ass.

He made a low groan deep in his throat as he pushed me back against his car, pressing his whole body to mine. "I love being married," he whispered, kissing me forcefully, as if he'd somehow forgotten what we were here to do. Clay was pretty easily sidetracked.

I laughed and pushed him away. "Come on, let's get this done," I suggested. "But, Clay, if David's here we just leave, okay? I don't want you to get hurt." I frowned; visions of my stepdad hitting him filled my head again. I definitely didn't ever want to see him get hurt again.

"Everything will be fine," he assured me, taking my hand and leading me up the drive towards the house. We stopped at the front door and both looked at each other awkwardly. "Maybe we should knock instead of just walking in?" he offered, looking a little unsure. I shrugged but nodded at the same time. It seemed incredibly weird having to knock on your own front door, but technically this wasn't my house anymore so we should respect that. He smiled sadly, his hand tightening on mine as he reached out and rang the doorbell.

Linda answered the door almost immediately. She smiled and threw her arms around Clay, her eyes already swimming with tears. "Oh, Clay! I've missed you," she gushed.

He chuckled, patting her back, looking extremely confused as to what his mom was doing at my parents' house. "Hey, Mom, I've missed you too."

She pulled away and grabbed me into a hug too. "Riley, are you okay?" she asked, holding me tightly.

I looked at Clay, bemused. "I'm fine, Linda. How are you?"

"Riley!" I heard my mom screech from inside. I looked round to see her running down the hallway, grinning moronically. She grabbed both Clay and I into a huge bear hug. She was almost jumping up and down with excitement.

"Hi, Mom," I greeted, pulling away.

She gripped hold of my hand, pulling me to her side as she smiled at me warmly. "I've got you some boxes. Linda and I have started packing up your stuff to make it easier for you," she said, smiling over at Linda.

"You did? That's great. Thanks, Sandra, thanks, Mom," Clay said.

My mom's hand tugged on mine as she nodded over her shoulder. "Come in the lounge, we have something for you."

Something for us? What does that mean? I shot a look at Clay who stayed close by my side as we walked. His body was a little tense, his shoulders stiff as he looked around discreetly, as if he was expecting David to jump out and grab me any second.

I followed behind our mothers, confused as to what was happening. As we stepped into the lounge, I gasped. On the coffee table in the centre of the room was a pile of presents. Some of them were covered in gold paper, and others in red and white spotted paper.

Are they for us? "What's this?" I asked, confused.

"Well, Linda and I wanted to get you a little something. We missed your wedding so we bought wedding presents, and then you need housewarming presents," my mom explained, pointing out the two separate piles of presents.

That's so sweet! They bought us presents? The fact that they were accepting of us being married and moving out brought a lump to my throat. Emotion bubbled up inside me, and before I could get hold of it, I started to cry. Clay turned and kissed the side of my head, wrapping his arm tightly around my waist as I sniffed and struggled to compose myself.

Linda grinned and sat down on the floor next to the table, patting the space next to her for me to sit. "These ones are the wedding gifts," she said, motioning towards the gold wrapped ones. I laughed quietly and looked over at Clay as he settled himself on the floor. Chewing on my lip, I sat in the space next to him and smiled gratefully as Linda picked up two presents, handing one to each of us.

When I ripped open the paper, a silver photo frame sat there, already housing a picture of me and Clay together from last summer. My heart swelled at how thoughtful it was. "I love it, thank you." I held it out to show Clay.

He smiled and nodded, turning his attention to the gift he had in his hands. He recoiled slightly as he tore of the paper to reveal a china figurine of a couple kissing, but he quickly plastered on a fake smile. "Thanks guys that's... nice." His smile didn't quite meet his eyes, but I prayed they didn't notice. I had a feeling he would insist that this decorate the inside of a closet or something.

To take the attention off of him, I quickly opened the last gold one. Nestled inside the layers of paper was a beautiful silver marriage certificate holder. I gasped, my eyes prickling with tears as I imagined our marriage certificate housed in there. "This is great. Thank you so much!"

Mom took it out of my hands and smiled down at it. "There's a bit here, you have to get it engraved with your names and the date of marriage. We didn't have time to get it done."

"Thank you, that's really nice of you," Clay said, pulling me into a hug and wiping my tears with his thumb.

"Now the housewarming ones," my mom chirped, smiling excitedly. "Now, we only got these this morning, and they didn't have much choice so it's just a start for you," she mused, handing us one each. I watched Clay open his first.

He gasped and held out two sets of bed sheets and duvet covers.

"We went for plain colours because we didn't know what you'd want to do with your room," Linda chimed in.

I swallowed the lump in my throat. *I only told my mom last night that we needed them, and they both go out this morning to buy them? Man, we have great parents!* I smiled gratefully, unable to speak. "Open yours, Riley," Linda prompted, patting it.

Inside mine I had pillowcases and kitchen towels. "Guys, seriously, this is extremely thoughtful, thank you so much." I shook my head in awe that they would go out this morning and buy them because they knew that these were the only things we didn't have in our apartment.

Linda waved her hand at the last two presents on the table. "There's two more, they're both the same so you'll have to open them at the same time I guess."

As instructed, I opened one while Clay did the other. They were a set of cream towels of all sizes. I pulled Linda into a hug. "Thank you," I whispered, fighting tears again.

"You're very welcome, daughter-in-law," she replied, pulling away with a smile. I laughed and went to hug my mom.

"Thanks, Mom, these are really great," I said, wiping my face on my hands.

She cupped my face in her hands, planting a soft kiss on my forehead before pulling back and smiling down at me. "Right come on you have a lot to pack, you'd better get going if you want to be done before your fathers are home," she suggested, nodding towards the stairs. "We'll pack these things back up then make some drinks or something."

"Okay thanks," Clay agreed, taking my hand.

When we got upstairs it was clear that our moms had made a great start packing. My clothes were already neatly folded into two giant suitcases, and they had started on my DVDs and CDs too. However, we still spent almost two hours packing the rest of my things before we were done. I helped Clay load it all into his car, and then we moved on to his house, spending another hour packing up his things. Finally, after what felt like forever, we were done and had two car loads of stuff. It was almost three o'clock. I hugged my mom and Linda tightly, promising to call them Thursday. They insisted they would come round after school on Friday to have a look at our new place.

Clay and I headed in our separate cars to our new place. When I pulled up beside him, he opened my door for me, smiling happily. "Hey, Mrs Preston," he greeted.

"Hey, Mr Preston," I replied, chewing on my lip. *Man, I love my new name. I don't think I'll ever get tired of it.*

He took my hand, playing with my fingers as his green eyes locked on mine.

"Listen, why don't we go up and make sure everything is open and stuff before we start bringing all our boxes up?"

I could tell that he had something else he was thinking about, but when I gave him a quizzical look he just shook his head and motioned over his shoulder towards the building door. I smiled and nodded in agreement, letting him lead me through the little entrance hallway and up the stairs to our new home. I was so excited that butterflies were swooping around in my stomach like crazy.

When we got to our door, Clay handed me one of the keys. "You do the honours, Riley Bear." He winked at me playfully and stood back, leaning against the doorframe casually.

I grinned excitedly and jammed the key into the lock as quickly as I could, pushing the door open, eager to get inside and make it home. As I took a step forward to go in Clay grabbed my hand, pulling me to a stop as he shook his head. I looked at him curiously, but just as I opened my mouth to ask him what he was doing, he bent and knocked my legs out from under me, pulling me into his arms. I squealed, shocked, and threw my arms around his neck.

"Part of my job, remember?" he teased, carrying me over the threshold and kicking the door shut behind him.

Damn, he is so sweet! I sighed contentedly and felt everything settle into place, my whole life now seemed so complete while I was here in his arms. I had never felt so completely happy in my life. Squeezing myself to him tightly, I pressed my lips against his, kissing him passionately.

"How about we unpack later and christen the new bed first?" he suggested, already heading towards the bedroom.

I giggled and nodded eagerly, kissing him again, wondering just how I got so lucky as to have Clay Preston fall in love with me.

• • •

A COUPLE OF HOURS later we were *still* unpacking. "Oh my goodness, how the heck long is this gonna take?" I whined. I was currently walking around in nothing but his t-shirt, and he was wearing a pair of low slung jeans that made his body look so hot I could barely keep my eyes on the clothes I was trying to hang in our closet.

"I don't know, Riley Bear, hopefully not too much longer, I want to see that sexy booty of yours rocking my t-shirt on the sofa. We haven't had a movie night in a long time," he replied, grinning wildly. The doorbell rang making me jump excitedly at the sound. *Our first visitors!* "Go on then, I know you want to be the first to answer the door." He laughed.

Needing no more encouragement I ran out of the room, pelting down the hall and throwing the front door open. Two guys and one girl stood there, probably all in their early twenties from my quick estimations.

"Well hello," one of the guys purred. I noticed that they were both looking me over slowly; suddenly I became very aware that I was only wearing Clay's t-shirt that came to about mid-thigh. *Crap, I should have put on some jeans!*

"Hi," I greeted, trying to hide my embarrassment by tugging on the bottom of the shirt, trying in vain to make it longer.

The girl frowned, disapproval clear across her face as she slapped the guy on his chest. "Jeez, don't eye-rape the new neighbour," she scolded. I giggled uncomfortably, chewing on my lip.

The other guy who hadn't spoken yet pouted at her playfully. "Oh, Sissy, but she's so damn hot," he responded. He turned to me and cocked his head to the side, his eyes inquiring. "Please tell me you live here with your twin sister and that you like to have random threesomes with guys who live in your building."

I practically choked on my laugh. *Wow, a couple of perverts live in our building!*

"Craig! Seriously what the hell is she gonna think of us if you don't shut your filthy mouth?" the girl snapped, slapping his chest again.

I shook my head quickly in answer to his question. "No, I don't live with my sister. I'm Riley Preston. Do you live here?" I asked, smiling, but already knowing the answer, he'd already said he lived in the building.

The girl nodded. "Yeah I live in 2B, directly opposite," she replied, pointing to the door across the hall. "I'm Sissy Tompkins." She stuck out her hand politely, and I shook it in return.

"And we both live in 1A downstairs, right underneath yours. And I would definitely like to be underneath you," one of the guys chimed in, holding out his hand.

I laughed and shook it quickly. "Not gonna happen, buddy. I'm married," I rejected, grinning as all three of their faces turned to shock.

"Married, what? How old are you?" Craig asked.

"I'm seventeen. My husband, Clay, is eighteen." I shrugged. *This is where they're going to say 'wow you're young to be married' or 'are you pregnant?'*

Instead of saying that though, the other guy held out his hand. "I'm Kane. Your husband is one lucky dude to be married to a stunner like you," he said, looking me over again.

Sissy slapped him again. "Stop perving on the new *married* neighbour!" she cried incredulously.

I laughed and shook my head knowing that she would be doing some perving when she saw Clay anyway. "Don't worry about it," I assured her. "Oh and, by the way, Sissy, I'll forgive you for drooling." I smiled wickedly.

"Drooling? What are you talking about?" she asked, confused.

I turned around, looking up the hallway towards the bedroom. "Clay, babe, come meet our new neighbours."

A hanger scraped on the rail as he answered, "Yeah all right, Riley Bear, I'll be right out." I could hear him shutting the closet door so I stepped back so she could get the full view of my sexy ass husband as he walked down the hallway. I watched Sissy's face, grinning wickedly. I knew the exact moment she laid eyes on Clay because her expression turned from confusion to hunger in a matter of seconds. She flicked her eyes to me then back to Clay, taking in all his shirtless, low slung jeans glory.

He wrapped his arms around me from behind. "Hey, guys, how you doing?" he asked, sticking his hand out in greeting.

"Hey, good to meet ya. I'm Craig, this is Kane, and Sissy," Craig introduced, pointing at everyone in turn.

Sissy didn't speak. Her eyes were roaming Clay's chest slowly, as if she'd never seen a half-naked man before. I smiled. I didn't mind if people looked as long as they didn't touch. I trusted Clay wholeheartedly, I trusted him with my life, I always had done.

"Er, Sissy, you've got a little something here," I joked, rubbing my bottom lip.

She shot her hand up to wipe her mouth before laughing when she realised she'd been caught. "Right! I'm so sorry," she apologised.

I like her already. "Don't worry about it; I have that problem myself all the time." I winked at her knowingly.

She flushed, nodding. "I bet you do! Damn."

Clay's mouth pressed against my ear. "Did I miss something?" I shivered as his hot breath blew down my neck.

"No, baby, it's just a girl joke," I replied, turning and kissing his cheek.

Sissy cleared her throat, clearly uncomfortable after staring at my husband. "So we just wanted to say welcome to the building and if you need anything let us know okay?" She smiled awkwardly, turning to leave and grabbing Kane's sleeve.

"Great thanks. And it was nice to meet you," I called as they made their way down the hallway.

Kane turned and smiled. "Oh and if you have any hot ass single friends, send them my way," he requested, winking at me.

Craig slapped him on the back of the head. "*Our way,* dude!" he corrected, shaking his head. I laughed and closed the door, shaking my head. They seemed like they would be a lot of fun to have as neighbours.

As soon as the door closed, Clay's arms wrapped around me, trapping me against the wall with his body. "Hmm I could sense some hormones in the air there, not that I blame those guys, I mean, I am married to the sexiest girl in the world," he whispered, kissing down my neck and running his hands slowly up my thighs.

I grinned and tangled my hand into the back of his hair. "Hey, Clay, do you know that when you move into a new house you have to make love in every room for good luck?" I asked breathlessly as he nipped gently at the skin on my shoulder.

"Mmm, I didn't know that. Does a hallway count as a room?" he asked, his breath tickling my skin against my neck giving me goosebumps.

"Oh heck yeah," I breathed. He laughed and kissed me softly, stealing my breath and melting my heart.

• • •

THAT NIGHT CLAY ordered takeout seeing as we hadn't had time to do our grocery shopping yet. *Wow this moving out business is way more tiring than I thought, but that could be because I haven't slept very well for the last three days.* We were now curled up on the sofa watching TV. We'd finished bringing good luck to our home a little while ago and were now just chilling out together.

It felt so nice just to cuddle, knowing that no one was going to come in or say anything. We didn't have to do anything or pretend for anyone. I loved it. I loved him. "I'm tired, baby," I mumbled, rubbing my eyes and yawning.

He smoothed the hair back from my face. "Let's go to bed then, Riley Bear. We have school tomorrow." I groaned and rolled my eyes. I didn't want to go to school. I wanted to hang out in our new place and go to the grocery store and look at some paint samples. He sighed as I pouted at him. "Riley, I need to go in tomorrow. I have a game on Friday, well, if I'm still allowed to play after skipping for two days." He bent forward and kissed my forehead softly.

I nodded, trying to hide my disappointment. "Okay fine, but you're buying me breakfast tomorrow morning before school." My eyes were starting to droop now, every time I closed them they became harder to open again after. *Jeez, this boy is just too comfortable.* I snuggled into his chest, preparing for sleep. He chuckled and pushed me away from him gently, easing himself off of the sofa. He reached down and slipped his arms under me, carrying me into our bedroom and sliding into the bed easily, settling me against him.

"I love you," he whispered, tucking the sheets under my chin.

I yawned. "I love you more."

"Not possible," he breathed in my ear as he snuggled closer to me, melting our bodies together.

chapter
twenty

A relentless buzzing woke me from my slumber. I groaned and turned quickly, realising it was cell phone vibrating against the wood of my bedside cabinet. My head was spinning slightly where I woke from the deep sleep I was in. I glanced at the clock to see it was just after two in the morning. *Who on earth is calling me at this time of night?*

I grabbed my cell phone quickly before it woke Clay and immediately pressed the answer button, climbing out of the bed quietly. I snuck out of the room before putting the phone to my ear.

"Hello?"

"Hey, Jailbait."

Oh my freaking God! "Blake? What the hell are you doing calling me? You're not allowed to call me," I hissed, looking back into the bedroom, praying I didn't wake Clay. If he knew Blake was on the phone we would be down the police station within five minutes, and I was too damn tired. I'd tell him in the morning. I knew he'd be annoyed that I didn't wake him straight away, but the boy needed to sleep too.

"I want to see you." His voice was different, his words not quite properly formed, slightly slurred.

Is he drunk? "Seriously? This needs to stop! I'm not interested, I'm with Clay. You need to stop calling me," I berated, shaking my head in disbelief.

"I can't, Jailbait. I've tried, but I just can't. I want you."

"Well that's too damn bad! I'm with Clay, I love him and that's it," I said sternly.

"Leave him. I can make you happier than he can," he pleaded.

Yeah right, as if! "Blake, what the hell are you talking about? You barely know me; we went on two dates, that's it, just two. You need to leave me alone. I already have a restraining order out against you; you're not even allowed to call me!" I retorted, shaking my head fiercely. *What do I need to say to this guy to make him understand?*

"No, the restraining order means I can't come near you, or contact you in a threatening manner. You could come to me, that doesn't violate the order," he countered, his voice cocky as if he was incredibly pleased with himself for finding a loophole.

"I don't want to see you!" I hissed. *Damn it, maybe I should just tell him to go jump in a lake or something, maybe that would make him understand.*

"Jailbait, come on now. We had fun, didn't we? I promise I'll never hurt you again. I'm so sorry about what I did, I shouldn't have done it. It's just Preston; he just drives me fucking crazy! This is all his fault, everything was great until he started sticking his fucking nose in," he spat angrily.

Wow he is so deluded. "No everything wasn't great, Blake," I corrected. "I'm sorry but you need to get over this little obsession with me. Honestly it's freaking creepy." I shuddered, wrapping my arm around myself as the room suddenly seemed to cool by a couple of degrees.

"Creepy?" He laughed. "That's too funny, I'm not creepy," he mused, still laughing.

No, you're a freaking psycho! "I'm going back to bed. Stop calling me." I disconnected the call not waiting for his answer. It immediately buzzed again in my hand so I turned it off. I guess I needed to get a new number or something.

I drank a glass of water trying to calm my nerves before slipping back into bed with Clay. "Hey, where'd you go?" he asked sleepily as I snuggled close to his side again.

Oh no, I don't want to tell him now, I'll tell him in the morning. "Bathroom," I lied. He kissed my nose, and I pushed all thoughts of Blake out of my head and went back to sleep for another couple of hours.

· · ·

THE ALARM WENT off at seven, and I rolled over and pressed my face into Clay's chest, needing more sleep. "Morning, Riley Bear," he chirped.

I groaned, squeezing my eyes shut tighter. "Why the hell are you always so freaking cheerful in the morning?" I asked, defeated, as I pulled a pillow over my head to block out the remaining light.

"I get to wake up next to the most beautiful girl in the world. That kind of puts a happy twist on my morning," he replied, shrugging and pulling the pillow away from my face.

My heart throbbed at how cute that was. "Yeah well I get to wake up to you, but sorry, baby, I'd still rather have an extra hour of sleep," I teased, rubbing my nose against his.

He smiled. "School today, Mrs Preston. I can't wait," he said excitedly as he rolled on top of me, grinning like a mad man.

I groaned. "Why can't school start at like ten thirty or something?" I whined, turning my nose up. I really wasn't a morning person, unlike Clay.

"Oh come on! You're not excited about people asking about us being married?" he asked, sitting up on the bed and rubbing a hand through his hair, ruffling it up.

"Of course I am, but jeez I'm gonna get some death glares today. I bet the cheerleaders push me down the stairs or run me over in the parking lot or something." I pouted thinking about it. They were going to seriously hate me today.

Clay laughed and shook his head. "They won't. Come on, I'm starved. Let's get dressed so we can go eat," he pleaded, pulling me up and throwing me his begging face that I couldn't say no to. I rolled my eyes and allowed him to pull me up and to the bathroom to shower.

• • •

AN HOUR AND A half later we stepped out of Clay's car into the school parking lot. I clung to his hand as people stopped talking to look at us. I was right; the cheerleaders, especially Zoë, looked like they wanted to kill me. I groaned as Clay led me towards the building.

"Damn, look at their faces!" I whispered as we walked past a group of glaring girls. Clay laughed and pressed his lips to mine as we walked past them. The taste of his lips made me feel better instantly and made me forget about the hateful looks from jealous girls as we walked through the school.

We went to the office first. The lady smiled as we walked in. "Good morning, Clay, Riley," she greeted cheerfully.

"Morning, Mrs Stevens. Riley and I have new addresses and stuff to report," Clay said confidently, pulling out the letter from the agent with our new address and stuff on the front.

"You have new addresses?" she questioned, heading to the filing cabinets behind her and pulling out Clay's file from the 'P' drawer before heading to the 'T' drawer for mine.

"Yeah, and I have a new name too," I added, eyeing my file.

"New name?" she repeated, looking at me like I was crazy.

I nodded. "Yeah Clay and I need to be filed together now, both under P." I grinned and bit my lip. She was the first person we had officially told at school, other than people who were at the wedding.

She laughed. "I'm lost, honey."

"We got married," Clay stated proudly, pulling me closer to his side, grinning.

Her easy smile fell from her face. "You're kidding me."

I shook my head leaning over her desk and taking the change of information form from the pile of papers she had sorted out. "Not kidding," I confirmed, grinning happily.

I let Clay tell her all about it as I wrote all of our new information down in the relevant boxes. I loved filling in the form as Mrs Preston and my next of kin as Clay. It was a nice feeling; I even had to make up a signature too for the bottom of the form.

"Damn I should have practiced before I signed this. This signature's terrible," I whined, turning my nose up at my name scrawled on the bottom.

Clay laughed. "You mean you haven't been signing Riley Preston on your notebooks since first grade like all the other girls?" he asked, faking hurt.

"Sorry, baby, but you just didn't do it for me then." I winked at him teasingly as I edged closer to him.

"Well I'm glad I do it for you now." He smirked at me as the receptionist transferred all of the information onto the computer.

"All right well that's all done then, Mr and Mrs Preston," she said, shaking her head, still looking a little bemused as she photocopied our marriage certificate for the file.

"Awesome, thanks." Clay wrapped his arm around my shoulder and led me out into the hall. Rachel was standing outside the office, leaning against the wall, flirting her butt off with Tom. When we walked out she grinned over at us knowingly.

"Hey you two. Finally pried yourselves out of that new apartment huh?" She waggled her eyebrows suggestively making me blush.

"It was hard, but I guess we needed to," I answered, laughing.

"Heads up!" someone shouted loudly. Clay jumped up in the air and caught a football that literally seemed to come out of nowhere. *Damn that's sexy!*

"Sorry!" a guy winced, running over and slapping Clay on the shoulder apologetically.

"No problem, Travis. Maybe you need to work on your arm though because that throw sucked," Clay teased, cocking his head to the side, smirking.

I rolled my eyes. *If he's going to be talking football then I'm out of here!* "See you later, baby." I linked my arm through Rachel's and blew Clay a kiss before walking off up the hall.

• • •

THE MORNING WENT better than expected. The teachers seemed a little shocked when I told them all about my new name, most of the time they forgot anyway and still ended up calling me Miss Tanner. It would take a while for me to get used to my new name, so I could hardly blame a teacher who didn't really seem to believe me in the first place.

At lunchtime all everyone wanted to talk about was our wedding and what it was like. Every single person in the school seemed to have watched the video of it. Luckily, the unofficial first dance video stayed private, thank goodness.

The girls were gushing about my rings, and Rachel recounted Clay's proposal word for word. How she remembered it I had no idea because she was wasted that night too. I sat there with a proud smile on my face the whole time; I didn't mind being the centre of attention like I thought I would. I was so happy to be married to Clay that I wanted everyone to know it.

When the bell rang signalling the end of lunch, Clay walked me to study hall, kissing me outside the door gently, making himself late for class no doubt. "I love you," he murmured against my lips, brushing my hair away from my face.

"Love you too, Clay."

He smiled and turned, running off towards the locker rooms to get changed for gym. I sighed dreamily, watching until he was out of view and then heading to a desk at the back, pulling out my English assignment from my morning class. A few minutes later a chair scraped back next to mine making me jump.

I looked up to see a guy I didn't know sitting down next to me; he was quite cute I guess, with dark blond hair and brown eyes. Rachel would totally say he was hot; maybe he'd give Tom a run for his money.

He smiled. "Hey, I'm new here. My names Andy Sanders."

"Riley Preston." I nodded in greeting. *Why the hell is he sitting next to me? Almost the whole room is empty, yet he has to choose the seat next to me?*

"So how'd you break your arm?" he asked, nodding at my cast.

I smiled uncomfortably. "Banged it on a wall." I turned back to my English essay, hoping that would be the end of the conversation.

"That sucks. Did it hurt? I've never broken anything before."

I winced, thinking about the pain when it happened. "Yeah it freaking killed, but it's okay now, just annoying with the cast on really," I admitted.

"I'll bet. So, Riley Preston, does the cast stop you from going out on dates and stuff?" he asked, grinning at me.

Dates and stuff? Holy crap, is he asking me out?

"Study hall is for studying, not socialising!" the teacher hissed from the front.

I smiled gratefully at her and went back to my essay, not speaking again for the rest of the hour. Thankfully I got out of rejecting the new guy; I hated to turn people down. It wasn't really his fault, he didn't know I was with Clay, hell he probably didn't even know who Clay was if he was new.

When the bell rang I gathered my stuff quickly, hoping to escape before he spoke to me again... but I was too slow. "Hey do you think you could tell me how to get to the language block? I have French there next period," Andy asked, looking at me hopefully.

"Er, yeah, actually I have that too. You can come with me." I grabbed the last of my things and headed out of the door with him hot on my heels.

"So you never answered my question before. Does the cast stop you from going out on dates and stuff?" he asked, smirking at me.

I squirmed uncomfortably and opened my mouth to tell him I was hopelessly in love with my husband but thanks for the offer when I heard someone shout my name. I breathed a sigh of relief and turned in the direction of the voice. It was Rachel. She was walking towards me slowly with a seductive smile on her face as she took in the new guy I was with.

"Hey, Rach. Um I need the bathroom. Do you think you could show Andy to French? He's new." I raised one eyebrow conspiratorially, knowing she would definitely like to show him around.

She nodded, chewing on her bottom lip flirtatiously. "Absolutely I can. Nice to meet you, Andy. I'm Rachel. How are you finding it here so far?"

I smiled at her gratefully as I turned for the bathroom. I didn't really need to go but turning down guys wasn't really my specialty. Jokes and stuff I could handle, but I hated to upset people, especially new guys. Hopefully by the time I got to class Rachel would have diverted his interest onto her so I wouldn't have to actually say anything.

~ Clay ~

"SERIOUSLY THOUGH, you're a married man who has his own place with his wife and you're eighteen," Zane said again, looking at me disbelievingly and shaking his head in disapproval.

"Zane, come on, do we have to keep going over and over this? Yes, I like being married to Riley. No, it wasn't a mistake," I confirmed for what felt like the hundredth time today.

He nodded, running a hand through his hair. "Don't get me wrong, I like Riley a lot, and damn if you weren't in the way I would *so* tap that. But yeah diverting from the point here, what I mean is... how the hell can you be happy that you get to sleep with just one girl for the rest of your life, instead of nailing anything that moves like before?" he asked, looking at me like I'd lost my mind.

"Because that one girl is Riley," I answered simply. I didn't know how to explain it other than that. Riley was just special, she always had been, and if I'd known that one day she would want to be with me then I would have waited for her. I would have never messed around with those other girls if I knew I had a shot with my dream girl, but you can't change your past, and she didn't think any less of me for sleeping around thank goodness.

"Right then, boys, out onto the field for practice!" Coach shouted, interrupting our conversation. I smiled, grateful for having to do something else other than answer idiotic questions about Riley and our marriage. "Clay, a word, please," Coach barked as I tried to make it out of the door without being seen.

I sighed and Tom slapped me on the back, shooting me a sympathetic smile. I hung back and waited until everyone had left the room before speaking. I knew I was in for it for skipping the last couple of days. "Yeah, Coach?"

"So there's a couple of things we need to talk about I guess," he said, raising his eyebrows looking at me sternly. "The first being, where the hell were you for the last two days? I needed you in practice to help train the new guy. I understand you got married and stuff but damn it, Clay, the team needed you too."

I nodded and tried to look apologetic even though I wasn't sorry I was off for two days. I had a lot to sort out and I got to move into a place with the girl of my dreams, I refused to feel bad about it.

"We had things to sort out. Sorry about that, won't happen again," I confirmed.

"Good. The second thing is about what happened Friday night during the game." He shook his head, frowning angrily.

I took a deep breath; I knew he'd need to talk to me about that. "Yeah I'm sorry that you had to take me off half way through, but I had some things that needed to be taken care of." I frowned, trying not to get angry at the thought of Blake going near Riley again.

He snorted. "Clay, for goodness sake, I'm not talking about having to take you off during the game! I meant about what happened. I heard about Riley's arm and what's going on with Blake Chambers. I know you two have your differences and most of that is probably my fault. If you need to talk to anyone, or you ever need help, then you come to me all right?" He squeezed my shoulder reassuringly as he looked into my eyes.

I smiled gratefully. "Thanks, I appreciate it. The police are involved now so everything's fine." I nodded, hoping that my words were true and that everything was fine now.

"That's good. So come on then, star player, let's get out there and make you sweat," he suggested, nodding towards the field. I smiled and we started walking out of the locker room heading towards the practice field. "Make sure you help the new wide receiver for me, okay? He's played a lot for his last school so we're lucky to have him, but I don't think he's too confident," Coach requested, slapping my back as we got to the edge of the field.

• • •

THE NEW GUY WAS pretty good, but Coach was right, he lacked a little confidence in his ability and was a little hesitant to go in heavy for the ball. Overall, practice was good; Coach rode us pretty hard which was probably my fault for being off for two days. Most of the time that we were practicing I couldn't take my eyes off the hot little thing that was sitting in the bleachers talking to Rachel. *Christ, my wife is so beautiful.* I felt something smack into my chest and I crashed into the hard ground, knocking the wind out of me. I groaned. *Shit, I need to keep my head in the game! Wow that hurt!*

"Sorry, you okay?" Andy asked, looking at me apologetically as he pushed himself up off of me and held out his hand to help me up.

I nodded, trying not to wince. "Yeah, no problem. I wasn't watching so you were right to take me out. I should be grateful it was you instead of one of the other guys, otherwise they probably would have broken a rib to teach me to pay attention," I joked, slapping his shoulder and flicking my eyes to Riley who was standing up looking at me worriedly. I waved my hand to show her I was fine. The silly girl worried about me too much, that's for sure.

"Right, that's it for the day," Coach shouted.

"Yeah you're a little distracted. That's your sister isn't it?" Andy asked, nodding towards Riley and Rachel.

"Sister?" I repeated, confused.

"Yeah, Riley, she said her name was Riley Preston. You're Clay Preston, aren't you?" he clarified. "So, er, what's the deal with that... stay away from my little sister or else kind of thing?" he asked, frowning.

He thinks she's my sister? I laughed and shook my head. "Riley's not my sister, she's-" Something crashed into my back sending me sprawling to the floor again. I groaned and heard laughter from on top of me.

"Damn it, Tom, leave him alone!" Riley shouted angrily from the sidelines.

"Uh-oh the Mrs is mad!" he mocked, laughing as he got up.

I smiled to myself. "You don't want to see her mad, trust me. That girl's like a freaking firework when she blows," I joked, shaking my head, laughing and pushing myself up from the floor.

"Yeah? All spark then fizzles out?" Tom joked, grinning.

Out of nowhere Riley slapped the back of his head making a resounding crack. He winced and hissed through his teeth. "No, more like if you mess around with me you'll get burned, dipshit," she growled angrily.

I laughed and shook my head as Tom looked at her apologetically. "Come on, Riley, I missed taking his ass out for the last two days."

"Aww you missed my ass, Tom?" I teased.

"Man, you're freaking hilarious," he replied, shaking his head, laughing.

Andy was just standing there watching the exchange. I suddenly realised that he was smiling at Riley a lot. *Oh hell no! Is that why he was asking what the deal was with my sister? Was he asking if he could date her or something? No freaking way he's getting a crush on my girl because that's just plain awkward!*

I grabbed her hand and pulled her to me, making her squeal. "No! You're filthy!" she whined as I put my muddy arms around her, pulling her body to mine and making her shirt dirty too.

"You like me dirty," I whispered, smirking at her.

She narrowed her eyes looking sexy as hell. "Well you're right there, I do like you dirty," she breathed. I smiled and inched my face closer to hers. I'd missed her like crazy all day and couldn't wait to take her home. Her mouth was an inch from mine, and I could smell her sweet breath blowing across my lips making my mouth water. "But I don't like *me* dirty," she added, pulling her face away just as my lips were about to touch hers.

I looked at her shocked as she stuck her tongue out at me. *Damn tease.* "Oh you are so in for it, Riley Bear," I warned. She giggled and turned and ran off across the field. I gave her a little head start because I could run a lot faster than her. "You'd better run, Riley!" I shouted after her. I smiled as I heard her laugh louder. "Excuse me." I waggled my eyebrows at the boys who were watching her run off.

I took off in a sprint and slowed down as I started to catch her too fast. I wanted her to get a little way from the school so we could be on our own, even if it was only for a minute. When she was halfway across the field I sprinted to her side and gripped her waist, rubbing my sweaty face on her cheek making her squeal.

"Clay!" She squirmed, giggling.

I slipped my hands down to her ass and picked her up. Her legs instantly wrapped around my waist where she seemed to fit perfectly, like she was made for me or something. "You need to practice running faster if you don't want me to catch you, Mrs Preston," I teased.

She grinned and shook her head, wrapping her arms around my neck. "Oh I wanted you to catch me, trust me." Her lips brushed against mine as she spoke.

I kissed her, savouring every second of it, making up for lost time. It was hard seeing her today in lessons and in the hallways. Not being able to talk to her and hold her hand when I wanted to. I walked slowly back towards the guys, still kissing her as she tangled her hands into my hair, pressing herself to me closer.

"Cut that crap out!" Coach shouted across the field. I could hear all the team hissing and booing jokingly. I smiled as Riley pulled back and blushed like crazy. She moved her legs as if she was getting down so I put my hand on her thigh wrapping it back around me again not letting her away from me.

She smiled and put her forehead to mine. "I love you, Clay," she whispered. Her eyes burned into mine.

"I love you too. So much." As we got to the group I noticed Andy was looking at me strangely. *Oh crap yeah, he thinks that Riley's my sister.* I laughed; I guess it did look a little twisted with her wrapped all around me like this. I guess I'd better explain. "Andy, this is my wife, Riley. Riley, this is Andy, the new wide receiver," I introduced, nodding at him.

She smiled a little uncomfortably. "Yeah we met already. So you play on the team, Andy?" she asked politely.

His eyes widened. "Wife? You two are married? That's why your name's Preston? I thought... yeah okay that makes sense I guess... I should um... go get showered." He shifted on his feet awkwardly as he spoke. I immediately knew that he'd already hit on my girl at some point today.

He turned and started walking off. Zane slung his arm around his shoulder. "Don't worry about it, man, we'd all tap that if she wasn't married. Clay's not offended," he joked, winking at me playfully.

"Your friends are a bunch of man-whores." Riley laughed, pressing her forehead to mine as I started to walk again.

I nodded, readjusting my grip on her. "I know. I'm so glad I never viewed women as sex objects."

She giggled, hugging me tightly. "Want to go grocery shopping after you're done here?" she asked excitedly.

"Sure. Are you going to cook something nice for me tonight like a good little wife?" I asked, grinning.

"Sure, baby, whatever you want." She pressed her lips to mine again, ending the conversation. When we got to the locker rooms I pressed her against the wall outside, kissing her deeply. I almost forgot where we were I was getting so into it. *Jeez my wife drives me wild!*

"Clay, put your girl down and get the hell in here and shower, I don't have time to wait around for you two to finish making out!" Coach barked from the locker room, laughing along with the rest of the team.

I grinned sheepishly and let her down, missing her contact immediately. I brushed some of the mud from her shirt. "Wait here for me okay?" I instructed, looking at her sternly. I hated to have her out of sight; if anything happened to her I would literally lose the only thing that ever mattered to me.

"I'm actually going to go to the library quickly and return my book for History; I forgot to do it earlier. I'll be back by the time you get out of the shower though."

"All right, we'll meet here then." I kissed her forehead and decided to have a cold shower today. I had a while to wait before I could get my hands on her again, I didn't want to walk around the store feeling like a freaking horny jackrabbit or something.

After she'd left, I showered quickly then dressed along with the rest of the team. "So are you having a housewarming party or what?" Tom asked excitedly, rubbing a towel in his hair to dry it.

I frowned. Riley and I hadn't spoken about it, but I didn't really want people coming in and messing up our place. *Wow I'm really getting responsible in my old age, married life is turning me into a bore!*

"I don't know, man, probably not. Our place isn't that big for a lot of people. We could have a few people over for a movie and takeout or something," I compromised. *Yeah I'm pretty sure that Riley will be up for that.*

"Wow, movie and takeout, you two are so adventurous as a couple," Tom mocked.

"Whatever, you're just jealous. How you getting on with Rachel anyway?" I asked as we stepped out of the locker room door. I immediately looked around for Riley, but she wasn't back yet. I glanced at my watch it was almost quarter to five. *Where is she? She should have been back from the library ages ago.*

Tom sighed. "I don't know. She blows hot, then cold. I don't know what I'm doing wrong and what I'm doing right with that girl. She's making me insane." He shook his head, frowning.

I smiled wickedly. "From what I've heard you do something very right with your hands, but don't tell her I told you. Riley told me not to say anything about it." I laughed as I punched him on the shoulder.

His eyebrows knitted together in confusion. "With my hands? What the hell do I do with my hands?"

I shrugged. "No idea," I admitted. "But apparently Rachel really likes it, so maybe you should focus on that." I waggled my eyebrows as he realised what I was talking about.

"Oh that! Yeah she does like that. Damn, she told Riley? Wow I must be good," he boasted, laughing and looking a little proud of himself.

I held up one hand to stop him talking. "I don't want to hear about it. That's what I told Riley, and that's what I'm telling you. I'm just passing on valuable information to help you win the girl," I said, winking at him. "But please don't tell Rachel. I don't want Riley in trouble for violating the girl code or whatever the hell they have." I didn't want Riley in trouble with her friend because I'd let it slip.

"I won't," he assured me. "I'm gonna call Rachel now and see if she's free tonight. I'll let you know how it goes tomorrow. Thanks, Clay!" He pulled out his cell phone, grinning as he walked off talking to her.

I smiled and waited another few minutes before I started to get a little worried about Riley. *Where the hell is she? When I could stand it no more, I* slipped my phone from my pocket and called her cell. The recorded message instantly told me that it was switched off though. I started to panic as I ran towards the library. *Oh crap, why is her cell phone off? Blake wouldn't have come here though, not into the school. He would know I was with her; he wouldn't dare cross me again surely.*

I burst into the library at full speed, almost taking the door off of its hinges. Riley was laughing with the librarian as she helped her put books back on the shelf.

They both looked at me as I ran in, probably making myself look like an utter moron. "Hey, you. Wow, you showered fast," Riley mused, looking at me confused.

The panic instantly fizzled out, and I breathed a sigh of relief that she was safe and had just lost track of time. "Fast? It's almost ten to five, Riley Bear."

She winced and looked at me apologetically. "I'm sorry, I didn't realise. I was helping Mrs Sing with the books."

I smiled and shook my head, trying not to let her see that I was in total overprotective husband mode right now. "It's no problem don't worry."

"Well you two should get going then. Thanks for your help, Riley, and if you're serious about the help then I'll see you tomorrow," Mrs Sing chirped, smiling happily.

Riley nodded eagerly. "I'm totally serious. It beats sitting in the wind watching Clay get smashed around. I hate seeing that." Riley winced as she put the books she was holding back onto the cart and walked to my side.

"I'll bet, see you tomorrow then," Mrs Sing called, smiling kindly.

"Yeah bye." Riley slipped her arm around my waist, clamping herself to me. I smiled and we walked towards the door, I looked at her curiously wondering what was going on. She smiled. "I volunteered at the library after school when you have practice. I hope you don't mind," she explained.

Oh that's what that was! "Yeah? That's a good idea, though I'll miss not seeing you sitting on the sidelines." I pouted jokingly.

She laughed. "Well if I'm not there you'll be able to concentrate and play properly. I hate to tell you this, baby, but since we got together, your game stinks," she teased.

I burst out laughing. "Way to give me an ego boost, Riley Bear." I rolled my eyes. "I was worried when you weren't back, I thought something had happened," I admitted.

"Clay, stop worrying, you'll give yourself an ulcer," she scolded, rolling her eyes.

"I called you but your cell was off. Does it need charging or something?" I asked, shrugging off her comment. I knew I was annoying her because of how worried I was, but that was my job now. Wasn't a husband allowed to worry about his wife?

"Oh shit," she muttered, stopping and looking at me uncomfortably.

I smiled and looked at her waiting for her to tell me she'd lost yet another cell phone or something. That was one of Riley's things; a cell phone never lasted more than six months before it was broken or lost. She had always been the same.

"I turned it off last night, I forgot to tell you. I'm so sorry, I meant to tell you and then you distracted me with all the chat and the shower this morning, then I just forgot," she rambled. *Riley never rambles, what the hell is she talking about?*

I frowned, waiting for her to continue and say something that made sense. "Riley, what?"

She closed her eyes, looking a little pained. "Blake called me again during the night; I didn't want to wake you. I'm so sorry I meant to tell you this morning I promise."

Anger burned through my veins. "What the hell? He called you again?" I shouted.

She winced and looked at me apologetically. "Clay, please don't be angry with me. I meant to tell you."

I sighed and wrapped my arm around her tightly. "I'm not angry with you, Riley Bear, I'm angry at him," I explained, trying to control my voice as every fibre in my body was trying to force me to get in the car and go and beat the life out of him.

"I'm so sorry for always being trouble," she said sadly.

I pulled back and cupped her face in my hands. "Don't be silly. None of this is your fault. Blake must be unhinged or something to keep on like this." I gritted my teeth so I didn't spit his name. "You should have woken me last night though. Why did you even answer the call?" I asked, shaking my head in disapproval.

"I didn't know it was him. It rang and I answered it quickly so it didn't wake you up. I'd already answered before I realised it was him." Her eyes were filling with tears now.

I bent my head and kissed her lips softly for a second. "What did he say?" I asked, not really wanting to know, but needing to.

She shrugged, gripping fistfuls of my shirt and holding me close to her. "The same old thing; he was sorry, he wanted to see me."

"Did he threaten to hurt you or anything?" My whole body was tight with stress.

She shook her head quickly. "No, nothing like that." She pressed her face into the side of my neck, and my arms immediately engulfed her, clamping her to me, wanting to keep her safe from all harm.

I sighed, "We need to go report this." *When the hell is this going to stop! Surely having a restraining order out against you and having the crap beaten out of you would kind of tell you that the girl wasn't interested. I just don't understand why the hell he's still doing this.*

She groaned and pulled back, begging me with her eyes. "Clay, I just want to get back to normal. Please? We need to get food and start behaving a like a married couple, not spending the evening down the police station. How about I just dump my sim card and get a new number?" she offered, looking at me hopefully.

I sighed and thought it through. He didn't know where we lived, he wouldn't know her number so he would have no way of contacting her again, and the police probably wouldn't do anything for a phone call anyway. They had more or less already told us that he needed to violate the order in a big way before they could arrest him. I would definitely like to speak to him again though...

"I've got a better idea. How about we swap cell phones for a few days? Then you don't have the hassle of telling everyone about a new number," I countered. That wasn't the exact reason, but she didn't need to know that, the real reason she wouldn't really like. If I had her phone and he called I'd still get to speak to him and tell him exactly what I'd do to him if he came near her again.

"Baby, that's not a good idea. We should just get rid of it or something then he can't call again," she rejected, shaking her head.

"Report it or swap numbers, your choice," I bargained, raising my eyebrows at her, knowing she wouldn't want to report it tonight. She was desperate to start living like a married couple and to be honest so was I.

She thought about it for a minute while I waited patiently. I knew I'd won, I just needed to give her time to think it through, I knew her too well. "Okay fine, but if he calls again then we get rid of it and report it."

"Absolutely," I confirmed. I kissed her forehead and led her towards the door. "Come on then, Riley Bear, let's get to the supermarket and get supplies because you're making me steak tonight."

"Am I now?" She laughed. I nodded and gave her my begging face that she could never resist. "Damn it, not the face! Fine I'll make steak." She rolled her eyes, grinning.

chapter
twenty-one

Friday went just as fast as the day before; people were still excited about us being married. Riley was still getting death glares from a lot of the girls, or so she told me anyway, I didn't see anything. Being married didn't stop them flirting with me and offering to do all sorts of slutty things in the supply closet or in the bathrooms the same as they used to. They seriously didn't get the hint at all. No one compared to Riley, they never had done. I had always made it clear to all of the girls I slept with that I wasn't interested in a relationship. Why they'd still slept with me after I told them that I had no idea, but it never used to put them off at all. If anything, it seemed to make them even more eager, wanting to be the one that would make me commit to something.

Now that I was married though, the attention seemed to have doubled. It was almost as if they were determined to split us up. There was no way I was letting that happen though, Riley was my dream girl so I wasn't giving her up for anything in the world.

I sat back on the sofa and watched her painting yet another paint sample on the wall of the lounge. They all looked the same to me, light green, dark green, warm green, cold green. To me they were just green, all the same. *What the heck does it matter if 'Apple Whisper' was slightly fresher than 'Mint Breeze'? And what does fresher mean anyway? Wow, I suck at decorating!*

"Well? Which do you like, baby?" Riley questioned, looking at me again, scrunching her nose up, looking adorable like she always did when she was trying to decide something.

Crap, which one is it she said she likes better? Wow I should have listened more instead of watching her ass! "Umm, well the apple one is nice-" I started. She subconsciously frowned a little meaning I chose the wrong one. "But I like the mint one better," I added quickly.

She smiled and looked back at them. "Yeah? I think I like that one too."

I laughed and nodded slowly; looking at the ten different shades of green she had painted on the wall in little squares. "Awesome, well Mint Breeze it is then for in here and Biscotti for the kitchen. That's two rooms sorted then, three more to go," I joked, raising my eyebrows at her.

She sighed contentedly and plopped down on my lap, smiling. "Can we paint tomorrow?" she asked excitedly.

"Sure, whatever you want," I agreed. She bent her head and pressed her soft lips to mine. I wrapped my arms around her, pulling her closer to me, running my hands down her back slowly. The doorbell rang and she jumped back, looking at me worriedly. "Everything's going to be fine." I moved her off of my lap and headed towards the front door.

When I opened it I was greeted by both of our mothers standing there, smiling happily. My eyes flicked behind them to make sure they definitely didn't bring my dad or David, they said they wouldn't but Riley had been worried about me getting hurt all day. When I was satisfied they weren't with them I grinned and opened the door wider to let them in.

I smiled. "Hey, Mom. Sandra."

"Hi, Clay. Oh this looks so nice!" Sandra cried as she came in, kissing my cheek on the way past, looking around the hallway, grinning proudly.

"Thanks. Riley's right in there." I pointed down the hall to the lounge at the end. She smiled and headed there instantly.

I turned back to my mom who pulled me into a huge hug. "I've missed you. Are you two doing okay? You need any money or anything?" she asked, looking at me worriedly as she cupped my face in her hands.

"We're fine, Mom, honestly. I won some money in Vegas; we're all set I promise," I confirmed.

She smiled with teary eyes. "It's not the same without you at home. Your father's incredibly sorry about what he did. He wanted to come today, but I told him to give it a few days." She looked at me pleadingly, silently begging me to show some compassion.

I stiffened as memories of him slapping Riley taunted me. I wasn't ready to forgive him. If I saw him at the moment, I knew I wouldn't be able to restrain myself so it was best he stayed away for a while.

"Yeah, I don't want to see him." I shrugged, ignoring how my mom's face fell.

"I can understand that, but you two will talk eventually, won't you?" she asked, swiping a tear that fell.

I frowned uncomfortably. I didn't like to see my mom sad, but I couldn't get that image of Riley's red cheek out of my head. "Eventually." I shrugged, hoping that eventually was a long time away.

She smiled and looked up the hallway towards the lounge. "So are you going to show me around?" she asked.

I smiled, grateful of the change of subject. "Absolutely." I shut the door, and we headed into the lounge to see Sandra and Riley talking about the paint again. I groaned quietly. *Damn it, please don't start this again! Mint Breeze will do!*

Riley smiled as she chatted with our moms. "I'm going to make coffee, guys." I excused myself as they started discussing colours for the bedroom.

I took my time making drinks so I didn't get caught up in yet another boring colour discussion. When I went back into the lounge, they were just coming out of the bathroom, still chatting animatedly. I watched them in awe. They were all talking at the same time seeming to have no problem listening and talking at the same time. *Wow I would love to be able to multitask like that!* I couldn't help but smile when I saw how happy Riley was talking to them and showing them around proudly. She missed her mom, she missed David too, but she refused to admit it. She plopped herself down at my side so I wrapped my arm around her.

"So you have a game tonight, Clay, we're not going to make you late are we?" Sandra asked, looking at her watch worriedly.

I shook my head and waved dismissively. "Nah. You guys are fine; I don't have to leave until six," I replied, eyeing the clock to see it was only just after half past four.

Sandra grinned and settled back with her coffee. "This place is adorable, and you two look so happy," she cooed.

Riley grinned at me making my heart beat a little faster. "We are happy, Mom," she confirmed, squeezing my hand tightly. "It wasn't a mistake. I know you two probably think we're too young, but I promise we're not." She shook her head fiercely. I could see by her expression how much she believed in what she was saying, that belief made my heart soar in my chest. She was so confident in us, I loved it.

"It's a little weird to think that my son's married and that I have a daughter-in-law, but you two were made for each other. Everyone could see it, it was only a matter of time," my mom said, shaking her head, looking amused.

Sandra laughed and nodded in confirmation. "Love doesn't have an age." She shrugged.

I smiled at that. I agreed completely.

"So this place is so sweet, and you've settled in nicely I see," my mom teased, grinning at us sitting on the sofa together.

Riley nodded, taking a sip of her coffee. "Yeah, we're pretty much unpacked now. We're going to be painting tomorrow if you want to come and help," she suggested.

"I'd love to come and help," my mom confirmed before turning to me and smiling hopefully. "Do you think I could bring your dad, Clay? I know he'd want to help too."

I frowned. *No freaking way, that's too soon.* I opened my mouth to say no, when Riley squeezed my hand. I turned to her; she was pouting at me pleadingly. I knew she didn't like the idea of me not seeing my father. We'd spoken about it a lot, and she kept asking me to let it go for my mom's sake. She'd argued her point well, asking how I could forgive David for hitting me when all my dad did was slap her once, but it was different. It didn't matter about me, but if someone hurt Riley that was a different thing all together.

Riley was killing me; she knew I didn't want to see him so why was she looking at me like that? I knew she was just trying to help and didn't want me to lose my family, but it would be so hard being in the room with him.

"Please, Clay, for your mom," she whispered, absentmindedly twirling my wedding ring around my finger as she held my hand.

The last of my will power crumbled when she pouted at me. *I guess I can let it go for my mom.* I sighed and nodded. "Fine, bring him, but if he says even one thing that I don't like he's out of here," I agreed, looking at my mom warningly, she'd have to make that clear to him before he came here. I wouldn't allow him to even look at Riley harshly again.

My mom grinned at me happily; I rolled my eyes and looked at Riley. "You know that's the right thing to do," she whispered, squeezing my hand reassuringly.

"I know," I mumbled grudgingly.

After another few minutes Riley and our moms all went to cook some dinner, I rested my head back on the sofa and listened to her laughing in there with them. She sounded so happy that it made my heart ache. I loved to make that girl happy. I flicked on the TV watching sports until Riley plopped herself on my lap making me jump.

"Scared ya," she teased, laughing.

I smiled and wrapped my arms around her. "Yep, little wife, you did." I rolled my eyes playfully.

She grinned. "I'm still not used to that at all."

"Being called my wife?" I asked, brushing her hair behind her ear as I kissed her cheek.

"Yeah, it's going to take a little while."

I grinned wickedly. "Well then it's a good thing I want to be married to you for a little while."

"Just a little while? I've got news for you, buster, you're stuck with me forever." She slapped my shoulder lightly as I pulled her closer looking right into her seemingly bottomless blue eyes.

"I'm pretty sure I can cope with that, Riley Bear." I pressed my lips to hers as someone cleared their throat theatrically. I sighed and pulled away looking up at our moms watching us from the doorway, both of them giving us the 'that's so cute' face.

"Food's ready," Sandra chirped, grinning happily.

"Awesome." I laughed and helped Riley off of my lap following her into the kitchen and sitting down at the island so we could eat off of the counter top because we didn't have a table or dining room.

BEFORE THE GAME was due to start I was stood in front of the bleachers with Rachel and Jeff. Clay was standing in front of me protectively as he scanned the crowd for Blake. He had taken it one step further today; I wasn't sitting by the entrance of the locker rooms like last week. I was actually sitting behind the coach's bench so that he could keep an eye on me while Clay was playing.

"Okay, I don't think he's here," Clay confirmed. "If you see him or anything then you go straight to Coach Bradley all right? And if it's during a break then you come to the locker room to find me." He bent his knees, looking at me sternly, his green eyes hard and firm.

"Yes, dad," I joked.

He grinned and shook his head. "It's not a joke. I'm worried about you."

I wrapped my arms around his neck. "I know you are, I'm just trying to lighten your mood. I promise to go straight to the coach or come to find you in the locker room if he comes near me or calls me again." I crossed my heart with my finger, smiling reassuringly.

He nodded, seeming satisfied but there was still tension in his shoulders. "Okay good. Love you." He kissed the tip of my nose and stepped back, scanning the crowd again quickly before he turned and ran off towards the middle of the field where the rest of the team were warming up.

As he got a little way away I wolf whistled loudly. When he turned back to me I looked at Rachel pretending to be annoyed. "Rachel, that's my husband you're whistling at!" I scolded, faking anger, making both her and Clay laugh. Once he was gone I sat down next to Rachel and sighed, watching as he made it to the centre of the field with his teammates.

"Wow your boy's overprotective," Rachel said, shaking her head but smiling at the same time.

I nodded in confirmation. "I know, I swear he's going to give himself a heart attack if he keeps this up." I frowned, watching as he jumped on the spot and swung his arms around, getting ready to play.

As I sat there watching him, I suddenly wondered how I had never realised how handsome he was before I went on that vacation. I had always known he was hot, but I had never once looked at him lustfully. Of course I had been able to see the attraction that he held for other girls, but he was never that boy with me. He was always just my best friend and one person I knew I could rely on more than any other. It was funny how that evolved over that month away. I was so grateful for that vacation because it made my feelings for him surface, but part of me couldn't help but wish I'd looked at him like that before. We'd wasted so much time being friends when the whole time I had the perfect boy right in front of me and I just couldn't see him.

The game went without a hitch, we won which I was happy about but I hated to watch him play. I'd never tell him, but I would literally rather be anywhere than watching him get smashed to the floor and jumped on. He'd even been trodden on a couple of times. How he enjoyed playing the brutal game I had no idea.

After the game he jogged over to me. "Hey, did your man do good or what?" he asked, smirking at me cockily.

I laughed and nodded. "Yeah, your game didn't stink as much today," I teased.

He smiled and kissed me lightly. I noticed he was being careful not to touch me as he was covered in mud and sweat and I was dressed ready to go out. "So I'm gonna go shower. Are you gonna come and wait in Coach's office for me?" he asked, looking at me hopefully.

I turned my nose up distastefully. *Sweaty, smelly office? No thanks!* "How about I go with Rachel and Jeff to the restaurant," I suggested. Instead of going straight to the party tonight, a bunch of Clay's friends and mine were heading out for dinner, kind of a celebration for our wedding which would now also be mingled in with celebrating winning the game.

Clay frowned, clearly uncomfortable with having me out of his sight after Blake calling the other night. "Okay I guess, but stay with Jeff."

"I will, baby. Stop stressing." I went up on tip toes and pressed my lips to his. When I pulled away I grinned. "Go shower, you smell bad," I lied. He actually smelt incredible, sweaty and dirty certainly suited Clay for some reason.

He laughed and slapped my behind gently before turning to Jeff. "Watch her for me?"

Jeff nodded, patting his shoulder reassuringly. "Sure, Clay, don't worry."

I watched as Clay frowned and turned to run off towards the lockers. When he was out of sight I followed Rachel and Jeff to his car in the parking lot. I sat in the back and smiled as Rachel fiddled with the stereo finding The Black Eyed

Peas and turning it up full blast. Jeff groaned and rolled his eyes as both of us girls sang the song, badly I might add.

When we pulled up at the restaurant Jeff shook his head. "Well thank God we're not going somewhere further away; I don't think I could have stood anymore of your singing." He turned his nose up.

I laughed and got out, linking my arm through Rachel's as she stuck her tongue out at him. "Oh you love my singing and don't pretend you don't," she teased, linking her free arm through his and pulling him to the door.

We got a table for eleven and sat at the back, fooling around until the rest of the guys all turned up. Our party tonight was actually everyone that went to Vegas. It was nice to see everyone all together again. It really was like some sort of wedding party or something. Andy came too because Clay wanted to try and bring him out of his shell a little and make him fit in with the team more.

Tom slid into the seat next to mine quickly and smirked at Clay who frowned and went to sit on the other side of the table. "Oh poor baby's put out he doesn't get to sit next to his wife," Tom mocked, throwing a breadstick at Clay.

"Whatever, you're just jealous that I get to take her home." Clay waggled his eyebrows suggestively.

Tom laughed. "Well at least someone's getting some tonight," he muttered, shooting a sly look at Rachel from the corner of his eye.

I elbowed her in the ribs, smiling. Tom liked her, Clay had told me, but he'd made me promise not to interfere. I was desperate to tell her and play matchmaker because she liked him too, but she wasn't ready for a full time boyfriend. Tom was so adorable, I really liked him, I would love it if they got together properly.

We were all laughing and behaving like children while we waited for our food to come, the boys all teasing each other about mistakes they'd made in the game tonight. Even Andy was joining in which was nice. The team all accepted him; they were a decent bunch of guys really.

"Tom's looking hot tonight," I whispered to Rachel. It was killing me not to interfere, but I'd promised Clay. I decided that this wasn't really interfering though. I was just giving her a little nudge in the right direction.

She looked at him; he was sitting there laughing hysterically at something one of the boys had said. At the exact moment she looked at him, he choked on his drink where he was laughing and almost spat it everywhere. Coke even dribbled down his chin.

Wow so smooth, Tom, I'm here trying to help you out yet you can't just keep yourself in check for a minute or two! I laughed as Andy slapped him on the back, laughing wickedly.

"So attractive," Rachel confirmed, laughed and shaking her head.

"You know you want him right now even with the drool," I teased.

She rolled her eyes but scooted her chair closer to mine, leaning in conspiratorially. "You know I went out with him last night? Well, it was actually really fun, I had a great time, and we didn't have sex so that wasn't what made it good. Usually I base a date on how the night ended, but that's the first time I've actually enjoyed a date even though we didn't get past first base." She blushed a little and looked at him again.

I grinned. *That sounds promising.* "He's a really lovely guy. Maybe you should give him a chance. Did he ask you out again?" I mentally crossed my fingers that he did.

She nodded. "Yeah he asked me to go out with him tomorrow night." She bit her lip, looking at him thoughtfully.

"And what did you say?" Hope was bubbling up inside me.

"I told him that I'd think about it. I don't want to get tied down to one guy. I did that before, and when he cheated on me it hurt so much that I swore never to let another guy have that power over me again. That's why I just use guys to get what I want," she replied, frowning.

She'd told me all about this guy that she used to date last year. Apparently he'd cheated on her and ripped her heart out, and she then swore off of guys so that she wouldn't get hurt again. "But what if he didn't hurt you? You can't go through life scared to take a chance," I persuaded. I glanced at Clay nervously. *Bordering on interfering, Riley, be careful not to break your promise!*

She sighed. "Yeah maybe you're right." She nodded, biting her lip, looking at Tom again. He looked at her at the same time and smiled his cute dimpled smile. She would be really crazy not to give him a chance. I kind of wanted to shake some sense into her, to grab them both and lock them in a room together and not let them out until they'd talked. She should just tell him what she'd told me, admit to him about this other douchebag that hurt her, and then he could reassure her that he genuinely liked her.

I sighed and pushed myself up from the seat as they started flirting with each other from each of my sides so I was caught in the middle. I smiled at Clay as I went to walk past him to the bathroom. He grabbed my hand and pulled me down onto his lap, wrapping his arms around me.

"Where are you sneaking off to?" he asked, running his hands down my back, making me shiver.

I looked into his green eyes and smiled seductively. "I was just going to the bathroom; want to come with me just in case I need help buttoning up my jeans?" I flirted.

He grinned and nodded eagerly. "Hell yeah I do, just in case you need help of course." He leant in close to my ear. "You go first, and I'll follow you in a couple of minutes," he breathed, nibbling on my earlobe.

I giggled and kissed him before pushing myself up from his lap. I practically skipped out the back towards the bathrooms. I waited around the corner out of sight for him to follow me when the coast was clear. I could barely breathe through the excitement that I felt inside.

I heard him approaching, and I giggled uncontrollably. *Damn I hope we don't get caught!* He walked round the corner, and my heart stopped.

It wasn't Clay. It was Blake.

chapter twenty-two

Blake's hand closed around mine as he pulled me forward, clamping his other hand over my mouth before I even had a chance to scream. There was a fire exit just off to the left out by the bathrooms, so he pushed the bar down to release the door and shoved us both through it, slamming it shut behind him.

As soon as he released his grip on me I backed away from him quickly, looking back to the door to see it was one of those that only opened from the inside. There was no handle or anything from this side. Blake was standing off to one side, blocking the only way to the front of the restaurant. I would literally have to walk past him to get back to the front door. No one was around; we were just out the back of the restaurant by the dumpsters in the middle of a little dark alleyway. There was no way I could run, and no one around to help.

Oh shit, what do I do? How do I get hold of Clay to come and help me? I discreetly patted my pocket, hoping that my cell phone was in there. Even as I was doing it though, I knew it was hopeless; my cell phone was in my purse which was back in the restaurant where I was sitting. *Damn it, I'm so freaking stupid!*

I took all of this in within a couple of seconds even though it felt like forever that I'd been standing here thinking of ways to escape. Blake was just standing there smiling at me, a nice smile too, playful even. I swallowed around the lump in my throat. *Wow he is seriously bipolar or something. Has he forgotten he's not allowed to be near me and that I'm with Clay?*

"Hey, Jailbait," he chirped, stepping closer to me. I whimpered and stepped back bumping into the chain-link fence behind me. "Don't look so scared of me. I won't hurt you again, I promise," he murmured stepping closer to me.

I could smell alcohol on his breath again. He actually looked a little rough; he wasn't clean shaven like normal, he had a couple of days growth there. The clothes he was wearing were rumpled and creased, like he'd had them on for a couple of days or slept in them or something.

"Blake, this isn't allowed. You're not supposed to be near me. Why did you follow me here?" I said breathlessly as I started to panic. *I just need to stay calm and keep him talking or something. Clay will come to the bathrooms looking for me in a minute or two, and when he realises I'm not there waiting for him he'll check outside. Stay calm, Riley.* I silently scolded myself for not taking my purse to the bathroom so I could have called him for help.

"I didn't follow you, I was here first." He smirked at me as he brushed his hand down the side of my face. I shrank back away from his hand, and a look of hurt crossed his face. "Why are you so scared of me still? I told you I won't hurt you again," he mumbled, looking at me apologetically.

"The last time I saw you I got slapped in the face twice and the time before that you broke my arm! How can I not be scared of you?" I asked acidly. *Shit, what on earth am I doing provoking him? I should just be talking to him calmly until Clay comes out for me. I need to keep him talking.* My heart was crashing in my chest, and my breathing was coming out in little shallow gasps making me feel slightly light-headed.

"And I apologised for that. Are you going to hold it against me forever?" he replied, cocking his head to the side, giving me the innocent little boy look.

"Blake, it's just that we shouldn't be talking." I looked around desperately. *Where the hell is Clay?*

"I just wanted to say hi seeing as you don't like to talk to me on the phone anymore." He pouted as he pressed his body against mine. His fingers linked through the fence either side of my body so I was now pinned against the fence with no way of getting past him at all.

"I just... we... you," I stuttered, trying not to cry.

He smiled. "I'm here having dinner with my sister and her boyfriend. They're a little worried about me apparently. I told them there was nothing to worry about that I was just missing my girlfriend," he said quietly.

I groaned internally. *What the hell is he thinking?* "Why are they worried about you?" I asked, trying to buy some time and keep him talking so he wouldn't hit me again or kiss me. Hell, maybe he'd even try for rape this time, we were down a deserted alley, this was the perfect chance for him to do it.

"I'm not sleeping very well, and I've been drinking a little lately. It's only to keep my mind off of you. I can't stop thinking about you. I've never wanted any girl as much as I want you." One of his fingers trailed up my hip, hooking in the belt loop of my jeans.

"Maybe you should see someone about it," I mumbled. My voice was barely above a whisper. I kept my eyes glued on the fire door; someone must have realised I wasn't back by now, surely. How long had I been out here? It felt like forever, but had it even been a minute or two yet?

"I am seeing someone about it, I'm seeing you. A little time with you should do the trick." He smiled and inched his face closer to mine. I turned my head away and closed my eyes as I put my hands on his chest and tried desperately to push him away from me.

He almost growled as he grabbed my hands and moved them off of his chest, pressing his body back to mine again. He linked his fingers through mine. He wasn't trying to hurt me; he was just holding my hands softly.

"What the hell is wrong with you, Jailbait?" he asked angrily.

I risked a glance up to his face. He was frowning at me, clearly annoyed. I felt his fingers brush over my rings on my left hand. I swallowed loudly. "I just... Blake, this needs to stop. I'm not your girlfriend," I whispered nervously.

His fingers were still touching my wedding and engagement ring as he pulled my hand up to look at it. He frowned, seeming confused. "These are pretty," he stated, ignoring my remark about me not being his girlfriend.

It's like he has selective hearing and can only hear what he wants to. "Yeah." My heart was banging so loudly in my chest I wouldn't be surprised if he could hear it.

"Where did you get them? Have you always worn these?" he asked curiously.

Oh God I'm not going to lie about being married to Clay, even if he gets angry about it. I'll never deny my marriage; it's the best thing that ever happened to me. "They're wedding rings." I gulped, watching as his face snapped up to mine, his blue eyes seeming to harden as his jaw tightened.

"Wedding rings?"

I nodded. "Yeah I got married in Vegas last weekend."

His hold on my hand tightened, almost crushing my fingers. I winced, trying not to whimper. "You got married? Is this some fucking joke? Because if it is it's not funny," he growled, looking at me warningly.

"It's not a joke," I said breathlessly whilst trying to pull my hand from his hold.

"You married him? Preston. We're talking about that fucking punk Preston again right?" he shouted, shoving me against the fence harder as he slammed his hand against it level with my face, missing me by mere inches. I whimpered and tried my best to stay calm.

"Clay and I are married now, Blake, so you need to leave me alone." I tried to sound more confident that I felt, but I was pretty sure I didn't pull it off though. I felt sick. My legs were shaking so badly that I wasn't sure how much longer they would support me.

Suddenly he laughed and shook his head. "This is some sort of sick joke. You can't be married, you're not old enough." He rolled his eyes, his face softening.

The click of a door sounded behind him so I breathed a sigh of relief. He was standing too close to me for me to see Clay yet, but I smiled with relief, waiting for Blake to be yanked off of me. He wasn't. Instead a woman spoke.

"Blake, what on earth are you doing out here? We were waiting for you, the food's here."

He turned back and looked over his shoulder. As he moved I saw a pretty girl with black hair standing in the doorway looking at him like he was stupid or something.

That must be his sister, they look a little alike.

"Hey, Michelle, yeah sorry I was just talking to Riley." Blake wrapped his arm around my waist, pulling me forward towards his sister.

She smiled politely. "Oh really? You're Riley?" *Wow he obviously hasn't told her anything about the police or the restraining order.* "It's nice to finally meet you, I've been hearing a lot about you from Blake. You're the first girl he's ever talked about." She smiled affectionately at her brother.

I put on a fake smile and pulled away from Blake towards his sister, holding out my hand to her. "Nice to meet you, Michelle."

She grinned and shook my hand, looking at my cast a little bemused. I moved so I could step past her into the building positioning myself so that she was between me and Blake so I could make a run for it. The warmth of the restaurant surrounded me, and my body started to relax because of how close Clay was. He was just in the other room, I could scream his name and he'd be here in an instant. My heart was returning to normal just at the thought of him alone.

"Maybe you could come over to the house for dinner one night," Michelle suggested.

Blake smiled happily. "She'd love to, right Jailbait?"

I smiled weakly. "I've got to get back to my friends. They're going to think I fell in the toilet or something." I nodded towards the restaurant.

"Okay well arrange a day with Blake. I'm glad you're back from your vacation. He's been a real grouch without you," she said, slapping Blake's shoulder but smiling happily at the same time.

He told her I was on vacation? Seriously he is so deranged! "Nice to meet you," I mumbled as I turned and walked off as fast as I could.

As I got to the table I grabbed Clay's hand and pulled him to his feet. He looked at me guiltily. "I'm sorry, Riley Bear, I got caught sneaking into the girls' toilets. The manager guy made me come back to my seat. What took you so long anyway?"

"We need to leave right now." I stepped closer to him, pressing my face against his chest. I could feel the tears starting to build in my eyes.

"Riley, what's happened?" he questioned, hugging me tightly. His voice sounded slightly panicked and stressed.

"Please, we need to leave right now. Will you get my purse? We need to go." I was going to have a full blown meltdown any minute and I didn't want to do that here. I also didn't want Clay anywhere near Blake, I knew he would probably beat the life out of him, and he almost got into trouble with the police for that last time. I couldn't have him in trouble for defending me.

"Okay, Riley Bear." He pulled away from me and bent down under the table, grabbing my purse from the floor. He pulled out twenty bucks and handed it to Tom. "Here, pay for our food okay? We've got to go."

"Everything okay?" Tom asked, sounding confused.

I kept my gaze firmly fixed on the floor, trying to control my breathing as the tears started to fall down my face. "No idea, Riley wants to leave. I'll speak to you later," Clay said quietly, probably so I couldn't hear what he was saying.

He wrapped his arm around my waist and I immediately turned for the door walking quickly with him at my side. When I got to his car the tears were rolling down my face. I swiped at them angrily. *Why the hell do I have to be so freaking weak and cry all the time?* He waited by my door, just watching me, looking slightly pained as I climbed in the car. He shut the door after me and jogged round to his side. He climbed in and started the car.

"Riley is everything all right? Has there been an accident or something? Has someone been hurt?" he asked desperately.

I shook my head. "No nothing like that. We just need to leave here, I'll tell you in a minute. Drive east," I instructed, nodding down the road.

He frowned looking even more confused. I glanced out of the windshield; I could see Blake's car parked a couple of spaces down from Jeff's. I briefly wondered how I'd not noticed it when we pulled up, but quickly remembered I was fooling around with Rachel, singing and teasing Jeff.

As we passed it, I prayed that Clay didn't see his car. If he knew that Blake was in there then he'd go back in after him, and I couldn't have that. Luckily though he didn't notice because he was too busy shooting me little worried glances as he drove down the road.

"What's happened, Riley? You're scaring me." Clay took my hand as he drove.

"Don't freak out, okay? We need to go to the police station." I swallowed my silent sobs.

"Why?" His face hardened immediately. "Did he call you again?" His other hand tightened on the steering wheel.

I gulped and shook my head. "No, he was at the restaurant," I whispered.

The car suddenly swerved on the road, making me clutch at my seat as he slammed on the brakes. "What the hell? He was at the restaurant? Did you see him there?" he shouted angrily.

"Please calm down! You can't just stay stopped here in the middle of the road." I winced as I looked over my shoulder at the couple of cars who also had to slam on their brakes and were stopped behind us, honking their horns angrily. One of the cars pulled around us, the driver shouting profanities as he drove past.

Clay frowned angrily and pulled over to the side of the road so the cars could get past, all of them glaring at us angrily. "He was there?" Clay repeated.

"Yes," I whispered.

"Why didn't you tell me I could have gone and sorted it out." He was clearly annoyed; his eyes were tight with barely contained fury.

"That was the exact reason I didn't tell you. You can't just go and confront him, you'd get in trouble!" I cried, shaking my head fiercely. I couldn't even think about him getting into trouble, or even worse than that, getting hurt.

"Did he see you?" he asked quietly.

I nodded. "Yes. Can we go to the police station and report it, please?" I begged. I didn't want to talk about this to Clay; he was one step away from driving back to the restaurant, I could tell by his face. I'd tell him once we got to the station.

"There's something to report?" Clay asked, looking at me intently, as if he was trying to drag the truth from my eyes. I squirmed in my seat. I hated to lie to him, but I couldn't tell him yet. When he found out he was going to go crazy and it would be better if Blake was in custody when Clay found out.

"Yes," I confirmed. "Can you drive us there without getting us killed?" I teased, trying to lighten the mood in the car. You could practically cut the atmosphere with a knife he was so tense.

"I think I can manage," he mumbled, starting the car again and pulling out. I looked out of the windshield all the way there, I could feel Clay's intense gaze almost boring a hole into the side of my face so I kept my eyes firmly fixed out the front. How we didn't die on the way there I have no idea because he hardly looked at the road.

When we pulled up in the parking lot about fifteen minutes later I was calm again. Just being near Clay made me feel better, and we were about to report it. Hopefully they could do something about it now, and he'd stay away from me.

Clay unbuckled my seatbelt and gripped hold of my waist pulling me onto his lap, wrapping his arms around me so I couldn't get away from him. "Did he hurt you?" he asked. His voice shook with anger.

"No," I whispered, pressing my face into the side of his neck.

"You spoke to him?"

I nodded. "He grabbed me while I was waiting for you near the bathrooms and dragged me outside through the fire door," I muttered against his neck. I felt his body jerk in his seat as his muscles tightened all over his body.

"What did he say?" he asked, gripping my shoulders and pushing me away from him so he could look at my face.

"Not much, he knows were married now. He saw my rings, but he thought I was joking." I looked at Clay apologetically. He didn't deserve all of this hassle. I had so much baggage. We should just be like a normal married couple in the honeymoon phase, not heading off to the police station to report things like this all the time. Clay deserved better than me, he deserved everything.

"But he didn't hurt you?" he questioned, cupping my face in his hands looking at me worriedly.

I shook my head and bent forward, pressing my lips to his softly. "He didn't hurt me, I promise. Come on let's go report it and then get some food, I'm starving," I suggested, trying to change the subject from the crazy guy who was harassing me.

• • •

WE WERE AT THE police station for almost three hours; they had no one to take our report so we were waiting for almost two hours for an officer to be free. I sat there munching on a packet of chips that Clay had bought from the vending machine. When we were finally interviewed I had to run though everything again and again. The whole time I could almost feel the hatred coming from Clay in waves. His hand was a tight fist on his leg. If he saw Blake at this exact moment in time I was pretty sure he'd kill him.

Finally, after what felt like forever and a day, we were done. Once I signed my report, we left and headed back to the car. I settled back in my seat and closed my eyes. It was almost midnight now, and I was starving and tired, I just wanted to curl up in a bed with my husband and have him hold me.

"You still hungry, Riley Bear?" Clay asked as he drove towards our apartment.

"A little but I can wait until breakfast." I shrugged; I didn't even really have the energy to eat now anyway.

"Okay, we'll go straight home then." He took my hand, stroking the back of it with his thumb. It didn't take very long to get home; there was no traffic around at that time of night so we were home within ten minutes. I followed Clay wearily up to our apartment and sighed as I plopped down on the edge of the bed. I couldn't even be bothered to take off my clothes.

Clay smiled and pulled my shirt off over my head throwing it on the floor before pushing on my shoulder making me lay back onto the bed. His hands trailed down my body to the waistband of my jeans. He unbuttoned them and slowly pulled them off before hovering above me his green eyes burning into mine making my stomach flutter.

"Promise me that he didn't hurt you," he whispered.

"I swear." I nodded; I gripped my hand around the back of his head and pulled his mouth to mine. The damn boy was so stressed his whole body was tense. I kissed him, hard, showing him how much I loved him and needed him. He responded immediately, kissing me with exactly the same intensity making my heart speed up in my chest.

I ran my hands up his back under his t-shirt and gripped his shoulders. "You're so tense, Clay. I could help you with that you know," I whispered. I wasn't tired anymore; my body was definitely wide awake.

"How are you gonna do that, beautiful girl?" he questioned, kissing down my neck and across my collarbone, leaving a burning trail across my skin.

"I have my ways." I rolled so I was on top then sat up on his stomach straddling him, smiling down at him wickedly. I needed to take his mind off of Blake, and I knew just how to do that.

chapter twenty-three

I woke early the next morning so excited that I wanted to jump up and down. We were decorating today, but first we needed to go and buy the paint. My mom and Clay's parents were coming over at about eleven so we needed to get everything ready by then. I was a little nervous about Richard coming because I knew that Clay hadn't forgiven him at all and didn't want to see him. Hopefully they would be all right today; I decided to keep them separated today so that we could keep the peace. Though maybe I'd have to bribe Clay using sexual favours to give his dad another shot, it would kill his mom if they didn't speak again. Richard was actually a genuinely great guy; it was just a shock for him, us just announcing we were married like that. At least he wanted to work things out with Clay, not like David who still refused to even acknowledge that we were married.

I turned carefully and looked at the clock; it wasn't even seven in the morning. I sighed. *I guess I should let him sleep for a little longer.* We'd fooled around until well after one o'clock this morning so he was bound to be a little tired. I rolled back over to face him and buried my face in the crook of his neck as I traced my fingers across his chest and abs slowly, making my mouth water. *Jeez, my husband is seriously yummy! Should I lust after him this much? Should I just want to jump his bones all the time or am I a little perverted?*

I traced my fingertips down a little lower, following the line of muscle near his hips, the V shape that led down to his groin. That was my favourite part of his stomach. I felt my passion for him spike as he made a little contented sigh in his sleep and tightened his arm around me. *Yeah, I can wake him up now; we can maybe just come to bed early later if he's tired!*

I shifted and straddled him pressing my body against his as I kissed him lightly on the lips. He looked so beautiful when he was asleep, so peaceful and just freaking perfect. He stirred a little in his sleep, his arm wrapping around me pulling me closer to his body. I smiled and kissed him again. He moaned quietly and kissed me back softly.

His hand moved up and tangled in the back of my hair. "You need to get off of me. If my wife catches you in here she'll kick your ass," he mumbled huskily as I kissed down his neck. He still hadn't opened his eyes.

I grinned against his skin. "I bet I could take her."

"I don't know, Riley's pretty feisty when she wants to be," he teased, tickling his hands down my back.

I pulled back and grinned at him. "Then we'd better be extra quiet so she doesn't hear us," I joked, raising my eyebrows, biting my lip looking at him flirtatiously.

He grinned and flipped me onto my back quickly, making me squeak in surprise as he hovered above me. "You think you can be quiet?" he replied, grinning at me knowingly.

I bit my lip as I wrapped my legs around his waist; I nodded, trying to look confident. "Yeah. I bet you can't make me scream."

He laughed. "I'll take that bet." He crashed his lips to mine, and I felt my heart skip a beat, I was so excited I could barely breathe. I knew I'd lose the bet; I always lost Clay's bets.

• • •

AT JUST AFTER ELEVEN the doorbell rang. I jumped off of the sofa to answer it, but Clay grabbed my hand pulling me behind him. He was worried about Richard hurting me, I could tell by the way his jaw was set. We both walked to the front door, and I saw his body stiffen as he opened it to show the three of them standing there. Richard was at the back and was looking extremely reproachful and apologetic.

"Hey," Clay mumbled, opening the door and still holding me half behind him. My mom smiled and walked in like she owned the place. She had an armful of old paint splattered sheets and was wearing a pair of dungarees that I only ever saw come out when she was decorating.

"Morning. Not interrupting anything are we?" She smirked at me as she walked into the lounge dumping the sheets on the floor. We'd already moved a lot of the furniture into the middle of the room this morning after we got home from the store with the paint.

I grinned and looked back to Linda and Richard; Linda smiled at Clay gratefully as she kissed his cheek. She looked really uncomfortable, and I guess

237 · Kirsty Moseley

was kind of in the middle of the two main men in her life. If they couldn't make it up then she would find it extremely hard.

"Hey, Mom," Clay nodded; I noticed that he put on a forced smile as his dad stepped over the threshold.

"Clay, Riley." Richard nodded in greeting looking at both of us apologetically. "I'm so sorry about what happened. I shouldn't have done that. I would never hurt you, Riley; I can't believe I did that. It was just heat of the moment. I shouldn't have."

Where I was pressed against Clay I felt his body tense up even more, he was like a snake poised for the attack. "If another moment like that happens again then you and I are going to have a problem," he growled angrily, his voice full of acid.

Richard shook his head. "It won't. I'm so sorry, and thank you for letting me come and help today. I really appreciate it; I don't deserve you to forgive me."

"You're not forgiven!" Clay snapped, looking at him warningly. He still hadn't shut the front door, he looked like he was contemplating throwing his dad back outside and slamming the door in his face. I winced at how uncomfortable this conversation was, and squeezed Clay's hand to get his attention. He looked back at me so I gave him the puppy dog face, begging him with my eyes to let it go. He sighed and turned back to his dad. "But thank you for helping with the painting," he mumbled grudgingly.

Richard smiled at me gratefully, and I smiled back. He was a lovely guy at heart and was like a second dad to me, I didn't want to lose him from my life either if I could help it.

"I'd better go see what your mother's doing, probably spilling paint on your floor knowing her," Richard said, excusing himself sheepishly and heading into the lounge at the end of the hall.

I put my hand over Clay's on the door and pushed it shut. He sighed and turned back to me. I was extremely proud of him, I knew that he didn't want to see his dad again and the fact that he was putting that aside, made him even more of a man to me.

"That was the right thing to do," I whispered, stepping closer to him.

He nodded, frowning. "I guess."

"Thank you for doing that for your mom, I know you didn't want to." I wrapped my arms around his waist and nibbled on his jaw lightly. Clay always seemed to like that.

"I didn't do it for her, Riley Bear; I did it because you wanted me to. It's killing me to have him in here after what he did to you," he mumbled, tracing his fingers across my cheek as if the mark would still be there.

I pulled back and looked at him. "Well then thank you for doing it for me." I kissed his lips lightly, just marvelling over how lucky I was to have him love me like he did.

He sighed and nodded, pressing his lips against mine for a second before pulling away and smirking at me. "Come on then, my dad's right; you know your mom's going to be spilling paint on the floor."

I laughed and followed him into the lounge where they were busy arguing playfully over who gets the biggest roller and who has to paint in the edges. Richard smiled sheepishly as we walked in, he looked terribly uncomfortable and I actually felt a little sorry for him.

I cleared my throat, wanting to take away some of the tension in the air. "Richard, do you think maybe you could help Clay move the rest of the furniture into the middle of the room before we start?" I asked, patting Clay on the butt playfully.

"Sure." Richard smiled happily.

I heard Clay groan quietly beside me so I gave him a little shove in the direction of the bookcase. I headed over to join the argument over who gets the rollers and who gets the paint brush, all the time watching Clay as he moved the larger pieces of furniture with his dad. They seemed to be making a little small talk, some of it about football and school. Clay seemed to be making a real effort, and I was immensely proud of him for it.

The police called later that day to tell us that they had arrested Blake for breaking the terms of the restraining order but because he hadn't actually hurt me or threatened me, that the case wouldn't be dealt with quickly. They'd let him out on bail, and he would have to go to court in about a month. Though even that seemed a little pointless, the most likely punishment he would get would be a fine, or the most would be community service.

To say that Clay was less than happy about it would be an understatement. He'd actually smashed the glass he was holding against the wall in anger but, in the cold light of day, there was nothing either of us could do about it. Hopefully now that Blake was actually going court that it would give him a little heads up that I wasn't interested. He wouldn't come near me again I was sure of it, if he did then the police would take him in again and this time they would hold him until his court case. They'd told him that too so he was very aware of the situation; he couldn't be that stupid so I relaxed slightly.

Clay and I finally started living like a married couple - we even had our first fight, but to be honest it was kind of forced because we both found it funny. He argued that I hadn't washed the dishes; I argued that he didn't put his clothes in the laundry. We shouted for about a minute before we both burst out laughing and ended up making love in the dirty laundry still arguing back and forth; which, in a weird way, was kind of sexy.

The apartment was incredible, and I loved waking up to him knowing that he was mine and always would be. His parents and my mom had been over

239 · Kirsty Moseley

for dinner one night. David still refused to speak to me or Clay. My mom said that he would come round eventually, but I didn't hold up much hope for it. I loved him like a father, and I would always think of him as my dad, but he was making me choose and I would choose Clay every time. David just didn't seem to understand the situation at all, all he saw was that his seventeen year old daughter had run off and got married in Vegas.

By the time the decorating was finished, Clay and I seemed to be on a paint fume high. I was ecstatic when it was finally done, and we could just relax and enjoy our apartment. Clay's football team were doing great too, there was some sort of competition they were entered into, and they had sailed through to the finals which was a week from tomorrow. He was training like crazy, every day after school he would go to an hour and a half practice. I thanked my lucky stars that I'd arranged to volunteer at the library because that would kill me to see him tackled and taken out for an hour and a half every day. Working at the library for the week had been like a godsend.

I couldn't wait for the football season to be over with, it was a constant worry about him from start to finish, but he just didn't seem to understand that. I hated to see him wince when he moved or be covered in bruises from a rough tackle, the sooner it was over and done with the better in my opinion. Other than that though we'd been living together for exactly two weeks and life couldn't be any more perfect. Life as Mrs Clay Preston was like living a dream.

Today was Friday, and I couldn't wait for the weekend to start. Last weekend we'd been painting and had his parents and my mom round so we couldn't just chill and spend time together. This weekend we were free to lounge around in our pyjamas eating ice cream until it came out of our ears if we wanted to. Clay had been working so hard at practice all week that he deserved to be pampered for the weekend, so I was going to do exactly that. I had lots of massages and bubble baths planned for us. We just needed to get through one more practice with him not being hurt too badly, and then the weekend could start.

I kissed his lips one last time and skipped off towards the library, ignoring the wolf whistle that he sent in my direction as I walked away. I smiled to myself and pushed the door open, looking back over my shoulder to see him standing there at the other end of the hallway with his hand on the door, making sure I went in okay before he went to practice.

"Go," I mouthed, pointing to the door, trying to look stern.

He smiled. "I'm going," he mouthed back, still standing there waiting for me to go in. He was so overprotective still that it was plain ridiculous, but it made him feel better so I didn't keep complaining about it. He raised an eyebrow at me and smirked looking so hot that my tummy quivered with butterflies. *Just an hour and a half and counting and then the weekend will start!* I sighed and headed into the library knowing he was going to stand there until I went in so I might as well concede and let him win.

Mrs Sing smiled at me warmly as I walked in. "Hi, Riley."

"Hey, so what shall I do today?" I asked, looking at the stack of returned books that were sitting there ready to be put away.

She smiled and nodded. "Returns, if you don't mind." She looked at me apologetically but to be honest it was quite fun in a bookworm kind of way. Much better than sitting in the cold listening to Clay get shouted at and smashed to the floor, so I was grateful for whatever I could do.

I loaded them onto a trolley and set to work putting them in the right places, taking my time with it in case she didn't have anything else for me to do and sent me to the field or something. Just before four o'clock I couldn't string it out any longer so I headed over to the desk looking at her hopefully.

"Anything else need doing?" I asked, desperately looking around for a job.

"Actually I have a lot of book requests that students have placed that I need to order from the central library. Would you mind doing that for me?" She pulled up another chair next to her and flicked on the laptop.

I breathed a sigh of relief and headed round to the desk sitting in the chair next to hers, filling in the form for the requests. After about five minutes the library phone rang. She answered it smiling, and I tried not to listen to her conversation, but I couldn't exactly help it, she was sitting next to me. Something about an order that she'd placed being over budget, but she was adamant she'd checked it and that it was within the limit that she was given. Finally after a few minutes she agreed to go and speak to the principal about it in person rather than over the phone.

She looked at me apologetically. "Sorry, Riley, but I can't leave you in here on your own because of health and safety. It's after school hours now so the school could get in a lot of trouble if you fell and hurt yourself and no one was here with you."

I groaned internally but nodded, putting on a brave face. *There's only twenty minutes of practice left now so at least I won't have to watch for that long.* "It's okay. I'll go see how Clay's doing." I shrugged, reluctantly pushing myself up from the chair and grabbing my schoolbag.

"Have a great weekend. You have anything planned?" she asked as she grabbed her purse and followed me out of the library, flicking off the lights and locking the door behind her.

I smiled happily. "Nope, and it's going to be awesome."

She laughed and rolled her eyes. "Young love, I remember those days. You make the most of it while you can because the honeymoon stage doesn't last forever."

I grinned. "I know, but whatever stage comes after that will be fun too." I skipped off towards the parking lot making her laugh and head in the other

241 · Kirsty Moseley

direction towards the principal's office.

I squinted when I got outside; it was a lot brighter than the dingy library so I needed to let my eyes adjust. I set off walking through the parking lot towards the school field on the other side. I heard footsteps behind me so I stopped and looked around wondering who on earth could be here at this time of day. The whole school usually left this place as soon as possible, no one ever hung around after unless there was a club or sport that they were attending. I flicked my eyes around the parking lot but couldn't see anyone at all. I was just being stupid, I knew that, but I couldn't slow my heartbeat down as I turned back and walked a little faster towards the field.

Suddenly someone grabbed me from behind, an arm wrapped around my waist and another clamped over my mouth muffling my scream.

chapter twenty-four

~ Clay ~

Finally coach blew the whistle signalling the end of practice. I smiled gratefully and rubbed my sore hands together; brushing off the dirt from the last tackle I'd taken. Coach Bradley wanted to run through all of our plays, and lucky me had gotten volunteered to play the opposition for most of them. Therefore I'd spent a lot of the last hour and a half pushing myself up off of the floor. I silently thanked my lucky stars that Riley was inside because she would have been freaking out today. The practice was brutal.

I guess Coach needed to work us hard, next Saturday was the final of the State Championship, and we wanted to win. It meant a lot to the whole school, not just the players, so we wanted to do well. We were ready for it after all of these extra practices. As long as none of us got injured in the week leading up to it then we should be able to walk an easy victory.

Coach Bradley waved me over as everyone headed in to shower; I lagged a little behind letting the rest of the team head in so he could speak to me in private.

He smiled as I got to him. "Great practice, Clay. I just need you to keep your eye on Andy, he's still lacking in confidence. I need him to be top of his game ready for Saturday." He patted me on the back, looking at me hopefully.

"I'll talk to him. Don't worry, Coach, everything will be fine. It's going to be a breeze," I said, waving my hand dismissively. We definitely had the better team, and our record this season was relentless and would have The Crows scared of us ready for the match next week.

Coach smiled. "Clay, I just wanted to thank you for all of your hard work over the last year, I know you always put in a hundred percent but this year you've really made my job easy for me. You're one hell of a captain," he enthused. "You're definitely sure you don't want to try out for college ball? I know I could get a couple of scouts to come and look at you, I could pull in a few favours," he offered, looking at me quizzically.

I smiled gratefully but shook my head. I didn't want to play professionally, that was never my intention. I wouldn't have the commitment or the dedication for this to be my life full time. My interests were more mechanical; since I was a little kid I'd always had a fascination for all things robotic or machine. Riley used to tease me about it because I would get a new toy for my birthday and then immediately take it apart to see how it worked instead of playing with it. The apprenticeship I had been offered was actually more like a dream job to me, and I knew I would enjoy going to work every day. *Well, unless I have to leave Riley naked in bed in the morning then I'm pretty sure my job will become a pain in the butt!*

"I'm sure thanks, Coach. I don't want to do this forever; it's just fun for me." I shrugged.

He smiled sadly and nodded. "I wish I had your talent, Clay. It's nice for me to be able to teach such a mature and talented young man, so thank you." He squeezed my shoulder and nodded towards the changing room door. "Go get showered and take your girl home, I know that's the only thing you're thinking about right now," he teased.

I smiled gratefully; I'd been waiting for practice to finish since I put on my uniform an hour and a half ago. This weekend Riley had promised it was just us, and I was certainly planning on making the most of my wife for the next two days.

I stood under the spray of the shower, wincing, letting the hot water pound onto my shoulders and back. *Damn, my whole body hurts. I need to get rid of all of these aches and pains before I see Riley; she's like some damn mind reader sometimes and always knows when I'm hurt.*

I dried and changed quickly and headed to the library to meet her. When I pushed the door though it didn't open. I looked at it confused and tried it again, but it was locked. *What the hell?* I squinted through the door, but even the lights were off. *Why the hell would the library be locked? She always waits in there for me. Maybe she finished early. Mrs Sing might have had something to do tonight and need to leave early.* I sighed and headed back towards the field, assuming that she must have come out while I was showering and we'd crossed paths. She was probably sitting on the bleachers reading or starting her homework or something.

When I got to the field I scanned the bleachers for her, but there was no one there at all. *Where the hell is she?* Coach walked out of the changing rooms and looked at me confused. "I thought you left already," he mused, frowning.

"I can't find Riley. Have you seen her come back here? The library's closed." I was starting to get a little worried now. She knew I would be stressed if she wasn't there so she wouldn't have gone too far without sending me a message or something.

Coach shook his head. "I haven't seen her, she hasn't come back here. She's probably waiting in the car for you." He shrugged.

I tried to make myself relax. *He's right she's probably waiting at the car listening to music or something. Calm down, Clay.* I nodded and turned and ran off back towards the parking lot again. Even as I was running towards it I could see she wasn't in the car. I started to feel sick. She wouldn't do this without good reason, not with the whole Blake thing hanging over our heads; she didn't like to make me worry.

I pulled out my cell phone and called her, but it went straight to voicemail. My heart was starting to beat a little too fast as I turned in circles, scanning for her. Suddenly I spotted something off to one side over along the side of the school. I took off in a sprint towards it, and before I even got there I knew it was Riley's schoolbag. I grabbed it off of the floor with shaky hands.

"Riley!" I shouted as loud as I could, hoping she had just dropped her bag or something and was just playing some sort of trick on me. If she was there was seriously going to be a huge argument because this was scaring the shit out of me. "Riley!" I shouted again as I pulled out my cell phone, trying again to call her as I sprinted back towards the office to see if anyone had seen her.

As I burst in through the office door I saw Mrs Sing just walking out of the principal's office, smiling as they spoke. I walked up to them quickly interrupting their conversation. "Mrs Sing, where's Riley?" I asked desperately. I noticed my voice was so tight with stress that it didn't even sound like mine.

She smiled politely and looked at me confused. "She went to meet you about three quarters of an hour ago."

I groaned and gripped my hands into my hair. *Where the hell is she?* "She didn't come out to the field; I just found her bag in the parking lot," I choked out.

Principal Owens stepped forward and gripped my shoulder, frowning. "Have you tried calling her?" he asked.

I nodded. "Yeah I just got her voicemail," I whispered. I needed to get out of here and look outside again; I couldn't stand in this little dull office anymore, I was going out of my mind.

What do I do if Blake has come here? What if he got to her while I was practicing and no one knew? Mrs Sing said that she came to find me forty five minutes ago; if it is him he could have done anything to her by now. I could feel the rage boiling up inside me; if Blake had touched one hair on her head I was killing him this time. There was no way I was letting this one go, not again, he needed to back the fuck away from my wife because this was beyond crazy.

~ Riley ~

I GLANCED OVER AT Blake while he was driving. I felt sick. *Clay's going to go crazy when he realises I'm not at school. Jeez, he's going to worry himself into an early grave about me!* Blake had a small smile on his face as he drove us to goodness knows where. I just sat there quietly, not wanting to upset him or anything. He'd practically carried me kicking and screaming into the car, but no one had been around to see or hear, so no one would even know I was gone until Clay started to look for me.

Luckily I'd learnt a lesson from the last time that he grabbed me. I'd been carrying my cell phone in my pocket instead of my purse so I knew I had that on me. But I couldn't exactly call anyone while he was with me, I didn't even know where we were going so I didn't want to risk pulling out my phone and wasting the one phone call I would probably get time to make.

He hadn't hurt me at all, just bundled me into his car and had ordered me to stop crying. As I sat there, I tried desperately to control myself, I didn't want to get upset and give him an excuse to hurt me. I just needed to play along, keep him talking, and look for an opportunity to call Clay. Clay would then call the police and everything would be fine. I just needed to stay in control of myself, not upset him, and pray that he wasn't driving us too far away.

He glanced over at me and smiled. "How was school?" he asked casually, as if this whole situation wasn't happening at all.

I gulped and willed my voice to come out more confident than I felt. "It was okay."

"That's good. You've been hanging around in the library a lot after school," he stated. My blood seemed to run cold in my veins. *Oh God, has he been watching me at school? Wow, this is actually worse than I first thought.*

"I have a job there volunteering," I replied quietly as I rejected yet another call that was vibrating against my leg in my jeans pocket. I felt sick that I was doing that to Clay, but I needed to find out where we were going first, I couldn't risk letting it carry on vibrating in my pocket because Blake might hear it. I couldn't just press answer because Clay might shout through the phone or something and then Blake would find it and I would lose my only chance.

"Yeah you said before that you like reading, I bet that suits you working there." He smiled over at me as he pulled into a crappy street that I had no idea what it was called.

I nodded and looked around for some sort of street name or something so

I could get my bearings, but there wasn't any. My heart sank a little more. *Right I just need to go for it and ask him where he's taking me.*

"Where are we going?" I asked, trying not to sound too interested but just enough to play along.

He smiled. "My place. I thought you might like to come hang out or something. We could get a takeout if you want," he suggested happily.

Holy crap he really has lost the plot! What on earth is wrong with him that he would think that bundling me into a car is normal? "I'm not hungry," I mumbled.

He indicated and pulled into a driveway on the left. Again I looked around desperately for a street name. My mind was whirling with thoughts as he cut the engine. *Will Clay know where Blake lives if I just tell him we are at his place? What if he doesn't? What am I supposed to do once I get inside with Blake... carry on pretending that this is normal and keep him talking? What if he wants to make out, or more?* I swallowed a sob at the thought of what he would probably want from me if we were alone at his house. *Alone. Oh God, what if we aren't alone? Michelle might be in there! Please let his sister be here so I can ask her for help and tell her what he's been doing!* Hope was bubbling up inside me at the new thoughts.

Blake turned to me and smiled. "You've not been to my place before, hell, I've never had any girl over so this is a first for me." He laughed quietly and actually looked a little nervous about it.

I gulped and nodded quickly, not knowing what to say. I was actually terrified of going inside with him. At least while we were in the car it provided some measure of safety, we were in the street so he couldn't exactly force himself on me, but once we were inside it was a different story.

He pushed his door open so I quickly weighed my options. *Could I outrun him if I ran down the street screaming for help? Would anyone even hear me or see me; because I hadn't seen one single person outside, people were probably at work or something.* The only other thing I could think of was to lock myself in the car, but I didn't have the keys. I debated how hard it would be to hotwire a car. It never looked too hard in movies, just rub two wires together and the car started. It was worth a try surely...

When his door closed I slammed my hand down on my door lock before scooting over to his side and doing the same with his lock as I looked around helplessly. I pulled the sun visor down hoping that a spare key would fall out like in the movies but, of course, that didn't happen.

My eyes fell on the steering column, and I wondered how I was supposed to get the plastic cover off so I could get to the wires inside. I yelped when his hand slammed down on the roof of the car making a loud bang reverberate through the car.

"Open the door, Jailbait," he called calmly through the window, pointing at the door lock.

I looked at his face and shook my head, now crying helplessly. His eyes were hard and I immediately knew that I shouldn't have done this. I should have just played along and gone inside with him in the hope that Michelle was home. *Jeez, I'm so freaking stupid. Hotwiring a car? Wow, I've lost the plot too!*

"Open the fucking door, Riley," he growled, his breath fogging up the glass as he glared at me warningly.

"Please, Blake, I just want to go home," I begged, still clawing at the plastic edge of the steering column trying to get the damn thing off. I was a total damsel in distress, and the first thing I was doing when I got out of this situation – if I actually got out of this situation – was Googleing how to hotwire a car because that little titbit of information would be handy to know right about now. He shoved his keys in the lock so I pressed my hand down on the button so it wouldn't come open. My heart was crashing in my chest. All I wanted to do was curl into a ball on Clay's lap and sob.

When he couldn't open the door he moved away from the car, and I just watched him with my heart in my throat. *What is he doing? Is he leaving me in the car?* I glanced around quickly trying to look for the nearest house that seemed like someone was inside, looking for a tell-tale sign, maybe a car in the driveway or a TV playing or something. I was mentally planning to run to the house and tell them to call the police. My only comfort that came out of this situation was that the police would now be able to hold him until his trial in a month's time. Blake would be off the streets and Clay and I would be worry free, at least for a little while.

I felt sick. I could barely breathe as I put one hand on the door lock and the other on the handle of the car, ready to burst out of the door and run as soon as he was far enough away from me. Three houses down had a car in the driveway so that was where I was headed. *Just a couple of hundred yards, I can run that easily.*

A few feet away from the car he bent down and picked something up off of the grass before turning back to the car again. An angry frown lined his forehead. My eyes flicked down to his hand quickly, trying desperately to see what he'd picked up. He was holding a big stone. I frowned, confused. *What the heck is he going to do with that?*

He stopped by the side of the car and cocked his head to the side, looking at me intently. "Are you going to open the door, Jailbait?"

I shook my head, swiping at the tears that were just falling uncontrollably down my face. He rolled his eyes and brought his arm up above his head. I suddenly realised what he was doing and barely had enough time to turn away and cover my face before his hand, and the stone, smashed into the driver's side window. The sound of breaking glass was quickly followed by it spraying over my lap and shoulder, scraping my exposed skin in a few places.

I screamed as I heard him fumbling with the lock. My instincts kicked in then so I grabbed the door handle, pulling with all of my might to keep it closed as he fumbled with the handle on the other side. Even as I was doing it I knew it was useless though. I only really had one good hand, and I was nowhere near strong enough against him. He yanked the door open effortlessly, almost making me tumble out of the car at the same time because I was holding so tightly.

His fingers closed around my upper arm, pulling me up as I lurched out, heading face first towards the ground. Blake made a sort of angry snarling sound as he jerked me upright, pushing me back at the same time so I fell back against the car. My head flew back, hitting the car and my neck burned with that whiplash feeling. I whimpered as little lights danced at the corners of my eyes.

"That was so fucking stupid, Riley!" he ranted. "Now I have to fix my car!" His hand tightened on my upper arm, his nails digging in as he stepped closer to me, pressing me against the car with his body.

Clay, please help me! I screamed it over and over in my head, but I knew it was pointless because he didn't even know where I was.

"I... I'm sorry," I mumbled, trying to stop the tears from falling.

Instantly his face softened. He sighed and brushed his hand across the side of my face lightly, wiping my tears away. "Just don't keep doing things like that. What's the matter with you? I told you I won't hurt you again, but you just won't forgive me. How many times do I need to say sorry?" he asked softly, bending his head and kissing my cheek gently. Bile rose in my throat at the feel of his lips against my skin.

"I want to go home. My parents will be worried about me," I whispered. I knew I couldn't mention Clay at all. He seemed just to snap at the mention of his name so I couldn't risk him going crazy again.

"They won't mind you hanging here with me for a little while. I haven't seen you for ages." His hand traced down the side of my leg as he pressed his body harder against mine. His nose ran up the side of my jaw, inhaling deeply. "You smell so good. I've missed your smell," he whispered.

I nodded slowly, trying to think of something else. "Is Michelle home? I'd like to meet her again," I said weakly, my voice breaking as I spoke.

He shook his head and kissed the side of my neck. "Nope. She's staying at Martin's for the weekend. It's just gonna be me and you this weekend. No one to disturb us, some alone time, finally." His hand slipped round to my ass, squeezing tightly. He pulled away from me quickly and gripped my arm again, practically dragging me towards his house.

I closed my eyes and let him lead me along, knowing there was nothing else I could do. As soon as we were inside the door, I stopped in the hallway, and he finally let go of my arm. I flicked my eyes around, shocked. It looked so normal inside. I didn't really know what I was expecting it to be like, but the inside of his house was actually pretty cute looking, homely even.

"Blake, can I use the bathroom?" I asked weakly, putting on a fake smile.

He smiled in return. "Sure. My house is your house. It's down the end there." He nodded down the hallway and then turned back to the front door, flicking the lock. I jumped as it clicked into place; it felt like the sound echoed through my whole body and gave me goosebumps at the finality of it.

chapter
twenty-five

I swallowed loudly and turned, looking up the hallway for the bathroom. I spotted a door at the end so I quickly walked towards it, praying he wouldn't stop me. I silently hoped that maybe there was a window or something in there so I'd be able to get out and run to that house a couple of doors away.

"Don't be too long, Jailbait," Blake called.

I gulped and forced a smile as I nodded. As soon as I was in the bathroom I spotted the window and my hope spiked to new levels. I ran to it quickly, yanking on the handle, but it didn't open. *Locked? Damn it!* "Shit," I mumbled, pressing my forehead to the glass. I pulled out my cell phone from my pocket praying that Blake wouldn't hear me talking in here; if he did then it would be game over.

I dialled Clay's number quickly and held my breath as I moved as far away from the door as possible in case Blake was listening or waiting for me outside. I knew I would only get a couple of minutes so I needed to be quick, and very, very quiet.

Clay answered almost immediately. "Riley?" he cried desperately.

Hearing his voice made a sob rise in my throat. I squeezed my eyes shut, wishing I was home with him starting the lazy weekend that I'd planned for us. "Yeah. Shh, baby, listen to me," I implored. "Blake came to the school, and he forced me into his car. I'm at his place, do you know where that is?" I whispered.

"He fucking what?" Clay screamed. I winced as my ears started to ring because of how loud he'd shouted.

"Baby, shh. I don't know how long I've got on the phone! I'm in the bathroom. Do you know where he lives or not, because I don't know where I am."

He answered immediately. "Yeah, yeah I know where he lives. I'll be there as soon as I can, but I think he lives like half an hour away. Can you stay in the bathroom?" he asked, sounding almost frantic.

I knew I wouldn't be able to stay in the bathroom for long; Blake would get suspicious soon so I'd have to go out, but I didn't want Clay to be worrying more than he needed to so I decided to play along and try to keep him calm. "I should be okay to stay in here. I've locked the door," I lied. "Please hurry. Call the police they'll get here quicker."

"I'm going to kill him this time," Clay growled. I could just imagine the murderous look on his face right now; I knew he meant it and the thought made me feel sick. I couldn't have Clay get into trouble and go to jail for me.

"Clay, call the police, baby. Go call them right now, okay? Then they'll be able to hold him until the trial. Don't come here on your own, promise me," I begged, swiping at the tear that fell down my face.

"The police are useless, Riley, they've done nothing to stop this at all!" he cried angrily.

Oh shit, he's going to come here on his own. He has no intentions of calling the police because he wants to beat Blake senseless. "Clay Preston, don't you dare do this! You call the police right now or I swear to you I'm going to be so pissed off. Don't risk this, please; I can't have you in trouble. Just call them and let them handle it," I begged fiercely.

"Riley-" he started, but I cut him off quickly.

"No, Clay, you do this for me, I'm going to hang up the phone now so you can call them. Don't you dare come here on your own!" I hissed, trying to sound stern.

"No, don't hang up!" Clay shouted desperately. "Riley, just keep the line open so I can hear you're all right. I'm still at the school so I'll call the police from here, just don't hang up on me okay?" he asked.

I gulped. "Okay, baby."

I slumped down to the floor and rested my head back against the wall, listening as he was talking to someone off of the phone. He sounded so desperate that it was painful to hear him panic so much. I could hear the principal's voice too so I knew he was doing as I asked, he wasn't coming here on his own. I was grateful for that.

After a couple of minutes Clay came back on the phone, talking soothingly about what we were going to do at the weekend, I knew he was trying to keep my mind of off everything and keep me calm, and I appreciated the small gesture. Suddenly I realised that I could hear the sound of a car engine in the background and the principal's voice was gone. *Is Clay coming here?*

My heart literally stopped because I didn't want him anywhere near Blake.

Not that I didn't think he could handle himself, because I knew that he could, but I just hated the thought of him being even a little hurt or then getting into trouble for fighting or something. Clay continued to talk to me calmly about how his football practice went, how they were going to thrash the other team in the final game, how the coach had asked him to talk to Andy. I knew he was just doing it to distract me from the situation.

"Clay, are you coming here on your own?" I whispered, praying he would say no. He didn't say anything so I took his silence as a yes. He didn't like to lie to me so usually he just avoided the question he didn't want to answer or changed the subject. I felt my heart sink. "Please don't. Please let the police handle it, Clay. Please, baby," I begged, grabbing a wad of tissue to wipe my constant stream of tears.

Suddenly a loud, incessant banging started on the bathroom door, making it shake on its hinges. I yelped in surprise, which of course started Clay panicking down the phone, shouting desperately for me to tell him what happened. I couldn't speak. My eyes were fixed on the door as it rattled on its hinges again.

"Jailbait, open the fucking door!" Blake shouted angrily from the other side.

I pushed myself up onto my feet, standing in the corner, pressing my cell phone too hard against my ear making it feel a little numb and my eardrums to ring from Clay's constant steam of panic that was blasting through the earpiece.

What do I do? Do I go out there and try to keep him talking, or do I just stay locked in here and hope that he can't get in? What if I don't open the door and he gets in here anyway – he'll be even more pissed and I'll get hurt again.

"Jailbait, I swear to God you need to open this fucking door right now!" Blake barked, banging the door hard again.

I turned to look at the window, fruitlessly trying it again before I made my decision. I gulped and knew I needed to open the door. How long would the police be? If I could just keep him talking until they got here...

"Clay, I need to hang up and go out before he breaks the door down!" I hissed down the phone, getting ready to disconnect the call.

"No! Riley, don't hang up, just put your phone in your pocket and keep the line open! Please? I'll be quiet, please just don't," he cried desperately.

"JAILBAIT!" Blake screamed angrily.

"I'm coming now!" I called, squeezing my eyes shut and willing myself to be strong. The banging stopped almost immediately, but I could still hear it in my ears. The sound was terrifying, and I knew I'd be hearing it in my dreams for a while after all this was over. *Hell, I bet I'll never be able to lock a bathroom door ever again after this!*

"Don't hang up," Clay begged again.

"Okay, baby, I won't. I need to go out now," I whispered, swiping at my face trying to stop crying, but it was useless. "I love you, Clay."

"I love you too, Riley Bear. I'll see you soon, and don't worry, everything will be just fine," he assured me softly. I gulped and carefully pushed my cell phone into the pocket of my jeans, praying that it wouldn't disconnect by accident or something because then Clay would freak the heck out.

Blake banged on the door again, just once, making me jump. I gulped and clasped my hands together holding my wedding ring tightly as I took the three steps towards the door, feeling my heart sink with every inch I got closer to it. I held my breath as I flicked the lock. As soon as the lock clicked, the door was wrenched open and Blake stood there glaring at me accusingly. He looked so livid that the hairs on the back of my neck prickled with fear.

"Sorry," I muttered, looking at the floor. *How did he get so messed up? What on earth is wrong with him that he's doing this to me? He barely even knows me, and he's acting like we've been dating for years or something. He really is deranged.*

He stepped closer to me and put his finger under my chin, forcing my face up. I couldn't make my eyes meet his though, so I focussed my attention on his lip ring instead, trying not to break down in hysterical sobs and wail for my husband to come and take me away.

"Have you been crying, Jailbait?" he asked. It surprised me how soft and tender his voice was after how hard his face had been when he opened the door. I nodded and bit my lip, not quite trusting my voice to speak. "Why?" he asked, brushing my hair behind my ear softly.

"I want to go home. Will you just take me home to my parents' house? I shouldn't be here because of the police and everything; I'm not allowed to see you," I mumbled, begging him with my eyes.

He frowned and shook his head. "Well that's just stupid. This whole thing has been blown way out of proportion. I told you I was sorry for hurting you, maybe you should just cancel the restraining order or something. Then there would be nothing in our way so we could move on," he suggested, shrugging. *Does he really think that it's just the restraining order in our way? Wow, just wow.*

I gulped and grasped for anything to say to make this situation better. But what do you say when you don't want to upset a sociopath? "You broke my arm, Blake," I whispered.

He almost growled as he gripped his hands in his hair looking extremely frustrated. "That was an accident! I'd been drinking, I didn't actually mean to hurt you, it just happened!" he cried, clearly annoyed with my comment.

Crap, I need to just change the subject because this is just making him madder at me! "I know it was. It's fine, let's just forget it," I offered, putting on a fake smile and sniffing through my semi-blocked nose. "Why don't you show me around or something?"

His face softened, and he broke out the heartbreaking smile that he first caught my attention with when I met him. "Yeah, I'd like that. Let's start in the kitchen, and I can make drinks and stuff. You hungry?" he asked, taking my hand and immediately tugging me up the hallway.

How long have I been here now? Are the police almost here? Please, please let them get here before Clay does! I desperately tried not to think of Clay bursting in here on his own and beating Blake to a pulp and then being towed away in handcuffs or something.

"Jailbait? I said are you hungry." He squeezed my hand a little and I quickly snapped back into myself. I needed to stop spacing out and stay in the moment so I could keep him calm! *Relax, Riley, everything's fine. Tonight Clay will kiss everything better and hold you when you wake up screaming because of this whole waking nightmare.*

"Er, not right now, but after we've looked around then maybe we could make dinner together or something?" I suggested, knowing that would kill some time.

He smiled happily as he grabbed two cans of Coke from the fridge, passing me one and gesturing around the room. "Kitchen," he stated, before pulling me back out of the room. I didn't even get a chance to look around before we were back out of the door. "Lounge," he said, waving his hand at the room. He pulled me back out again and towards the stairs. I groaned inwardly. *This is going to be the quickest house tour in history. So much for my great killing time plan!*

Probably less than a minute later he stopped outside another door. "And this... this one's my room." He smirked at me as he pushed a key into the door, unlocking it.

I felt my body jerk at the thought of going in his room. Why hadn't I thought this through? Why did I ask for a tour? Maybe he completely read something into it, thinking I wanted to see his room or something! *Damn it, Riley, you're so freaking stupid sometimes.*

He smiled at me as he pushed the door open, gesturing for me to go in first. I swallowed my sob and forced myself to walk over the threshold. I just prayed that he would wave his hand around again like he did for every other room and then we could go and make dinner or something. My eyes flicked to his bed and I bit my lip hard enough to draw blood, willing myself not to panic and pass out or something leaving myself completely exposed and vulnerable to him.

His room was a typical boy's room, just plain, and painted a royal blue, a little messy, but not unlike what Clay's room used to look like at his parents' house.

"Like it?" he asked.

I tried not to flinch as his hand rubbed the small of my back softly. I nodded and put on a fake smile. "Yeah, it's nice."

He grinned happily, and I noticed that his eyes flicked to the bed too as he stepped closer to me. *Oh God here it comes.* "You didn't see my favourite part yet," he murmured, looking at me so intently that it made my heart stop at the passion on his face. His favourite part? I looked around the room again wondering what it would be, maybe a games console or something probably in typical boy fashion.

He laughed and took hold of my shoulders turning me around so I faced the wall behind me, the one that the door was on. I felt my heart stop as my blood seemed to run cold. This situation was so much worse than I thought. I was in some serious trouble, and I needed to make sure that Clay didn't come anywhere near Blake, because this guy was crazier than both of us gave him credit for.

chapter

twenty-six

I couldn't take my eyes off of the wall. There were pictures everywhere of me, not just me though, that was the scary thing. Clay was there as well. There were pictures of us together, laughing or hugging, but in every picture Clay's face had either been scratched out leaving it white, or burned out leaving a ragged hole. I knew it was him because of his clothes and where we were. These weren't pictures of us as kids; these were pictures of things we'd done recently. Us at the football game, us at the store, at the movies, and other just random things. There was even one of us loading paint cans into Clay's trunk so I knew that one was less than a week old.

How long had he been following me, taking these pictures? Why hadn't I seen him? He literally must have been following me all the time. The ones that scared me the most were the ones of me or Clay at our apartment. There was even one taken from the street outside where Clay was closing the drapes in just his boxers so he must have been ready for bed. That meant that Blake was camping outside our apartment at night with a camera, just waiting. He knew we lived together.

I felt light-headed, and my lungs were starting to burn because I just couldn't remember how to breathe. Every inch of the wall was covered in photos of me. Why would Blake take Clay out of the pictures though? And in such a violent way too - did he want to hurt Clay? Panic was making my palms sweaty. What if Clay came here without the police and Blake went crazy? He had totally lost his mind, so he could literally do anything.

He was looking at me, obviously waiting for some sort of reaction and I didn't know what to do. How could I pretend this was normal? How could I put on a fake smile and pretend like this didn't make my blood run cold in my veins? I couldn't, my reaction was already starting, and I had no control over it at all.

I felt the scream trying to force its way out as I clamped my jaw tight so all that came out was a little whimper. *Oh crap, oh crap, OH CRAP!* My hands were shaking, my legs felt weak, and all I wanted to do was run from the house screaming for Clay to run as far away from here as possible so Blake didn't do anything to him.

"This one's my favourite." He moved me forward, closer to the sick shrine on the wall as he rubbed his hands up and down my arms softly. I struggled not to cringe away from him as bile rose in my throat. He pointed to a picture of me sitting on the bleachers on a game night. I was laughing at something, you could see I was wearing Clay's jersey, but I had a jacket over the top so that's probably why he didn't scratch off Clay's number or something. There was another photo of me overlapping this one, obviously cutting off who I was sitting with, but I knew it would be Rachel; I always sat with her at the games.

Blake sighed contentedly behind me. "You look so happy here. I love it when you smile. It lights your whole face, makes you look so damn hot. Actually, I love all the pictures, but that one is special," he whispered. His breath blew down my neck as he pressed his chest against my back.

"Because Clay isn't in it?" My voice broke when I said his name as I tried desperately not to have a full blown panic attack. As soon as I said the words, I immediately wanted to punch myself for mentioning his name. *Why? Why did I say that? Wow, I'm so stupid!*

His hands immediately tightened on my arms, his fingers digging into my skin making me wince. He made an angry snort. "That fucker ruins all the pictures; I never get a nice one of you on your own. Little shit. You need to stop hanging around with him, Jailbait!" he ordered, his voice hard and accusing.

How long had I been here now? It was literally only a few minutes since I'd called Clay, how long would it be before the police turned up? The police couldn't possibly have seen this shrine on his wall; otherwise they would be taking my complaint more seriously.

The pain in my upper arms started to get worse as his grip tightened on me. "Blake, you're hurting me," I whispered as my eyes filled with tears.

He huffed out a deep breath, letting go of me. He ran his hands through his hair roughly as he stepped to the side, his eyes piercing into mine with a harsh intensity that made my stomach ache. "Why do you have to hang around with that asshole? Why not someone else? A girl? Any other guy than Preston!"

Jeez, he has such a problem with Clay. What on earth is this really about? There has to be more to it. "Blake, why do you hate him so much?" I whispered, turning away from the wall of photos. I couldn't look at it anymore, it was making me feel light-headed, and I didn't want to pass out with him here and leave myself vulnerable.

His whole posture tightened as his hands clenched into fists. "He took everything from me! He took the only things I've ever cared about. He's living my fucking life!" he shouted, making me flinch from his anger.

What? What had Clay done to him? "What do you mean?" I asked, trying to keep my voice calm hoping to calm him down.

He growled in frustration and slammed his hand down on the dresser. "When my parents died the only thing I had left was football," he started.

I nodded. He'd told me that before, that he got injured and Clay had taken his spot while he recovered and then when Blake came back they had to share the running back position.

"So when he took my spot on the team I had nothing left. I was in such a bad place and that was the only thing keeping me sane and grounded, but that asshole stole it from me! I ended up missing my shot with the talent scouts because Coach decided to play Preston instead of me on the day they came, so I didn't get any college offers. I got stuck in a dead end job, earning shit money and no hopes for anything, all because of him. Everything's his fault, and now he's trying to steal you! You're the only girl I've ever liked, and he wants to take you away from me too!" He was clenching his jaw so tightly that I could see the muscles clenching.

I shook my head in rejection. He had twisted everything in his mind to make it Clay's fault when in reality it was no one's fault, he just had some terrible luck, that's all. "Blake, none of that is Clay's fault. He didn't ask to take your spot; he didn't ask to be played on those games when the scouts were there!" I cried, swiping at the tear that fell down my face.

His eyebrows knitted together. "I don't give a shit if he asked for it or not! Everything he has should be mine, he has everything and he takes it all for granted. He doesn't even care what I went through. Not once did he say sorry to me, not once!" He stepped closer to me, and I instantly flinched back from the anger on his face. "Well he's not taking you away from me. You and I are meant to be together, Riley, and I won't let him ruin it," he stated matter-of-factly as he brushed his hand across my cheek, wiping my tears. I pressed back against the wall, trying to squirm away from him.

"Blake, please. You need some help. Something's not right, and you need to talk to someone about it. They can help you," I whispered desperately.

I just prayed that Clay was listening to this through my cell phone so he would know not to come in the house on his own. If he could hear how crazy Blake was talking right now then he would know to just stop the car and wait far away, because Blake sounded like he genuinely wanted to hurt him. The thing that broke my heart though is that I knew Clay better than that, I knew he would come for me, if he arrived here before the police did then he would burst in here on his own with no care for himself.

Blake laughed quietly before bending down and kissing my cheek lightly. "I don't need to see anyone, silly, I just need to spend some time with you; you'll see I'm not such a terrible guy. Just give me another chance and I'll prove to you what a great boyfriend I can be." He stepped closer to me and pressed his body against mine lightly, pinning me against the wall.

I felt sick; my whole body was shaking as his hands moved to grip my waist softly. He smiled and pressed his forehead against mine as one hand slipped down to my ass and the other went around my waist holding me in place. I whimpered and bit the inside of my mouth hard enough to draw blood, just so I would have something else to think about other than the lust I could see in his eyes.

"Let's just put the past behind us and start over, please?" he whispered, his lips brushing against mine as he spoke. *Oh God, please don't let him rape me, please!* "Please, Jailbait? Give me another chance, I promise I can make you happy." His arm tightened on my waist, clamping me closer to him.

I swallowed my sob and took a deep breath. "Okay, Blake, sure. We'll start over," I whispered, knowing my voice would break if I tried to speak properly.

He grinned and pressed his lips against mine, kissing me fiercely. I whimpered, turning my head to the side quickly. I felt sick that he'd done that. I was married, and he'd just kissed me. I felt dirty and shameful - but I knew that was nothing compared to what I would feel like if I didn't get the heck out of his bedroom.

He almost growled in frustration as he pressed me harder against the wall. "Kiss me then for fuck sake," he demanded.

I grasped at anything I could say to change the subject and get his mind onto something else. "Blake, I'm hungry now. Do you think we could go downstairs and make something for dinner?" I asked quickly as he gripped my chin, pulling my face around to his again.

He sighed and frowned, obviously annoyed that I was making him wait. He looked at me for a long time, it felt like forever, and finally he smiled. "You're hungry?" he teased playfully.

Oh jeez, he really is bipolar! I nodded quickly. "Yeah. Are we going to get a takeout? I could go get one while you choose us a DVD or something to watch," I offered hopefully. *Please say yes and then I can get the heck out of this house!*

He smiled. "I'll cook something, I like to cook actually. I might even impress you with my culinary skills." He took my hand and nodded for the door. I smiled gratefully and felt some of the tension leave my body just because we'd be further away from a bed. Hopefully we'd be in the kitchen for a while cooking, and that would give the police time to arrive.

When we got to the kitchen, he headed straight for the fridge. I hung back, looking around at the back door; it was off to one side, about ten feet from me. I debated as to whether I could discreetly go and check if it was unlocked, or if that would totally give me away. Just as I decided it was worth a try and started inching towards the door, he turned, smiling at me happily. I stopped in my tracks, hoping he wouldn't have noticed anything.

"How about I make chicken stir fry?" he offered, holding up a packet of chicken.

I nodded quickly. "Yeah sure. You can cook that?" I asked, wanting to keep him talking as long as possible so it would string it out.

He laughed and threw the ingredients on the side, grabbing prepacked noodles and vegetables from the fridge. "Like I said, I'm a pretty good cook," he boasted. "Michelle's terrible so I do most of the cooking." When he had everything he wanted, he pushed some mushrooms towards me and a chopping board. "Want to help?" he asked, grinning happily.

I gulped and nodded wondering how he could be so casual about all of this. He really must be crazy, and I didn't think jail time would help him at all. He needed to talk to someone and maybe have some sort of medical help, because something was seriously wrong with him. Maybe losing his parents like that had done some damage to him inside and no one knew. Maybe it was some sort of attachment disorder or something, which was why he seemed to latch onto me and get so possessive so quickly. I actually felt a little sorry for him, if he was ill then this wasn't actually his fault, maybe he was a nice guy but just couldn't help it because he was sick.

He smiled and stepped closer to me, his side brushing against mine as he started cutting up the vegetables. I reached for a knife from the block and wondered if I should just turn around and threaten him with it, demand that he open the door or I'd stab him or something. I had a sinking feeling that wouldn't work though; I wouldn't be able to stab someone which would probably be evident on my face as I spoke the words.

No. I decided I should just stick to the original plan and try to keep him talking until the police arrived. I flicked my eyes to the clock on the wall; it was almost five o'clock now. I had called Clay about fifteen minutes ago so hopefully it wouldn't be that much longer before the police arrived. He hadn't hurt me, and I didn't think he would if I just played nice and pretended everything was okay. If I freaked out and started threatening him with a knife or something there was no doubt in my mind that he would hurt me if he was provoked.

I forced myself to make small talk with him while he cooked. The whole time I made sure to position myself as far away from him as possible without being too obvious. When I finished cutting the mushrooms, I slid my knife over to the edge of the counter and put a dishcloth over the top of it. If I needed it I knew where it was, but I was praying it wouldn't come to that. The police would be here soon, so that was just a precaution. The thought of hurting him made me feel slightly sick. He needed help, there was clearly something wrong with him.

After another five minutes or so, there was a knock at the door. I held my breath and flicked my eyes to the clock. It had been twenty minutes since I'd called Clay, so that had to be the police and not him, he'd said that the school was half an hour away from Blake's house so it was too soon for it to be Clay.

Blake frowned, his eyes flicking to me for a couple of seconds. "Stay here and watch the food for me while I get the door." He nodded towards the pan on the stove.

I smiled sweetly. "I'm not too skilled at cooking, I'll probably burn it. How about I just get the door?" I suggested, already walking towards the hallway quickly.

He grabbed my hand and yanked me to a stop; he tugged on my hand making me slam against his chest roughly. "Watch the food, Jailbait. I'll get the door," he said sternly. He pushed me back towards the stove, and I tried not to show any reaction. *Maybe as soon as he leaves the room I should run out of the backdoor.* I nodded, and he smiled before turning and heading out of the kitchen to go and answer the door.

As soon as he was out of sight I ran to the backdoor, trying the handle only to find that it was locked. I groaned and looked around desperately for the keys. My gaze fell on a little key hook just off to the side, a set of keys dangled there. I felt my heart skip a beat as I grabbed them quickly. My hand was shaking as I tried to look for the most likely key. I could hear Blake fumbling with the lock and chain on the front door, so I knew I needed to be quick. Just as decided to try the gold key first, a loud crash and a groan of pain, sounded from the hallway.

My breath caught in my throat as I looked towards the hallway door. Did the police have him? Could I just walk out of the front door now instead? I could hear sounds of a scuffle coming from the hallway so I fumbled with the key, deciding I just needed to get outside. I tried desperately to get it in the lock, but my hands were shaking too much.

Just as the key slid in, I heard someone shout.

"Where the fuck is she?"

I felt the colour drain from my face as my muscles all seemed to stiffen at once. That was Clay's voice, I would know it anywhere. I pushed the key into the lock so I wouldn't have to find the right one again just in case we needed to make a quick exit, and then ran to the hallway door so I could see what on earth he was doing here. I just prayed the police were here as well. *Please don't let him have come on his own, please!*

As I got to the door I saw Blake on the floor, Clay was on top of him, straddling him, his face murderously angry as he punched Blake over and over.

Oh God, he's going to get into trouble this time!

"Clay!" I screamed, trying to stop him before he went too far, he was showing no signs of stopping at all, and I was actually a little scared for Blake. Maybe Clay didn't realise he was sick, maybe he just thought he was trying to hurt me, or maybe he just didn't care either way.

Clay looked up at me quickly, his eyes widening as his body seemed to relax. I smiled weakly at him. He had never looked so beautiful to me; he looked like an avenging angel or something. The fury that was on his face softened as he looked at me, the corner of his mouth twitching with a smile. I felt my panic start to recede as I looked at him; Clay was here so I knew everything was going to be fine. Everything was always fine when he was near me, my world would always be that little bit more complete.

Suddenly Clay was thrown back, slamming against the wall; Blake pushed himself up quickly, obviously taking advantage of Clay's distraction. I screamed again as Clay's head hit the wall hard, his eyes squeezing shut as he hissed through his teeth. *Oh no, he's hurt!* My heart was trying to break out of my chest. I couldn't see him hurt, I just couldn't. I tried to run forwards towards him, but Blake was on his feet now, blocking my way.

"You little shit, Preston! What the hell are you doing here? Just get the hell out, she doesn't want you near her anymore!" Blake shouted, grabbing the front of Clay's shirt and yanking him to his feet roughly, slamming him against the wall again. The sound of the crash reverberated up the small hallway, seeming to bounce off of the walls and make it twice as horrifying.

I gripped Blake's arm tightly trying to get his attention so he wouldn't hit Clay. He turned to look at me, a sneer on his face. He looked so hateful that it scared the life out of me. I knew there and then that he didn't just want to hurt Clay, he wanted to kill him, I could see it in his eyes. He genuinely had lost it and somehow had pushed the blame for everything that was wrong in his life, onto Clay.

"Please don't," I begged as uncontrollable tears rolled down my face.

He almost growled in anger as he shook his head. He didn't say anything, just brought his arm up and slapped me hard across the face as I tried to pull him away from Clay. Pain exploded in my head, making my eyes get watery as I stumbled against the wall, dizzy and disorientated.

I didn't see what happened next because my eyes were a little blurry, but something knocked me to the floor. A loud crash and sounds of breaking wood came from my right, the direction of the kitchen, so I knew the scuffle had moved in there. I pushed myself up on my hands and knees and looked in the direction of the crash.

Clay had obviously gotten over the initial shock of the bang to the head.

Him and Blake were now rolling around the floor, fighting. It was horrifying to watch, not like when you see a fight on TV or anything, this was scary and I could hear the sounds of the blows, each one seemed to echo through my head making me feel sick.

Blake shoved Clay off him and pushed himself up to his feet. He looked a little unsteady as blood dripped from his nose and a cut under his eye. Quick as a flash, Clay jumped up and rammed into him, throwing them both over the top of the kitchen counter scattering the cooking food and plates all over the floor as they just continued to fight.

"Stop it!" I screamed as I crawled into the kitchen. I couldn't bear the thought of Clay getting hurt, and although he looked like he was winning, I hated it. It was breaking my heart watching this, and I couldn't cope with it. I needed to get him out of here and wrap my arms around his waist and sob onto his shoulder.

They didn't pay one bit of attention to me as they shouted at each other, reining blow after blow down onto each other's faces and bodies. Suddenly the front door slammed against the wall behind me and I heard feet running up the hallway.

I barely had time to look around before three people ran past me into the kitchen. Arms wrapped around my waist, hoisting me up to my feet and holding me steady. I looked up at the guy holding me, he smiled reassuringly, and I noticed his uniform. I felt my body relax as I realised the police were here. It was over. They would look in Blake's room and see that he needed help; they would take him somewhere and give him the attention he needed.

"Are you okay, Miss?" the guy asked.

I nodded and leant on him heavily as my legs threatened to give out on me. I looked back to see the three officers that had run into the kitchen had stopped and were looking at Blake and Clay who were still fighting on the floor.

"Stop immediately and stand up! Face the wall and put your hands on the back of your head!" one of them commanded.

Oh no, Clay's going to get into trouble! But I knew it couldn't be that bad really. They would take into consideration that Blake already had the restraining order out against him; they would know that Clay was coming here to protect me. He would get another telling off for fighting, but they would know that he was defending me so there was no way he would be in serious trouble for his. I hoped not anyway.

The two boys immediately stopped struggling. Clay was on top of Blake, pinning him to the floor. He looked up at the police officers who were both standing there, looking at them sternly; baton's poised at the ready in case they had to intervene. Clay nodded and let go of Blake, climbing to his feet slowly.

I looked at every inch of my husband's face worriedly. He didn't look too bad at all. His lip had split, and his jaw had a big red patch on it that was probably going to bruise, but other than that though, he looked his perfect, beautiful self. The fear and panic started to ebb away as I finally realised that it was over. I smiled sadly and relaxed against the officer who was still supporting a lot of my weight. Maybe something good had come out of this after all; Blake was finally going the help that he desperately needed.

Clay moved over to the wall and did as he was told, spreading his legs and putting his hands on the back of his head. Blake pushed himself up from the floor, he definitely looked worse than Clay. *My boy is definitely a badass.* Blake looked at me and frowned before shaking his head and bending down quickly, grabbing something from the floor.

I saw the officer closest to him move and step forward as he shouted, "Knife!" *Knife? What the hell?*

Blake turned quickly; I just had time to see a flash of the blade that I had hidden under the cloth on the counter. "No!" I screamed as I thrashed to get out of the officers hold. There was no indecision on Blake's face, he looked so angry, so hard, and like a totally different person from the one I had met only a short time ago at the football game.

Everything seemed to be happening in slow motion as Blake stepped towards Clay and shoved the knife into the side of his chest. It felt like my world stopped spinning. I couldn't breathe, and the panic started to take over.

I could hear the officers shouting at Blake to drop the knife, as they all converged forwards, fumbling with their weapons that were strapped to their sides. They all seemed like they were so far away from me, like I was listening to them from underwater or something.

All my brain could register was how Clay flinched and seemed to crumple slightly as he slumped against the wall. Blake leant against him heavily, and I saw him pull his arm back again, making Clay yelp in pain as he pulled the knife back out of his side.

Blake stepped back slightly, still pinning Clay against the wall as he threw his arm forward again and shoved the knife deep into Clay's lower back.

chapter twenty-seven

I was vaguely aware that the guy that was holding me up was shouting orders and shoved me against the wall, putting his body in front of mine. There was a loud bang, a scream of pain, and then the cops all rushed forward. They grabbed Blake, practically throwing him to the floor as they all literally jumped on him, pinning him down as he thrashed and tried to get up screaming like a crazy person.

None of that properly registered in my brain though. The only thing that registered was that my husband was slowly sliding down the wall, his face a picture of pain. I felt my heart breaking. I couldn't move, I couldn't cry, I couldn't even breathe. My whole world was shattering around me; all my hopes and dreams were slowly fading into insignificance. All of the plans we had made were slowly disappearing with every inch that he sank towards the cold tiled floor.

My whole body felt numb, my legs felt like jelly and were threatening to give out on me at any second. I still hadn't taken a breath. Everything was still happening in slow motion. Clay was still falling to the floor, and I could do nothing to help him. I couldn't take it back, I couldn't rewind time and make that knife pierce my skin instead, I couldn't save him from the look of pain that was etched across his face. I was useless, a stupid, useless girl, and this was entirely my fault.

Blake had hurt Clay because of me, he had stabbed him because of me, even the knife he'd used was the one I had left it on the side when we were cooking. Everything was my fault. I couldn't be more to blame unless I had pushed the knife into him myself. I had killed my husband, my best friend, the love of my life; he was dead because of me and I would have to live with that knowledge for the rest of my life. I didn't even want to think about living now that I would be without Clay, how could I? He was everything good that was in my life, my whole life had been centred around him, and now he was gone. How could I live like that? I knew the answer to that question, I couldn't.

Clay hit the floor with a thump that seemed to make my whole body go cold; I could feel my hands shaking. He was gone. I was alone. I'd lost him.

Suddenly his arm twitched, and he groaned. My heart jumped in my chest as my eyes widened in shock. *He isn't dead?* I swallowed the sob that was trying to break free and shoved myself away from the wall, but the cop just pushed me back pinning me there.

What the hell is he doing? "Let me go! He's hurt; I need to go to him!" I screamed, thrashing against him, trying to get myself out of the little cage he seemed to have made against the wall.

He shook his head. "Just wait until he has the cuffs on," he ordered sternly.

Cuffs, what the hell? I'm not waiting for Blake to have the cuffs on; I need to go to Clay! He groaned again and I felt hope bubbling up inside. *Please, please, please let him be okay. I'll do anything, anything in the world, please.*

"Get off me! Let me go!" I screamed, trying to duck under his arm.

He easily restrained me again though before I got more than a few inches away from him. I scowled at him. If he didn't let me go I was going to knee him where the sun didn't shine, there was no way he was keeping me away from Clay. He looked over his shoulder and I flicked my eyes in the direction of Blake. The two cops were still trying to restrain him as he shouted that it wasn't his fault, that Clay deserved it, that he had broken in here and attacked him, and he was acting in self-defence. I heard the snap of cuffs, and they yanked him to his feet, shoving him face first into the wall, making him hiss in pain.

"He's secure," one of the cops shouted. He moved Blake slightly and I saw a streak of red on the wall near his leg. Is that his blood? Have they shot him? I thought back to the loud bang, and as I looked at one of the cops standing there, he was indeed putting a gun back in a holster on his hip. I frowned. *If they have guns why couldn't they have shot him before he stabbed Clay? They could have stopped him before he hurt anyone!*

I looked back at the guy holding me, glaring angrily. "Now you can let me go! I need to see Clay!" I cried desperately.

He nodded and let go of me instantly. For a second I swayed on my feet, and I wasn't even sure I could stand on my own. He grabbed my arm to steady me, but all I could think about was Clay. I threw off his hold and ran across the room, almost falling down at his side. He was gasping, sucking in small little ragged breaths. His eyes were squeezed shut; there was blood all over his shirt, soaking into the white material making him look like something out of a horror movie.

I bent my face down to his, brushing his hair back as I thought desperately of what I should do. Should I apply pressure or would that make it worse? Should I roll him onto his back or would that make it even harder for him to breathe?

"Clay? Baby, can you hear me? I'm here; you're going to be okay. Oh God, please be okay," I whispered as I brushed his hair off his forehead.

He groaned, and I saw his eyes flicker, it seemed like he was trying to open them. I could feel the grief and horror of the situation washing over me, but I refused to let it. I needed to be strong for him; he needed me so I wasn't going to succumb to the sadness, at least not in front of him. He needed to believe everything was going to be fine, even though the dark stain on his shirt was getting bigger and bigger by the second as he lost more blood. I looked up at the cops; two of them were leading a limping Blake out of the room, practically dragging him along as he carried on screaming that he'd done nothing wrong.

Anger was burning inside me making my stomach shake, and I could almost taste the hatred in my mouth. I wanted to grab the knife that was in the middle of the kitchen and cut him into little pieces, but I needed to stay with Clay, I couldn't leave him. The police would lock Blake up and throw away the key for this. All of the sympathy and pity that I had built up for him since I arrived at his house was gone now; all I was left with was raw hatred.

I looked back at the cop who had been holding me; he was talking quickly into his walkie talkie as he made his way over to where Clay and I were on the floor. "Please help him," I begged as I squeezed Clay's hand.

The cop nodded. "We will. The ambulance is on its way," he replied as he gripped Clay's shirt and lifted it. I winced, unsure as to whether I could look and see the wound on his body, but I just couldn't keep my eyes in check. They wandered down there of their own accord and what I saw made my heart break even more. I swallowed loudly and forced my face to remain emotionless. I couldn't break down, I needed to be strong. There was a deep, ragged gash on the middle of his lower back, just above the waistband of his jeans. Blood was flowing freely from it and was pooling in the curve of his back.

"Get me a cloth or something," the cop ordered, nodding his head towards the kitchen cupboards.

I dragged my eyes away from the most horrifying and heartbreaking thing I had ever seen in my life, and pushed myself off of the floor, running over and pulling open every single drawer until I found the ones with the dishtowels in. I grabbed a handful of them and ran back to Clay as fast as I could. The cop was looking at Clay's side now; he took the towels and pressed one against the wound on his back as he clenched his jaw looking slightly worried. I looked at him pleadingly, silently begging him not to let my husband die.

I looked back at Clay as his breathing became even shallower and more ragged. His face was relaxed now, as if he was merely sleeping, so peaceful and perfect. Well, apart from the slight red tinge to his jaw from fighting with Blake. I kissed his nose lightly. "I love you, baby. You'll be fine, I promise. Tomorrow I'm going to make you chocolate chip pancakes for breakfast, I'll even burn them slightly just the way you like," I whispered, smiling sadly as I squeezed his hand again.

I could hear the cop talking to one of the others, something about a punctured lung, and how he needed a chest tube quickly before he went into cardiac arrest. He sounded slightly panicked as he asked how long the ambulance was going to be. The other guy was helping him work on Clay, but I couldn't take my eyes off his peaceful face. I traced my finger along the bridge of his nose, the curve to his lip, his cheekbone, memorising him all over again as they continued to fuss around me.

After what felt like just a few seconds someone grabbed me, pulling me to my feet and away from Clay. I gripped his hand tighter as I thrashed trying to get back to him, I didn't want to leave his side, not for a single second in case he woke up.

"Ma'am, the medics are here, you need to move and let them do their job!" someone ordered. "Please step aside." His grip on my upper arms tightened as he held me away from Clay's unconscious form.

I looked around and noticed that there were indeed two new guys in blue uniforms. They immediately started fussing over Clay. I tried to block out what they were saying, I didn't want to hear that because it would make me lose the marginal control I had over myself. I just focused on Clay's face as they cut his shirt off him, prodding at his body. A small whimper left my lips when I saw one of them grab a scalpel and a little piece of tubing, heading towards Clay's already bloody chest with it.

After the longest most painful time of my life, they finally agreed that he could be moved. Apparently the tube that they had inserted had worked and was helping him breathe. His heart rate was strong. One of them said the most beautiful word I had ever heard in my life, the best word that had ever been invented in the history of the world: stable.

I felt my body relax; I laughed quietly to myself and looked at the ceiling, repeating the words 'thank you' over and over in my head. But the medics still looked extremely worried. There was an intense concentration on their faces as they discussed how best to move him without causing any more damage. One of them ran off and came back with a spinal board and neck brace. I frowned, not understanding what was going on. *They said he's stable, so why are they still so tense?*

The cop that was holding me turned me around to face him. "Ma'am, is there someone I should call? His parents? Yours?" he asked, looking at me sympathetically. I looked back over my shoulder as they rolled Clay onto the yellow board, strapping him in with little black straps. *Why are they being so careful?* "Ma'am?" I felt pressure on my arm so I looked back at the cop; he seemed to be waiting for me to answer something.

"Is he going to be okay? They said he was stable, that means that he's okay, right?" I whispered.

He smiled sadly. "They're doing everything they can; they'll know more once he gets to the hospital. But if you could just tell me if there is someone I should call..." He trailed off, looking at me expectantly.

My mind was scrambled, I could barely even think about anything other Clay, but his parents somehow registered in my mind, they would need to be told. I smiled at him gratefully and reached into my pocket pulling out my cell phone. I was barely holding on to my sanity, and if I had to tell them what had happened I would lose it, and I couldn't do that. I held the phone out to him. "Clay's parents' cell phones are in there under Linda and Richard. My parents are in there under Mom and David," I muttered, looking back to the medics as they put the last couple of straps on Clay's lifeless body.

"Okay, I'll call them and tell them what happened and tell them to come to the hospital to meet you. Are you going in the ambulance or do you need a ride?" he asked, watching as they lifted the stretcher off of the floor.

I quickly stepped forward keeping pace with them, not wanting Clay out of my sight for a second. "Can I come with you?" I begged the medic.

He smiled and nodded. "Sure, Ma'am."

I trailed along next to Clay, sitting in the little seat opposite him in the ambulance, trying to stay out of the way while the medic inserted needles into the back of his hand, attaching some clear fluid to the IV. I just sat there emotionally numb. I didn't know what to do, what to think, what to say, so I did nothing. I thought nothing. I just refused to acknowledge how grave this situation was, refused to acknowledge how the medic's forehead was creased and how his movements were a little tense. Clay would be fine; he wouldn't leave me on my own.

When we got to the hospital, Clay was rushed in with about five people all fussing over him as they sped him through the hallways and into one of the emergency rooms. I pushed the door open wanting to go in with him, but a nurse put her arm around my shoulder smiling sympathetically at me. I wanted to scream at her to stop smiling like that. Everyone was being so sad and worried, so sympathetic and apologetic, it was scary. I didn't want to think about what could happen, all I would let myself think was that Clay would be fine, and tomorrow I would apologise over and over for this happening, and he would kiss my nose and tell me that it wasn't my fault and that he loved me. That was all I would let myself think about for now because the thoughts I had at the back of my brain were actually too horrifying to acknowledge.

"If you could just wait outside while the doctors are assessing him. Someone will be out to talk to you as soon as possible." She smiled and guided me over to a row of plastic chairs off to one side.

I nodded weakly and sat down, trying to keep my breathing steady and my heart at a normal pace. Everything was fine; I just needed to keep control of myself because behaving like a panicked stupid child wouldn't help anyone in this situation, especially not Clay.

I couldn't sit still, so I stood up and started pacing the hallway. I looked at each one of the paintings in turn as I walked past, thinking of anything else other than how long it was taking for them to come out and speak to me. Wasn't the saying, 'no news is good news', wasn't that how it went? So surely it was good that no one had come out yet, I nodded to myself and chewed on my lip. After a couple of minutes the cop from the house turned up. He smiled at me sympathetically as he sat down on the chair I had just vacated. He didn't say anything, just sat there watching me with a concerned expression on his face.

I turned to look at him. "He's fine, they're just being cautious. He's just fine," I told him sternly. I gulped at how my voice sounded, so thick and husky that it didn't even sound like mine.

He smiled weakly and nodded. "I'm sure he is, Ma'am,"

I nodded in confirmation and switched to chewing on my nails instead of my lip as I just continued to pace the hallway. My heart was crashing so loud in my chest that it was almost deafening, my stomach twisting, my whole body felt cold, but I put on a smile anyway. I just needed to think positive, if I willed everything to be fine then it would be. Then Clay and I could just go home and have the weekend we had been planning. The lazy weekend where we did nothing but make out and watch TV, the perfect weekend with the perfect guy.

I heard someone crying, and I looked up to see Linda and Richard running down the hallway towards me. I smiled reassuringly but kept my eyes firmly on Richard. Linda had totally lost it, and I refused to let her drag me down with her.

"What happened? They said Clay had been stabbed?" Richard asked breathlessly as he gripped my shoulders a little too tight for comfort.

I gulped and nodded. "He did. He's in there now with the doctors, but he'll be fine."

Linda looked at me, her eyes pink and bloodshot. "They said that? Have they been out to speak to you?" She sniffed.

I shook my head. "No they haven't yet. But it's Clay, he'll be fine. You know him, he's strong, he wouldn't let something like this hurt him. He wouldn't," I stated, my voice sounded surprisingly calm and assured. Linda smiled weakly in response.

I turned and resumed pacing as the cop spoke to them. He was telling them about how they had received a phone call from the principal of the school informing them about what had happened, how they had been dispatched to Blake's house, but they had arrived after Clay and the boys were already fighting. When he got to the part about Blake grabbing the knife I made myself walk further up the hallway so I couldn't hear it, if I heard it then I would start to picture it, and I couldn't do that and remain in control.

Ten minutes later the door to the room opened and a man in his mid-thirties walked out looking around. Linda, Richard, and the cop all jumped up from where they were sitting. The doctor looked around until he saw me. I couldn't move, I was just frozen in place, my feet felt like they were stuck to the floor. He wasn't smiling, his eyes were cautious and controlled. My hands started to shake.

He ignored Linda and Richard who were looking at him expectantly; instead he walked up to me. His eyes travelled from my face down to my hand. He seemed to nod a little in confirmation.

"I notice that Clay has a wedding ring on his finger. Are you married?" he asked, looking at me intently. I nodded, still unable to speak, I couldn't even breathe properly, my heart felt like it was going to break out of my chest making me feel a little light-headed. "Okay, so you're his next of kin then. I need to talk to you about his condition."

I felt numb inside, like this was happening to someone else, I felt detached and emotionless. I had no idea what he was going to say, but I knew that Clay wasn't dead, I would know if he'd died, I would have felt it, wouldn't I? Didn't they say that? That you always know when something has happened to the one you love? If Clay had died then it would have killed me as well, wouldn't it? God wouldn't be that cruel, to leave me here without him, would he?

The doctor put his hand on my arm and I let him guide me to the chairs on the side of the hallway. My feet felt like ten ton weights so each step was a struggle. Linda and Richard followed behind us. Linda was sobbing her heart out on Richard's shoulder, and I couldn't help but feel lonely. I needed Clay to be here for me like his dad was for his mom. I sat down and looked at the doctor expectantly, not knowing what on earth he was going to say, but the sad look on his face was telling me that this wasn't good news.

The doctor smiled grimly. "We've managed to get the bleeding under control now. The knife pierced his lung, but we've inserted a chest tube so that's helping him breathe. His lung should be fine; we'll have to leave the tube in for a couple of weeks until it's repaired," he stated.

That's all? A chest tube for a couple of weeks? I felt my stomach start to unwind itself as happiness started to build up inside me. He was lucky, *we* were lucky and I would never take a minute of his time for granted again. I would cherish every second of him from this day forward because every single one of them was precious, I'd never realised just how precious until now.

I smiled and nodded. "Can I go in and see him? Is he awake?" I asked, grinning from ear to ear.

He shook his head. "He's unconscious at the moment. He's lost a lot of blood so we're trying to replace it as quickly as possible. There's something else that I need to talk to you about."

I frowned and nodded, not liking the sound of that at all. "Okay," I whispered as the smile slowly fell from my face.

"The knife that went into Clay's lower back has severed his spine," he said softly.

I felt my heart sink. That couldn't be right. Severed his spine? Did that mean he was paralysed or something? That just couldn't be right, Clay would never let that happen, he would never allow something like that happen to him. He would rather die than not be able to walk; I knew that because that was the type of person he was. He hated to rely on people or burden them; he would hate to have a disability.

"You can fix it, right?" I whispered as Linda started to wail.

The doctor looked at me apologetically. "There's something we can try, we have an extraordinarily gifted surgeon here who specialised in experimental surgical procedures. His name is Doctor Kirk, and he'd like to look at Clay and see if there's something he can do to help," he said, his eyes boring into mine.

I nodded and willed myself not to break down and sob, I needed to be strong now for Clay so I couldn't let myself fall to pieces. "Okay, when can he look at him?" I asked, swallowing loudly. The numbness was back now, and I was grateful for it. The emptiness was easier to cope with than grief. I couldn't let the grief and horror drag me under, I wouldn't let it.

"He's already assessed his injuries, and he thinks there's a chance he can limit the damage and possibly make it so that he would be able to regain the feeling in his legs. The only trouble is, the surgery is very risky, the operation is highly invasive, and Clay has already sustained a lot of damage to his body. It could make it worse, or even kill him," he said sadly.

I closed my eyes and tried to pretend like he hadn't said the K word. I couldn't even let myself think about Clay dying, I refused to acknowledge that. He wouldn't leave me, he was my husband, and he wouldn't ever leave me on my own like that.

"But it might help him walk again?" I whispered, not trusting my voice to speak properly. I opened my eyes looking at the doctor hopefully.

He nodded. "Yes, it's the only chance he has of being able to walk again. Without the surgery he'll be paralysed from the waist down. With the surgery there's about a fifty percent chance that he would regain feeling in his legs,"

Richard shook his head, stepping forward, his eyes firmly locked on the doctor. "But you said he could die," he interjected, his hand tightening in

Linda's hair as she sobbed louder. His whole body was tight with stress, and I could see he was doing the same as me, clinging to the edge of the cliff trying not to let go and completely breakdown.

The doctor nodded. "Yes, the surgery is risky, there's around a thirty percent chance that he wouldn't make it through the operation," he answered matter-of-factly, in the seemingly detached manner doctors always had.

Oh God, please, please don't let my baby die please! I cleared my throat, needing to ask something. "But there's a fifty-fifty chance that it'll fix him?" I asked, needing confirmation.

I already knew what needed to happen. If Clay was awake for this decision he would have already consented to this. He wouldn't want to be stuck in a wheelchair for the rest of his life, and he would want to take the risk. He was strong, I had every confidence that he wouldn't leave me. He'd promised we would be together forever so there is no way he would let himself die on an operating table.

"That's right," the doctor confirmed. "As his next of kin I need you to make the decision on his behalf because he's currently unconscious. You'll need to sign a consent form," he said, looking at me intently.

I nodded quickly; Clay would want this, there was no doubt in my mind that he would want to try everything, no matter what the risk was. "Okay, do it," I whispered.

Linda pushed herself away from Richard quickly and looked at me with red rimmed puffy eyes as she swiped at her nose with a tissue. "What? You can't do that! Did you not hear what he said, Riley? There's a chance he won't make it through surgery!" she cried, frowning at me angrily.

I nodded. "I heard every word he said, Linda, I'm not stupid. But Clay would want this, you know he would. If he were awake then he would sign the form himself and you know it," I said fiercely.

She shook her head. "You don't know that! Why can't you wait for him to wake up and then let him make the decision with his life? It's not for you to decide," she snapped, looking at me as if this was my fault. Guilt flared up inside me again, because technically this *was* my fault and she obviously knew it.

I gulped and looked at the doctor. "Can we wait and let him make up his own mind?" I asked.

The doctor shook his head quickly. "The longer you wait for the operation the less chance of success. Every hour you wait the chances of it working reduce, if you leave it too long then it could be impossible to repair it. I recommend that we move quickly," he said sternly.

I nodded and looked back at Linda. That was out of the question, we couldn't wait because then there might not even be a choice to make, it might be too late by the time he woke up. "We can't wait. Clay would want this, Linda.

You know him, he wouldn't want to be stuck in a wheelchair, you know that," I said fiercely. I turned back to the doctor. He'd said it was my decision, and I was making the choice Clay would make himself if he were able. "What form do I need to sign?" I asked, looking down at the papers in his hand. The quicker I signed it the quicker they could go in there and save my husband from a life he would be miserable in.

He nodded and pulled out a yellow form holding it out to me with a pen. Linda practically screamed as she stood up and shook her head, looking at Richard desperately before turning back to me. "No! You can't do that, Riley, you can't risk it! If he doesn't go into the surgery, then he'll survive. If you send him in there, he might not come back out! Don't you understand that?" she cried, looking at me almost hatefully, as if I was purposefully trying to hurt Clay.

"Linda, think about what Clay would want, not what you would want. You know Clay would want this! Do you think I honestly want to sign that form knowing there's a chance that he might not come back out of there? Of course I don't, but I'm thinking about Clay right now not me. He would want this, and you know it," I retorted, reaching for the pen and form to sign.

I scribbled my name on the bottom in the next of kin box as Linda thrashed wildly in Richards arms, crying hysterically. I swallowed loudly and passed the form back to the doctor feeling my heart break. *Have I just signed a death warrant for my husband? Is that definitely what he would want?* I pushed the last thought away, I was one hundred percent sure this is what my best friend, and love of my life would want. I didn't doubt that decision for a second.

The selfish part of me didn't want to sign it, just in case I lost him. If he didn't go in for the surgery he would survive, and I would still have Clay by my side, a little changed, but I would still have him. The surgery was a risk and one I would rather not take, but I didn't doubt my decision for a second, this was one hundred percent what Clay would want for himself, I knew that with all of my heart.

The doctor stood up and smiled. "We'll scrub up and take him to surgery within half an hour." He turned to walk away, and I glanced at Linda and Richard who were hugging each other and watching his back as he walked up the hallway.

Richard just looked like he was in shock and didn't know what to think. Linda, however, looked murderously angry. Suddenly her face brightened and she pushed herself out of Richard's arms, taking a couple of steps in the direction of the doctor.

"Wait!" she shouted, making him stop and turn to look at her. She pointed at me accusingly, but her eyes never left the doctor's. She had a fierce determination on her face. "She can't legally sign the forms. She's underage so their marriage isn't legal. She's seventeen, and they used a fake ID to get married. I'll take it to a lawyer if I have to." She took a deep breath and looked at me, her eyes hard and calculating. "She can't sign that form. She's not next his of kin. I am," she stated triumphantly.

chapter twenty-eight

I stood there looking at her in shock, my mouth hanging open like a complete and utter moron. What on earth was she talking about my marriage wasn't legal? Of course it was legal; I was his wife in body and spirit. So what if we used a fake ID to actually go through with the ceremony. She accepted it, and so did Richard. For the last couple of weeks she'd been telling me how proud she was that we were married and happy, and now she was taking it all back?

I looked at the doctor, waiting for him to tell her that she was talking trash, that if Clay and I chose to give ourselves to each other then that was good enough for him. He looked between the two of us, his gaze flicking down to my ring on my finger again before looking back at me.

"Is that true? You used fake identification to get married?" he asked, eyeing me cautiously.

I gulped and nodded. I didn't like the way he was looking at me, he didn't look like he was going to be jumping to my defence anytime soon. "Yeah but that doesn't mean that I'm not his wife. Clay and I said those words to each other, and we both meant them. He's my husband, and that's final."

Linda stepped forward towards the doctor, swiping at her teary face. I noticed that she didn't even glance in my direction. "I'll take it to a lawyer if I have to," she repeated.

I looked at her unable to believe what I was hearing. She was seriously going to stop Clay going in for surgery and risk him never being able to walk again? She knew what type of person he was; she knew he'd hate his life if he had to spend it like that. I couldn't let that happen. She was thinking about herself, not Clay. She wasn't thinking about how his life would change and how he would never be able to walk or run or do the things that he loved to do the most.

The initial shock was disappearing to be replaced by anger. No, it wasn't anger, it was blind rage. "What the hell are you doing?" I screamed, grabbing her arm and yanking her around to face me so I could look into her face when I told her she was being a selfish bitch and that Clay was going to hate her when he woke up and found out what she'd sentenced him to.

She glared at me with watery eyes, her face was desperate and sad, but I just didn't care, this wasn't about her and she needed to woman up and grow a pair. "I'm not signing that form, and neither are you," she stated, her voice breaking slightly.

I gaped at her incredulously. "You're being selfish, Linda! You think Clay's going to thank you for this? You think he's going to turn around and say 'Gee thanks, Mom, I know I'm never going to be able to achieve my dreams but you did the right thing in committing me to a wheelchair for life.' You seriously think your son is going to be grateful to you for this?" I cried, throwing my hands up in exasperation.

"At least he'll be alive!" she shouted, her face going slightly red as she started to get angry too.

"He'll wish he wasn't, I would bet my life on it. You think you know him, but you don't. If you think this is the decision that Clay would make for himself, then you don't know him at all," I growled. My hands were itching to grab her and shake the life out of her, to slap her face until she saw sense. She was going to ruin my baby's life, and there was nothing I could do about it.

"If he goes in there then there's a thirty percent chance he won't come back out!" she shouted, sneering at me.

I felt my heart start to break as I thought about that chance, but I quickly dismissed it. Clay wouldn't let that happen, he wouldn't because if he left me then I would have to kick his ass and that wouldn't be pretty. I shook my head. "That won't happen. It won't," I vowed confidently.

She wrenched her arm out of my grasp. "You're the one being selfish here, not me. You just want to send him in there so you won't have to be stuck with a guy in a wheelchair for the rest of your life," she growled, her face hard and hurtful.

My whole body went cold before white hot anger coursed through my veins. Before I knew what I was doing I stepped forward and slapped her hard across the face making a loud crack echo down the hallway. My palm stung but I ignored it. "Don't you ever doubt my love for your son! I will always love Clay, and I don't care if he can't walk, but *he would*, and that's the point here! You think I want to risk his life? Is that the type of person that you think I am, Linda? You think I want to purposely put him in danger, well I don't. I don't want him to go in there at all because I could lose him, but I need him happy and this life you're sentencing him to is going to make him miserable. I hope you can live with that." I turned to look at Richard; he was just standing there with his mouth open, staring between the two of us. He seemed to be stuck to the spot. I wasn't even sure he was breathing. "Richard, you can sign the form too," I said, looking at him pleadingly. He was my last hope here, if I could just convince him to sign it instead...

Linda turned and glared at him. "If you dare sign that form I will never forgive you," she hissed, lifting her chin and looking at him warningly.

When did she become such a bitch? "If you don't sign that form your son will never forgive you," I countered, just as confidently.

Richard looked confused; he was pale, his eyes flicking between the two of us so fast that I would have laughed if the situation weren't utterly heartbreaking. He sucked in a deep breath through his teeth and gripped his hands in his hair before turning to look at the doctor. "How long will be it before he wakes up so he can decide for himself?" he asked weakly.

I looked back to the doctor expectantly. He had just remained silent through this whole exchange, standing there watching us scream at each other in the hallway. "It could be a couple of hours, or it could be a couple of days. There's no way to tell for sure."

I gulped and looked back at Richard, pleading with him silently. "If you wait for him to wake up then there might not be a decision to make. Please think about Clay, please?" I begged, willing myself not to cry. I was slowly losing the control that I had over myself as I imagined the heartbreak I would see on Clay's face when they told him he would never walk again.

Linda made a snorting noise deep in her throat. "Richard, if you sign that form and kill my son I will never forgive you, never," she warned.

He opened and closed his mouth a couple of times but didn't say anything. As I stood there watching him struggle to decide, I prayed with every bone in my body for him to make the right choice.

He didn't.

"I won't sign the form either. Clay should make the decision himself," he whispered as a tear fell down his face.

I closed my eyes as emotions washed over my body so fast that I could barely even register what they were. Most of it was sheer and utter desperation. I could barely cope with the crushing weight of them all. I felt like I was dying inside, dying for Clay who was going to have to live through the rest of his life being unhappy and missing out on the things he valued the most. *How can two people not know their son like this? How can they think they would want this for himself?* I knew why Linda was doing it, the thought of losing him was all she as thinking about. She wasn't thinking about long-term, and how this would change him, how it would affect his life.

I blew out the breath I didn't even realise I was holding and turned to the doctor. "Are you sure I can't sign the form? To Clay I'm his wife, in spirit I'm his wife, and I know he'd want this."

He shook his head. "I'm sorry but if you used a fake ID to get married then in the eyes of the law your marriage isn't legal. We had something like this happen before, not the same circumstances but the same underage marriage thing, and they actually brought in lawyers to sort it out. I'm sorry, but the law isn't on your side. I have to go with the next of kin, and that's a parent." He looked at me apologetically. Maybe he could see my point, maybe he would make the same decision as me if he was in my place, he never said, but that was the look that was on his face.

"Can you wake him up early so that there's still a chance he could have the surgery?" I asked hopefully.

"It doesn't work like that; his body has gone into shutdown mode so that it can repair itself. He'll wake up when he's able to," he said softly.

"How long can the surgery wait?" I asked, praying he would say he had plenty of time to wake up and sign the form so that he could still have a good chance of walking.

He shrugged, looking at me apologetically. "It's hard to say, but Dr Kirk said the sooner the better. The chances of success diminish with each passing hour, after a couple of days then there will probably be no chance of success at all."

I nodded and swallowed my sadness. If there was nothing I could do, then I needed to go and see Clay so I could beg him to wake up early. "Can I see him?" I asked. He nodded and motioned up the hallway. I turned back to Linda and Richard who were now hugging and crying together, and again I was struck by a wave of loneliness. "I hope you can live with yourselves after this. When you see how unhappy Clay is I hope that this day sticks out in your mind as the day you could have done something about it," I said emotionless as I turned and stepped closer to the doctor. I heard Richard groan and Linda started to sob hysterically again, but I couldn't bring myself to feel sorry for them, not even one tiny bit.

The doctor turned and headed up the hallway with me following behind him. My heart sank with every step. He pushed open the door to a room on the right hand side of the hall, and I stepped in tentatively behind him. My eyes settled on the bed and as soon as I saw Clay laying there I suddenly doubted that I was strong enough for this. Was I strong enough to keep up this cool calm exterior when all I wanted to do was sink to my knees and sob until I couldn't breathe? My legs were threatening to give out on me, my hands were shaking, and my stomach twisted in knots as my whole body went cold.

He was laying there with an IV line in both hands, blood going in one and fluid going in the other. He was strapped to a heart monitor that was steadily beeping next to his bed, the little green line making little peaks against the black screen. There was a clear plastic tube going into his mouth that was attached to a ventilator, another tube protruding out of his right side, near his ribs, which was obviously the chest tube they had said about that was fixing his collapsed lung. The sight of him being so helpless and frail was almost enough to send me over the edge. I fought desperately to hold onto the control I had over my emotions. I needed to be strong for him; he needed me so I couldn't let myself break down.

I pushed my legs forward and almost stumbled to the side of his bed. His eyes were closed; he looked so peaceful, like he was in a deep sleep. If it weren't for the tubes and wires attached to his body then I would have just shook him awake. It looked like he was faking sleep, like he was just fooling around and trying to scare me to death.

I dragged my eyes over every inch of his face and the exposed skin on his chest. My hand found his and I brought it up to my face, being careful of the tubes. I kissed his wedding ring before turning his hand over and pressing my face into his palm, closing my eyes against the pain that was trying to consume me.

"I need you to wake up, Clay. It's really important. Can you hear me? If you can hear me then I need you to wake up, baby. Please? Please open your eyes for me," I begged, pressing my lips against his palm. He didn't move. All I could hear was the steady beeping and the suck and wheeze of the ventilator as he breathed. "Clay, this is so important. Can you wake up? For me, baby, please?" I whispered, finally opening my eyes to look down at him. "Wake up damn it! Clay Preston, you need to open your eyes and help me! I can't do this on my own so you need to wake the hell up!" I cried desperately as I pressed my forehead to his. I felt a single tear dribble down my face, it dropped onto the tip of his nose so I kissed it away quickly, trying to compose myself.

I heard the door open again but I didn't bother turning around. I knew it was Linda, I could tell by the ragged sobs that were coming out of her. I didn't even want to see her, if I saw her then I would get angry again and there was nothing I could do about it now. Instead, I just focused my attention on Clay, trying to wake him so he could sort this mess out himself.

He didn't wake up though. I stood there feeling numb, holding his hand to my face just staring at the heart monitor, somehow hypnotised by the line and the way it moved so steadily.

No one said anything. Richard dragged a couple of chairs over to the side of the bed and touched my shoulder to get my attention, but I refused to look at him. When Clay woke up, if he told me that I was wrong and that he wouldn't have gone in for the operation, then I'd take back everything I said to them. I'd apologise and beg for their forgiveness, but until that time I wasn't even going to acknowledge their presence.

After about an hour the door opened and I flicked my eyes up to see if it was another nurse or doctor. They'd been coming in pretty regularly to check the printout for his heart monitor and to increase or decrease the dosage on his drip.

It wasn't a doctor though; it was my mom and David. They both looked so sad that I almost lost it and burst into helpless tears, but I caught myself just in time. My mom ran into the room and hugged me tightly, a little too tight for comfort, but I couldn't be bothered to protest so I just let her do it.

She whimpered, her fingers biting into my back as I just stood there numbly, not even having the will to hug her back. "Oh God, is he okay? Why is he attached to all these machines?" she asked breathlessly, her face stained with tears.

"He's going to be fine," I mumbled.

Her eyes were searching my face, checking to see if I was all right probably. "Are you okay, Riley? Do you need a drink or something? You look like you're going into shock or something. Why are you so calm?" she asked, rubbing my back in small circles.

I cringed away from her hand, I didn't want her touching me and comforting me. I wasn't the one that needed her attention, Clay was. "I'm fine, Mom."

I could hear David and Richard talking, the conversation was getting heated as David was asking about the surgery and why he was not already having it if it could help him walk. I turned my head to look at him properly for the first time in over two weeks. He looked murderously angry as he glared at Richard.

"What the hell do you mean; you're waiting for Clay to make the decision? You don't need to wait for him to wake up, are you crazy? Of course he's going to want the operation! This is Clay we're talking about, that boy isn't happy unless he's doing something physical, you know that. Hell, I know that, and he's not even my son!" David cried, looking between Richard and Linda in disbelief. I smiled at his angry face. I'd missed him so much this last couple of weeks, and here he was echoing my exact feelings to Clay's parents. He looked up at me, his eyes wide and a little scared. "Riley, you need to send him in for the surgery. You can't do this to Clay," he said, looking at me pleadingly.

I bit my lip and shook my head as my eyes met his. "They won't let me," I croaked. I was slowly losing it. Looking at David was making me lose the control I had over my emotions; I could feel my cool calm exterior crumbling into a quivering mess. My heart was thumping in my chest and I just needed him to hug me and tell me that everything was going to be okay. David was always the one I could depend on, David and Clay were the two men in my life, and I would love them both forever. I just needed a hug from my dad.

"What do you mean they won't let you?" he asked, frowning and looking confused.

A tear fell down my face as I pushed myself away from Clay's side for the first time since I had walked in the door. I threw myself at David, wrapping my arms around his waist as I sobbed into his chest. He gasped, obviously a little taken aback before hugging me fiercely, taking most of my weight as my legs seemed to give out underneath me.

He pressed his cheek to the top of my head and rocked me gently. "It's okay, pumpkin. Everything's fine, shh. It's okay," he cooed softly as I just continued to sob uncontrollably.

I breathed in his smell, the scent of axe mixed with apple shampoo that was unmistakably my stepdad. I gripped the back of his shirt tightly as he stroked my hair, still rocking me like a three year old.

"Let's go sit outside for a while and get some fresh air," he suggested, trying to pull me towards the door.

I dug my heels into the floor and shook my head quickly, pulling away from him. There was no way I was leaving Clay. I needed to be here when he woke up, I needed to be the first person he saw when he opened his eyes. "I don't want to. He might wake up."

He smiled down at me reassuringly and wiped my tears away with his thumbs. "They'll call you, Riley. Come on, just for a couple of minutes," he insisted, giving me a persuasive smile.

I broke into a fresh round of sobs, shaking my head. "They won't call me; they don't even want me here," I muttered, my voice barely above a whisper.

David glared at Richard, he looked incredibly angry; he always was protective of me and always stepped in if someone was hurting me. He opened his mouth to say something, but my mom stepped forward and spoke first. "Riley, I'll stay here with Clay. I'll call you if he wakes up. I promise you I will," she said, nodding fiercely.

I smiled at her gratefully and nodded. I didn't like crying in this room. I was worried that Clay could somehow hear me. If he knew I was upset then that would upset him, and I couldn't have that. "I'll just be in the hallway. I don't want to go too far, just in case," I croaked, my throat sore from all the crying.

David led me out of the room, my arms still tight around his waist. He pulled me over to the plastic chairs and smiled at me sadly. I pulled my knees up to my chest and put my head on his shoulder as he murmured soothing words, stroking my back. After a couple of minutes I started to calm down a little. The empty, numb feeling was starting to return and I was actually quite grateful that it was because the grief and sadness of this situation was almost too much to bear. Add on top of that the fact that this was entirely my fault and that Clay was hurt because of me, that he would never walk again because of me. The feelings were killing me slowly, and I couldn't deal with it.

"Why won't they let you send him in for surgery, Riley? As his next of kin why can't you just go tell the doctors that you want him to have it?" David asked quietly, his hand cupping round the back of my head, holding me to him tightly.

I sniffed, wiping my face with the back of my hand. "Linda told the doctors that our marriage isn't legal. Apparently because we used a fake ID then it doesn't count. I can't sign the form, I tried," I whispered, gripping his shirt that was wet with my tears.

"Not legal? Is that right though? Yes you used a fake ID, but Linda and Richard have accepted it for the last two weeks, as has your mother. The marriage wasn't annulled or protested, and you've been living as man and wife for over two weeks. Surely that counts for something?" he questioned.

I jerked back to look at him. I felt a bubble of hope. *Is that true? I would give anything for that to be true!* "Really? Oh God, Daddy, please, please say that's true," I begged, gripping his shirt tighter.

His face softened, and I knew it was because of what I had called him; I hardly ever called him that. A few times it had slipped out over the years, every time it looked like it made his heart melt. He stroked the side of my face lightly. "I'll look into it for you. I'll call Ron, he's a lawyer, he'll know if there's anything we can do."

Oh please, please, please let that be true! I nodded quickly and even laughed at the hope that I felt inside. Everything was going to be fine; David would sort everything just like he always did.

His smile faded, and he looked at me so sadly that I almost broke into a fresh round of sobs again. "I'm so sorry that I pushed you away like that, Riley. I cut you both out. I shouldn't have done that, and the things I said..." he trailed off, clenching his fist tightly and squeezing his eyes shut angrily. "The last words that I said to Clay were that he was a stupid little prick," he whispered. "I'm so sorry, so, so sorry. I hope I get a chance to take it back and apologise to him. I love Clay for you, Riley; he's the best man I could ever imagine for someone as special as you are. You two are perfect for each other, and I overreacted. I wasn't thinking about you two, I was just thinking about myself and what I had lost. But I love that boy like a son, I always have and I always will." A tear slid down his cheek as he spoke. This was the only time I had ever seen him cry. His chin quivered as he looked at me with eyes so sorrowful that it was almost as if he was the child and I was the adult. He was begging me with his eyes for my forgiveness; he looked like he was torturing himself over it.

I could forgive him, of course I could, he was my dad, and he always would be. I knew that Clay had already forgiven him because he was the one that convinced me to let it go and look at it from David's point of view. "Clay knows that you didn't mean it," I whispered, nodding reassuringly.

He looked at me, hope evident in his eyes; he really wanted that to be true. "He does?" he croaked, his voice weak and thick with emotion.

I nodded and smiled weakly. "Of course he does. Clay loves you too."

He smiled then and rubbed a hand over his face, wiping the couple of tears that had leaked out. "I was just so angry at him. All I could think about was that you two had run off and gotten married and taken away one of the most special things a dad could have in his life."

I looked at him quizzically. *What did we take away from him?* "What do you mean?"

He smiled and stroked my face again lightly, just looking at me tenderly. "Every dad wants to see their daughter marry the man of their dreams. I wanted you to have the big wedding with the fancy cake, with your whole family watching and smiling. I wanted to walk you down the aisle in your beautiful white dress. I wanted to smile, and when the vicar asks, who gives this woman to be married, I wanted to proudly step forward and say I do, because that's my daughter," he whispered, smiling wistfully.

I smiled at the little fantasy that had started to play out in my head. I imagined the proud smile he would have on his face as he placed my hand in Clay's and I could suddenly understand why he was so upset. It didn't excuse his behaviour, but it explained it to me finally.

"That sounds nice," I admitted, swallowing the lump in my throat.

He nodded. "Yeah but that doesn't matter right now. What matters right now is getting your husband that surgery, because Clay is going to be devastated if he can't walk." He winced as he said it and I smiled gratefully that he just knew him so well, that he was thinking about Clay and no one else, and also because he had called Clay my husband. He was finally acknowledging our marriage. He stood up and held a hand down to me. "I'm going to go outside and make some calls. Do you want to come out for some fresh air or are you going back in?"

The thought of being more than a few steps away from Clay made my stomach twist in knots so I shook my head and motioned towards his room. "I'm going back in."

He smiled and kissed my forehead. "I'm going to call Ron; I'll be back as soon as I can. Be strong, Riley, and don't let them beat you down. You and Clay belong together, and you'll get through this." He turned and walked off up the hallway; I waited until he was out of sight then took a few deep breaths before pushing the door to his room open again. I strolled casually to the side of his bed, refusing to look at Linda or Richard, just focusing my attention on the love of my life.

I sat there holding his hand for what felt like forever before David walked back in, he shook his head at me looking defeated and sad and I knew what Linda said was true. Our marriage wasn't legal. I nodded in response; I think I always knew it, deep down I knew that it was hopeless. I looked back to Clay and rested my chin on the side of his bed, watching the rise and fall of his chest, ignoring the whispers of the conversations going on in the room around me. I didn't care what they said anymore, it didn't matter, the only thing that mattered to me was that Clay open his beautiful green eyes.

The minutes turned into hours, and before I knew it, the nurse came in and said that only one person could stay with him tonight. I glared at Linda warningly. *If she dares tell me to leave I'm picking up Clay's IV pole and beating her to death with it. There's no way I'm leaving this room.*

She looked at me challengingly for a minute, but I didn't back down. She must have seen it in my face that I wasn't leaving because she gave me a small curt nod before turning to Richard and standing up. "Let's go, we can come back in the morning," she muttered.

"Thank you," I said weakly. I knew it was probably hard for her to walk out of here and leave him - maybe she was a stronger person than I was because there was no way I could force myself to leave this room.

"See you in the morning," she replied, gripping Clay's hand and kissing his cheek before turning and walking out of the room, crying again. Richard, my mom and David said their goodbyes, and then I was finally alone with my husband.

I pulled my chair closer to him and sat awake the whole night, whispering that I loved him and telling him all the things we would do when he woke up. I listed all of his favourite foods that I would cook for him, all the stupid TV shows he liked that I would watch with him when he was better, and how I wouldn't even complain about them. Lastly I talked about how our marriage wasn't legal so he was going to have to marry me again, but how this time I wanted the big wedding that David had talked about.

I threatened that if he didn't wake up within an hour, that I planned on spending all of his Vegas winnings on the biggest, most extravagant wedding I could think of. When he didn't wake up within the assigned deadline, I gave him another hour and added something else onto the list that I would waste money on, trying to shock him into waking up.

Ten threats later and he still hadn't woken up. Our wedding plan now included: A Chanel wedding dress, Gucci suits, elephants to take us to the church, money bouquets, chocolate dessert bowls, iPod's as table favours for our guests, and a whole heap more. I was going to have to send Clay back to Vegas to pay for it all if he didn't wake up soon. I smiled a little at the thought, knowing that I didn't need any of that stuff. All I needed was for him to wake up, get better and be happy.

Linda and Richard came back in the morning. My mom and David brought me a change of clothes and food. I took it to the bathroom, changing into the fresh clothes but dumping the food into the trash. I couldn't even think about eating, my stomach was already full of worry, nerves and knots; I couldn't possibly fit anything else in there too.

Just after lunchtime the same cop that was at Blake's house came in. He told us that Blake had been charged with defying a court order, breaking the terms of a restraining order, aggravated assault, attempted murder, and kidnapping. Apparently he was currently in a facility for the mentally ill; it had taken them a while to charge him because he needed treatment for a gunshot wound to the leg. As the cop was telling us, I just sat there silently hoping he rotted in jail for what he did to Clay. I had no sympathy for him at all anymore; he should have been the one lying in the hospital bed, not my baby.

I tuned out as Richard started quizzing the cop about why they had not acted sooner, how this could have happened; he wanted to make a formal complaint against the police for hesitating and allowing Clay to get stabbed not once but twice. I didn't listen to the conversation, those things weren't important to me right now. It was too late, and I just couldn't think about it.

My tired brain was slowly zoning out. I sat there like a zombie, unable to take my eyes off Clay. I didn't want to eat or drink, people fussed over me, but I couldn't answer their questions. I didn't have the energy to fake a smile and put on a show for them. With every minute that Clay lay there motionless, I was slowly dying inside.

Exactly twenty-seven hours after the knife pierced his body, his hand moved in mine. I gasped and looked down at it shocked. *Did that really just happen or did my sleep deprived mind make that up?* My heart was crashing in my chest as I looked at his fingers, willing them to move again so I would know I wasn't just losing my mind. As if on demand, his index finger twitched a little and I jumped out of my seat excitedly.

chapter
twenty-nine

"His hand moved!" I cried, looking at his face eagerly, waiting for him to open his eyes.

Linda and Richard jumped up too, and we all leant over the bed just waiting. When his hand tightened on mine, Linda laughed quietly, and Richard pressed the call button the wall to get the doctors' attention.

The same doctor from yesterday came rushing in. Obviously his shift had ended and started again, and that made the time seem even longer somehow. A nurse came in behind him; they both looked at us curiously.

"His hand moved," Richard explained.

I couldn't take my eyes off Clay; I daren't even blink in case I missed anything. I couldn't breathe as I stood there waiting and waiting. After about a minute his eyelids fluttered. The doctor walked around the bed to the machines, checking the printout of his heart monitor.

Suddenly it happened, and I dragged in a ragged breath as my fear and worry loosened slightly. I worked hard to keep the horror and sadness off of my face as Clay's eyelids fluttered twice before opening. I smiled weakly as he groaned and raised his hand to pull at the tube that was going down his throat.

I took his hand quickly and brushed his hair back from his forehead. "Shh, Clay, it's okay. Everything's okay. They'll take that out just don't worry," I cooed soothingly as the nurse and doctor stepped forward to the edge of the bed. His eyes met mine, and I saw panic and fear there which broke my heart. "Everything's okay, baby," I lied. He squeezed my hand hard as they pulled out the tubes from his throat making him gag and cough as he gasped for breath. They fussed over him for a couple of minutes while he just gripped my hand as if his life depended on it.

Once the tubes were out the doctor stepped closer to him, shining a light in Clay's eyes before smiling sadly and putting his penlight back in his pocket. I felt sick because I knew what was coming next. They were about to tell him and I was about to watch his heart break. Was I strong enough to be here when they told him? Could I watch them rip his heart out without breaking down and making it worse for him? I didn't want to be here, but Clay's green eyes met mine so I knew I needed to stay. It would hurt like hell to watch, but I would never leave him when he needed me. I needed to be strong for him, I refused to cry and make this worse for him by being weak.

I sat on the chair next to his bed as the doctor and nurse looked at Linda, silently asking for permission to tell him the news. She nodded and they stepped forward again. Clay didn't pay any attention to them; instead he tugged on my hand, making me move closer to him. I smiled weakly and pressed my lips to his dry chapped ones for a second before pulling back. "I love you, Clay," I whispered fiercely.

He smiled his heartbreaking smile that I had missed so much for the last day. "I love you more, Riley Bear," he croaked, his voice sounding raspy and sore. My stomach seemed to flutter that the first words out of his mouth were the sweetest words in the history of the world. I would never take a single one of his words for granted again; this situation had just shown me that I loved him more than I even knew.

The doctor cleared his throat. "Clay, we need to talk to you about what happened," he said confidently.

Clay tore his eyes from me to look at the doctor. I couldn't listen, I couldn't hear it again. As the doctor told him about his injuries I kept my eyes on Clay's face, watching as emotions crossed his face so quickly I could barely even register them. Confusion, horror, fear, desperation.

He turned his head and looked at me, his eyes pleading with me to tell him he was fine, that this was a lie or a joke. He had never looked so vulnerable and scared, and I hated his parents more than ever for it. I nodded in confirmation watching his face fall as he slowly started to accept it, his hand was squeezing mine so hard it felt like he was going to break my fingers, but I just didn't care.

The doctor still wasn't done though. He was still telling him about the operation and how it was risky and running through the chances of success. When it got to the point about the next of kin, Clay's eyes snapped to me.

"Tell me you signed the forms, Riley. Tell me they did the operation. Please... please tell me," he begged, looking at me desperately.

I shook my head slowly, swallowing my horror at how scared and hurt he looked. "I couldn't, they wouldn't let me. I'm not your next of kin," I whispered. Each word seemed to burn its way out of my throat.

He looked at me confused. "Not my next of kin? Of course you are, you're my wife," he rasped, looking at me confused.

I reached out and my hand and stroked the side of his face. "Our marriage isn't legal, Clay. They wouldn't let me sign it. I'm so sorry, baby, I tried, I wanted to." I flicked my gaze to Linda, trying to kill her with my eyes because the look on Clay's face right now was pure agony and heartbreak, and it was all her fault.

"So, the operation didn't happen?" Clay asked, still looking at me, ignoring everyone else in the room. "I can't walk now? That's it?"

I didn't know what to say. I leant forward and kissed his forehead softly, making his hand tighten on mine. "You didn't have the operation, but if you want to have it now then there's still a chance it'll work." I turned to the doctor, looking at him for confirmation, "Right? He can still have it, can't he?"

He nodded and stepped forward, cocking his head to the side, looking at Clay intently. He cleared his throat, obviously trying to get his attention again, but Clay's eyes were fixed firmly on me, the heartbroken look on his face caused me more pain than I had ever experienced in my life.

"I'll get Dr Kirk to come in and talk to you if that's what you want, Clay. He's the surgeon who would perform the operation. He'll be able to run through things better than me," the doctor said, touching Clay's arm lightly.

Clay didn't say anything, just nodded and gulped noisily. I pressed my forehead to his and looked into his eyes. I could see my exact feeling mirrored there, he was terrified, his eyes glassy but he was trying not to cry.

"I love you," I whispered, kissing his lips lightly.

He closed his eyes and nodded. "You too, Riley."

"Everything's going to be fine," I said, willing my voice to sound more confident than I felt. The doctors had said that the surgery needed to happen as soon as possible, was twenty-seven hours too late? He smiled weakly and nodded, wincing as he moved. I hissed through my teeth at the pain on his face. "Don't move, just keep still and they'll probably give you something for the pain."

He ignored my advice and tugged on my hand, making me step impossibly closer. "Our marriage isn't legal?" he asked, his voice barely above a whisper.

I flicked my eyes to Linda. She was just watching us with her mouth open, silent tears falling down her face as she gripped at her shirt, just above her heart. All I could think was two words: selfish bitch. I gulped and looked back to Clay, forcing a smile. "No, baby, it's not. But on the upside, now we get to have another wedding night," I teased quietly, trying to bring a bit of normality to this whole horrifying ordeal.

He laughed a little before wincing again, squeezing his eyes shut, his jaw tight. "Pervert," he whispered through clenched teeth.

"Yeah, you know me." I nodded, fighting the tears that were making my eyes prickle.

When his jaw unclenched he looked around the room for the first time, they stopped at his parents, and he forced a tight smile. Linda stepped up to the bed next to me. I went to step back so she could have more room to see him, but Clay's hand tightened on mine not letting me move away from him.

"I'm so glad you're awake, Clay. I've been so worried, we've all been so worried," she said, her voice hitching where she was crying so hard.

He nodded. "Yeah, sorry." He smiled awkwardly at Richard because their relationship was still a little strained. "Hey, Dad."

I felt slightly awkward where I was pressed half against Linda. I couldn't even look at her, I was trapped between her and the wall and I just wanted to shove her far away from me. I could barely breathe with her so close to me, like I had suddenly developed claustrophobia or something.

"How are you feeling, okay?" Linda asked, brushing her hand up and down Clay's arm lightly.

He laughed humourlessly. "I just found out that there's a good chance I might not be able to walk again, how do you think I'm feeling?" he asked, closing his eyes and shaking his head as if that was a stupid question. I could feel his hand shaking in mine, the sweat on his palm was making his hand slick against my skin. His fingers found my wedding ring and he twirled it around my finger absentmindedly.

Linda sucked in a deep breath and looked at him, her guilt and sadness clear across her face. "I'm so sorry, Clay. We thought it was what's best for you. There was a chance you could die; we didn't want to send you in there with the odds so low. That wasn't our decision to make. We don't get to play God with your life. That was your decision to make, no one else's. I couldn't let Riley sign the form," Linda said quietly, continuing her relentless stroking of his arm.

I swallowed the hatred I could feel trying to come out of me. I tried to keep in mind that she was just scared, that she hadn't purposefully tried to hurt Clay, she had thought she was doing what was best for him. She just didn't realise that she couldn't see past her own feelings, her own pain, she didn't make that choice for him at all, she'd made it for herself.

He looked at her, confusion colouring his voice as he spoke, "What does that mean? Couldn't let Riley sign the form? Wait. You... you stopped her from sending me in for the operation?"

Linda glanced at Richard, her eyes filling with tears again as she nodded. "We thought it was best to get you well. It wasn't for us to make that decision with your life, Clay," she said again.

He groaned and shook his head. "Why? Why would you do that? You think I want this? You think I want to live like this?" he asked angrily. The steady beeps of the heart monitor started to speed up as his breathing started to accelerate and get shallower.

Clay's parents and I all looked at the little green line that was spiking faster and faster. "Calm down, Clay," I begged, bumping Linda with my hip, telling her to move as I leant over the bed more, stroking the side of his face trying to get him to calm down.

His eyes met mine. "You wanted to send me in for it but my parents didn't let you?" he whispered, raising his hand weakly. The IV line obviously made it harder for him to move it because he was a little uncoordinated and it took him a couple of attempts before his hand gripped around the back of my head. He pulled my face up level with his. "They didn't send me in there, and now there's a chance that I'm stuck like this?" he asked. I nodded, knowing I wouldn't be able to speak. I had no words for this. All I wanted to do was turn around and scratch Linda's eyes out. He drew in a jagged breath, his eyes locked on mine. "Tell them to leave, Riley," he ordered, tightening his hand in the back of my hair.

I gulped and turned my head to the side looking at Linda and Richard, they were hugging, both of them crying. Linda was literally trembling from head to toe. "Why don't you go wait outside or something," I suggested quietly. I knew they wouldn't want to leave and at least Clay and I could talk privately about it.

"Not outside, go home," Clay growled. His eyes were still firmly fixed on me, as if he couldn't even bring himself to look at them or something.

Richard cleared his throat awkwardly. "Clay, we thought it was the best thing for you, we had no right to risk you like that," he said, looking between me and Clay, a pleading expression on his face.

Clay finally looked away from me; his gaze fell on his parents, his face hard and angry. "You think that wasting time waiting for me to wake up was what's best for me?" he asked, looking at them in disbelief. "You should have let her sign the forms, you should have let her..." He trailed off, his voice breaking.

"I'm so sorry," Richard whispered.

"Just get out. If I can still go in for the surgery then I'm going in for it. How could you not know that's what I would want?" Clay asked weakly. Richard opened his mouth to answer, but Clay cut him off. "Just get the hell out!" he yelled. His heart rate spiked again on the monitor.

I gasped and pulled away from Clay. I needed to get them to leave before he ended up even more sick from the stress of it all. "Just go, please?" I begged, flicking my eyes to the heart monitor, drawing their attention to the little number in the corner that was creeping higher and higher by the second.

Richard winced as he looked at it and then grabbed Linda's hand and practically dragged her from the room. I flinched as I could hear her wailing from outside the door. I turned back to look at Clay. He was just lying there staring at the ceiling, his jaw tight, his eyes just focused on one spot as if it was telling him the secrets of life.

"Are you okay? Does it hurt?" I whispered, fussing with the sheets, not knowing what else to do or say.

"I'm okay. What happened, Riley Bear?" he asked, finally turning to look at me.

I closed my eyes. *How am I going to explain all of this to him? How can I even look him in the eye knowing that this was all because of me?* "Blake, he... he grabbed a knife and he," my voice broke and his hand gripped mine, squeezing gently, "he stabbed you in the side first. The doctors said that you had a collapsed lung, but they've put some kind of tube in to fix it, they said it was okay now."

He nodded. "He stabbed me in the back too." It wasn't a question, it was a statement.

I nodded, looking at him apologetically. "I'm so sorry. I'm so, so sorry. This is my fault. Everything, this whole situation is my fault. You're hurt because of me," I whispered, trying desperately not to cry.

He smiled and shook his head. "No, Riley Bear. Don't do that, this isn't your fault, don't feel bad." He tugged on my hand gently, his intention clear. I moved closer to him, bending over his bed and tucked my face into the side of his neck. The beautiful smell that was purely Clay Preston filled my lungs, and I smiled despite the guilt and pain I felt inside.

"I love you, Clay, and everything's going to be fine, I promise." I kissed the skin on his neck just as the door opened and the doctor walked in with another man hot on his heels.

I pulled back and tried to take in everything that they were saying. Dr Kirk wanted to do the operation almost immediately, there was still about a forty percent chance that it would work, but they had to get in there and see before he would know how much the operation would actually help. The chances of Clay dying were reduced too; his body had recovered slightly while he was in the coma so although there were still risks, as with any surgery, the risks were dramatically reduced.

I felt my body relax when they said that and I let out a breath I didn't even realise I was holding. They were running through the procedure, but I couldn't listen to that at all, all I let myself hear was that it was six hours long and that after the operation, they would have to wait a little while to see how successful it was.

"So, do you want to go in for it?" Dr Kirk asked as he finished explaining everything to Clay.

Clay looked at me before nodding. "Yeah, let's do it. I want to know I've tried everything."

The doctors all left to arrange everything for the operation, and he was to go down as soon as there was an operating room free. When we were on our own again, Clay smiled weakly at me. "You look like hell, Riley Bear. Did you sleep?"

he asked, tracing his finger under my eye.

I caught his hand and kissed his palm, pressing my face into it. "I'm fine, baby." I needed to tell him something, he needed to know this before he went in for the operation. I stood up so I was leaning over him, looking into his eyes so he knew I was serious. "Clay, if you let yourself die in there I swear to God I'm going to bring you back to life again, just so I can kill you myself. You understand?" I said fiercely.

He laughed quietly. "Hmm, I definitely like masterful Riley," he teased.

"Stop it, Clay, I'm serious. If I only ask one thing from you in my life, it's that you come back to me. I need you to promise me, promise me you'll survive this. I need to hear you say it, and then I can stop worrying because you've never broken a promise to me before, so I have a lot of faith in your word." I gripped the front of the hospital gown he was wearing; I needed him to tell me that so much, my whole body was on edge waiting for it.

He smiled and nodded, his hand moving up to cup the side of my face. "I'll be fine, I promise," he whispered, his eyes locked on mine and held a fierce intensity that made my heart start to speed up.

I smiled and pressed my lips to his again lightly for a couple of seconds before putting my forehead to his, just enjoying being close to him.

Half an hour later they were ready for him to go down to theatre. I held his hand as they walked him down the little corridor, his fingers gripping mine so tightly that I was almost losing feeling in them, but somehow it still didn't feel tight enough. When we got to the door, they stopped pushing the bed and looked at me expectantly so I knew I wasn't allowed any further with him.

I could feel the panic starting to rise in my chest because he was going to be out of my sight for so long. I looked at Dr Kirk, looking him over trying to see any doubt in his mind, to see if he was going to be able to save my baby and bring him back to me. He smiled and nodded reassuringly and I begged him with my eyes to keep Clay alive. This man now held my whole life in his hands, my hopes, my dreams, my whole future. All I could do was trust him.

I looked back to Clay, he smiled weakly, but his eyes told me that he was just as scared as I was. I took in a deep breath and pushed my shoulders back knowing I needed to show confidence, even if I didn't feel it. "I'll see you when you get out. Don't think you're getting out of marrying me again, buster, you know I never liked the name Tanner so I'm sticking with Preston. You make sure you hurry up and get better so we can get straight to the nearest church and get married again, you hear me?" I asked, raising one eyebrow trying to look stern.

He laughed quietly. "Whatever you say, Riley Bear."

I kissed him softly, savouring the feel of his lips, and I prayed that this wasn't the last time I got to speak to him, that this wasn't the last kiss we ever had. "I love you, Clay." I brushed my hand down the side of his bruised face.

He smiled his beautiful smile and gripped the back of my head, pulling me closer to him as if he was going to whisper in my ear. With his other hand he gripped my chin and turned my head to the side. Before I even had a chance to work out what he was doing, he sucked on the side of my neck, hard. I giggled, and he pushed me away slightly, a big smile on his face.

"Just marking my territory," he stated as I rubbed the freshly made hickey on my neck, trying to pretend I was angry, but I couldn't keep the smile off my face. The doctor cleared his throat so I pulled back and stood up, smiling down at Clay as they pushed the doors open and wheeled his bed down the corridor. Just as the doors were about to close Clay shouted me, "Riley?"

"Yeah?"

"I love you more," he called smugly.

My heart throbbed, and the doors to the corridor slammed shut leaving me on my own, staring at the place where I last saw the love of my life. I couldn't stay strong anymore; I sank to my knees and sobbed into the floor.

• • •

THE SIX HOURS were like physical pain. I felt like I was sitting balanced on the edge of a cliff, one wrong move and I would go tumbling over into a living hell. My parents and Clay's were sitting in the waiting room with me. No one really said anything and I was grateful that I didn't have to put up some sort of act for them. I just didn't have the energy anymore. I was so tired that my head was throbbing. My eyes stung, but while everyone else dozed in their chairs, I kept my eyes locked on the doors where he would come out of.

Just after 10 p.m. the doctor walked out of the door, his eyes locked first on Linda and then on me. I couldn't breathe. I couldn't move. This was it. These next couple of words would shape the rest of my life, either Clay survived the surgery or he didn't. At this point I couldn't bring myself to care about if the operation had worked, all I needed was Clay by my side, however he came I didn't mind, just as long as I still had him.

The doctor walked up to our group. Everyone else jumped out of their chairs, but I couldn't, I knew if I stood up I would fall to the floor. The doctor smiled and nodded. "It went very well. He's in recovery right now. There's a lot of swelling so we won't know how successful it was until that's gone down, but the early indications are that there's a strong chance of success," he said.

Richard grabbed Linda into a hug, David slapped the doctor on the shoulder laughing, and my mom looked at me, grinning from ear to ear. I closed my eyes and breathed a sigh of relief, my tired muscles relaxing. "He's okay?" I croaked. My heart was racing in my chest, my whole body was tingling. It was over, Clay was alive, we had a little while to wait to see if it had worked but he was alive and that was all that mattered to me.

"He's okay," Dr Kirk confirmed. "He's strong; he'll be out for a little while until the anaesthetic leaves his body, maybe an hour or two. When he wakes up it's best to keep him as calm as possible. The surgery was very invasive, he needs to relax and let his body recover. Tomorrow we'll run some tests and see how successful it was."

I gripped the arms of the chair and pushed myself up, immediately being grabbed into a hug by my mom. "But you think it went well? The surgery I mean?" I asked hopefully.

He nodded. "It went without a hitch; we just need to see how his body reacts to the repair now. I'd better go; they'll bring him out soon and move him back to his room."

"Thank you, thank you so much," I whispered, looking at him gratefully. *How can I ever repay this man that has hopefully saved my baby from a life that he'll be miserable in?*

"You're welcome, Mrs Preston," he replied, smiling, before walking away towards the nurses station.

I laughed at the name; at least he was acknowledging our marriage. I gripped my wedding ring tightly in my hand and turned to Linda and Richard. I needed to get this sorted out before Clay woke up, I needed to keep him calm and seeing his parents wouldn't really do that at the moment.

"I think it's best that you just stay away for a little while. I'll talk to Clay tomorrow, but the doctor said he needed to rest. I don't want him upset again so just let me talk to him before you see him," I instructed, praying I wouldn't have another fight on my hands. I really didn't have the energy for that right now.

Richard nodded in agreement. "Yeah. Thank you, Riley. We were only trying to do what's best for him."

I didn't really know what to say about that. They were doing what was best for them, not Clay, but again, I couldn't get into that argument with them right now. "I'll talk to him about it. Maybe you should go home. I'll call you if there are any changes," I said, rubbing my temples, trying to relieve the pounding in my head. I hadn't slept for over thirty-eight hours, and wow did I feel it kicking in now.

Linda pushed herself away from Richard and wrapped me in a hug, but I couldn't hug her back. The best she could expect from me was that I didn't push her away. In my eyes that was more than she deserved from me. "I'm so sorry. I should have listened to you, he wanted the surgery, I should have listened!" she wailed, her fingers digging in my back where she was hugging me so tightly.

I nodded. "Yeah, you should have," I confirmed. I swallowed my angry, bitchy retort. I'd already said my piece to her, they would both probably suffer the consequences of it now, Clay certainly knew how to hold a grudge when he wanted to. There was a good chance that he wouldn't want to see his parents again. My influence on Clay was probably the only chance they had right now, and to be honest, I didn't feel particularly charitable towards them at that precise moment. "You should go home before he comes out."

They nodded, both saying their goodbyes and walking out slowly, leaving me with my parents. Finally, after what felt like forever, they wheeled Clay out of the operating suites and back into the same room he was in before. He had even more tubes and wires sticking out of him this time. His face was pale but yet strangely peaceful as he lay in bed. My parents weren't allowed into his room because visiting hours were over so I pulled the chair up by the side of the bed again and held his hand.

When he finally groaned and opened his eyes I smiled and leant over to him. "Hi. Thanks for not breaking your promise," I whispered, looking at him gratefully. He smiled weakly, pulling the little oxygen mask off of his face. He tried to speak but all that came out was a croaking sound, probably from the tubes he'd had down his throat from the surgery. "Shh, baby, everything went good they said. You just need to relax and rest, and tomorrow they'll run some tests to see how it went. Just get some sleep for me, okay? I'll be right here all night," I assured him, squeezing his hand as I kissed his forehead.

He smiled and instantly closed his eyes. He looked exhausted. "You sleep too, Riley Bear," he rasped, his voice barely above a whisper.

I smiled and nodded. "I will, baby. I'll see you in the morning." I kissed his hand and rested my chin on the side of his bed. I felt sleep coming to take me and I couldn't fight it anymore. I knew that tomorrow was going to be another long day, either everything would go as planned, or it wouldn't. Either way, we had a lot of work to do to get Clay over this; this was far from over for either of us.

chapter thirty

I woke in the morning and could barely move; I groaned and lifted my head from the side of Clay's bed, rubbing my aching neck. My back seemed to pop as I sat up. *Wow, not a good idea to sleep bent over leaning on the bed!*

My eyes immediately found Clay; he was awake and just staring at me, a small sad smile pulling at the corners of his mouth. "Hey," he whispered.

"Hi, why didn't you wake me if you were awake?" I asked, rubbing my hand up his arm and trying to stifle a yawn. My whole body was hurting and aching, my eyes were still stinging, and I could do with another few hours' sleep at least, but I tried not to show it on my face.

He stroked my cheek with the back of one finger. "You know I like to watch you sleep," he said quietly.

I laughed and turned my head to kiss his hand. "I know, pervert, but I would have much rather you had woken me up so I could have talked to you. I've missed you. You were asleep for a long time you know," I scolded playfully. He smiled but didn't say anything. His eyes were tighter than normal; his face was defeated and sad. I swallowed loudly. "What's wrong, Clay?"

He sighed deeply. "I can't feel my legs," he replied, looking away from me.

I felt my heart sink. *Did it not work? Has he gone through all of that pain for nothing? Did he risk his life and nothing has changed?* "Clay, let's just wait for the doctor, okay? He said they needed to wait a while before doing the tests. Maybe the swelling hasn't gone down yet; maybe you need more time to get over the surgery. It's only been a few hours," I said, trying to keep my voice level and devoid of any emotion.

He nodded, but it didn't look like he believed me. "Yeah I guess."

"Please, baby, just don't start stressing about it yet. Let's just let the doctor do his thing and do the tests when you're ready to do them, okay?" I begged. "You could be working yourself up into a state for nothing. The doctor said you needed to stay calm and rest."

He nodded and squeezed my hand, putting on a fake smile and looking back to me. "Yeah okay." He sighed and looked over my face slowly. "You still look tired, Riley Bear, you should sleep some more."

I kissed his hand and shook my head. "If you're awake then I'm awake."

"Riley, what if it doesn't work and I can't walk anymore? What do I do then?" he whispered. He looked like he was a couple of seconds from completely breaking down, and it was scaring me a little. Clay was always so strong, he was always the one in control and looked after me, and right now the roles had totally reversed for the first time.

"We'll deal with that if it happens. Let's just not think about it right now, all right? What's the point in worrying about something that won't even happen?" I asked, trying to sound positive.

He closed his eyes and pulled on my hand. "Come lay with me for a little while. You should go back to sleep, you look like hell, Riley Bear."

I laughed and tried to look offended. "That's not the way to talk to the girl you're in love with, Clay. If you're trying to get in my pants then you're going about it all wrong," I teased, climbing on the bed carefully, settling myself along his side but barely touching him, staying as still as possible.

"I might not be able to do that again, Riley, did you think about that?" he snapped.

I frowned at his anger but didn't say anything; I wasn't sure what I could say to make him feel better, so I just put my arm across his chest and kissed his shoulder. He hardly ever shouted at me or anything, so him doing it now just showed me how upset he actually was. If he needed someone to shout at and get his anger out on then I could be that person for him, I'd be anything he needed me to be.

• • •

AFTER ANOTHER HOUR of us just lying in silence, the doctor came in to do his rounds. He smiled as he walked in and I pushed myself up out of the bed, barely able to breathe. *Is this it, is he going to do the tests now?* I stood back as he looked at Clay's IV, detaching him from all of the tubes and wires. He checked his eyes and his catheter before he smiled and came back up to the side of the bed.

"Okay, so the operation went well, Clay. I'm hopeful that there should be a marked improvement; I was able to repair everything that I could see. What I'm going to do is send you down for an MRI scan now and then when you're back I'll do a couple of physical tests," he said. A nurse walked in with a couple of orderlies and went to the head of Clay's bed.

"Can I go with him?" I asked, not wanting Clay out of my sight for a second more than necessary.

"Sure, you can go to the waiting room with him, but you won't be allowed in the room while they do it." The doctor smiled and nodded and the two orderlies started pushing the bed out of the room. I ran to catch up with it and held Clay's hand all the way there, kissing him lightly when we got there.

I sat there in the waiting room, trying to look at a magazine while I waited for him to come out, but I couldn't even tell you what the magazine was called. I was flicking through the pages without even looking at them properly, just so I would have something to do with my hands to stop them shaking.

Once we were back in his room, we had to wait a little while before his surgeon came back in. I just held Clay's hand tightly, trying to talk to him, but he just answered yes or no to everything I said. My attempts to distract him weren't working at all. He was so distant and quiet that it was making the hairs on the back of my neck stand up. My heart was aching because Clay was keeping his feelings bottled up, he never kept things from me, but he was obviously doing it now. Every time I looked at him it seemed like he was sinking further and further into a depression and there was nothing I could say or do to bring him out of it.

Dr Kirk came back in and did the physical tests on Clay's feet and legs. He kept poking him with a sharp needle like thing, putting some sort of cloth that he had dipped into a liquid, onto various parts of Clay's legs, asking him if he could feel the cold. To every question Clay answered no, and I saw the devastation building in his eyes with each passing second.

The doctor threw the things in the trash and smiled reassuringly. "There's obviously some swelling still there, that's clear from the MRI, I had a look at that before I came in. It could just be too early to tell," he offered, his voice still hopeful.

"What does that mean?" Clay asked, looking a little confused.

The doctor sighed and looked at him apologetically. "It's just a wait and see thing. I'm sorry, I know that's hard to do, but there's not much else we can do at this point but just wait and see how your body reacts. The more the swelling goes down then the more we'll be able to see how much mobility there is there," he explained, scribbling on Clay's chart.

"How much mobility, what does that mean? That even if it was successful then I wouldn't be back to normal?" Clay asked, trying to move in the bed as he hissed through his teeth and squeezed his eyes shut.

The doctor pushed on his shoulder. "Just stay still. Give your body a chance,

Clay. This isn't an overnight thing. I know it's hard, but you need to be patient and rest as much as you can."

I stepped forward again and stroked his face. "Clay, just relax. Please listen to the doctor, he knows what he's talking about," I begged desperately.

The doctor smiled at me. "We'll leave it another day and then send you down for another MRI and CT scan tomorrow once the swelling has gone down some more. This is perfectly normal, Clay. Just be patient, I know it's hard but it's the only thing you can do right now." The doctor patted him on the shoulder. He waited a few seconds, scribbling on his chart again before nodding. "I'll let you two have some privacy, and I'll come back later. Any problems press the buzzer." He nodded to the little hand held button hanging on the wall.

When he walked out of the room Clay turned to look at me. The look on his face broke my heart a little more. He was so sad, sadder than I had ever seen him look. I knew then and there that if I could take his place, I would do it in a heartbeat. He looked like he knew his fate already; he had already given up hope of being able to walk again.

"Everything's fine, baby. We just need to wait a little while; those tests don't mean anything, Clay. Just wait for the swelling to go down like he said, don't get yourself upset about it, okay?" I begged, hearing my voice break a little even though I was trying to be strong.

Suddenly his face turned from sad and desperate to angry. When his eyes locked on mine they were hard and accusing. "I need you to leave, Riley," he growled.

I gaped at him, shocked. *What the heck does that mean? Oh God, he's blaming me for this, he thinks this is my fault because if Blake wasn't stalking me then he wouldn't have gotten hurt.* It was my fault, I knew that, and I would never forgive myself, but the hard look on his face was actually like physical pain.

"What?" I whispered, looking at him like he was crazy. *He doesn't really want me to leave, does he?*

"You need to leave. Now," he repeated.

"Clay, baby, please. I'm sorry. I'm so, so sorry," I whispered. The tears that I had held at bay while I was in front of him, now started to fall uncontrollably down my face.

He shook his head. "You don't need to be sorry, Riley. Just leave," he said sternly.

"I can't," I whispered. How long did he want me to leave for, how long would it take him to forgive me for what Blake did to him because of me? An hour? A day? A week? I couldn't make myself walk out of the door and leave him, I couldn't. *Is this why he's been cold and distant with me all morning? Because he was angry with me about it? Has he been planning this all morning?*

We both knew that this was my fault, but I never thought in a million years that he would ask me to leave him. If there was one thing that I would bet my life on, it was that Clay would never cut me out of his life, never. But that was exactly what he was doing. I looked at him pleadingly, my heart breaking. The pain was unbearable. I wasn't going to live through this; this pain was going to kill me. To be apart from him would kill me. Surely he wasn't this angry with me; surely he'd forgive me, wouldn't he?

"Why? Please let me stay, I know this is my fault, but please, Clay, I love you. I'm so sorry this happened to you!" I cried, bending and putting my face in the side of his neck, being careful of all the needles he still had in the back of each hand and the tube sticking out of his chest.

His hands tangled in the back of my hair as he kissed the top of my head. "I don't blame you, this wasn't your fault. But I can't love you, Riley. I'm sorry, but you need to go so I can concentrate on recovering without having to think about you all the time."

I gripped the front of his hospital gown, holding onto it for dear life. If I let go I didn't know what I would do. Could I live without Clay in my life, even for a second? Those few hours when I wasn't sure if he'd make it, or the hours when he was in surgery, those were the worse of my life, and I knew that if he'd died I would have wanted to die too.

I thought about what he said. *He wants to concentrate on recovering? What is that supposed to mean? He isn't making sense. If this isn't because he's blaming me then what is it about?*

"Why?" I screamed against the skin of his neck, making his hand tighten in the back of my hair as I sobbed uncontrollably.

"I can't have you here while I'm like this. I can't have you tied to someone like me," he whispered.

Suddenly everything clicked into place, as if someone had flicked on a light switch in a darkened room. Everything made sense in an instant. He *did* want me, but he thought he was doing this for me. I pulled back to look at him, shaking my head incredulously. This was some kind of sick way of letting me go because he didn't want me to have to be with him if he couldn't walk. Was he seriously thinking I wouldn't want to be with him because of that? Did he not know me at all? All these years he'd known me, but yet he thought I would walk away because there was a chance he would be in a wheelchair for the rest of his life? I could feel my anger building up inside. There was no way this was happening, no way in hell he was sending me away from him for my own benefit.

"What the hell are you talking about, Clay? Are you kidding me right now? Tell me why you want me to go, tell me why you don't want me anymore!" I cried, swallowing the lump in my throat.

There had to be something else, that couldn't be the reason. Clay had always been selfless and put my happiness over the top of his, but he had to know that this would kill me. He wouldn't make me leave because he thought he was doing the right thing for me, would he?

He sighed and turned his head away from me. "Just go, Riley."

"No," I said fiercely.

"Just get the hell out! I don't want you here! I don't want you stuck with a fucking cripple just because you feel guilty or something stupid. I don't want to take everything away from you; I don't want to disappoint you because I can't make love to you anymore! I don't want to let this go on and then you leave me in a few years time for someone who can walk and give you children, someone who can give you everything you deserve out of life. It's going to be easier for me to get over you now, to do it all in one go, rather than start to rely on you and then you leave me. Just get out and don't ever come back!" he shouted, glaring at me angrily. He gripped hold of my arm and shoved me towards the door as one of the nurses came bursting in, obviously hearing his little outburst.

The nurse looked between us with wide eyes. "What on earth is going on in here? Clay, you need to calm down! You've just had surgery you need to relax and let your body recover!" she cried angrily as she headed over to his side pressing the button on the little heart monitor. The beeping was so fast that it actually scared the life out of me. Clay was gasping for breath as she pushed on his shoulder making him settle down. A little oxygen mask was quickly pushed over his mouth and nose as she looked at him worriedly.

"What's wrong? Is he okay?" I asked weakly. I had never been so scared in my life as the rapid beeping of his monitor seemed to fill the air, deafening me. Clay's eyes flicked to me, and I saw no indecision in his eyes. This was it, everything I thought would last forever, was over. He really wanted me to leave, and the look on his face broke my heart into a million pieces.

"Get out, Riley," he muttered weakly, pulling the mask off of his face.

"I love you, Clay," I whispered, begging him with my eyes. I couldn't leave him, not ever. He was my life, how could he not understand that? There was no way I would leave him for someone else in a couple of years, no chance of that happening at all. I loved him with all of my heart, and it hurt me that he would doubt me like that, he should know me better.

He shook his head. "You don't love me enough for this," he said breathlessly. He turned to the nurse who was trying to get the mask back on his face. "Make her leave. Get security, get her out of here. I don't want her here!" he shouted, making her recoil from the anger in his voice.

She turned to me looking at me apologetically. "Please leave. He needs to relax and you being here is working him up. Just leave, come back in a couple of hours." She put her hand on my arm and nodded towards the door, her eyes kind and sympathetic.

"I don't want her back in a couple of hours! Just get her the hell out!" Clay cried, gasping for breath as he tried to push himself up in the bed but by the looks of it he was too weak as he instantly slumped back down again, hissing in pain.

I looked from the nurse to Clay and back again. *I have to leave; I'm doing that to him, making him feel like that. I'm making him worse, making him ill. He needs to relax, the doctor had said so.*

"I'll go. Look after him," I whispered as I turned and ran out of the door as fast as my legs could carry me.

~ Clay ~

I WATCHED HER HEART break before she turned and ran out of the door. I clenched my jaw tight so I didn't beg her to come back. I couldn't breathe; the pain in my heart was a hundred times worse than any physical pain I could ever feel. I'd just lost the one thing that I needed out of life, the one thing that mattered to me, hell she was the *only* thing that mattered to me in life. Not only had I lost her, but I'd actually pushed her away. I'd made her leave when she didn't want to, and that hurt even more. I hated myself because I'd hurt her by setting her free. If I could take her heartbreak as well as my own, I would. I would lay down my life for her in an instant and I always would. I would do anything to make her happy, even if it destroyed me in the process. In time she would get over this and find someone else, and he would give her everything that I couldn't anymore. The thought was agony, but I wouldn't have it any other way. Riley deserved the best out of life, and a husband in a wheelchair wasn't that.

The nurse tugged on the mask, pulling it out of my hand and pressing it back over my mouth and nose again. "Try and calm down, if your heart rate gets any faster you'll go into cardiac arrest," she said sternly.

Cardiac arrest? A heart attack, hell that sounds awesome right about now, hopefully it'll kill me and I won't have to live one day without my girl by my side. I closed my eyes, trying to block out the pain of it, but I couldn't, all I could see was Riley telling me she loved me, flashes of our wedding and the day after when we woke up in the hotel and realised we were married, thoughts of making love to her for the first time. All these memories were flashing through my brain making it even more painful.

I would have lived every day of my life making her happy, but it wasn't enough, I wasn't enough for her now, and I was doing the right thing letting her off. She didn't deserve a life sentence being tied to a guy in a wheelchair. I'd thought about this since the moment I woke up this morning and saw her sitting there on the chair, asleep at my side. I knew she wouldn't want to go, but if I couldn't walk again then I wasn't what was best for her anymore. Sure, everything would have been fine for a year or two, but after a little while she would have started to resent me for holding her back and then she'd leave me. It was best to set her free now, and then I could learn how to deal with this on my own. I'd be on my own sooner or later anyway, so why delay the inevitable?

After a little while the nurse pulled the mask off of my face and looked at me sympathetically. "Are you okay? Can I get you anything? Call someone?" she asked kindly.

I shook my head and forced a smile. I couldn't hold it together for much longer; I didn't want anyone here when I lost control. "I'm fine; can I just have a minute?" I asked, my voice husky and filled with emotion.

"Sure. If you need me then press the buzzer, all right?" She smiled and put the call button on the bed next to my hand.

"I'm fine now, thanks," I lied.

She took one last look at me before she walked out. As soon as I the door closed I couldn't hold it anymore, I gripped my hands in my hair, and I sobbed. I sobbed for what I'd lost. I sobbed for what I gave up. I sobbed for what could have been. I hadn't cried since I was a kid, but I couldn't stop. I prayed for death because that would have been easier than dealing with this, this was like living in hell on earth, and I wasn't strong enough for it.

After I calmed myself down I laid there numb, staring at the ceiling waiting for death to come and get me and take me out of here, to stop the pain and fill the gaping hole that used to be where my heart was. My parents came, but I couldn't even bring myself to talk to them, couldn't even shout at them for not sending me in for the surgery. I couldn't even utter a single word because they didn't matter. Nothing mattered apart from Riley, and she was gone. I just stared straight ahead and blocked out their words, replaying images of Riley in my head.

The doctors and nurses fussed over me for a couple of hours, I heard someone mention something about me being on suicide watch or something, but that didn't matter either. How they expected me to be able to kill myself when I couldn't get out of bed was beyond me. Maybe they were worried about me starving myself to death or something stupid. I just lay there, dead inside, my thoughts only with her, only ever with her just like they always had been.

A couple of hours later and I heard a commotion in the hallway outside my room. I didn't bother to open my eyes, what was the point? There was no point; there was no point in anything.

The door to my room started to open but then abruptly closed again. "You can't go in there," the nurse said sternly. *Oh great, another fucking visitor. Why can't they all take the hint and just leave me alone?*

"I need to talk to him."

My breath caught in my throat. That was my angel's voice and it hurt to hear it. *Why is she here? Is she really going to make me ask her to leave again? Can I do it again? Can I say the words and rip my heart out for a second time?*

"He doesn't want to see you," the nurse said sternly.

"I don't care what the hell he wants. He's seeing me!" Riley protested as the door burst open.

I flicked my eyes to her and instantly felt sick with guilt. She looked so sad that it made my arms ache to hold her and make her feel better. Her face was all puffy and red from crying, and I felt like a piece of shit. I wanted to throw myself at her feet and beg her to forgive me. The selfish side of me was rejoicing that she was here, but the more rational, sensible part of me was wishing she would leave and never come back. That was what was best for her and I needed her to be happy, that was the only thing I needed out of life.

The nurse looked at me worriedly from the doorway, so I waved my hand dismissively, signalling that it was fine for her to come in. She frowned but walked out, letting the door swing closed behind her.

Riley stared at me, her whole posture angry and tight. "I know you don't want to see me, but I have something for you," she snapped as she strode over to me and emptied the contents of a shoebox into my lap. She threw the empty box against the wall angrily as she glared at me.

I glanced down at my lap, confused. *What the hell is all this junk?* There were movie stubs, a quarter, a couple of buttons, an old shirt of mine. A ring box, postcards, a little stuffed dog, a flattened helium balloon with happy birthday printed on the side. There were birthday cards, Christmas cards, photographs of us together and a couple of folded up pieces of paper, amongst a ton of other little knickknack things. I picked up the paper and opened them to see a couple of drawings that I'd done as a kid, letters that I'd written her asking her to come and play. There were little notes that I'd written for her recently telling her that I loved her.

I looked up at her confused. *Why has she kept all of this stuff? It's all just junk that should have been thrown in the trash years ago.* "What's all this?" I asked, my voice shaking slightly where I was trying not to cry again. I refused to cry in front of her, she hadn't seen me cry since I was nine years old and I wasn't going to let her see it now.

"That, Clay Preston, is everything important that has happened to me in my life up until this point. Every single thing in there involved you, and I kept all of this stuff because it means a lot to me. My whole life is in that box up until this point," she replied, her voice breaking slightly as she spoke. "And this," she continued, holding up her left hand and pointing to her wedding ring, "this is my whole life up until the day I die."

Oh God, she's killing me! How can I get her to understand that I'm doing what's best for her by setting her free? "Riley, I-" I started, but she cut me off.

"You look me right in the eye, and you tell me that you don't love me, and then I'll walk out of this door never to return again. But you'd better make it convincing, Clay, because I always know when you're lying to me," she challenged, looking at me fiercely.

I gulped. There was no way I could say those words to her, I'd never be able to say those words to her. "Riley, please," I begged.

"Do you love me, Clay?" she asked, looking me right in the eye. A tear slid down her cheek, and I longed to kiss it away.

I knew I couldn't lie to her, I could never force those words out of my mouth, and even if I could then she knew me too well, she'd see through it immediately.

"I will always love you, Riley Bear," I said honestly.

She swiped her face with the back of her hand, wiping her tears away. "Then don't you dare insult me again by telling me that I don't love you enough for this!" she hissed through her teeth. I'd hurt her by saying that I could tell.

"I want what's best for you. I'm thinking of you," I whispered.

She shook her head angrily. "You think being miserable and living without my other half is what's best for me? Where are you getting this crap from, Clay? You're always what's best for me, always!" she said, sniffing loudly.

"Maybe not anymore."

She stepped closer to the bed, looking right into my eyes making my heart speed up, and I was glad I wasn't hooked up to that monitor anymore so she didn't know. "Stop being such a damn hero! I love you; I want to be with you. If you don't want me then this is another matter, but that's not it is it?" she asked, looking at me hopefully. "You're my life, Clay. You always were, and you always will be."

I gulped. I could see the truth in her eyes. She always was stubborn; it was one of the things I loved the most about her. "You're my life too," I admitted quietly.

I felt like such a coward for doing this, I felt so selfish in keeping her, when she would be happier without me. I should be brave enough to let her live a full life with someone who could give her everything, but I wasn't. I couldn't say the words again; I wasn't strong enough to cut out my own heart for a second time.

She smiled and stroked the side of my face. I couldn't help but close my eyes and savour the feel of her skin against mine. An hour ago I never thought I would get to touch her again so I was making the most of it now. "No more stupid talk about me leaving you. No more talk about you not being the best thing that ever happened to me. No more talk about what's best for me," she said sternly.

"I don't want this for you, Riley," I whispered, looking at her pleadingly.

She cupped her hand around the side of my face and looked right into my eyes. "I want this for me. I want you. For better or worse, until death do us part, that's what we promised. And the last time I checked, you were still alive."

"Barely."

She smiled and traced her thumb over my bottom lip softly. "Barely is enough for me, Clay."

I sighed sadly. "But I want to be the one to take care of you. You deserve someone to look after you; it shouldn't be the other way around. That's a husband's job; it's always been my job to look after you."

She smiled and shook her head at me. "I love you more than anything, Clay. I'll always love you, and as a couple we're supposed to take care of each other," she whispered. Her eyes were burning into mine making hope bubble up in my chest; she genuinely didn't want to go, I could see it in her eyes. She really wanted me, wheelchair or not.

I couldn't speak. I knew I had the most amazing girl in the world. I loved her with every bone in my body; I just prayed that I was enough to make her happy, that the changed version of me was enough for her. I took her hand off my face and interlaced our fingers, my fingertips seeking out the wedding band that I had put there. I couldn't find the words to say to her, I had nothing; nothing at all was going through my brain. All I could focus on was her, her beautiful face and how much I loved and needed her.

"I need you to say those five words to me, Clay. I need to hear it, right now," she said, looking at me pleadingly.

Wow my girl is demanding, wasn't it usually three words that a girl wanted to hear? I smiled teasingly. "Five words? Oh wait, you mean, go buy me some candy?" I joked.

She laughed and shook her head, biting her lip as she climbed onto the bed next to me, crushing half of the stuff that she had thrown at me when she walked in.

I smiled even wider. "Jelly doughnuts rule, so there?" I offered.

She giggled and looked me right in the eye. "If you don't get it right this time, I'm never kissing you again," she warned, raising one eyebrow playfully.

I grinned and put one hand around the back of her head, pulling her closer to me, our lips almost touching. Her smell filled my lungs making the hair on the nape of my neck stand up with excitement. "I love you, Riley Bear," I whispered.

She seemed to breathe a sigh of relief. "I love you too, Clay."

I tightened my hand into the back of her hair and pulled her mouth to mine roughly, kissing her so hard that it probably hurt her lips, but I was almost desperate for reassurance. She didn't complain or pull away, quite the opposite in fact, she pressed her body against my side as she kissed me just as fiercely.

She pulled her mouth away from mine, pressing her forehead to mine as we both gasped for breath. I didn't let go of her hair, just held her close to me as if she was the only thing holding me to this earth. In reality she always did feel like that to me, like she was the very centre of my world, like she was the reason I was here.

"I love you, Riley Preston," I whispered.

She pulled back and shook her head. "Riley Tanner. If you want me to be Mrs Preston then you'll have to marry me again," she teased, smirking at me.

I laughed quietly; I would love to marry her again. There were parts of our wedding in Vegas that were a little hazy because of alcohol and I would love to have another shot at it, so I could memorise every detail of the day I became the luckiest man in the world.

"I'll think about it," I breathed, pulling her mouth back to mine again. She giggled and bit my bottom lip warningly. I pulled my head back a fraction. "Okay, okay, no biting. I guess I can marry you again," I whispered against her lips, grinning like an idiot.

"Good boy," she breathed as she crashed her lips to mine again, ending the conversation.

chapter thirty-one

She pulled away after a couple of minutes, just as I was getting really into it, but I guess I couldn't exactly lay there making out with my wife all afternoon. I felt sadness hit me again when I remembered that we weren't actually married, but that was easily fixed if she really was up for it again. I'd stall it for a little while though, just to make sure that was what she honestly wanted, I didn't want to tie her to me if she didn't want to.

She smiled and shifted on the bed, pushing her hand under her hip and pulling out a badge with 'C & R, Best Friends 4eva' written on it. I'd made that for her when I was seven years old when I got a badge maker as a gift for Christmas. She laughed and pinned it on the front of the hospital gown I was wearing.

"I was such a dork as a kid," I admitted, laughing at it. It was actually pretty embarrassing that she'd kept that all these years.

She smiled. "You're a dork as an adult too!" She stuck her tongue out at me and went to grab the shoe box that she'd tossed against the wall earlier. I scooped up all of the worthless crap that was spread over my lap. There were things I didn't even remember and some stuff I couldn't even understand why she'd kept it. I held up a pebble, raising at eyebrow at her in question.

She smiled and took it off me, putting it back into the box. "You brought that back from the beach for me when you went on vacation one year," she explained, shrugging.

I grinned; she was so freaking sweet to have kept all of this stuff. It made me feel incredibly special that Riley had kept all of these things, just because they reminded her of me. She was almost done putting it back into the box now.

I grabbed a wad of tissue from my lap. "Please tell me this isn't from when I had a cold or something." I looked at it disgusted.

She laughed, shaking her head. "Nope. Open it and see."

I frowned and opened the tissue, praying there wasn't something gross inside it. A little white thing was nestled in the middle; I frowned at it, having no idea what on earth it was. I prodded it with my fingertip. It was hard and smooth. "What is this, Riley Bear?"

She laughed and bit her lip. "That's your tooth."

I dropped it on the bed and pulled my hands away as quickly as I could, wiping them on my clothes. "Seriously? That's gross! Why did you keep my tooth? Where did you even get it from anyway?"

She smiled and took the tissue, scooping the little while lump back inside without touching it. "You gave it to me. Remember when I was saving up for that Malibu Barbie doll? I was whining that it was taking me forever to save my allowance money and that the stores would sell out," she explained. "Well you went home and pulled out your wobbly tooth, you gave it to me and told me to put it under my pillow and pretend it was mine, so that the tooth fairy would give me some money to put towards the doll."

I laughed. *Did I? I don't remember that, it sounds like something I'd do though.* "Wow, I was a good friend, huh?" I teased.

She smiled and put the box on the chair, climbing back onto the bed with me, wrapping her arms around me gently. "The best," she whispered, kissing me again.

We laid there for a long time, looking through all of the worthless crap that she called treasure, her telling me what some of the more random things were and what they meant. Doctors and nurses came and went; I was given painkillers which I was grateful for.

After about two hours of small talk, she turned and looked at me thoughtfully. I gulped. Was she going to take it back now? Was she going to tell me that she wasn't sure she could love me now that I couldn't walk?

"Baby, can I talk to you about something?" she whispered, looking decidedly uncomfortable.

I nodded, unable to speak through the lump that was rapidly forming in my throat.

"Okay so..." Her nose crinkled up like it did when she was thinking about something extremely hard. "I was thinking about your parents."

I felt my body relax because this wasn't about us, it was about my parents. "I don't want to talk about it, Riley Bear."

I was too angry at them to talk about them right now. They'd come here earlier, and I couldn't even bring myself to shout at them, to blame them for leaving the surgery and potentially ruining my chances of walking. I didn't want to see them, I didn't want to talk to them, I couldn't even be bothered to argue with them about it. Their decision had left me in this situation. Deep down I knew that I would have never known if the surgery would have worked if I'd had it hours earlier, but those precious few hours might have made all of the difference and that thought would haunt me forever.

She stroked her hand across my chest, playing with the badge. "Clay, I know that you're angry, and goodness knows I'm angry too... but they weren't stopping it to hurt you. Look, I don't want to fight their corner, I'm so angry at them that I actually can't believe I'm even talking to you about it. But, just think about it for a couple of days, don't do anything irrational, they love you."

I sighed and nodded. "Let's just leave it Riley, okay? I don't want to be thinking about them right now."

She smiled and immediately settled back down at my side again, she was being so careful of me, every move was slow and deliberate, as if she was afraid to shift the bed in case it hurt me or something. I smiled down at her, trying not to laugh at the pained, worried expression on her face.

"What?" she asked when she caught me staring.

I sighed. "You don't have to be so careful of me, Riley Bear. It's not like it's going to hurt me or anything, is it? You could drop something on my foot and I wouldn't even know unless you told me." I tried to make it sound like a joke, but even I could hear the sadness in my voice. I was trying to stay positive, I honestly was, but I had no idea how I was going to cope with not being able to walk again. Not being able to do little things for Riley, like carrying the groceries when we went to the store, pushing the shopping cart, things people took for granted and never even thought about until you couldn't do them anymore. Everything was going to change now; nothing would ever be the same again.

She frowned and looked down at my legs. "Clay, stop thinking the worst. Give it a little while, all right?" she pleaded.

I nodded and kissed her forehead, putting on a fake smile. "Okay. I'm pretty tired; want to sleep with me for a little while?" I asked, stifling a yawn. From what she'd told me I'd been in a coma for twenty-seven hours straight, then knocked out for six hours, then slept the whole night, I should have had enough sleep by now, but I could feel my eyelids getting heavy.

"Sure, baby." She kissed the side of my neck, her hand finding mine, holding tightly. I couldn't stay awake even if I wanted to.

• • •

I WOKE UP WITH Something heavy on my crotch. I groaned as the throbbing pain started to get worse in my back. My whole body was starting to ache; I guessed it was time for more pain meds. How long had I been asleep? I shifted my arm, tightening it around Riley, trying to get her closer to me. I could tell she was still asleep because of how deep her breathing was against the side of my neck, I knew this girl like the back of my hand.

She snuggled into me tighter; the heavy thing on my crotch moved and went further down, pressing on my thighs, making the pain in my back worse.

I groaned and was just about to wake her up to ask her to get the doctor, when I realised that I could actually feel a weight on my legs. I raised my head and looked down a little shocked. Riley's leg was on top of mine. I could actually feel the weight of her leg that she'd casually slung over me in her sleep. *I can feel it? Holy shit!*

Excitement burst in my chest. "Riley!"

She jerked awake quickly and jumped a mile, almost falling off the bed because I'd practically shouted in her ear. "What? What's wrong?" she cried, looking at me with wide eyes.

I looked at her with her eyes all big, lines of sleep on her face, her clothes all wrinkled, and I burst out laughing. She had never looked more beautiful. I had no idea how that worked though, because I had the same thought every time I woke up and saw her in the morning.

She looked at me confused, and then I suddenly remembered why I woke her up in the first place. I felt the smile stretch across my face as I grabbed her hand and pulled her closer to me again. "I can feel my legs a little," I told her, watching as the words sunk in.

Her mouth dropped open; her eyes looked down towards my feet. Suddenly she let out an excited little squeal and clamped her hand over her mouth as she started giggling. She jumped out of the bed, bouncing on the spot like a little girl who'd just been given a puppy.

"Holy crap, Clay! Really? Oh thank God! Really?" Her hands hovered near my thighs, as if she wanted to touch me but wasn't sure if she should.

I laughed and nodded. I could feel relieved tears building in my eyes. It was a start, but it was a good start, wasn't it? She squealed again and then burst into tears, pressing her face into my chest. I stroked the back of her head as I tried to move my legs. I couldn't move them properly, but I could move my toes a little. It was like when you'd been sitting in the same position for a long time, and your legs went numb, you knew they were there, and you could move them a little, but you just didn't have much control over them.

I kissed the top of her head. Maybe it was all about waiting after all, maybe the longer we waited the better it would get. Hopefully this wasn't just it, a little feeling in my legs. Hopefully as the swelling went down even more I'd get more movement back.

She sniffed loudly and pushed herself up, wiping her eyes, a beautiful smile stretched across her face. "I'll buzz for the doctors," she said, her voice all husky and thick through sleep and crying.

I grabbed her hand to stop her as I suddenly realised something else I could feel too. "Er, Riley Bear, just wait a minute, okay?" I requested. *Wow, talk about embarrassing!*

She sniffed again, wiping her face with the sleeve of her sweater. "Why, Baby?"

I laughed and pulled her a little closer to me again. "Because I woke up next to you, beautiful girl," I croaked, trying to hide my face in her hair.

She looked at me curiously, one eyebrow raised, her red eyes confused. "So?"

I laughed and nodded down towards my feet again. She followed my gaze and started to giggle uncontrollably. She climbed onto the bed next to me again, blushing and biting her lip.

"Hmm... I do tend to have that effect on you in the mornings," she breathed, her hand sliding down my chest, heading towards the tent I was making with the blankets. I laughed as she kissed my neck, making my body feel a little hot. I wanted her. Even through the pain in my back she was still managing to turn me on. *Stupid freaking hormones!* If I could, I would pull the covers up over our heads and make love to her until the sun came up, but I guess it was one step at a time. At least I knew that wouldn't be a problem now.

I caught her hand, moving it away just as she got close enough to my crotch. "Not helping with the calming down thing there, Riley Bear." I laughed, trying to think of anything other than her, so I could calm my body down.

She smiled against my neck. "Okay, baby, think of something un-sexy," she teased, rolling away from me, propping herself up on her elbow, watching me with a huge smile on her face.

After a few minutes of lying there with my eyes closed, thinking about football, I was finally okay so she could call the doctors in.

THE DOCTORS FUSSED over him for the longest time. I watched them avidly, they were prodding his legs and feet, I chewed on my lip when I watched Clay wiggle his toes. I felt like my insides were going to burst with happiness. It was so crazy how something as small as a tiny movement can make everything seem right in the world. Another MRI scan was arranged; they wanted to leave it another hour or two so that the swelling would go down even more.

Clay had a happy smile on his face the whole time. He was clinging to my hand tightly, as if he was afraid to let go. I had been on a rollercoaster ride, my day went from bad - when I woke up and he couldn't feel his legs, to unbearable for the couple of hours I was away from him. But in that moment, none of that mattered. All that mattered was the laugh that I heard come out of Clay's mouth when the doctor nodded and told him that everything looked great.

He left to set up the scans, and I pulled the chair over to the bed again, kissing the side of his beautiful face as I sat down. "I told you to stop worrying," I teased.

"Yeah, yeah. No I told you so comments are required," he said, smirking at me. It was nice to see Clay coming back to normal a little; it broke my heart to see him so upset and sad. Clay hardly ever got sad about anything; he was always the strong one, so the look on his face for the last few hours had been slowly killing me inside.

After having the scans the doctor had given us the news that everything looked just as it should do. There was still a lot of inflammation around the operation site which would fade over time. The doctor was extremely hopeful that Clay would be able to walk again, but he warned that it would be a lot of hard work for him.

Everything was working out perfectly; as the hours wore on he could raise his knee a couple of inches, even though it hurt his back doing it. Apparently that was normal though, he'd just had major surgery so pain was to be expected.

They wouldn't let me stay at the hospital with him that night because he wasn't in critical condition like the last couple of nights. I didn't want to go home to our apartment, it didn't feel right staying there without Clay, so I went back to my parents' house. My mom had gone and picked up a few days' worth of clothes for me. It took me a long time to say goodbye to Clay. I felt like I left a piece of me behind when I walked out of the hospital, knowing I wouldn't see him again for a few hours.

It felt weird walking into my parents' house; it didn't feel like home anymore. It was surprising how quickly I had gotten used to living with Clay, I had lived in this house all of my life, but yet it felt strange to slip between the sheets of my bed. I hugged myself tightly and cried, but not with sadness this time, with relief. It would be a lot of hard work, but Clay was always a hard worker, I knew he would put two hundred percent into it. Clay was always up for a challenge, and he never failed.

• • •

HE STAYED IN the hospital for a total of twelve days. The doctors were immensely pleased with him; he was out of bed and in a wheelchair. He could move his legs, but it was an enormous effort for him, I could see the sweat form on his forehead when he tried really hard. I could tell he was getting frustrated about it, but the doctors had explained it was like a baby learning how to walk for the first time. The will to walk was there, and the knowledge, but he just needed to teach his body how to do it again. The trouble with Clay was that he never liked to rely on people. Clay was a giver, not a receiver, so it was hard for him to let me, my parents, or our friends, fuss over him and do things for him.

Another thing that pissed him off: he missed the big football game. Our school had to play in the final of the state championship without their captain and had just managed to scrape a win. He was incredibly annoyed that he'd missed it, but the whole team, including the coach, had come to see him that night. They had all crammed in his room, shouting and dancing around in celebration. They were thrown out by an angry nurse within ten minutes, but Clay enjoyed it while it lasted. They left him the trophy, which took pride of place on his side table next to his bed.

After the twelve days, Clay was moved to a rehabilitation centre. Apparently he would stay there for about six weeks, where they would work with him extensively, training his muscles again. His brain needed to reconnect with the damaged nerves and learn the whole process of putting one foot in front of the other.

I was allowed to help him with his therapy. They taught me how to help him stretch his muscles, but mostly I was just moral support. I was currently standing at the end of the exercise room, watching as Clay adjusted himself ready to get up to try again to walk. His therapist said he needed to do little bursts and then rest. He'd only been here for a week, but so far he was up to seven steps at a time before he had to stop and rest.

"Hey, Riley Bear, I've got an idea," he said quietly, looking around sheepishly, probably to make sure no one could hear what he was saying.

"What's that, baby?"

He adjusted the footrests on his wheelchair and put his feet on the floor, positioning himself between the two rails so he could hold on if he needed to when walking.

"How about for every step I take, you take off one item of clothing back in my room?" he suggested, smirking at me as his eyes raked down my body slowly.

I laughed. Only Clay could think about sex while trying to do something so serious and important. I had the strong feeling that he'd been getting a little frustrated that we hadn't done anything more than kissing for the past three weeks. "An item of clothing, really?" I asked, raising one eyebrow. I looked down at myself and mentally counted what I was wearing, thankfully it was quite cold today so I had on jeans, a tank top, shirt and one of his hoodies over the top. Including underwear and four items for shoes and socks, I was wearing a total of ten things today. "Hmm, maybe you could get me to my underwear," I teased, pulling at the zip of the hoodie, looking at him through my eyelashes.

He smirked at me and shook his head slowly. "No way, Riley Bear, I'm getting you naked today. How many?" he asked.

"Ten."

He grinned, seeming fairly excited about the challenge. "Easy," he mused.

I stood at the end of the rails, giggling as a determined expression crossed his face, and damn that boy, he made the ten steps no problem. *Hmm... maybe this is a good way to motivate him; I'll wear more layers tomorrow!*

He laughed and looked at me cockily. "Awesome." He turned to his therapist who was oblivious to our little deal. "I think I've done enough for today, I'm gonna go back to my room," Clay told him.

I laughed and shook my head, "No way, baby, I promise I'll do that, but you still need to go swimming and stuff before you're done," I said sternly. I wasn't letting him off of his training schedule; he could wait a couple of hours to get me out of my clothes.

He pouted at me. "Fine, I guess I still get to look at you in a bathing suit so that's not too bad," he replied, rolling his eyes playfully.

I'd been swimming with him every day too, it was apparently one of the best things to do to build up his strength and control without actually putting weight on his back. It was fun too; we got to mess around in the water for a little while, well, until we got told off by the therapist for making out in the pool.

The police had been keeping us updated on the investigation for Blake. Apparently he was pleading guilty to all charges, so there would be no trial for it. He was kept in holding while he waited to be sentenced. A month after it all happened; the same cop from Blake's house came to the rehabilitation centre to tell us that Blake had been sentenced to six years in a mental institution for the numerous charges he'd pleaded guilty for. It hardly seemed like anything at all, and he'd be out sooner than that too for good behaviour.

While he was in there, he would undergo extensive therapy to help him. Apparently he was ill, they had prescribed him medication for his condition, but due to patient confidentiality the police weren't allowed to tell us exactly what was wrong with him. I was guessing it was some sort of Schizophrenia or Paranoia disorder. Those type of things fitted with the whole situation, the way he blamed Clay for his life going wrong, also for the stalking, the physical violence and the mood swings. I guess we'd never know for sure. As long as he was getting help then there was nothing else we could do about it, at least he was being punished for everything he did.

We didn't dwell on it; we had too much to worry about without thinking about Blake. Instead, we focused all of our energy on getting Clay better. It was working; it would be a long time before he was back to normal, but he'd get there, eventually.

chapter thirty-two

I almost skipped to the car. I was so excited I could barely stop my hands from shaking as I started the car. I probably should have let David come with me after all, like he'd offered, but I'd wanted it for it to be just me and Clay. Everything was set up at the house; all I needed to do was go to the rehabilitation centre.

I drove there, practically bouncing in my seat. When I pulled into the parking lot, I smiled and grabbed my cell phone, sending Clay a quick text to say I was here. He liked me to do that so he could come and meet me out the front or in the reception.

He'd been doing so well lately, it was still an effort for him, walking wasn't quite the unconscious action that it used to be, but it didn't cause him pain now, which was a monumental step forward. He still got tired quickly, which frustrated him. He hated that he needed help, he hated to ask anyone for anything. I saw on his face how much it pained him to have to ask me to sit down with him and take a break, when we were walking around the grounds or something.

I made a slow walk to the front door, giving him time to cover the short distance from his room to the entrance way so he could meet me. As I pushed the door open, I saw his blond head come around the corner at the end of the hallway. A beautiful smile stretched across his face that I couldn't help but mirror.

Today was a momentous day. Today Clay was coming home.

"Hey, beautiful girl!" he chirped as he got up to me and wrapped his arms tight around my waist.

"Hey, baby." I hugged him back, still being careful of him. It scared me, being close to him, just in case I hurt him or something. I sighed contentedly as his familiar smell filled my lungs. I hated to leave him at night-times, but I wasn't allowed to stay here with him at the centre. Tonight would be the first time in two months that I would get to sleep in a bed with the love of my life, and I couldn't wait to fall asleep in his arms.

He pulled back and cupped my face in his hands, his green eyes burning into mine; they showed a happiness that had been growing more and more each day. He'd been counting down the days until he could come home. It had felt like forever, but finally it was here.

"I had a dream about you last night," he whispered, kissing my lips gently.

I smiled against his mouth as I gripped the side of his shirt, wanting desperately to pull him closer to me, to crush his body against mine. We hadn't been together for a long time, not through lack of him wanting to though. He'd practically been begging for attention, but I just couldn't bring myself to take things further than a quick fumble with him. I was terrified of hurting him. What if it was too soon and it caused him more problems? That thought never left my mind and made me feel nauseous. It definitely wasn't that I didn't want his body, because Clay Preston was a serious hottie, he literally drove me crazy with desire, but I loved him too much to rush anything.

"Oh you dreamt about me? What were we doing?" I teased, raising one eyebrow at him.

He smirked at me, kissing me again lightly. "This," he whispered, pulling me closer to him. "And this," he purred, kissing my neck making my stomach get butterflies. "And this." His hands slipped down to my butt, squeezing gently.

I tried to control my body's urges and rein in my raging hormones, but it was hard. "Oh really? Right in the middle of the reception?" I asked breathlessly as his tongue trailed up the side of my neck.

He laughed and pulled back. "No, we were back in Vegas actually."

I smiled when he mentioned Vegas. *Jeez I wish I was back there with him right now.* It felt like we were different people back then, two teenagers without a care in the world, not like now.

"Maybe we could go there again one day. You could win some more money at cards," I teased, pulling away as he nibbled on my earlobe.

He grinned and took my hand, nodding. "Definitely."

I raked my eyes over him slowly, taking in every flawless inch of him. He looked incredibly handsome today in just a plain grey t-shirt and light blue jeans. His hair was getting a little long and he kept brushing it back off of his forehead. Without him saying anything, I already knew that one of the first things he would want to do when he got home was have a haircut, he always had hated his hair getting long.

"Shall we get started then?" I asked, nodding back towards where the training room was. He smiled and nodded, leading me through the hallway toward the changing room, so we could do his last training session before he was finally discharged.

• • •

AFTER TWO HOURS of swimming and him doing some weights and resistance training, he was finally signed out of the centre to be an outpatient. They'd given him a training routine that he was to continue with on his own. I smiled when I scanned it over; swimming was on there five days a week. That was definitely my favourite thing we did together, I also liked the massages I had to give him after to relax his muscles. I was just glad he couldn't see my face when I was doing that, I would imagine that I looked like some sort of desperate horny beast or something when I rubbed my hands over his body.

After we'd packed up his stuff, I sat on the bed watching as he checked all his cupboards, making sure he had everything. He liked to have independence. I got the distinct impression that he liked it when I let him do little things on his own, instead of fussing over him too much. He'd told me once that the way his mother fussed over him made him feel less of a man in some way, I didn't ever want to make him feel like that so I wanted him to do what he could.

Clay had finally started speaking to his parents again a couple of weeks ago. I think because he was getting better he had decided to try and get on with them, if things hadn't worked with the operation, I would bet that things would be very different. I was pretty sure that if he was in a wheelchair then he would always have in the back of his head of what could have been, so he wouldn't be able to see them again. Things were strained with them; everyone was a little uncomfortable because although he was talking to them, he hadn't forgiven them.

I personally hadn't forgiven them either, and I didn't think I ever would be able to. I had always liked Linda and Richard, but when I looked at them now, all I could see was them letting down their son and being selfish. The way that Linda had dismissed my relationship with her son had hurt me to the core, and I would never be able to forget it. So I put on a fake smile and pretended everything was fine with them. If I had to do that for Clay so he could have a relationship with his parents, then that was what I would do.

When he looked like he was finally done packing up, I went to get up off of his bed but he shook his head, putting his hand on my shoulder. "No way, Riley Bear. If this is the last time I'm in this room then I'm making the most of the bed before we go," he stated, smirking as he stepped closer to me, his face inches from mine.

My mouth started to water at the thought of his body, but I couldn't do that, not yet, not until he was totally okay. He kissed me, hard, moving closer to me so I had nowhere to go but onto my back on the bed. He grinned against my lips as he lowered himself down on top of me, kissing me deeply. The kiss was so good it made me feel like my toes were curling up.

I moaned into his mouth as his hand slid down my body, gripping my thigh, moving my leg so it wrapped around his waist. I instantly panicked that I would hurt him and pulled away quickly, just in case.

He groaned and put his face in the side of my neck. "Riley!" he whined.

I stroked the back of his head. "I'm sorry. I just... Clay, it's just..." I mumbled, searching for the right words.

He sighed and kissed my neck gently. "Yeah, I know."

I gripped my hand in the back of his hair. "I just want to wait a little while. Just in case. I'm sorry," I said honestly. I really was sorry, this whole situation was my fault and maybe I was just making it worse for him instead of helping him. Maybe I should just give him what he wanted; goodness knows I wanted it too.

"You don't have to be sorry, Riley Bear. I know what you're thinking about, and it's okay," he whispered, kissing me again. He rolled off of me and gripped his arms around my waist, pulling me on top of him instead. I instantly took my weight on my hands and knees so I didn't hurt him. He laughed and ran his hands down my back, gripping my hips and pulling me down onto him. "I know you're worried about hurting me, but I think this position would work exceptionally well. I could just lie back and let you do all the work," he teased, waggling his eyebrows at me.

I laughed uncomfortably. "Clay, just a little longer, please?" I begged. I needed him to stop doing this to me because every time he did my will to say no crumbled a little more.

He smiled his sexy little smile that I loved so much and nodded. "Know what I really dreamt about last night?" he asked, changing the subject.

I lowered myself down on him a little more, still being careful. "What, baby?"

He smiled and tucked my hair behind my ear, his fingertips brushing across my cheek lightly, making my skin tingle where he touched. "We were in Vegas like I said, but we'd just gotten married again."

I smiled. "We did?" My heart was starting to drum in my chest. I didn't think Clay wanted to marry me again, usually whenever I mentioned it he changed the subject immediately. I figured that maybe he felt a little rushed, maybe he was secretly glad we weren't married so young and that he'd escaped by having it not be legal.

He nodded and kissed the tip of my nose. "Yeah, and you looked beautiful in your white dress."

I gulped. Was he ready to talk about it now? "I didn't think you'd want to marry me again."

He frowned and looked at me like I was crazy. "Riley, are you kidding me? Of course I want to marry you again; you're the love of my life. I just wanted to wait a little while before we spoke about it, I just wanted to make sure that you were okay being tied to someone like me."

Someone like him? He thought he was doing this for me again? Did he really still not understand how much I loved him? "Why wouldn't I want to be tied to the most perfect boy in the world?" I asked, trailing little kisses along the line of his jaw, making his hands tighten on my hips.

He moaned breathlessly, pulling on my ass again so I pressed against his crotch harder. I could feel how excited he was, and I started to feel guilty again. He was a guy and he hadn't had any physical attention for eight weeks, this was probably killing him.

"I was wondering, Riley Bear..." He trailed off as I bit his chin lightly.

"Wondering what?" I whispered, licking the rim of his ear.

"Riley, I can't concentrate while you're doing that!" he moaned. I laughed and pulled away from him slightly, looking him in the eyes, nodding for him to continue. He took a deep breath, looking a little nervous as he took my left hand, rolling my engagement ring around my finger. I didn't wear my wedding ring anymore; I'd taken it off and had it hanging on my necklace instead, because technically we weren't married. Clay refused to take his off though.

"Riley, I know I already asked you once before and you said yes, but things have changed a little since then," he started. I swallowed loudly. *Is he going to say what I think he's going to say?* "But I love you more than anything in the world. I will always love you, and I wondered if you would do me the honour of marrying me... again."

I couldn't breathe; I felt the smile stretch across my face as a hundred butterflies seemed to take flight in my stomach. Clay Preston wanted to marry me again, and I couldn't be happier about that fact. He was just looking at me worriedly so suddenly I realised I hadn't actually answered his question.

I bent my head and kissed him softly, relishing in the feel of his lips against mine. Kissing Clay just seemed to make everything right in the world. With his lips against mine, I felt like the luckiest and most special girl in the world because the most amazing boy loved me and wanted me. He kissed me back immediately, tangling his fingers in the back of my hair, pulling me impossibly close to him.

By the time I pulled away, we were both a little breathless. I looked him right in the eyes and smiled. "Of course I'll marry you again, Clay," I whispered. He clearly had no idea how much I loved him, I would do anything for him and yet he still worried that I would change my mind. Maybe he'd gone crazy or something.

He laughed, grinning as ran his hand down my back. "Thank you, Riley

Bear. I'm gonna be an excellent husband, you won't regret it."

I brushed my nose against his lightly. "I know what kind of a husband you'll be, baby." He would be the best husband in the world; I knew that from personal experience.

~ Clay ~

I COULDN'T BE HAPPIER. I had the girl of my dreams sitting on top of me, and she'd just agreed to marry me again. Nothing could make this moment better. I trailed my hand down her back until I got to the waistband of her jeans. Scratch that, we could be naked, that would make this moment better.

"Are you ready to go, baby?" she asked, stroking my face softly.

I nodded; I couldn't wait to get out of this place. I'd been here for six weeks, and although it was a nice place, I just needed to get out, to be with my girl in familiar surroundings, start to move on from this, and look to the future.

She smiled and pushed herself off me, I resisted the urge to pull her back down on top of me again. I had missed her like crazy last night, the same as I had done every night since she first left when I was in the hospital. Riley felt like home to me, and I couldn't get enough of her time or attention. She held down a hand to me, and I took it, letting her help me off of the bed and onto my feet. I hated that I needed help for things, but I guess there was nothing I could do about it. I just needed to accept that, until everything was back to normal, then there would be little things that would have to change. My body was getting stronger every day, if I carried on with the training the way I had been doing, then in a few months everything would be perfect again.

She went to grab my suitcase so I took her hand, kissing the engagement ring that she still wore, before taking the handle of the case. It was a pull along so I wouldn't have to lift it anyway, she was just being over cautious as usual.

I said my goodbyes to all of the staff on my way out, ignoring the one nurse that I tried to stay away from because she was an obsessive flirt. She really was terrible, she wasn't too bad in front of Riley, but in the evenings she bordered on sexual harassment.

I couldn't keep the grin off of my face as I walked out of the front door for the last time, heading over to Riley's car. She was obsessively tapping away on her phone, she looked so happy that it made my heart drum in my chest.

Riley drove us back to her parents' house. We were going to be staying there for a while so I could recover a little more. Our apartment was on the second floor, so Sandra and David had offered to let us stay at their house for a month or so, so I wouldn't have to trudge up and down stairs to get home each time. Apparently they'd converted one of the downstairs rooms into a bedroom for us.

As we pulled up, I glanced over to my parents' house next door. I didn't really want anything to do with them anymore, but Riley being Riley, had convinced me to give them a second chance. I knew they didn't do it on purpose, but I just didn't understand how they could not know that the operation was something I would have wanted to happen. Riley wouldn't tell me exactly what happened while I was in a coma, but the general gist was that my mom had told the doctors that she was seventeen and that her age made our marriage illegal. I had a feeling there was more to it than that, I think that Riley was more upset with them than she let on, but if she didn't want to tell me then there was nothing I could do about it.

I got out of the car and held Riley's hand tightly. I couldn't wait for just some me and her time. I knew she was going to make me wait to get my hands on her, but at least I got to hold her tonight while I slept which I was excited about. I could wait for sex; I could wait forever if she wanted to. I was actually thinking of suggesting we wait until after we were married again, so that I could give her the proper wedding night that we missed out on last time because she'd fallen asleep in the bar.

As we walked up to the front door, she looked strangely excited. She pushed open the door and nodded for me to go in first. As I walked in, the room exploded into cheers and clapping. I jumped a mile until I looked around and spotted all of our friends standing around wearing pointy coloured party hats. Balloons were pinned on the walls and numerous homemade banners hung there saying welcome home. I grinned as I understood why Riley had looked so excited. She'd arranged a welcome home party for me.

I laughed and pulled her closer to my body, kissing the top of her head and she hugged me, grinning happily. *Jeez, I have the most perfect girl in the world!*

Tom and Ben came bounding over and pulled me into a hug. "Finally you're out!" Tom chirped, grinning like an idiot.

I looked around and saw practically the whole football team standing there, eating, drinking, and laughing. I felt a little overwhelmed that all of these people would turn out for me. I really had some great friends.

"Yep, finally." I hugged them both back, still a little shocked that they were all here, I wasn't expecting this at all. Tom pulled me away towards the food, Riley winked at me and mouthed that she loved me as she blew me a kiss. I laughed and followed him over to the table of junk food that had been laid out for us, all of my favourite foods where there, she'd gone to so much effort, and I was a seriously lucky guy to have her.

My parents were here as well, they literally only said hi and welcome home before they excused themselves back to their house. I had the distinct impression that they knew not to push it too far, they could probably sense that I wasn't ready for much yet, and I was grateful that they were giving me some time to work out everything on my own terms.

David and Sandra where there too. I headed over to them as soon as I broke free of Tom and Ben's grasp. I hugged Sandra and held out a hand to David, but he pulled me into a hug instead. I'd been getting on remarkably well with them in the last few weeks; they really were great people and had come to visit me every other day at the centre. In fact, everyone had been great; my friends came to visit every weekend too just for moral support. In some ways, I hadn't realised how lucky I was until this all happened.

"David, do you think I could have a word with you in private?" I asked. There was something I needed to do, and I wanted to get it out of the way.

"Sure. Want to go out on the porch or something?" he suggested, nodding to the side door.

"Yeah, great." I gulped nervously. My hands were starting to sweat. I followed him out of the house, promising my friends that I'd be right back as they questioned where I was going. When we got outside I headed straight over to the porch swing, needing to sit down for a few minutes.

David sat down next to me, looking at me curiously. "Is something wrong, Clay?"

I shook my head and wiped my hand over my face trying to calm my nerves. "No, I just need to ask you something, and I'm a little nervous about it," I admitted.

He laughed and patted my knee. "You can ask me anything. What's up?"

I took a deep breath. "Okay, so you know I love Riley, right?" I started. He nodded, frowning, obviously confused as to where I was going with this conversation. "Well, I know we're young, but I really wanted to ask you for your permission to marry your daughter. I know I should have asked you before, traditionally I should have asked you a long time ago, but it's better late than never, right?" I winced, feeling guilty that we'd run off to get married. Riley had told me that David felt a little cheated last time, and that was the reason he was so angry that we were married.

He laughed, seeming a little relieved. "You had me scared for a minute there!" He sat back against the swing and ran a hand through his hair. "Clay, I know you and Riley are meant for each other, and I couldn't wish for a better guy for her, I honestly couldn't. This whole thing has just shown me how short and fleeting life can be. When you find someone you love, you should hold on to that as tightly as you can, because you never know what's just around the corner." He blew out a breath and raked his hand through his hair. "The only hope I ever had for her was that she be happy in her life, and you make her happy." He patted my leg again affectionately.

I grinned. "So, that's a 'yes, Clay, you can marry my daughter'?" I asked, then as an afterthought I added, "Again."

He nodded. "Yeah, Clay, I'd be honoured to call you my son in law... again."

I smiled and held a hand out to him, relief washing over my body. He gripped my hand tightly, a broad smile stretched across his face. "Thanks, David. We won't be running off this time. I want us to get married here, in a church this time. I'm sure Riley would love to have you give her away," I said.

He laughed. "I guess I'd better break out the wedding fund I've been paying into since I married Sandra, huh?"

I smiled. He'd been paying into a wedding fund for Riley? I wasn't too surprised though, to be honest David doted on his daughter and I'd never seen a more devoted dad than him, even though she wasn't even technically his daughter.

"I guess you'd better," I laughed. I noticed that he hadn't let go of my hand which was a little strange.

His face tuned serious. "Clay, I love you like a son I really do. I know you love my daughter, which is the only reason I would consent to you two getting married so young." His eyes bored into mine, and I shifted a little uncomfortably on the swing under his intense stare. "But if you hurt my daughter, I swear I'll kill you myself, understand?" he asked sternly.

I wanted to laugh, but because he was being so serious I kept my face straight as I nodded. "Absolutely. I'll never hurt her, I promise," I vowed.

David nodded in approval and finally let go of my hand, his face softening again as he smiled so I knew the threat was over. He was just looking out for his daughter, and I couldn't help but admire the man, maybe he loved Riley as much as I did, I quickly dismissed the thought, no one loved anyone as much as I loved Riley, it just wasn't possible.

"Thanks for letting us stay here," I said, leaning back against the swing, smiling gratefully.

"It's nice having you here again. You stay as long as you need to, okay?" He patted my knee again.

I was about to answer when the screen door opened and the love of my life walked out, looking at us curiously. I smiled and she headed over to us, sitting in the space between me and her dad. "Everything okay?" she asked, looking between the two of us worriedly.

I nodded and slipped my arm around her shoulders. "Everything's perfect, Riley Bear."

David stood up, kissing the top of her head. He smiled at me happily. "Don't stay out here too long you two. There's a party going on in there. People came here to see you, Clay," he instructed as he walked into the house.

Riley pulled her knees up, curling into me as I tightened my arms around her. I sighed happily as we just sat on the swing for a little while, neither of us talking. I just held my girl tightly in my arms. Everything was just as it should be.

chapter thirty-three

Everything was set up, there was nothing else I needed to do or worry about. All I needed to do was relax, enjoy and memorise every single second of today.

We'd been planning this for the last two months, and finally it was here. Things were back to normal now, my back and legs were in perfect working order, and we were back living in our own place. I had graduated high school and was due to start my dream job in three weeks' time. Riley had her senior year starting in a month. It would be weird her going off to school and me going to work, I was used to seeing her all day every day, so that was going to be a big step. I had a feeling it would just make us appreciate each other more when we did finally come back together though.

Tom was standing next to me, cracking little remarks about me still having time to call it off and run away. I knew he was joking though, he knew how much I loved Riley so that wasn't something that would be happening.

I fiddled with my cravat, making sure I looked all right. I wanted everything to be perfect today, Riley deserved a perfect day. She'd been a rock for me since everything happened, so strong and supportive that she took my breath away.

I flicked my eyes around the room. People were sitting on the benches, chatting and smiling, all dressed up to the nines. My family and Riley's, all sitting on the wooden benches, eagerly awaiting the show.

Sandra was sitting at the front, tissue in her hand, dabbing her eyes already, with a little happy smile on her face. I caught her eye and she grinned at me, sniffing and looking at me affectionately. I guess she always knew this day would come, she always told us that we would get married one day, and here we were.

I couldn't wait for this ceremony to be over. Not that I wanted to wish it away or anything, but I just couldn't wait for her to be Mrs Preston again. It's surprising how quickly you got used to everything and when I found out that she wasn't technically my wife, that was a little soul destroying. I needed to get my ring back on her finger, and fast!

Also, once the wedding and the party after was done with, I'd get to take my girl to a posh little hotel room with the big four poster bed that I'd booked, and we'd finally consummate our marriage properly. Then after that we would have two weeks of heaven on a beach, alone. I couldn't wait for that.

I heard a rustling from behind me so I glanced back to see the Priest standing there, his book in his hand ready. He gave me a small smile, and I felt my heart speed up. *Does that smile that mean that she's here?* I took a calming breath and glanced at Tom; he grinned and slapped me on the shoulder. It only seemed right that he would be my best man for the second time, not only was he my best male friend, but tradition said he needed to hook up with the bridesmaid, and I was pretty sure that Rachel would kick my ass if I chose someone else.

They had been dating exclusively for the last four months. They had hooked up a lot before that, but Rachel had told Riley that she decided to go for it and give him a chance after I had my accident. She said that she realised that life was too short to be worrying about getting hurt and that she needed to take a chance before someone else nabbed him; apparently those were her exact words.

The music started, signalling that they were here. I laughed quietly under my breath; my hands were sweating, my feet itching to run to the front door so I could see her quicker. The waiting felt like agony. I hadn't seen her since last night because she wanted to stick to tradition and so had kicked me out of our apartment for good luck. She had the girls stay over instead. I couldn't help but call her last night though; just to make sure she hadn't changed her mind and was going to stand me up. We'd ended up talking for over an hour about random nothingness before she fell asleep whilst talking to me, I could hear her heavy breathing through the phone.

I heard Tom make a low groan beside me so I flicked my eyes to his face. He'd turned around and was watching the other direction, a lustful expression on his face, a small smile tugging at the corners of his mouth. I turned back to see what he was looking at and realised it wasn't a what, it was a who. Rachel was walking down the aisle in an off-white dress with a yellow ribbon tied around her waist. Her hair was pulled up in an elegant twist; she looked beautiful, even I could see that. She smiled at Tom, blushing slightly as she walked up the aisle.

When she got to the end, she stood on the other side of the aisle, before turning back to look at the door expectantly. *Oh God, this is it!*

When I saw her step round the corner my breath caught in my throat. She looked beautiful as I knew she would, but I never could have imagined just how utterly breathtaking she would look. The ivory, off the shoulder silk dress clung to the top half of her body before flowing out at her hips. Layers and layers of silk fell to the floor and trailed behind her a little way. It moulded to her in all of the right places, showing off everything she had to offer, but at the same time concealing everything so only I knew what was underneath.

She looked like something that had walked straight out of one of the bridal magazines she'd been fussing over for the last two months. The veil covered her face but was still thin enough that I could see her every feature. Her hair had been pulled up at the back, with loose curls escaping around the front. She was carrying a bouquet of yellow tulips, her favourites. She looked stunning, and I really was the luckiest guy in the world.

David smiled down at her proudly, his arm looped through hers as they started walking towards me. I couldn't take my eyes off her. My mouth was dry, my hands sweating even more than they were earlier, and I could barely stop myself from walking down the aisle and meeting her halfway just so I could be closer to her.

David looked up at me and smiled happily, and I couldn't help but grin back at him like the cat that got the cream. I could see Riley chewing on her lip as she walked towards me, a little blush on her cheeks as people all "Ahh'd" as she walked past them. It seemed to take forever for them to get to me. When they finally stopped at my side, I was attacked by her familiar scent. I resisted the urge to moan in appreciation. She looked so incredible that I couldn't help but rake my eyes over every inch of her. Her dad lifted her veil, folding it over the back of her hair and Rachel stepped forward, taking her flowers.

Riley looked back at me, and I felt the proud smile stretch across my face that this girl was mine. "Hi," I mouthed to her.

She smiled her beautiful smile. "Hi," she mouthed back.

The Priest cleared his throat quietly so I looked away from the love of my life as he started to give his little "We are gathered here today" speech. Finally, he was done talking and looked at David, I saw that David's eyes were all glazed over with tears as he smiled down at his daughter and put her left hand in mine. I gave him a small reassuring nod as his eyes met mine in a silent exchange; I knew exactly what he wanted to say, he was begging me with his eyes to look after her. He didn't need to say anything; I would always look after Riley, always.

Riley kissed her dad's cheek just before he stepped back and wrapped his arm around Sandra, who was still crying silent tears with a happy grin on her face. I squeezed Riley's hand gently, and she sighed contentedly as we both turned back to the front to make our promises to each other.

I made sure I memorised every single second of the wedding, every word, every gesture she made, every breath she took. I'd missed most of this last time in Vegas because we were drunk, I wanted to be able to picture this moment with crystal clarity.

I slipped the ring on her finger for the second time. This time it was unquestionably legal; her parents had consented so there was nothing to stand in our way this time.

"I now pronounce you husband and wife. You may now kiss your bride," the Priest said, smiling and nodding at me.

About time!

I smiled and leant in closer to her, her blue eyes met mine, and I let out a sigh of relief that we were married. She was Mrs Preston again; all was right in the world.

As my lips touched hers, she made a small whimper noise and I stepped closer to her, kissing her more forcefully. Her hand gripped the side of my grey suit jacket as she kissed me back just as passionately. I pulled out of the kiss and put my forehead to hers. She didn't open her eyes straight away, her hand tightened on my jacket, pulling me closer to her as a smile pulled at the edges of her lips.

"I love you, Riley Bear," I whispered.

Her eyes finally fluttered open, and her gaze met mine; her eyes held so much passion and love that it almost shocked me to the core. I still couldn't wrap my head around the fact that this extraordinary girl wanted me; I genuinely didn't know how I got so lucky.

"I love you too," she murmured.

I grinned proudly and pulled away, taking her hand in mine as I turned back to look at everyone that had come here today to support us and watch us commit to each other. My parents sat just behind me, both smiling at us, I smiled back and flicked my eyes around the rest of the church. All of our friends were here, family I hadn't seen for years, even a couple of the teachers turned up today too.

I smiled down at Riley again. "Are we ready then, Mrs Preston?" I asked, motioning my head towards the room at the back of the church where we were supposed to go to sign the register for our marriage. She smiled and nodded so I proudly led my wife back there, followed by Tom and Rachel, and Riley's parents who were all acting as witnesses and would need to sign the marriage certificate too.

David slapped me on the shoulder proudly, giving me a small nod. "Welcome to the family, Son," he said, holding out a hand to me. I shook his hand and laughed. I had been part of their family for years, but those words were nice to hear.

When we were all signed and legal, we made our way back through the now empty church. I held Riley's hand tightly, watching every move she made in her beautiful dress. When we stepped out of the church doors, confetti and rice were thrown at us from all angles; some of it even went in my mouth. I couldn't help but laugh as Riley giggled like crazy next to me. I kissed her again as it all fell down around us. I could hear the click of the cameras everywhere. I pulled back and looked at Riley, she had the biggest smile across her face, confetti was all in her hair, little coloured bits of paper over her shoulders and even a piece of it stuck to the side of her cheek. She had never looked more beautiful to me.

My whole life had been building up to this point. Standing here in a rain of coloured paper, I felt like I had truly come home. This was the happiest moment of my life, and I was suddenly glad that the last marriage wasn't legal. Not many people can say they get to marry the girl of their dreams twice.

I took her hand and led her to the car that was waiting at the bottom of the steps for us and would take us to the after party. Just a few more hours and then I would finally get my hands on my wife again, I personally couldn't wait.

After the food and the speeches, the music started. I recognised the song immediately. It was the song that was everything that Riley was to me. James Morrison, 'You Make It Real'. I took her hand and smiled. "Want to dance?" I asked, nodding towards the dance floor.

She nodded eagerly and stood, allowing me to lead her over to the empty dance floor. I felt so proud to be leading this girl out to dance, presenting her as my wife for the first time. I really was the luckiest guy in the world to be married to my best friend, not many people could say that.

I pulled her into my arms, and we swayed to the beat. I felt myself being drawn into her eyes; she had the most beautiful big blue eyes that I had ever seen. I could almost drown in them they were so inviting. I traced my hand up her back slowly, loving the feel of the silky material under my fingertips. She looked incredible, and I would remember the way she looked right now for the rest of my life.

"I love you, Clay," she whispered, pressing herself to me tighter.

I smiled and brushed my nose against hers, letting her perfume fill my lungs, making my whole body tense up with excitement. "I love you more, Mrs Preston," I mumbled through the fog of desire that was clouding my brain.

We'd agreed on the 'no sex before marriage' thing that I suggested, I think she was happy I suggested it to be honest because she was terrified about hurting me. The trouble was though that as soon as I'd suggested it, I'd wanted to take it back. It had been way too long since I had my way with her. Riley was an incredibly beautiful girl, she literally drove me wild with desire for her, waking up next to her every day for the last two months had been like torture. Not that we hadn't been fooling around, I couldn't completely cut her out cold turkey because that would kill me, but I hadn't made love to my girl for over four months now. I couldn't wait for tonight, my mouth was watering at the thought of it alone.

I brought my mouth down to touch hers softly. As soon as my lips touched hers she made a sexy little moan in the back of her throat and kissed me back fiercely. I smiled against her lips. *Hmm, maybe she's just as eager as me for this party to be over.* I could hear the click of cameras around us, people making Ooh's and Ah's but all I could focus on was the taste and feel of my wife's mouth on mine. I pulled her impossibly closer to me, almost losing myself in the kiss.

The rest of the night passed quickly, there didn't seem to be enough time to talk to people, and dance with all of the people I was traditionally supposed to. I watched as Riley danced with her dad, they were having a little heart to heart on the dance floor, I could tell by the way she gripped his shoulder and had happy tears in her eyes. She adored her dad and most of today wouldn't have been possible without him. When he said he'd break out the wedding fund, he really did, everything we wanted was bought and paid for immediately. He really was a great guy, and I was lucky to be able to call him my father-in-law.

When the party was finally over, and we had said goodbye to everyone, I took her hand and led her slowly up the stairs of the hotel. We'd conveniently booked the honeymoon suite of the hotel that we had the party in, so we wouldn't have to travel anywhere after. As we walked up the stairs, I could barely breathe through my excitement. Was it normal to be this excited to see a girl naked? Maybe I was a little strange, but it was Riley that made me this way. The girl literally drove me crazy, she always had done.

As we got to the hotel room door, I suddenly got nervous. What if the accident was going to stop me from doing what I wanted to do tonight? I knew I would have no 'elevation' issues, because that had been fairly obvious in the last four months. One of her smiles and I was giving her a soldiers salute, but what if I couldn't actually 'perform'. Even if I could perform, then I was sure to be out of practice, maybe it would suck for her, and I'd let her down.

I could feel my hands shaking as I fumbled with the key, trying to get it in the lock. I gulped. *Oh man, this is bad; I'm going to let her down on the most important night of my life.* Why had I suggested no sex before marriage? I wanted to punch myself for being so freaking stupid and not thinking everything through. *Idiot, idiot, idiot!*

The lock clicked and I pushed the door open. She smiled her sexy little smile, and I noticed that she looked a little nervous too, but her fears were probably more along the lines of her hurting me, I knew she was worried about that because we'd spoken about it numerous times before.

She went to step into the room so I grabbed her hand to stop her. She frowned, looking at me with the most adorable little confused expression on her face, and I couldn't help but kiss her. I bent slightly and slipped one arm around the back of her legs as I kissed her. She realised what I was doing and pulled out of the kiss quickly.

"No, Clay! For goodness sake, are you crazy!" she cried, pushing me away.

I smiled reassuringly. "It's fine, Riley Bear, I promise," I whispered, kissing her again. I gave her a couple of seconds to get into the kiss before I swept her into my arms, doing it quickly, before she had a chance to protest. It didn't hurt, I'd spoken to the doctors about it and apparently I was fine doing this, but I guess that didn't stop her worrying about me, nothing would probably ever stop this girl from worrying about me. That thought was extremely comforting.

She squealed against my lips but didn't struggle, probably in case she hurt me or anything. I smiled and pulled back, carrying her over the threshold of our hotel room. We'd already been married once, but I wanted to do everything that I could to make this right and traditional this time.

"Clay, please don't hurt yourself," she begged, wrapping her arms around my neck as I kicked the door shut behind me.

I kissed her again and carried her over to the bed, so eager to get her out of her dress that I could barely think about anything else. She giggled as we plopped down onto the bed. I didn't break the kiss as she pushed my suit jacket off of my shoulders, letting it fall off onto the floor. She nibbled on my bottom lip wanting me to deepen the kiss, so I slipped my tongue into her mouth. The minute her taste touched my tongue I was so hard it was almost painful against the material of my pants.

I needed her so much. All I wanted to do was grip fistfuls of her dress and rip the damn thing off, but I knew I couldn't do that. I rolled onto my back, pulling her on top of me and started working on the long row of little buttons that she had going down the length of her back. Trailing my fingers over the skin there lightly, making her shiver and moan into my mouth.

She was wriggling on top of me, and I was so excited that I was actually scared I was going to finish before she even touched me or got my clothes off. I gulped and tried to calm down before I embarrassed myself and ruined it for her, I tried taking deep breaths as she kissed down my neck. She was pressed against my crotch; the pressure of it was driving me mad.

Finally, I finished with the last button on her dress. Just as I was about to slip the material off of her shoulders, she sat up and shook her head. "I'll be right back, okay?" she asked, tipping her head to one side, looking stunningly beautiful.

I gulped, unsure if I would be able to speak. "Yeah," I croaked, my voice not even sounding like mine because of how hot she'd made me.

She smiled nervously and climbed off of the bed, grabbing her little overnight bag that had been brought here for us by Tom this morning. Holding her dress closed against her body, she disappeared into the bathroom. I sat up on the edge of the bed, looking down at my crotch. "Calm down, Clay, for goodness sake," I muttered to myself, shaking my head at my body's reaction to her presence.

I forced myself to stand up and pulled off the cravat and waistcoat I was wearing, throwing them over the back of the chair. I untucked my shirt and unfastened a couple of buttons, trying to think of anything other than Riley so I could calm down a bit. I headed over to the light switch; thankfully it was a dimmer switch so I turned the lights down low and shut the drapes. I mentally slapped myself for not doing the whole candles and rose petals thing again for her.

I busied myself in the room, fiddling with the bed sheets, moving our luggage over to the side of the room. She'd been in there forever, what was taking her so long? Was she having second thoughts or something and she wouldn't want me to make love to her tonight? Maybe she was just as nervous as I was...

I spotted a bottle of champagne on the side and two glasses. There was a note there with it. I picked it up and read it; apparently it was from David and Sandra so we could toast our marriage. I smiled, that was incredibly thoughtful of them to do that.

I picked up the bottle and unwrapped the foil. Just as I pulled off the wire cage that covered the cork, I heard the bathroom door open behind me. I turned to look at her. At the exact same time that my mouth dropped open, the cork popped out of the bottle, hitting the ceiling, but I couldn't even drag my eyes away from her to see if it was spilling everywhere.

She had changed out of her dress, letting her hair down in loose waves around her shoulders. She was wearing a strapless white corset that made her breasts look twice their normal size, and showed a strip of her toned stomach. She had on white matching panties and white stockings that had a lace strip at the top, held up with sexy little suspenders attached to the bottom of the corset. She looked incredible. She leant against the doorframe, cocking her head to the side, doing that little looking through her eyelashes thing that I loved.

She looked like an angel. One of those sexed up, fallen from heaven Angels, that you would cut off your right arm to be with.

I gulped and tried to think of something intelligent to say, but nothing came out. The only thing I could think was 'fuck yeah' but I couldn't exactly say that, so I said nothing.

She smirked at me, a knowing look in her eyes. It was then that I realised I was just standing there with my mouth and eyes open wide, staring at her like a freaking moron. I was actually surprised I wasn't drooling, but then again I hadn't wiped my mouth, so maybe I was and I just didn't realise.

"I take it that you like my wedding night underwear?" she teased, pushing away from the doorframe, biting her lip as she did a little twirl on her tiptoes. The back view was just as incredible as the front; her ass looked edible in the little white panties. I couldn't move. My feet felt like they were ton weights or something, I wanted to go to her and wrap my arms around her, but I couldn't move a single inch.

I nodded and gulped again, watching as she sauntered over to me, her hips swaying sexily. She stopped just in front of me, her eyes not leaving mine as she took the champagne bottle out of my hands and raised it to me in a toast. She brought the bottle to her lips, leaving the rim of the bottle pressed against her bottom lip longer than necessary as she looked at me suggestively, before closing her lips around it and taking a drink. Again, the only thing I could think was 'fuck yeah', so I said nothing.

She smiled and put the bottle on the side, gripping her hand around the back of my head, pulling my mouth to hers again. The scent of her hair and perfume was all around me, everything else disappeared in the room until all I could see, smell and feel was her. When her tongue touched mine, I could still taste the bubbles of champagne on her tongue. The taste of her mingled with the champagne, was exquisite, the most incredible thing I had ever tasted in my life.

She pulled away just as I was getting a little breathless. She stepped back, so I gripped my hands on her hips, my thumbs stroking the exposed strip of skin across her stomach where the corset didn't meet the panties. I couldn't let her move away from me, not when she looked like that.

She shook her head and pushed my hands off of her, stepping back again and leaning against the post of the four poster bed, crossing one foot over the other. She looked so sexy that my body was screaming at me to just take her. *So much for being calm and taking our time!*

"Take your clothes off, Clay," she purred seductively.

I groaned and started on the buttons of my shirt with shaky fingers. *Why is it when you are in a rush everything takes longer? Or did it just feel that way because I was so eager to be naked?* She watched me, chewing on her bottom lip, her hands behind her back, leaning on the post casually.

When I was down to my boxers I looked back to her, but she shook her head. "Everything," she ordered, nodding at them. I grinned. *Masterful Riley's back, I've missed her!*

I pushed them off, standing there completely naked as she raked her eyes down my body, with a small satisfied smile. I couldn't help but laugh at the lustful expression on her face. "You really are a pervert, Riley Bear," I teased.

She smiled and shrugged unashamedly. "Yeah, so what are you gonna do about it?" she answered, giggling.

Finally I could move my feet. I closed the distance between us as quickly as I could, wrapping my arms around her as I crashed my lips to hers. She moaned in the back of her throat as she slipped her arms around my neck, crushing her body against mine. The feel of her lingerie rubbing against my chest made me even harder, and I couldn't decide if I wanted to take it off of her, or leave it on.

I moved us over to the bed and settled myself on top of her, running my hands down her body, memorising every delicious inch of her. The feel of her under me again was incredible. I'd missed this so much. I knew I wasn't going to last long for the first time because of how eager I was, I was already halfway there, yet we hadn't even done anything. So I knew I needed to do a lot of work to make her enjoy it, before I allowed myself to indulge.

Her hand ran down my back, her fingers trailing over the scar at the base of my spine making me grind into her slightly. She moaned, and I suddenly made up my mind, the corset and stockings could stay, but the panties had to go. I slid my hands down her body, unclasping the suspenders, pulling her panties off slowly, trailing my fingertips down her thighs, making her raise her hips up in excitement.

I could barely breathe as I kissed down her neck, nipping on the skin lightly. When I got to the base of her neck I sucked hard and gave her the first hickey of our marriage, the first of many. I laughed and kissed further down, letting my lips and tongue explore every inch of my wife as she moaned and wriggled underneath me, moaning my name.

Once I'd made her climax, I kissed my way back up to her mouth, looking at her flushed face. She was more beautiful than anything I had ever seen in my life, the way she panted and looked at me, her blue eyes dancing with excitement, made the hair on the back of my neck stand up.

She smiled as she ran her hand down between our bodies, her nails scratching gently as she did so. I grunted at the feel of it, my mind going blank again as her hand got to where I so desperately needed it. She rolled me onto my back, a seductive little smile on her lips as she kissed across my cheek and down my jaw line. My arousal spiked as she nibbled on my chin. *Christ I love it when she does that!*

Her mouth was moving lower and lower, making the muscles in my stomach contract with every inch that her mouth moved. Her hair was trailing across my body, tickling and making me get goosebumps. When I felt her hot, wet tongue touch the tip of my shaft I knew I had to stop her. I held my breath and used every ounce of will power that I had to pull her away from me before she pushed me to the point of no return.

She looked at me confused as I rolled her onto her back again. I smiled at how flawless my wife looked right now, so incredible; I just couldn't believe my luck that this girl wanted me. The angels must have been smiling down on me on the day they decided that Riley and I would be neighbours all those years ago.

"I just want to make love to you now," I whispered, cupping her face in my hands, tracing my thumb over her cheekbone.

Her breath caught in her throat as she nodded. The lust I saw on her face matched my own. "Please be careful," she begged quietly.

I could see how much she wanted this too, and suddenly I realised that it didn't matter how long I lasted the first time, or if I did something wrong, because Riley loved me and wanted me as much as I wanted her. I felt all of my nerves and worry fade away as I suddenly remembered that this was Riley, my best friend, and the love of my life. I didn't ever need to feel embarrassed or inadequate around her because she would always love me regardless. If I messed up this time, then I would have a whole lifetime to put it right. But I could see in her eyes that whatever happened right now, I would never be a disappointment to her, and that thought made my heart fly in my chest.

I smiled reassuringly; I could see she was worried about me. "Everything's fine, Riley Bear. Everything's just perfect, just the way it should be. I love you so much," I said honestly. I couldn't describe to her how much I loved her, how much I would always love her, there were just no words to express it.

She smiled, her arms tightening around my neck, her eyes boring into mine and I knew what she was going to say before she even said it. Her eyes told me everything I needed to know.

"I love you too, Clay."

I smiled gratefully and bent my head to kiss her, preparing to start off a long night with her. This was our proper wedding night, and I didn't plan on letting her sleep for a single second.

epilogue

7 years later

"Mrs Preston, if you'd like to come in now."

I looked up at the same time as Riley did. She squeezed my hand and practically ran to the door, dragging me along behind her into the room. I smiled at her eagerness and closed the door behind me.

"Okay, so if you could lie down for me then and we'll get started," the lady instructed, nodding towards the bed. I sat down on the chair next to the bed, watching as Riley got herself comfortable. I grinned at her excitedly. This day felt like it had taken forever to get here. Ever since we got the appointment through, we'd both been counting down the days.

I held Riley's hand tightly as the lady squirted some clear gel on her stomach then rolled a little plastic thing over it. I wanted to look at the screen that the ultrasound technician was looking at, I really did, but I couldn't drag my eyes away from Riley's face. We'd been together for seven and a half years now, yet it still felt like yesterday that we first said those three little words. She was still the most beautiful thing I had ever seen in my life, and I was grateful for every single one of her smiles. I would gladly spend the rest of my life making her happy, and now I had someone else to look after too.

We'd been trying for this baby for over a year and a half. She'd left college and stopped having the contraceptive injection almost immediately. The trying had been extremely fun. I'd gotten to be the pervert that she usually made me into, but I had an excuse to hide behind this time. I was doing it all in the name of making a baby, and claimed it was nothing to do with the fact that my wife drove me wild all the time.

She bit her lip and looked at me, her eyes shining with excitement. *Jeez I hope it's a girl and she looks just like her mommy! Actually wait, I shouldn't really hope that she looks like Riley because then I'll be in deep trouble trying to keep the boys away from my little girl!*

I kissed her lightly as she squeezed my hand, making a little excited noise against my lips that made me laugh. She was ridiculously eager to be a mom. She'd been rubbing her tummy for the last eight weeks, since we'd done the test, cooing over the fact that she had a baby growing inside her, well, her exact words were 'a part of Clay growing inside her'. She was going to be a fantastic mother, and if I loved the baby even a tenth of how much I loved her then it would want for nothing.

A little "Oh!" from the ultrasound technician caught our attention.

Both of us looked at her worriedly, and I suddenly started to feel sick. Something was wrong. She'd pushed herself back a little in the chair, her fingers frantically tapping on the keyboard before she moved the little plastic thing to a different angle on Riley's stomach. *Oh God we're going to lose the baby or something. What if something has happened to the baby inside her stomach and it isn't growing properly? That would be awful for both of us but would probably kill Riley.*

"Is something wrong?" I asked quickly, squeezing Riley's hand reassuringly.

The lady looked around at us, an expression on her face that I couldn't quite work out, something crossed between nervousness and happiness. "That depends..."

That depends... What on earth was that supposed to mean? Either it was bad news and something was wrong, or it wasn't and I was making myself feel sick for nothing.

"On what?" I asked. Riley seemed to stop breathing on the little bed next to me.

The lady's eyes flicked between the two of us, a smile pulling at the corners of her mouth. "It depends on how you both feel about twins," she replied.

It felt like someone had slapped me in the face. No one said anything, the room was deadly silent. *Did I actually hear her right?*

Twins?

Two babies at once?

I could hear Riley giggling, she was squeezing my hand trying to get my attention, but I couldn't move. I felt like I'd been frozen on the spot, like time had stopped. How the hell could we have made twins? It felt like that saying about buses, 'you wait for one for ages, and then two come along at once'. I guess all that practicing for a baby had done its job better than we thought.

My mouth had gone dry. Twins. Possibly two daughters that I had to worry about looking like their mommy. *Wow, I'm in trouble!*

The lady turned the screen that she'd been looking at so that we could see the pictures. I could see an oval outline of her womb, then it looked like it had been divided into two, with two little shapes moving around inside, going in and out of focus.

I could hear Riley saying my name over and over, and I tried my hardest to look at her, but I couldn't get my eyes off of the computer screen. I could see the two little shapes there, the little grey blobs moving around. The ultrasound technician flicked a button and suddenly I could hear frantic beating sounds.

Two sets of nappies. Two babies waking up in the middle of the night. Two babies screaming for food...

I finally managed to drag my eyes from the computer and looked at Riley. My wife. The love of my life. Mother of my... *two* children.

"Looks like I got you good," I mumbled, not knowing what else to say.

She burst out laughing, stroking her hand down the side of my face. I was still a little shocked, but it was slowly sinking in. I was going to be a daddy, not once, but twice, all because of this amazing girl on the bed.

"I love you, Riley Bear," I vowed, meaning every single word.

She smiled and pulled me closer to her. "I love you too, Clay," she whispered.

"This means double the trouble," I joked, putting my hand on her stomach, ignoring the gel that squelched under my fingers.

"Yeah... but twice the fun," she answered.

I laughed and kissed her again. *Twins. I really am in big trouble.*

The End

Want to read more from the "Prestons"?

Free Falling (companion novel to Always You)

They say that your school years are supposed to be the best years of your life, and that you should make the most of them because you'll miss them when you're all grown up. Up until Maisie Preston's senior year, she would have totally agreed with that statement. Life was great; she had everything going for her, excellent grades, great parents, an annoying yet caring twin brother, and an impossibly sweet boyfriend.

Everything was perfect - that is until the arrival of Zach Anderson. A misfit delinquent that seemed to bring with him a lot of bad karma. Is it just a coincidence that his arrival marks a significant change in Maisie's life? Up until senior year, life was perfect, but things seem to be going downhill fast.

Out Now!

Other books by Kirsty Moseley

The Boy Who Sneaks in My Bedroom Window
Free Falling
Nothing Left to Lose
Enjoying the Chase
Reasons Not to Fall in Love (short story)
One Wild Night (Enjoying the Chase novella)
Poles Apart

www.kirstymoseley.com

CPSIA information can be obtained
at www.ICGtesting.com
Printed in the USA
FSOW01n0704300915
11694FS

9 781480 089136